DEFENDED

THE DEFENDER SERIES

BIRTH OF THE DEFENDER
PREQUEL

THE MISSION
BOOK 1

DEFENDED
BOOK 2

TREASONOUS ACTS
BOOK 3

IN EVIL'S GRASP
BOOK 4

MISSION ABANDONED
BOOK 5

BIRTH OF A REVOLUTION
BOOK 6

DEFENDED

THE DEFENDER SERIES

BOOK 2

Reggi Broach

second edition

Defender Christian Publications
Harrison, Tennessee, USA

Published by Defender Christian Publications, Harrison, TN, USA

First edition printed 2018.

ISBN: 978-1-950038-06-0 (paperback)
ISBN: 978-1-950038-03-9 (eBook)
ISBN: 978-1-950038-04-6 (hardback)
LCCN: 2017901519

PUBLISHERS NOTE:
This is a work of fiction. Names, characters, places, and incidents either are a product of the author's imagination or are used fictitiously, and any resemblance to actual persons, living or dead, business establishments, events, or locales is entirely coincidental. The publisher does not have any control over and does not assume any responsibility for author or third-party web sites or their content.

Defender Publications books are available at special discounts for bulk purchases, for sales promotions, or corporate use. Special editions, including personalized covers, excerpts of existing books, or books with corporate logos, can be created for some titles. For more information, contact R. B. Enterprises at:
SpecialSales@RBEnterprises.info

TABLE OF CONTENTS

"When justice is done, it brings joy to the righteous but terror to evildoers."

- Proverbs 21:15

ACKNOWLEDGMENTS

God has been immensely gracious to give me a job doing something I love. I pray that this endeavor brings honor and glory to His name. I want nothing more than to share Him with others.

I owe many people a great deal in bringing this second book to fruition. This book was originally part of Book 1, The Defender: The Mission. Thanks to Becky Chaffin, one of those who helped me with proofing and editing. She encouraged me to break the book into smaller chunks. She is a wise woman. Despite splitting the books, they are still sizable. Thanks also to Janelle Musick for editing this book and Book 1 (The Defender: The Mission). I've learned a great deal from both of you.

Thank you again, Chaplain Jerry Minchew, author of Knighthawke and Knighthawke Vanishing Shadows. Thanks, Vickie Minchew, for giving me the first read through when this was part of Book 1 and for your honest feedback. Your help has made this all possible.

My family has been instrumental in getting these books written and published. God blessed me with an awesome husband who puts up with my constant distractions when I ask him to proof scenes. He has done a fantastic job formatting the books and the cover. The man is so busy and still has time to help me with my projects. My girls put up with a lot too. I bounce ideas off them and Kayleigh helps me choreograph fight scenes. Rachel keeps me on target by scheduling "writing" dates with me. My niece Alea is another one of my trusted "grammar police" helpers. Thanks again to my son for letting me use his name. My brother, Nathan, was quite helpful with providing gravitational calculations necessary to the story.

I didn't say this in the acknowledgments of the first book and I should have. There just seemed to be so many people to thank, I hesitated to go any further. My entire family has offered me encouragement in this endeavor since I started it. I am glad my Dad and Mom raised me in the church where I first encountered the Creator and Savior. I'm glad they taught me right from wrong and respect for God's Holiness. With every step, I can almost feel my mother's watchful eye and my father's warnings about respecting God.

Commonwealth Interstellar Force Ship

Tech Specs: *SS Evangeline*

Explorer Class Ship with long range space, planetary atmospheric, and aquatic maneuvering capabilities.

Drive Capabilities:
- Tachyon
- Matter/Antimatter

Ship Weapons Capabilities:
- Minimal laser
- EMP and tachyon defensive weaponry
- Electromagnetic shields and deflectors

Personal Weapons Capabilities
- **Tri-Emp:** A personal weapon, projectile based with three levels of electro-magnetic pulse charge.
- **Laser Rifle:** a longer range weapon with a laser and Tri-Emp capabilities.
- **Personal Shield Generator:** a glove-like device generating a shield for personal use, capable of being adjusted to different sizes and sensitivity.

Ship Accessory Equipment
- **Shuttle:** can be flown in space, atmospheric, and aquatic environments. Used for ship to planet movements and short flights on planets. Mainly used as personnel transport, with limited cargo capacity. The co-pilot controls the computer, shield, and laser weapons.
- **Surf-ve:** an amphibious surface vehicle for transportation of personnel or cargo. It has a retractable canopy over the passenger compartment. The co-pilot's chair has computer, shield, and laser weapons control.
- **Whipper:** single person transport that uses anti-gravity hover technology. It can move and hover over land or water.

Personnel Accommodations:
- 14

Mission

To establish a Commonwealth presence on all technologically undeveloped worlds, or worlds that have not chosen to ally with the Commonwealth despite non-spatial developments. To report any world where the invasive forces of the Liontari have a foothold.

Crew Manifest

The crew is to consist of two teams. The primary team is the ship's crew, and the secondary team is the diplomatic mission team. Each team is to act as support personnel for the opposing team as needed.

Commonwealth Interstellar Force Headquarters				
Office of Personnel Raesii CIF Training Base CIF *SS Evangeline* Crew Manifest				
Name		Rank	Ship's Crew	Diplomatic Crew
Last	First			
Alexander	David	Captain	Captain	
Alexander	Brynna	Commander		Diplomatic Team Leader
Dominick	Lazaro	Lt. Commander	Chief Engineer	
Flint	Braxton	Lt. Commander		Architectural Engineer
Adams	Jason	Lt. Commander		Physician
Flint	Alexia (Lexi)	Lt.		Psychologist
Ryder	Thane	Lt.	Pilot	
Adams	Laura	Lt. JG		Nurse, Botanist
Holden	Marissa	Lt. JG	Navigation	
Dominick	Cheyenne	ENS		Linguistics
Ryder	Aulani	ENS	Comm & Computer Tech	
Holden	Jake	Chief Petty Officer	Security	

PART FOUR

UNKNOWN HISTORY

DREA III

The Evangeline's missions to Galat III and Medoris IV had been successful although somewhat trying and traumatic. The crew had discovered followers of their enemy, the Liontari, on Galat III. They promptly evacuated and reported the enemy's presence despite cryptic warnings from Arni Liontari, the self-proclaimed son of Pateras El Liontari.

Medoris had shown no signs of the enemy's presence, but Arni Liontari could somehow transport himself wherever he wanted to go. It was now becoming clear; the crew of the Evangeline was his new target. Their time on Medoris yielded new allies for the Commonwealth from several rather stout warriors and nomads, a peace treaty between the local populations and several steps forward in establishing some basic human rights. It also nearly cost them several lives.

The Evangeline's next stop was Drea III. Drea had a significant history. The Commonwealth had interacted with this world before. There were a long list of warnings concerning the planet's warlike and bloody history. Drea III was invited into the Commonwealth years earlier, but it was later determined they were not yet ready for it. The last contact was approximately fifty years ago. The planet had been in a post-Industrial age of development and was just starting space travel from a surprisingly advanced level when the Commonwealth introduced themselves the first time. Reports filed at the time, indicated the world still had a significant population of inhabitants with primitive beliefs. The introduction of the Commonwealth's existence and belief system caused a civil war among the inhabitants. The Evangeline was granted permission to approach this world again but was strongly advised to use caution.

The captain, commander, security chief, and ship's psychologist sat down together to work out their strategy. It was going to take four days to get there, so they had plenty of time to consider their options. This also gave Captain David Alexander time to consult with his superiors about how to handle his encounters with Arni. The reports Captain Alexander had filed were colorful, to say the least. The Captain, Lt. Marissa Holden, and Security Chief Jake Holden were the main ones to mention encounters with their enemy Arni Liontari. Unlike their departure from Galat III, Captain Alexander sent the reports without any disturbing dreams or words of warning from Arni in the middle of the night. The reports were sent off the same day the ship left Medoris IV.

The night before the crew would reach Drea III, Captain Alexander and his wife, Commander Brynna Alexander were off duty and asleep in their cabin when Admiral Deacons contacted the ship. Ensign Aulani Ryder was on duty at the comms station and her husband, Lt. Thane Ryder was the commander-on-duty when the Admiral's communication came through. Lt. Ryder put the Admiral on stand-by and hailed David immediately. David woke Brynna, quickly splashed some water on his face, and pulled his casual uniform on.

"Admiral Deacons, I apologize for keeping you waiting. We're on radically different schedules here."

"That's alright, Captain Alexander. It gave me more time to go over your reports. You're certain the Liontari influence is not on Medoris IV?" "Yes sir. The only thing they knew of the Liontaris surrounded us.

They attributed what they saw to the work of the "gods." They had never seen Arni until he showed up near us."

"Captain, you are sure you nor any of your people have been compromised?" Admiral Deacons questioned.

"There's no evidence to suggest anyone has been compromised. Everyone still vows loyalty to the Commonwealth." David started to say affected instead of compromised because the entire crew had been affected in some way, but he thought better of it. "Lt. Flint has interviewed anyone who was deemed to be "at risk" and has cleared everyone including me."

Admiral Deacons sighed a large sigh of relief. He set aside his role as admiral and took on the more personal role as David's Uncle Rob. "Oh, thank goodness. David... Son... I was afraid we'd lost you."

"There were a couple moments when I thought I was about to be lost to everyone, sir. The people on Medoris don't appear to have any knowledge of the Liontari, but the planet itself nearly wiped us out. We had a rough mission on this one, sir. Uncle Rob, maybe you were right about me. Maybe I am too soft."

"What do you mean, Son?"

"I nearly lost Brynna and Marissa. Then I nearly got myself killed.

I came close to getting Lazaro and Braxton killed."

"No, David, I was the one who was wrong. You aren't too soft. You can't be second-guessing yourself. This is not an easy mission. From what I've read, you've done an outstanding job. It looks like the Medorans are well on their way to becoming Commonwealth material. Son, we don't want to lose anyone, but you know, sometimes, we do."

"Yes sir, but nothing prepared me for getting a crew member back from the dead."

"Your physician is certain Lt. Holden was dead?"

David looked almost sick. "Absolutely. He performed a complete autopsy on her. Her neck was broken in addition to numerous other injuries which could've killed her. There is no doubt. She was dead."

The Admiral still eyed him suspiciously. "You're also certain about your doctor?"

David nodded. "Yes, sir." David hadn't had any reason to suspect the doctor. He had seen Marissa's lifeless body for himself. There were no doubts she was dead and no reason to suspect the doctor of deception. Admiral Deacons slowly shook his head. "There is no way we could have prepared you for this. We don't even know how to advise you on being prepared for any possible next time. The Admiral's board has referred your inquiry to the Defense Minister. You should be getting a response from his office in the next few days. In the meantime, your orders to avoid all contact still stand. If you do gather more intelligence be sure and pass it on in your reports, but don't prolong your exposure unnecessarily. Understood?" David nodded. "Yes sir!"

Having taken care of business, Admiral Deacons changed gears. "Are you and Brynna alright?"

David sensing the Admiral had metaphorically taken off his Admiral's insignia, changed gears to match. "Yeah Uncle Rob, we're fine. I've gotten myself in hot water with my first officer and my wife two or three times on this mission, but we've smoothed things over."

Brynna had slipped quietly into the "Living Room" area where David was sitting while he took the Admiral's communication. Sensing the laxness of the conversation, she grinned and leaned into the Admiral's view over David's shoulder. "Four times, if we're actually counting."

Startled by her sudden appearance, David momentarily forgot his focus on the Admiral. "Four?!? What else did I do?"

The Admiral smiled. He thought Brynna was good for David. She kept him on his toes. "How are you, Brynna? Are you keeping this young man in line?"

Brynna grinned mischievously. "I'm fine, sir, and I'm doing the best I can with what I have to work with."

The Admiral laughed. "David, I think you have some more work to do smoothing things over."

David's wry answer and the look of vexation on his face spoke volumes even though his words didn't. "Apparently so."

"David, in all seriousness, I suggest you spend time with your ship's psychologist, regularly. You are in the field, and your situation is beyond belief. Don't keep this stuff bottled up, or it will eat away at you. Even little things can pile up and become overwhelming. It's not weakness, it's a wise precaution. Brynna, that goes for you too."

Brynna and David both acknowledged the Admiral's recommendation. After a couple more minutes of informal pleasantries, the Admiral excused himself from the communication and allowed them to go back to bed.

Thirty minutes later the Admiral contacted the ship again and asked to speak to the security chief. The Admiral gave strict instructions to the bridge crew not to wake the Captain or

Commander, but to simply leave his second communication on the ship's log. Thane did as he was ordered, but he gave communications officer, Ensign Aulani Ryder a concerned look after putting the communication through to the chief.

Two hours later, Thane was waking the Captain and Commander again with a message from the Defense Minister's office. The Defense Minister would be hailing them in fifteen minutes. David and Brynna used the time to freshen up and grab a quick cup of coffee to clear the cobwebs from their brains. The two sat down and waited for the call to come in. A minute later Thane patched it through.

"Captain Alexander, Commander Alexander, I received your request to attempt to communicate with Arni Liontari and I must say we are extremely concerned. Considering your previous orders and the amount of information you have reported, it seems you have already had far too much contact with the enemy."

David didn't like the sound of where this was going and jumped in quickly. "Minister, the contact we have had so far was initiated by Liontari, not us, and we aren't specifically requesting you allow us to communicate with the enemy. We're just telling you the enemy has shared some of his goals with us and are requesting additional instructions. There is obviously an opportunity to gather some intelligence which could be useful. If our instructions remain the same, then we will follow them as ordered."

The Defense Minister scowled at David. "How can you say that? You obviously have not obeyed your orders already. You've spent enough time talking with Arni Liontari to gather this information. That was more time than your orders should have allowed."

David was starting to get annoyed and defensive. He kept his temper under control and turned the questions back on the Defense Minister. "Sir, have you read my entire report? When Arni showed up the first time, I was trapped in a ring of fire. I had nowhere to go, except to a fiery death. The second time I had been up for nearly thirty hours, my wrist and hand were broken, we had just found the body of one my crewmen. I suppose I could have tried harder to walk away, but do you suppose you'd be thinking very clearly under those conditions? When he shows up in situations like these, I just need to know if I should take advantage of the opportunity and ask questions, commit suicide to prevent being conscripted against my will, or attempt to kill a man who has the power to appear and disappear at will. Not to mention the fact he also seems to have the power of life and death in his hands. I admit, the second time I ran into Arni Liontari, my judgment may have been impaired by exhaustion, emotional trauma, and physical injury, but that's why I asked for additional instructions. If I am supposed to stay clear of him, then fine, I don't have a problem with it. However, I can't stay away from him, execute him, and interrogate him at the same time."

Brynna tried to keep a neutral look on her face, but David's rant had her in shock. The Defense Minister was significantly more than a superior officer.

The Defense Minister scowled at David for a moment before responding. "I see. We'll get back to you shortly." He promptly ended their conversation.

As soon as he was gone, Brynna blinked then looked at David. "What was that about?"

David looked concerned. "He's questioning my loyalty." David jumped up to finish getting completely dressed.

Brynna still felt stunned. David had never talked so harshly to a dignitary before, at least not as long as she had known him. "David, why did you react so... so... strongly?"

David looked at her with fire in his eyes. "If I give them any reason to think I've been compromised, he'll be contacting the Chief to have me thrown out the nearest air lock. I had to fight back hard and fast. If I don't get offended, then they may feel I'm hiding something. I need to get to the bridge."

Brynna stood there feeling slightly lost. It was the middle of the night for her and she had been awakened twice already. She wanted to go back to bed and get some sleep but knew at this point her mind wasn't going to let her sleep. She took a deep breath. "I'll finish getting dressed and meet you up there in a few minutes. You want me to grab you a little something to eat?"

David was already thinking about his next moves. "Huh? Uh... yeah, that's fine." And he was gone.

Thane and Aulani were not terribly surprised to see the Captain step onto the bridge. They were surprised by his mood. He immediately went to his duty station and started reviewing the ship's logs. Thane walked over to give him a shift report. "Captain, Admiral Deacons contacted Chief Holden after talking to you. He ordered me not to wake you, but to put the information in the ship's log for you to view later." Thane was fairly certain this was the information the Captain was searching for. "Should I have found a discreet way to let you know sooner?"

David's eyes locked on Thane's. "Are you asking me if you should have disobeyed the orders of a superior officer?

Thane looked sideways at the Captain. "No sir. I'm just asking if that is the type of information you need sooner rather than later."

David looked back down at his screen. "Good answer, Lt. Ryder, and yes, that is the type of information I would prefer to have sooner rather than later. Thanks."

"Captain, what was that last communication about?" Thane wasn't sure if he should ask, but he thought it couldn't hurt.

David eyed Thane suspiciously. Realizing he was being paranoid, he shook it off and answered the young lieutenant. "I'm not entirely sure, but I think my loyalty is under scrutiny." The Captain looked over at Aulani who was actively paying attention. "Is there anything else I need to know? Or maybe something you think I ought to know?"

Thane's eyes narrowed, "Not that I am aware of, sir." Now it was Thane's turn to be paranoid. "Why are they questioning your loyalty, sir?"

David sat back in his chair and swiveled into a position enabling him to see the couple more easily. "If you think about it, since Arni seems to have singled me out, that puts me at the greatest risk. I've had more dealings with him than anyone, except possibly Marissa."

Aulani looked back and forth at Thane and the Captain. "But, Lexi cleared you."

David looked at Aulani's trusting face. "And I'm the one who sent her report in."

The realization crept across her face then she brightened up again. "So, we need a system of checks and balances."

Brynna stepped onto the bridge and discreetly laid a pastry and a cup of coffee down beside David's elbow. David nodded to her then addressed Aulani's comment. "Exactly. Whatever you send out should be copied to whoever wrote the report and one other to verify accuracy. Everyone should be proofing two reports, their own and someone else's. Brynna, can you set that up? I don't want husbands and wives proofing each other's reports and let the Doc proof Lexi's. Aulani, I also need you to construct a program for scanning all incoming and outgoing communication. I want the program to look for hidden carrier waves or messages. Have it alert myself and the Commander immediately. A notation should also go into the ship's log the instant anything is detected."

Aulani was tense again, "Sir, do you suspect someone of something?"

"No, I don't. I do want to be prepared, just in case. I also want to make sure the guys back home know we can be trusted."

Aulani's tension wasn't so easily relieved this time. She set to work as the Captain ordered. Brynna was now at her own duty station working on a proofing rubric. David started working on a brief message to accompany the copies of the reports. He didn't want to wake any sleeping crewmen. This was important, but it was still something that could wait until the next duty shift. He didn't, however want them wondering why the reports showed up unexpectedly.

Thane was still standing there waiting for his orders. "Captain, is there something I need to be working on?"

David glanced up at him and thought. "Not at the moment, Lieutenant, but if you think of anything that might help, let me know." Thane moved back to his duty station and monitored the scanners.

It only took Brynna a couple minutes to put the rubric together. She forwarded a copy to the communications station for Aulani, or whoever was working at the comms station at any given time. David noticed she continued working on something. He finished his memo and sent it to Aulani for distribution, then moved over to Brynna's work station. He leaned over her shoulder. "What are you working on?"

Brynna continued working without looking over at him. "I'm creating a program to send a copy of all deleted log entries, and any manual changes into a secondary file only you and I can access. Basically, if anybody deletes a log entry, you and I will be notified. I'm also going to have an entry put into this file, so if anyone other than a file's originator makes copies, we'll be notified. It will automatically record the files Aulani will copy and redistribute. We expect that to happen, but if someone starts tampering with the files, or altering data, I want to know about it."

David nodded and responded softly. "Good idea. I don't like not trusting anyone on this ship, but there is always a chance somebody could turn."

Aulani whipped her head around suddenly, "Captain!"

David thought she had overheard his comment until he saw her communications terminal lit up. Aulani continued her explanation. "There's a communique coming in from the Supreme Executor's office!" David blinked as he processed the magnitude of her statement then moved over to stand in front of his duty station. He glanced at Aulani. "Get that monitoring program running to scan for secondary signals now!" Then David nodded for her to put the call through to the main viewer. A man's face appeared on the screen. It was not the Executor's face, but one of his officials. The man identified himself as Stuart Jacobs, the Executor's Administrative Assistant. Mr. Jacobs informed the Captain the Supreme Executor wanted to speak to him.

"Is this to be a private conversation, Mr. Jacobs? I am currently on the bridge with my first officer, my pilot, and my comms officer. Should I move to my office?"

David saw the man's eyes looking past the video recorder. Someone was feeding him information. In a second his focus shifted back to David. "No, Captain, that won't be necessary. This is not a restricted communication. I was informed you were not currently on duty. I was calling ahead of Executor Hale, so you could be made available."

David smiled cordially. "I appreciate your consideration in giving me a chance to make myself presentable. After the two previous communications, I decided now was not the time to be sleeping. I'm ready to speak to the Supreme Executor whenever it's convenient for him."

"Of course, stand by for Supreme Executor Luciano Hale."

David glanced over at Brynna. She quickly moved over beside him. The entire bridge crew stood at attention and waited for the Supreme Executor's face to appear on the screen.

Seconds later, the Executor appeared on the screen. "As you were, please. I don't care to stand on ceremony. Captain, Commander, I do have some questions for you."

Thane and Aulani nervously went back to their duties, but their attention was clearly divided. David and Brynna stood "at ease." "Of course, sir. What would you like to know?"

"Captain, you know as well as I do, not everything fits into a report. Your reports are meant to give us facts, but I need you to give me some speculation. What can you tell me about Arni that isn't in your reports?" Captain Alexander was caught off guard by being contacted by the highest authority in the galaxy. The question was very broad and unexpected. "Well, sir, I'm not entirely sure how to answer that question. I really don't know what his goals are, which is why I asked for further instructions. I do know he has not forced our cooperation in anything. He seems unusually interested in us, but it appears as though he's to trying to "win" our loyalty through acts of benevolence. I get the feeling he can't force us to do his will. For that matter, he told us he wouldn't force our cooperation. I didn't believe him at first, but his actions suggest he might be telling the truth. I am also aware he could be setting an elaborate trap for us. I considered trying to capture him, question him or even shoot him on sight, but we are talking about a man who we've seen manipulate matter on a cellular level. I don't know if capturing or killing him is even possible. I know I can ask him questions."

Executor Hale studied the young Captain carefully. "You didn't try to kill him because you were afraid you couldn't?"

David phrased his response carefully. "No, sir. I have never really been in a position to make such an attempt and my orders didn't address this possibility. I was simply weighing my options. I'm not afraid to try sir, if that's what you want me to do. I've sworn my allegiance to the Commonwealth Interstellar Force. I've given my life to serve it and I will give up my life if that's what is called for. It just seems inevitable we will cross paths again, and I want to be prepared for it."

Executor Hale continued to study David. He was leaning back in an executive chair, his elbows on the armrests, and with his fingers interlaced in front of him. His dark eyes seemed to look straight through David. Finally, he smiled and spoke. "You're Admiral Deacons' nephew, aren't you?"

David wasn't sure if this was good or bad. "Yes sir."

The Executor smiled a little more. It was a pleasant enough smile, but it still unnerved David. "Your uncle speaks highly of you and your wife. I thought perhaps his report was biased, but you seem to be unaffected by your interactions with the Liontari."

David glanced over at Brynna. "Thank you, sir." He wasn't entirely sure his response was the right one, but it was the best he could do.

"Captain, you wanted further instructions, here they are. I don't want you to go out of your way to hunt him down, but if he is ever present again, find out what you can about his plan. You are, under no circumstances, to try and capture or attempt to kill him. As a matter of fact, if his life were to be in danger, then do whatever you must to keep him alive."

David was taken aback. "Sir? You want me to protect the Commonwealth's biggest enemy?"

The Executor's smile faded. "Are you questioning my orders, Captain?"

"No sir, I just want to be sure I understand what you are ordering me to do, and not do."

The Executor's face relaxed again. "Captain Alexander, we are working on a plan to get to Pateras El Liontari, and I need Arni to be able to move about freely. I'm going to trust you to use your own best judgment on how much to allow yourself to be exposed to. Commander Alexander."

Brynna stepped forward. "Yes sir?"

"I hate to put you in this position, but maybe it will serve as an extra check and balance. It will be your responsibility to watch your Captain. If he strays from the path, execute him as you were ordered. Can you do that?"

Brynna didn't even glance David's direction before answering. "Yes sir! I can sir!"

On overhearing this part of the conversation, Aulani gave Thane a startled glance. He returned a stern look that said, "pay attention to your duties."

Executor Hale seemed satisfied. "Captain, Commander, I see why Admiral Deacons spoke so highly of you both. You are dedicated soldiers. I'm sure you both will make me proud. I'm going to give these same instructions to the other teams. We've had other teams report similar contacts with Arni Liontari. I appreciate all your efforts. Remember what I said. Don't kill him. No matter what, he must not die. I will continue to monitor your progress. Executor Hale out."

As soon as the Executor was off the channel, David leaped over to Aulani's station. Looking intently at her display, he asked, "Any signs of secondary transmissions?"

Aulani shook her head. "No sir. May I ask what you're looking for, sir?"

"I just wanted to be sure he wasn't telling me one thing and the security chief something else." Brynna stared at David. She knew this wasn't all he was looking for. Brynna sat back down at her terminal and started working on another computer program to help find what she knew he was really looking for.

David had one more instruction for Aulani. "Send the crew a message to expect a mandatory briefing after the start of the next duty shift. I want everyone to see the Executor's instructions." The Captain sat back down in his chair and mulled over the night's events.

Thane saw him staring off into space. "Captain, you've got three and a half hours before the next duty shift. Why don't you go get a nap? If I need to stay on duty longer, I can."

David looked over at Thane. "Are you trying to throw me off your bridge, Lieutenant?"

Thane's mouth twitched. "Yes sir."

David smiled. "You will let me know if anyone else important calls?"

Thane grinned. "Yes sir. Just don't get annoyed with me if I call you and tell you I updated the ship's log."

David moved towards the door, "Understood, Lieutenant. Brynna, are you coming?"

Brynna looked around at him. "I'll be about five or ten minutes behind you. I need to finish this."

"Okay. Thane, if you don't mind. Stay on duty until after the briefing since you already heard the Executor's instructions. No need to sit through it twice. Brynna, if you need to sleep in a little, you can."

Thane acknowledged the Captain's request. Brynna declined to sleep in. She told David she could take another nap later in the day, if needed. She felt it was important they both be present. David made a mental note to keep his own sleep schedule more in line with CIF headquarters.

David went back to his room and laid down again. He had trouble relaxing. That last conversation with the Supreme Executor should have laid his fears to rest, but they didn't. David got up and took a hot shower. He hoped it would relax him. When he got back into bed, Brynna was already there. She wasn't asleep yet either. Once he laid down she snuggled up to him. They both laid there thinking but saying nothing. David finally dozed off into a fitful sleep. He slipped in and out of dreams. He saw the dream about the wild dogs after they left Galat. He dreamed about the tornado that snatched Marissa only this time it was pulling him away from Brynna.

All too soon his alarm woke him. He wasn't sure if he was relieved to be awake, or not. The Captain forced himself out of bed and got dressed, again. He headed to the dining hall for breakfast and a large cup of coffee. As soon as everyone was assembled, David patched a feed into engineering and the bridge. He looked around the room. The room seemed slightly empty. With some of the crew attending the meeting remotely and the loss of the two temporary crewmen, Medoran locals Manton and Vesta, David felt like he was waiting for others to show up. He began the briefing by updating the crew on the new system of checks and balances he was implementing for the filing of reports and his expectations in regard to being notified about contacts from CIF headquarters. He also told the crew he was going to change the duty schedule to match CIF headquarters as often as possible. The Captain attributed the changes to his numerous communications that came in during the night.

The next thing he covered was his late-night conversation with the Supreme Executor. The crew had lots of questions, but the issue causing the most disruption was Executor Hale's adamant declaration to protect the life of Arni Liontari. David expected Jake to be the biggest objector, but his reaction was surprisingly mild. Jake once again had his chair tipped back on only two legs and balanced against the wall. When David showed the video of the discussion with the Supreme Executor, Jake sat his chair down and leaned forward on the table in front of him. David watched the expression on Jake's face go from curiosity to shock, then anger, and finally landed on acceptance. He never asked one question. The other crew members were shocked and did not recover so quickly. The crew had several objections to the Executor's orders. David gave them a moment to vent, then firmly backed the Supreme Executor's orders.

The last topic was a briefing on reaching Drea. The ship would enter the Drean system late this evening. David asked Lt. Holden to plot a course through the star system to keep the ship out of the line of sight of Drea III. He wanted to put the ship down on one of the planet's moons to monitor it from a safe distance before initiating contact. Once they put down on the Drean moon, the crew would then locate their target time zone and match their sleep schedules accordingly. The night watch would be minimal and would consist of two who would work late and two who would get up early. The schedule would rotate, so nobody would get used to the offset hours.

After the briefing concluded and everyone dispersed, David caught Jake. "Is there anything you need to tell me, Chief?"

Jake didn't hesitate. He knew exactly what the Captain was asking about. "It was just routine, Captain. Admiral Deacons just wanted to make sure everyone had been carefully scrutinized and cleared. The Admiral said you already told him you and Marissa were cleared by Lexi. He just wanted to be sure. I told him you and Marissa were perfectly normal. Is there a problem, sir?"

David's face still conveyed a very serious tone. "No Chief, I don't think so. My loyalty was being called into question last night and I think it's made me a little paranoid. The Defense Minister also contacted me and nearly accused me of treason. I didn't take kindly to that."

Jake nodded pensively. "I wouldn't appreciate it either, sir. Was there anything else? I recorded the communication if you want to review it."

David shook his head. "No that's alright. I may review it later. You can go on about your duties, Chief."

Later that evening, the Captain had the full bridge crew on duty as they approached Drea. Lt. Holden was able to keep the ship completely out of view from Drea III. The ship moved to land on the dry barren moon without incident. David positioned the ship in the shadows between two ridges on the moon nearest the planet. Once the ship had found a comfortable resting place, the thrusters were powered down. The crew suddenly noticed they were losing the artificial gravity. Thane had carried a cup of coffee onto the bridge and when the ship touched down the fluid bounced out of the cup. The moon they were on was very small and had only about ten percent of normal gravity. Thane grabbed the cup and using various acrobatic moves, tried to catch the slowly falling, hot liquid with his cup without losing his own balance or burning his hands. David grabbed his console and hailed engineering. "Lt. Commander Dominick! We've lost the artificial gravity up here. What's going on down there?"

Brynna sent out a ship wide warning to warn anyone who might not have noticed. Any number of accidents could happen. If anyone were working out in the gymnasium, they would be at serious risk for injury, not to mention if anyone happened to be showering. Everything would still gravitate downward but would bounce – a lot. The gravity being ninety percent short meant an object could bounce higher than normal and nine times more often than normal. A pillow wouldn't be a problem, but sharp objects could become deadly. The speed at which something fell would be three times slower. Trying to catch a falling object was not advisable, because one's own reactions would be equally skewed.

A second later, Chief Engineer, Lt. Commander Lazaro Dominick responded. "I'm sorry, Captain. I forgot to shut off the automatic gravity equalizer. Stand by for re-initialization of artificial gravity." A few more seconds passed. The bridge crew heard "Uh-oh" a thump and a loud "Ow! That didn't feel good."

Another voice laughed then asked, "Are you okay, Laz?" The voice belonged to the mission team's Architectural Engineer and the ship's Assistant Engineer, Lt. Commander Braxton Flint.

Lazaro hadn't closed the comm line. Lazaro's voice came back with, "I'll live, but that's going to leave a mark."

They heard Braxton's laughing voice again, "I didn't know you could move like that." Grins slowly began to emerge on the faces of the bridge crew who had all managed to keep their seats after the landing.

David was just as amused as the rest of the crew, but he had to maintain his dignity and bearing. It was, after all, a dangerous situation. He was also kicking himself for not making sure the gravity was maintained. The Captain finally called out to the engineering department again. "Gentlemen, is there a problem?"

For a split second, there was dead silence as the two engineers looked at each other and realized the Captain had heard their antics. Lazaro finally responded. "Uhhh... No sir, I just overshot the control panel by a little bit. Artificial gravity coming on now." A shrill chirping sounded throughout the ship to warn the crew gravity was resuming. The gravity began to build slowly until it matched the gravity on Drea III.

It was the chief engineer's job to get the crew ready for the gravity of their next destination by slowly altering the artificial gravity while the crew was in space, so it wouldn't be disorienting once they reached their destination. The ship had hand rails and hand holds along the walls and corridors to prepare for the possibility of losing the artificial gravity while in space. The crew had been trained on how to maneuver even in zero gravity situations. The bridge crew had adjustable arm rests that could move across their bodies giving just enough pressure to keep them in their seats.

David wanted to find the situation funny, but the risk to the crew's safety was simply too great to let this situation pass lightly. He stabbed the comm button again. "Lt. Commander Dominick, as soon as engineering is squared away, report to me in my office." David didn't wait for his reply before cutting off the connection. He hastily got up and headed to his office. The bridge crew's attitudes sobered.

Before he stepped off the bridge, David gave Brynna one last order. "Check with the rest of the crew for injuries then do a run through to check for damage." Brynna acknowledged the order and had Cheyenne start contacting the crew members who weren't in engineering or on the bridge. She sent all available crew members to do a sweep throughout the ship to look for damage.

Brynna finished getting the ship settled in. She made sure there were no exterior lights on and activated the ship's camouflage net. The veins running through the ship's hull served to feed more than the tachyon particles. It could match the ship's hull to the surrounding terrain colors. It didn't do a lot for close-up camouflage, but it worked well for hiding in space and at a distance.

David sat down at his desk and put his face in his hands. He allowed himself to laugh softly for a moment at the thought of his engineer flying across the room. He symbolically wiped the smile from his face when he heard the Lt. Commander at the door. The Lt. Commander had picked up on the Captain's mood from his last communication and made an appropriately official entry. "Lt. Commander Dominick, reporting as ordered, sir!" Standing at attention, the commander waited for the Captain's response.

Captain Alexander waited long enough for the commander to get appropriately nervous. Finally, he spoke, calmly and quietly. "Lt. Commander Dominick, would you mind explaining to me why my ship lost artificial gravity?"

Still standing at attention the commander began his explanation. "I'm sorry, sir. I failed to change the computer programming which defaults to planetary levels upon landing."

"Lt. Commander, you are a professionally trained ship's engineer. You have check lists, do you not? Check lists aimed at preventing just such a mishap. Am I right, commander?"

"Yes sir. I do, sir."

"Did you not use this checklist?"

"I – uh, I guess I got in a hurry and assumed the setting was correct, sir."

David's eyes narrowed, and brow furrowed. "You assumed it was correct? Commander, a check list is there to prevent assumptions. It is meant to make sure nothing is forgotten, overlooked, or missed. Do you realize what kind of accidents could have happened?"

Lazaro's mind jumped back to his attempt to get back to the console to adjust the artificial gravity and the fall he had taken. A look of pain and embarrassment crossed his face. "Yes sir, I'm sorry, sir. It won't happen again. You have my word."

"It better not. I'd hate to start requiring you to submit time stamped checklist log entries. You are a fine officer. This mission lends itself to a more relaxed atmosphere, but certain duties still require the most rigid and professional attitudes. Make sure you know the difference."

"Yes, Captain."

Lazaro and David had bonded during their ordeal in the Sorley camp. This made it difficult for the Captain to reprimand him. David's tone softened. "At ease, Commander. Are you hurt from your fall?"

"Just a couple bruises and my ego is slightly damaged."

"From your fall or from my tirade?"

Lazaro glumly responded, "A little of both. I'm sorry I disappointed you, sir."

David looked up at Lazaro. "Stay true to your word of not letting it happen again, and you won't disappoint me. Go let the Doc give you a quick once over, then make any appropriate apologies and we will let the matter go."

Lazaro snapped back to attention. "Yes sir!" David dismissed him.

Lazaro left the Captain's office and did as he was instructed.

Brynna walked into the office a minute after Lazaro left. She found David with his face buried in his hands. He didn't look up when she came in. When he didn't look up, Commander Alexander stood there a moment watching him. She watched him take a deep breath then his body began to shake slowly then more violently. The only sound he was making was a slight wheezing sound as the deep breath he had taken escaped from his lungs. She was clueless as to what was wrong with him. She finally stepped closer. "David?"

The Captain raised his head to look at her. Tears had welled up in his eyes and his face was flushed. He took another deep breath and laughed robustly. The tears in his eyes ran down his face. He wiped them away with his sleeve and continued to laugh. He was laughing so hard, Brynna thought he might fall in the floor. Brynna waited patiently for his laughter to subside. David finally leaned back in his chair and caught his breath. "Whew, I think I really needed that laugh."

Brynna gave him a puzzled look. "Exactly what was so funny?"

David laughed again. "I'm not sure I could explain it and give it justice. Between Thane's dancing around on the bridge trying to catch hot coffee and the ship's internal surveillance footage of what happened in engineering, I just had to laugh. Braxton was right. I had no idea Lazaro could move like that. The look on your face was even funny. The fact that I couldn't laugh on the bridge made it even funnier."

Brynna relaxed. She had thought something was terribly wrong when she first walked in. She was relieved, but slightly annoyed. She rolled her eyes and shook her head. "You're impossible. So, what was wrong with the artificial gravity?"

David scowled. "Operator error. It won't happen again."

"You didn't put him on report, did you?"

"No, but I made my point. Come look at this video feed."

The two enjoyed another moment of laughter before getting back to the seriousness of their mission.

Early the next morning Brynna met with Botanist, Lt. Junior Grade Laura Adams; Psychologist and Sociologist, Lt. Lexi Flint; and Linguistics Expert, Ensign Cheyenne Dominick to review what history they had on Drea III. According to the Commonwealth files, Drea III was just starting into space exploration when the Commonwealth introduced themselves. The planet had been apprehensive about their new visitors. The planet was not united under one government but had many governments. The Commonwealth tried to encourage a unification of the planet and introduced them to their language of Intergalactic Standard among other things. The smaller governments began to think this was a plot to destroy them and remove their power base. They formed an alliance, orchestrating a revolution against the larger nations. The larger nations embraced the Commonwealth and immediately started teaching the concepts and language in the schools. The Commonwealth spent ten years trying to work with the planet before a major war broke out. Once the war started, the Commonwealth pulled out and told the leaders who supported them they would return when the planet was united and open to the Commonwealth. There had been no other contacts recorded with Drea III in the last forty-seven years.

Cheyenne recorded communication signals throughout the night. The planet had learned a few things from the Commonwealth's previous interactions. Intergalactic Standard had been adopted as the primary language on the planet and was taught in all schools. Intergalactic Standard was a unique language in that it was specifically designed. It didn't just develop as most languages do. Several linguistics experts designed the language to be simple and easy to learn with as few basic rules as possible. They also designed it to have a lack of rule exceptions. Some languages have letters sounding one way in one word but pronounced differently in another word. Intergalactic Standard was not like that. One letter had one sound and no other, not even if combined with another letter. Brynna was glad to hear they would have little need of translators on this trip. Cheyenne wasn't. She enjoyed trying to work out translations.

Cheyenne was glad to report the planet managed to establish a "United World Council." The council didn't quite rule as one body, but it did bring the various nations together for common causes. The information was collected from various news reports. Cheyenne suggested this Council would be the one to contact initially. Considering their splintered history, Lexi agreed. Cheyenne, due to her expertise in linguistics was also quite adept in sociology. She noted the current planet was overall peaceful. There were no active wars going on, but there were still numerous reports of crimes, gang activity in locations of lower economic status and food riots in areas of extreme poverty and drought. Most of the planet was in good shape and from the little information Cheyenne gathered, the areas of deepest need were being supplied from other areas. She did notice the primitive beliefs they were warned about were still prevalent. There were news articles about a "religious" leader known as the Intercessor. His name was never mentioned only his title. He was a member of the United World Council. This gave the four women cause for concern, but it didn't cause them to alter their plans to visit the planet.

Economically the planet seemed to be in a period of financial recovery. There were areas which were in good shape and some areas still needing help.

The governmental structure on Drea III was made up of several nations with bicameral or tricameral legislative bodies. The secondary leaders of each of the nations served on the United World Council (UWC). The Council appeared to have no legal authority over the individual countries, but they could influence decisions and actions of the various nations. The UWC's responsibilities included facilitation and mediation between the countries they represented.

Over the next couple days, the crew continued to acquire as much data as possible then Brynna called everyone together for a full staff meeting. The information was presented to the crew. They were warned that, due to the presence of such a high ranking religious leader, the people may be superstitious and very protective of this leader. The crew was not to challenge this leader in any way until his role on the council was more firmly determined.

Jake had been reviewing the records about the planet's security forces and weapons technologies. He reported their "police" forces in most countries were trained to military level standards. Their forces were routinely armed with pistol sized lasers, knives, and electroshock projectiles similar to the crew's Tri-EMP's. They were also reported to have rather extensive and effective body armor.

Lexi reported their technology to be comparable to the Commonwealth. The only thing they seemed to lack was space exploration technology. The biggest question was why they no longer appeared to be pursuing space exploration. There were four large satellites rotating around the planet, though they gave the appearance of being dormant. No incoming or outgoing signals were detected from the satellites. The crew surmised that after the introduction of the Commonwealth, the planet's inhabitants decided their people were not ready to accept "aliens from space." The governments probably stopped all space exploration and the satellites were simply leftover from their attempts forty-seven years earlier. Scans indicated the satellites showed signs of being in space for forty to sixty years.

Brynna decided this mission would simply be a diplomatic mission. She doubted there would be much in the way of technology they could offer this planet. She advised the crew to carry weapons but do so as discreetly as possible.

The crew had matched their schedule with the time zone of the United World Council a couple days earlier, so they were now ready to make contact. The next morning, David launched the ship from the moon's surface and began to work the ship into a wide orbit around Drea III. He wanted the planet's inhabitants to have time to "see" the ship coming slowly. He didn't want them to think they were about to be attacked.

The ship's surveillance indicated the United World Council had just convened. Aulani hijacked their communications net and sent a signal to address the Council. Brynna interrupted their meeting.

"Greetings United World Council of Drea III. I am Commander Brynna Alexander of the Commonwealth Interstellar Force Space Exploration vessel Evangeline. This is my husband and the commander of the Evangeline, Captain David Alexander. We are here on a diplomatic mission from the Commonwealth. If you will permit us, we would like to-"

"Commander…" Brynna was interrupted by an older woman on the Council. The woman had salt and pepper colored hair pulled neatly in a tight bun at the back of her head. She sat in the center of a panel of what appeared to be the leaders of the council. "The Commonwealth has not been welcome on Drea III for nearly fifty years. Please move on out of our space and you can take your satellites with you."

At that moment, Security Chief Holden reported. "Captain! The satellites are active. I'm detecting a weapons lock!"

Brynna looked back at the Council. "Are you preparing to fire at us?

We will gladly leave peacefully."

David addressed Thane and Marissa. "Move us away from the planet and plot a course out of this system."

The woman on the screen answered Brynna. "We have no such weapons. Those satellites belong to your Commonwealth. You must leave quickly, or they will shoot you down. They were left behind when your people left our world the last time. They're meant to make sure we never leave our planet."

Brynna gave a disbelieving look to the woman then moved to her station. Jake piped up again. "Captain the nearest satellite is firing a laser cannon."

David quickly barked orders. "Evasive maneuvers! Raise the deflector shield. Brynna, get me the shutdown codes for those satellites. If those are ours, we should be able to shut them down." David punched the ship wide comm line. "Engineering prepare for emergency maneuvers. All hands brace for impact."

As Thane punched the controls, the ship lurched side to side. The artificial gravity countered the ship's movements, but such drastic moves were still felt. The laser cannon blast lasted about six seconds. In his attempts to dodge the blast Thane had moved the ship into a second satellites range.

"Second satellite powering up!" Jake bellowed.

David responded quickly and decisively. "Jake, fire ship's lasers at the first satellite. Thane, put us on a line right between those two satellites heading away from Drea III."

The woman jumped in quickly with a vital piece of information. "Their ranges overlap! You'll be hit by both satellites!"

David had to fight the urge to shove Thane out of the way and take the helm himself. "Belay that order. Head straight for the first satellite. Jake continue firing. Brynna, do you have that code yet?"

"Negative, Captain, still working on it." Brynna quickly responded.

The second satellite fired. The deflector absorbed some of the energy and deflected the rest. When David saw the laser bounce off the shield, he had an idea. "Marissa, can you find an angle to deflect that beam, so a primary beam bounces off us and hits a secondary satellite? I need it fast. Engineering, can we activate the tachyon drive?"

Lazaro responded. "No, Captain, not while we are using the deflector and firing lasers. It will take time to build the tachyon web and if we get hit during that time, we're instantly fried."

Thane piped up. "Captain! How close do you want me to get to this satellite?" If the satellite hits them at this range, the shields may fail.

David answered quickly. "Lieutenant, put us in a zigzag pattern working your way outward going in and out of the range where the satellites first activated. Jake, any damage to that satellite?"

"Negative, Captain, those things have shields comparable to ours." As Thane turned the ship again, the first satellite fired. Thane dodged, but the beam caught the edge of the ship which flipped the ship the way one would flip a coin. The ship went tumbling towards the second satellite. Thane struggled to stop the spiral and resume his course. Lazaro had stayed on an open channel and monitored what was happening on the bridge. He was also watching the engine readings. He found a brief opening in the activity and threw in a vital piece of information. "Captain, the deflector strength is down by 23%."

David acknowledged the engineer and moved on. Thane got the ship under control and turned it again, but he had lost a great deal of momentum. As they moved back in the general direction of the first satellite, David looked at the woman on the screen who had continued to watch the crew anxiously. "If we land, will it stop firing?"

The woman looked sorrowful. "No, I'm sorry. It won't. Even if you go out of its range, it will signal one of the others to destroy you."

David turned his attention back to his previous attempts to escape. The second satellite fired and hit the ship solidly. The entire ship shuttered and groaned under the stress. The deflector again absorbed some of the impact and deflected some. Lazaro updated the Captain again quickly, "Shields down to 61%!" David didn't take the time to acknowledge him but jumped to Marissa. "Lt. Holden, have you got that trajectory yet?"

Marissa responded. "Yes sir, sending coordinates to Lt. Ryder now. Sir, attitude and pitch need to be exactly right. I'm sending that information as well. But Captain, this position puts us in the range of both satellites."

David glanced at Thane and snapped, "Do it!"

Jake jumped in again. "Captain! The satellites need six seconds to recharge after firing." The second satellite hit the ship again just as Jake said the words. The Captain turned to Jake, "Cease firing at the first satellite and reroute power to the deflector. Lazaro, reroute as much power as you can to the deflector and the thrusters." Again, he didn't wait for a response. The ship moved slowly into the position indicated by Lt. Holden. Thane began adjusting the ship's attitude and pitch as instructed, but they were hit by another blast before he could finish. Thane fired thrusters again and moved the ship into position. The ship was finally where the Captain wanted it.

Lazaro piped up with another shield update, "Shields at 28%."

The Captain looked at Thane. "Make sure you keep us in this position, no matter what."

Thane nodded. "Yes sir!" Marissa linked her controls in with Thane's to try and hold the ship steady with him.

By this point the first satellite locked onto them again and fired again. The ship shuttered. Lazaro reported shield integrity down to 17%. David barked at Lazaro, "Reroute power from everything to the deflectors including life support."

The second satellite was due to fire again. Thane and Marissa were frantically realigning the ship for the next hit. The second satellite fired again as the ship settled back into place. The next six seconds seemed to be the longest the crew had ever experienced. The beam bounced off the ship and hit the first satellite squarely just as it was powering up to fire again. It caused the energy beam to feedback on itself and shorted out the firing mechanism. The thing still had a target lock on the ship. The crew watched and waited. The pulse never came and as the feedback loop worked its way through the satellite's circuitry, the entire thing finally shut down and the target lock was lost. The second satellite still had a lock on the ship and fired again after recharging. The ship had been knocked further away by the previous blast, so the hit was not as strong. It was still strong enough to finish off the deflector. Lazaro was quick to notify the Captain. "Captain, shields are down and we have damage to the net. The hull is intact, though."

The blast didn't hit the ship squarely and sent the ship tumbling again. Thane struggled to stabilize the vessel. With Marissa's help, Thane got it under control. The ship was now out of the second satellite's range. Scans indicated the satellite had transmitted the ship's coordinates to the first satellite which was no longer functioning. David really hoped the satellite didn't require a confirmation of target acquisition. The ship sat nearly dead in space, waiting and monitoring the second satellite. The satellite appeared to have shut down.

Once they decided the onslaught was over, David began to assess damage and consider his next moves. "All hands, report in to Ensign Ryder."

Brynna looked up at David. "Captain, I have the codes you asked for now." She looked almost sick to her stomach. Finding them after the ship was damaged and now out of danger was more irony than she cared for.

David looked at her. It took a moment for him to process the look on her face. "Input the codes and send them to all the satellites. I want them all shut down immediately."

David looked back up at the face of the woman on the UWC. Her face displayed obvious relief the ship had survived. David and Brynna both found it curious. She had plainly told them they weren't welcome, but she was glad to see them survive?

Before he could address the woman on the screen Ensign Ryder interrupted. "Captain, all hands have reported in. There were no injuries. Lt. Commander Dominick reports tachyon drive is not functional due to web damage to the hull. He says we can't leave this system until we make repairs. We have maneuvering thrusters and landing capabilities, but he advises we don't attempt to land until the deflectors are minimally recharged to prevent any potential hull breaches. The ship's structural integrity is intact; however, it may be weakened."

"Acknowledged, Ensign. Have the Lt. Commander do what he can and standby for further instructions." David turned his attention back to the viewer. "We apologize for the interruption. I believe we were attempting to introduce ourselves. I am Captain David Alexander of the Commonwealth ship the Evangeline. My wife, Commander Brynna Alexander is here on a diplomatic mission to Drea III."

The woman had relaxed and was now taking the same stance she had earlier. "Captain, I'm sorry for the frightening welcome you just received, but we want no ties with the Commonwealth."

Brynna stood to address the woman. "Our information says you are known as Moderator Saundra Tarmon. Is that correct?"

The woman seemed unsettled these strangers knew who she was. "Have you been spying on us?"

Brynna smiled. "Only if watching your own public information broadcasts is considered spying."

Brynna saw the woman relax again. She even smiled in return. "Yes, I am Moderator Tarmon."

Brynna continued trying to win the woman's trust. "Moderator, I accept you want no part of the Commonwealth, but I wondered if you would take the time to hear us out. If you still want us to leave, we will. We can leave the satellites dormant if that is your desire as well. We won't stay where we aren't wanted. We are searching for something and thought perhaps your people could help us. We also are now in need of a place to land and make repairs to our ship. We cannot leave this star system until the repairs are complete."

"Commander, I don't mean to be insensitive to your situation, but..."

A woman sitting next to the Moderator handed her what appeared to be a data pad. The Moderator frowned and gave the woman a disturbed look. She then turned her attention back to Brynna. "Standby Commander Alexander."

The screen faded to a default picture of the UWC logo. Brynna gave David a questioning look. David gave Brynna a shrug in return. In a moment, the Moderator was back and acting rather pensive. "Commander, Captain, we will meet with you and give you whatever you need. Here are coordinates for a private and appropriate landing site. We would prefer you come in from the ocean, so your landing isn't seen by the general population. The Commonwealth left a bad taste in the mouths of everyone on this planet. It would be best if no one knew you were here. You may carry whatever weapons you feel are necessary for your own safety. However, I must insist there be an armed escort with you at all times when you leave your ship. Do we have an agreement?"

David glanced at Brynna who gave a very slight nod. "Moderator, thank you for your offer. My wife will be responsible for the diplomacy. My responsibilities are for the safety of this ship and its crew. These terms are acceptable to both of us."

The Moderator nodded to the couple. "Would it be possible to ask you to wait until nightfall to come in? That would also help keep your presence undetected."

David glanced over at Aulani before answering. Aulani knew without David saying anything what he was asking. In a moment, she had an answer for him. "The Lt. Commander says he needs at least eight hours minimum to charge the deflectors and longer would be better."

David looked back at the Moderator. "After dark, it is. We will contact you before we begin our descent. We'll plan on beginning our repairs in the morning and to meet with you at your convenience."

The Moderator agreed and concluded her communication. As soon as she was gone Brynna looked at David. "Why do you suppose she changed her mind?"

Jake offered his thoughts. "Do you suppose it's a trap?"

It was David's turn to look pensive. "I don't know, but I don't intend to get caught unprepared."

Jake gave David a questioning look. "How do propose we defend ourselves against an entire planet, especially with a damaged ship?"

David studied Jake's face. "I want scanners trained on the area we're to land in. If there are significant troop or artillery movements near the landing site or our intended approach pattern, let me know immediately." David rotated his chair to face Aulani. "Ensign, monitor all communications going into and out of the UWC. I don't mean to eavesdrop, but I do want to know about anything pertaining to us. If the Moderator uses her communications access code elsewhere, monitor that as well. Enlist the help of Lt. Flint and Ensign Dominick if you need to." "Yes sir." Aulani proceeded to program the computer to notify her if Moderator Tarmon's code was used. For good measure, she did a search for the codes of the other leaders on the UWC and added them to her "watch list." Aulani programmed the computer to notify her if key words showed up. She contacted Cheyenne and Lexi and told them she was going to be forwarding transcribed copies of communiques for them to peruse. She explained what they were looking for and what steps she had already taken with the key word searches. It was doubtful the computer would miss anything, but one could never be too careful.

Later that evening, the crew was preparing to leave their standard orbit and put the ship down on the planet. David notified Moderator Tarmon of their intentions and continued scanning the area. Jake reported an increase in security around the perimeter. There was a visible showing of troops around their intended landing site, but nothing excessive. Everything could be attributed to a normal high security situation, not a show of force. If he had felt threatened, they would have located a remote place to put the ship down and made their repairs as quickly and quietly as possible. Technically, they could have made the repairs while in orbit, but it would have been extremely dangerous and time consuming. The repairs were going to have to be made outside the ship which would mean space walks in environmental suits. Making the repairs on the ground was much safer and faster.

Once the ship was cleared for landing by Lt. Commander Dominick and Moderator Tarmon, David gave the order. The ship didn't normally moan and groan during a landing. Because of the external damage to the ship, this time it did. The difference was evident on the crew's faces as they worked quietly and looked around every time they heard an unexpected noise. From the looks on their faces, David thought they expected the hull to break apart at any second. He didn't blame them for their thoughts. It had crossed his mind as well. The ship landed safely, and everyone breathed a sigh of relief.

A group of troops were standing in formation near their landing site.

David left Brynna in command on the bridge while he took Jake outside to greet the troops assembled outside the ship. He left strict instructions for her if something unfortunate were to happen.

Jason was at the helm with Marissa. Thane was sent to the shuttle with Braxton, just in case.

David opened the hatch slowly and lowered the stairs to the ground. He stepped out onto the platform slowly. Jake carried a multipurpose rifle in his hands, pointed down at the ground. He stepped out beside the Captain. The Captain held his hands open and raised slightly, so the troops on the ground could see he wasn't a threat. Jake stayed at the top of the platform while the Captain moved slowly down the steps.

A man who appeared to be in charge of the troops on the ground walked equally slowly towards David. The two met about halfway between the ship and the ground troops. The man spoke first. "I'm Colonel Aaron Bernt of the Cathal Security Force."

David responded in kind. "I am Captain David Alexander of the Co… uh the… Interstellar Ship, the Evangeline."

Colonel Bernt scowled at David's hesitation. "I know you're from the Commonwealth, Captain. Why are you trying to hide who you are?" David gave the Colonel a wry smile. "I apologize if I offended you, Colonel. Moderator Tarmon informed us the Commonwealth left a bad impression and advised us to keep a low profile. I didn't know if you had been informed exactly who we were."

The Colonel was still suspicious. "What are your intentions, Captain?"

The Captain spoke plainly. "My intentions tonight are to introduce myself then get some sleep before starting repairs on our ship in the morning. I also wanted to be sure you're here just as a precaution and not as an attacker. What are your intentions, Colonel?"

The Colonel finally smiled. "My intentions are similar to yours, Captain. I am here as a precaution and to be certain you aren't planning to attack us."

David smiled in return. It would appear they understood each other. "Colonel, my people intend to stay inside our ship tonight. As far as tomorrow is concerned, we have major repairs to tend to. Please let your superiors know even though we represent the Commonwealth, we are on a mission of peace. Our weapons are only for self-defense. We are not equipped for war."

The Colonel rocked on his heels. "Captain, you realize we only have your word for it, and you are a stranger."

David nodded. "I understand. I also understand you have no ships capable of space travel to use as a reference, but this ship is not big enough to carry weapons and troops sufficient to attack your planet. I suppose we could wreak some havoc for a time, but eventually you would find a way to take us out. We are also obviously crippled. Please take whatever precautions you feel you need to. We mean your people no harm. We will protect our own, and if we are asked to leave, we will do so."

Colonel Bernt studied David for a moment. The darkness and artificial lighting made it hard for him to see David as clearly as he would like to. "You're awfully young to be commanding a ship, aren't you?"

David smiled. "I am one of the youngest captains, but for this mission they didn't need people with lots of experience. I think they wanted the young and innocent or should I say naive."

The Colonel laughed. "That was a long time ago for me. Welcome to Drea III, Captain."

"Thank you, Colonel."

After a few more minutes of idle chatter, David returned to the ship and closed the hatch. Naturally someone stayed on watch all night.

The crew ate breakfast at sunrise while David and Brynna briefed the crew on the day's agenda and how to conduct themselves. The Captain instructed the crew to maintain the highest standards of military decorum. This society was far more advanced than the previous ones they had encountered. Customs and courtesies may differ, but the presence of military decorum speaks the same in any society. The Captain set the tone immediately at breakfast by using the crew's rank and last names again.

After breakfast, David and Jake headed out the same way they had the previous night. The Captain put the same security measures in place, and only Lazaro went with him to examine the ship from the outside. The troops had been stationed around the ship during the night at a discreet distance. Their "protectors" were not asleep, but their posture indicated they weren't on high alert. As soon as David opened the hatch, the men were suddenly very focused. These men were young and the only things they knew about the Commonwealth and off-worlders was what they learned in school. Naturally they were curious, but they also had orders to keep their distance. As soon as David and Lazaro started walking around the ship, one of their chaperons notified a higher-ranking officer who joined the troops in a few short minutes.

David got a better look at his surroundings with the morning light. They had landed at a military landing strip. There were other aircraft and hangars in the area around them. None appeared to be passenger aircraft.

Lt. Commander Dominick informed the Captain he would need to pull the Surf-Ve out of the hold to work on the edge and underside of the ship. As they discussed their intentions, Colonel Bernt arrived. David walked out to talk with him. He informed Colonel Bernt they would be pulling their surface transport vehicle out to aid in the repairs. He didn't want the Colonel or his troops to get nervous unnecessarily. The Colonel in turn, informed the crew the UWC board of directors would be there to meet with them that afternoon. David thanked the Colonel for the information and went back to the ship. He left Jake on look out while he went inside to talk to Brynna.

David found her at her station on the bridge. "Commander, I just talked to Colonel Bernt. He told me the UWC board of directors wants to meet with us this afternoon. I don't know what they plan on discussing, but as fond as they are of the Commonwealth, I think I am going to put as many people as possible into working on repairs. I want this ship fully functional as soon as possible."

Brynna readily agreed. "I hope we can find out why they dislike the Commonwealth so much. Maybe we can do something to improve relations. I've got Lexi working on pulling as many historical files as we can. I hope we can get the information together before our meeting this afternoon."

David assigned all the crew to either repairs or standing guard with the exceptions of Brynna and Lexi. The crew worked diligently making the repairs. Repairing the net was time consuming and tedious work. It would take at least two days to get it repaired, possibly longer. It wasn't a job he wanted to rush through. If it wasn't done right, the ship could rip apart the next time the tachyon drive was engaged. David took his turn standing guard and helping with the repairs.

It was late afternoon when a convoy of vehicles arrived carrying the expected officials. The delegation was escorted to a conference room in one of the buildings nearby. When David saw what he surmised were the expected guests, he stopped his work on the ship's hull, notified Brynna and went inside to get cleaned up. The crew had different levels of uniforms. Class One uniforms were the formal uniforms they had worn to the banquet before they launched. Class Two uniforms were a business type uniform. Class Three was a more casual and versatile uniform one would wear on the average day or if one expected to get hot or dirty. The crew wore this uniform routinely. Class Four was a combat type uniform which had a variety of sub-levels based on what type of situation they were in. Class Four might be white for snowy weather, camouflage based on the environment or black for police type actions in urban settings. David had been in his Class Three uniform and gotten quite dirty while working. He quickly showered and decided on the Class Two uniform.

Brynna joined him a couple minutes later and changed into her Class Two uniform as well. She hailed Lexi and Thane to inform of the appropriate uniform. Thane was going as a security officer.

The four finished getting ready just in time to greet Colonel Bernt. The Colonel was there to escort the Captain and his party to meet with the delegation from the United World Council. The four got into a vehicle with the Colonel and his own security officers and rode a short distance to one of the nearby buildings. Colonel Bernt led the crew to a conference room where the UWC delegation were already seated.

The room contained one large round conference table. The UWC board of directors consisted of three people. The woman they recognized as Moderator Tarmon stood up and waved the crew to seats on the other side of the table. "Welcome, please have a seat."

Brynna and Lexi took the two center seats facing the Moderator. David sat next to Brynna and Thane sat next to Lexi but didn't slide his chair forward. His primary duty was security, not diplomacy. David's chair was only halfway pulled up to the table. His job was a little of both. Once the crew was settled, the Moderator continued. "As you know,

I am Moderator Saundra Tarmon. On my left is Damarion Torrell, Vice- Chancellor of Raanan and on my right is Vice-Chancellor Irena Noe of Ketill."

Brynna stood and introduced herself and her party as well. Vice- Chancellor Torrell was confused by David and Brynna's roles. Brynna did her best to explain their symbiotic and alternating roles. Although he verbally declared understanding of her explanation, his face was not as convincing.

Brynna started to explain her mission and why they had approached the planet. Moderator Tarmon cut her off. "Commander, as we told you previously, your mission here is of no concern to us because the Commonwealth is not welcome here. We came to make sure your repairs will be completed as soon as possible, and you will leave and never return. Is there anything you need to speed things up?"

Brynna tried to hide her frustration. She looked over at David. "Captain, what is our expected timetable for completing repairs to the ship?"

The Captain slid his chair forward. "The repairs are going to take at least two more days. I'm sorry for the inconvenience. The repairs to the net are meticulous and tedious. If we could simply replace them, it would speed things up a bit, but we don't have enough spare material for this large of a repair."

Moderator Tarmon glanced at her companions. "What sort of material?"

"The ship's hull has a network of specialized conduits that carry tachyon particles. It has to be exactly right, or it won't function." David was careful not to give them too much information. With their dislike for the Commonwealth, someone could easily use the information to try and sabotage the ship and dissuade the Commonwealth from visiting again. "The tachyons create a field like those found in wormholes causing a bubble which pulls the ship through space surpassing light speed."

Before he could go any further in his explanation, he noticed the board members looking back and forth at each other.

After an awkward pause, David continued. "Are you familiar with this technology? We were of the understanding you hadn't ventured into space."

Moderator Tarmon got visual approval from her companions before answering. "We experimented with this technology for intra-planetary travel. It's possible some of our engineers could help your people."

Brynna gave David a questioning look. Why would they offer their help? The Commander turned to the Moderator and asked her the question she had just asked herself. "Moderator Tarmon, forgive me for asking, but why would you want to help us?"

Stress showed on the Moderator's face. "Forgive my bluntness, but we want you gone as soon as possible."

Brynna took this as her opportunity to ask the question she had been anxiously holding onto. "Moderator, apparently our historical logs are lacking. We knew nothing about those satellites in orbit around your planet and we don't understand what happened between you and the Commonwealth. We would be very grateful if you could enlighten us. What happened fifty years ago?"

The three looked at each other again. Chancellor Torrell volunteered to answer. "We started a space program seventy years ago. It got the attention of your people. They came bearing gifts to help us further our space program, but it cost us dearly. Your people tried to destroy our culture and governments. At first, we welcomed your people and their ideas. We adopted your language. The United World Council exists as a result of contact with your people. The larger nations embraced the Commonwealth's ideology, but the smaller nations thought it was a plot to steal power from them. It caused a world war. The Commonwealth declared us unfit to join them. They ordered us to stop all pursuits of space travel until they deemed us fit to join them. We refused to adhere to the Commonwealth's mandate and tried to continue our attempts to explore our own star system. The Commonwealth attacked our space exploration facilities. They destroyed the facilities from space. They killed thousands of innocent civilians. They placed those monstrous satellites around our planet to destroy any ship capable of leaving the atmosphere. After several tragic incidents, the entire planet quit trying to go into space. We focused our efforts on improving our home. And now here you are to bring more devastation to our world."

Chancellor Noe took up the dialogue at this point. "So, why have you come here? Are you checking to see if we are fit to join your Commonwealth now? Are you bearing more gifts?"

Before Brynna could respond Lexi pulled on her arm and whispered to her. Brynna nodded. She turned back to address Chancellor Noe's question. "Chancellor Noe, we knew nothing about your history with the Commonwealth. If what you have told us is accurate, then we are truly sorry for the bad blood between our two civilizations."

Chancellor Torrell jumped to his feet and his face turned blood red. "If it's accurate?!? Are you accusing us of lying?!?"

Brynna raised her hand to stop his tirade. "Chancellors, please, I mean no disrespect. All of this happened before I was born and while all of you were fairly young. History often changes based on who tells it and how many times it is told. Unfortunately, you are right about our current mission. We came to offer membership in the Commonwealth. We were sent to offer Commonwealth technology as goodwill gestures. We were sent to do exactly what you have just said."

The three dignitaries exchanged glances at Brynna's blunt admission. Moderator Tarmon took up the conversation again. "You admit this?"

Brynna responded honestly. "I have never had any intention of deceiving you. Yes, we were given permission to do what we needed to make an alliance work, but we were also told to walk away if it wasn't accepted."

Chancellor Torrell glared at Brynna. "Now that you have your answer will you leave peacefully?"

Brynna again responded candidly. "If that's your wish. I am truly sorry for what happened to you. We are not here to harm anyone. I appreciate your candor, but your information about the Commonwealth is fifty years old. I am having a hard time understanding how the Commonwealth would be guilty of such atrocities. I can't even begin to establish any kind of a relationship with your world without knowing what happened here. Please give us a chance to fix this."

The Moderator stared intently at Brynna. "We will return to the Council and discuss it. I doubt there is much you could say to change anyone's mind about the Commonwealth, but I will try. I will send Colonel Bernt with our answer."

"Before you take this back to your Council, I have a suggestion. Let's put the Commonwealth on trial just between us. Please invite other Council members if you like but give us a fair chance to debate the issue with you."

The Moderator was confused. David and Lexi were confused as well. Moderator Tarmon overcame her confusion. "How is this supposed to help?"

Brynna confidently replied. "If you aren't convinced we are truly here to help and establish good relations, we will leave quietly under cover of darkness again and no one needs to ever know we were here. If we convince you we have honorable intentions, then we get to present our proposal to your council."

Chancellor Torrell jumped in. "What if you find out your Commonwealth is not as innocent as you thought it was? What will you do then? Will you try to destroy us to keep their ugly secrets?"

Brynna started to respond until David touched her arm. Seeing he had something on his mind she begged the delegation's indulgence for a moment. David and Lexi leaned in close to discuss the matter discreetly. "Commander, what are you planning on offering them?" David whispered.

Brynna quietly told the two her intention was to leave and give them the codes to the satellites orbiting their world. David scowled at her. "You can't give someone access to CIF codes and weapons if they are self- proclaimed enemies of the Commonwealth."

Lexi backed David's objection. "Commander, he's right. You can't do this. It would be treason."

Brynna gave the two of them a stare suggesting she thought both had lost their minds. The two of them were thinking in turn Brynna had lost her mind. Brynna finally tried to put their minds at ease. "They would have to convince us the Commonwealth was, and still is, an evil force to be reckoned with. Are you two telling me you have doubts about the innocence of the Commonwealth?"

"No, of course not, but . . ." Lexi's voice trailed off.

David picked up her train of thought. "They aren't going to accept such a one-sided challenge. What hope would they have of convincing us we are in the wrong? Lastly, what if we were convinced the Commonwealth is up to no good? We would be honor bound to give them those codes."

Brynna shook her head. "Captain, what is it you think they can do with fifty-year-old codes giving them access to four, fifty-year-old satellites? It means they can start them up, shut them down or reprogram them to protect their own world. I don't really see a problem here. I also doubt their fifty-year-old knowledge could convince me of the Commonwealth's ill intentions. Do I have your consent to continue?"

Something about this idea was gnawing at David's insides. "Offer to leave the satellites shut down, not to give them the codes."

Brynna took a deep breath. "Yes, Captain." Brynna turned back to the delegation. "Moderator Tarmon, if you convince us the Commonwealth's intentions are not honorable as we have been led to believe, then we will leave and will leave those satellites dormant. We'll send out warnings to other Commonwealth vessels there are active satellites surrounding your planet and it should be avoided at all costs. You will have the option of exploring space again without anyone to stop you. I can't help you when you get outside this star system and run into other Commonwealth vessels. Would that be acceptable to you?"

Chancellor Noe gave the group a skeptical stare. "If we convinced you the Commonwealth is corrupt then why would you leave and return to your mission?"

Brynna didn't hesitate to answer. "The Commonwealth knows where we are. If we simply stayed here and didn't return, someone would come here to investigate. If we are convinced of your argument, then we would not want to bring your enemy to your doorstep. We would owe you the courtesy of at least protecting you. We would also need to return to the last two planets we visited and undo some damage. We would also be obligated to find out who's responsible for such travesties and try to put them right."

The three appeared pleased with her response. They discussed her suggestion quietly then gave her their answer. "We accept this challenge. I think the Intercessor will be equally pleased. We can begin in three days. We will send our engineers to meet with your engineer to see if we can offer any help with your repairs while we each prepare for this trial."

"The Intercessor?" Lexi wanted to know the role this religious leader played in their government.

Moderator Tarmon bit her lower lip. "The Intercessor is on the board of directors of the United World Council, but he is currently unavailable. He is the one who asked us to allow you to land. He will rejoin us in a few days. You can learn about him when you meet him."

Brynna smiled. "That's fine. We look forward to meeting him." The Moderator smiled as well. "I look forward to our debate." The meeting adjourned, and the groups went their separate ways.

As promised the next morning, two Drean Engineers presented themselves to the Captain and Lt. Commander Dominick. They introduced themselves as Robin Alberto and Hugh Kelly. They seemed a bit nervous. David didn't question their nervousness, he assumed it was simply because the ship represented a fifty-year-old danger to them. David did everything he could to put the two at ease.

Lazaro doubted the Drean Engineers would be able to help them at all. Since they had done no space exploration they would have little need to explore tachyon use. Once he had given the engineers the basic run-through of how the ship worked, showing them the damaged hull and conduits, he expected them to shake their heads and walk away. The engineers stepped away and talked privately for a moment. Lazaro and David were waiting patiently by the ship. Lazaro turned his head, so the approaching engineers could not make out what he was saying and spoke quietly to David. "Here we go. I doubt they understood half of what I showed them." David gave Lazaro a stern look.

When the two reached David and Lazaro, the female engineer was the first to speak. "Captain, Lt. Commander, may we take a piece of the damaged conduit back with us to our facility? We make similar conduit there, but if the molecular structure isn't a precise match, well... let's just say the results could be disastrous."

Lazaro suddenly looked like he had swallowed an insect. David covered for his stunned companion. "You have a facility already producing this type of conduit? Since you have no space travel, what do you use it for?"

Robin looked nervously at her fellow engineer. "Uh, Hugh? Are we at liberty to discuss this?" Robin Alberto was an attractive young engineer who had not been out of school for very long. She appeared to be very gifted in engineering. Her biggest flaw was a lack of experience and confidence.

David quickly put her fears to rest. "It's okay. This isn't something I need to know. I was just surprised and curious. If you talk to your superiors later and they say it's okay, you can tell us about it then. Please feel free to take a piece of the conduit. It might be better if you take a small undamaged piece, so you have a better sample. Isn't that right Commander?"

Lazaro had now recovered sufficiently to converse appropriately. "Yes, he's right. If you take a damaged piece, the molecular structure could have been altered enough to be incompatible with the undamaged pieces."

Hugh seemed reluctant to talk much. He spoke with Robin but said little to the crew. He was an older man. His hair was white. David wasn't sure what the life expectancy was of people here, but it was entirely possible Hugh had been old enough to remember the Commonwealth vividly. Hugh glared at Lazaro. He did know who they were and where they were from. He had been swallowing his pride by coming and helping the Commonwealth aliens. Now he was done. He spoke in a heavily accented Intergalactic Standard. "You think because we aren't a part of your Commonwealth we're not as advanced as you. We are an advanced society. We don't murder innocents like your people."

David had the urge to get defensive but chose instead to have compassion on the man. "I am truly sorry for whatever losses you have suffered. My engineer and I were not even born at the time those events occurred, so we have no knowledge of what happened here. I'm no killer, innocent or otherwise." For a split second, David paused. Memories of his early days as a wartime soldier flashed through his mind along with images of his dream from Galat. He took a second to shake off the images and continue his train of thought. "I promise you this. I will do whatever I can to make this right again." His tale was mostly accurate.

Hugh stepped closer to the Captain and in a flash landed a right cross to the Captain's jaw. The Captain found himself on the ground in front of Lazaro. Lazaro quickly bent down to help the Captain up but kept one eye on the angry engineer. Jake was on duty on the top of the ship, and when he saw the altercation he ran down the hull until it became too steep near the edge. He threw himself down feet first and slid down the steep section of the hull landing upright on the Surf-Ve which was parked at the edge of the ship's hull. He was now standing with his rifle pointed squarely at the visiting engineers. David heard him coming and while keeping his eye locked on Hugh's eyes, he ordered Jake to stand down. The Captain slowly got to his feet, allowing time for the situation to diffuse a little. He wiped a spot of blood from his busted lip. He seemed to be doing that a lot lately. "For an older man, you pack quite a punch. I assume this was… personal?"

Robin was standing frozen in fear. The troops around the perimeter were closing in quickly upon seeing the disturbance. Hugh still appeared to be shaking in anger. "My sister and her husband were in one of the buildings your people destroyed! Do you think you can fix that? They left behind two small children. Can you give them back their parents and the joy of their childhood?"

"Whoever was responsible for that action is long gone. I don't know who it was or why they committed such atrocities. We are not here to repeat their actions. My orders are to make friends or leave. Our weapons are minimal and for self-defense only. I will find out whatever I can and as I said, I will do whatever I can to make this right. Maybe I can't, but I will try."

The troops now surrounded the five of them, but they weren't sure who to point their weapons at. They were just as uptight by the ship and its crew as the two engineers, but their orders were to protect the crew and the ship. Colonel Bernt arrived in a personal vehicle about two seconds after the troops. The Colonel stepped down from his vehicle and demanded to know what was going on.

Hugh continued to stare in anger at David. David faced Colonel Bernt. "I apologize for the disturbance. It was my fault. It appears I am unfamiliar with the proper customs and courtesies of this world and I offended Mr. Kelly. I was just about to offer an apology to him for my offense." David turned back to Engineer Kelly. "I am truly sorry. We didn't mean to cause you any harm. I hope someday you can forgive us." The engineer's stare began to soften as the realization began to hit him, David really could not be held accountable for what others had done to him. The engineer reached out to shake David's hand. "Maybe you aren't the one to blame. I'm sorry I hit you. We will get your conduit to you late this afternoon."

David shook his hand warmly to let him know there were no hard feelings. Hugh reached over to his stunned co-worker and guided her away from the ship by the arm.

After the two were out of earshot, Colonel Bernt looked at David. "That didn't sound like a breach in customs and courtesies to me."

David gave the Colonel a wry smile. "No, I suppose it didn't, but I am reporting it to you as a misunderstanding."

The Colonel nodded. "I see. Perhaps when we are off-duty you can give me a better explanation."

"I'll do that." David smiled.

The Colonel had understood completely what David was and was not saying. David rubbed his aching jaw and headed inside.

Lazaro was nearly as stunned as Engineer Alberto. He glanced at the Colonel. "I hope he explains that to me when he explains it to you. I'm a little lost myself."

The Colonel laughed. "He's not going to explain anything to me. A Captain is never off-duty. He may get some sleep, but he's never really off-duty. All he told me is he doesn't want to get the engineers in trouble." Lazaro looked at the direction the Captain had gone, and then looked back at Colonel Bernt. "Is that what he said? I seem to have missed it." The Colonel returned to his car smiling at Lazaro's confusion. It was something only someone in command would understand.

A couple hours later Robin returned with two pieces of conduit. Lazaro scanned the pieces carefully and determined they matched the ship's original conduit perfectly. The craftsmanship was flawless and rivaled their own. The young engineer contacted Hugh Kelly to let him know the pieces worked, and in another couple hours the crew had all the conduit they needed. Lazaro carefully scanned every piece for flaws. One flaw or weak spot could be disastrous. He was also careful because of the grudge Hugh obviously carried against the Commonwealth. If he wanted revenge, the easiest way to get it would be to send a sabotaged piece of conduit. Lazaro didn't enjoy paranoia. He had to admit though, sometimes it saved lives.

Robin spent the rest of the afternoon working alongside Lazaro and Braxton. She was eager to see and understand their alien technology. She wasn't working with them to spy on them. She was genuinely curious. Spying would have given her very little information anyway. The Dreans were already using this technology only the application was different.

As the sunlight began to fade, Robin excused herself and headed home. Braxton and Lazaro headed back into the ship to eat and get some rest. Once they headed inside and the hatch was secure, Marissa also headed inside from standing guard.

The crew sat around together in the dining hall enjoying lighthearted conversation. The topic of choice seemed to be the Captain's bruised face. David sat there and quietly took the jovial haranguing. Jake was the one having the most fun. He laughed loudly about the "old" man putting the young robust Captain on the ground. Lazaro looked at the Captain. He had seen David's cat-like reflexes and knew it was not like him to get surprised like that. Finally, Lazaro was tired of Jake's lambasting comments. "Captain, I've seen you in action. Why didn't you duck when he threw that punch? You had to have seen it coming."

David continued eating. "I guess it was just an off day for me."

Brynna was getting just as fed up with Jake's attitude. Her eyes narrowed as she studied David's face. He was hiding something. "You're lying. You knew he was going to slug you, and you just stood there and took it. Why?"

David could have hidden his secret better if he had wanted to. It either wasn't that important, or a small part of him was annoyed with Jake as well. Now his face appeared even more guilty. Lazaro looked into David's eyes as well. "She's right, you did see that punch coming. Why didn't you stop him?"

David set his fork down. The crew stopped laughing and waited for his answer. David sighed. "The man had a fifty-year-old ax to grind. He needed a target and if it wasn't me, it might have been the ship or one of you. He also now knows I wasn't quick to retaliate. Jake could have killed him if I had given the word. That man knew what I could have done to him and what I didn't do. Now he has something to think about. The UWC Board of Directors has a report about the incident as well by now. They know I could have reported it to Colonel Bernt and I didn't."

Jake was finished eating and sitting in his usual position with his chair leaned back against the wall balanced on two legs. As soon as David finished speaking, Jake brought his chair back down on all four legs. "Are you kidding me? You let him hit you? Why did you let me sit here and make a fool of myself by laughing at you?"

David grinned. "You did that all by yourself." The room erupted in laughter. David picked his fork up again and started to take another bite but stopped. "Jake, you did a good job out there this morning. Thanks for having my back and using restraint."

Jake nodded. "You're welcome sir."

David headed to the gym for a light workout after his meal then back to his quarters. He showered and got into bed. He had assigned himself the early watch then guard duty after breakfast. Brynna came in and found him lying in bed staring at the ceiling with all the lights still on. "You aren't going to get to sleep very quickly like that." She quipped.

David glanced around the room and at his own posture. Looking back at Brynna, he gave her a weak smile. "I suppose you're right." David rolled onto his side and dimmed the overhead lights and turned off his bedside light. Brynna dimmed the lights even more to help him sleep without hindering herself. In a couple minutes David rolled onto his other side. He tossed and turned the entire time Brynna was getting ready for bed.

Brynna finally sat down on the edge of the bed and took his hand. "David, what's wrong?"

David's eyes made contact with Brynna's. Her face clearly told him not to play games or try to deny something was bothering him. She looked incredibly attractive in the gown she had chosen to wear to bed, but he knew she wasn't about to allow him to distract her from the question. David resigned himself to tell her what was on his mind. He sat up in the bed and propped up on his pillows. "I had flashbacks of my dream from Galat III while I was talking to the Drean engineers today. It was right after I said I had never killed anyone, guilty or innocent."

Brynna scowled. "David, the people on Galat were fine. You didn't do anything to harm them. They are still living their happy lives, benefiting from the technology we gave them. We didn't hurt them in any way. You're a good man. You would never do anything consciously to harm an innocent. Have you talked to Lexi about this?"

David smiled at Brynna. He reached up and caressed her soft face. He tried to massage the furrows out of her brow with his thumb. The furrows would not relax until he promised to talk to Lexi in the morning. Brynna turned out the remaining lights and cuddled up beside David. In a few minutes, they were both sound asleep. They seemed to both rest better together, rather than separately.

The next morning Lexi met with David while he was on guard duty. It gave Lexi a chance to get outside and the two could talk without anyone overhearing, so long as they kept their voices down. Lexi listened intently to the Captain's experience and offered a very viable explanation. She believed Arni planted these feelings of fear and doubt in David to interfere with him and his mission. Although the explanation sounded plausible, David was having trouble believing it. He affirmed her explanation to her satisfaction then made a mental note to hide his feelings better. He didn't want her or Brynna doubting his mental stability. He also decided to spend more time working out his anxiety on the punching bag in the gym. It seemed to be worth a little more than Lexi's suppositions.

With the help the local engineers had given by providing conduit, the repairs took a lot less time than Lazaro expected. Halfway through the next day they finished the repairs and started running tests to check the structural integrity of the network. The tests revealed the net was working perfectly.

Having completed the repairs, David got the crew working on some general maintenance of the ship including a good scrub down, inside and out. Every possible door and hatch was opened to give the ship a chance to "air out." The air filtration system kept the ship's air "clean," but over time, the air just felt stale. With the ship clean and in perfect working order, the crew was now able to concentrate again on their mission.

DEBATE OR TRIAL

Brynna and Moderator Tarmon decided the lighter format of a debate would be preferable to a trial. Moderator Tarmon suggested the meeting be set up in a banquet room as a debate with frequent breaks to discourage things from getting too intense. She also proposed a buffet be set up to encourage casual conversation and mingling. Brynna thoroughly liked the idea and gladly accepted her invitation to bring the entire crew. Both agreed the crew needed to get out and have some shore leave even if it was restricted to the banquet facility. Neither Jake, nor David, liked the idea of leaving the ship unattended, but felt it would be difficult to turn down the Drean hospitality.

The Moderator handpicked specific members of the council to attend. She chose those she considered more open minded. She wanted to be true to her word of giving their visitors a fair chance to be heard.

Brynna and Lexi spent their time putting together the history files pertaining to the Commonwealth's former contacts with Drea III and planning their presentation. Brynna tried to access the military files from the CIF database pertaining to the Commonwealth's prior contact with this world. She was met with a surprising amount of resistance. She was told the file was highly classified and her request would be referred to the proper authorities for consideration. She was also told to expect her answer in approximately six to eight weeks. The young commander started to withdraw her request, but something inside her really wanted to see that file even if it was received several weeks late.

David contacted his uncle to get the information for Brynna. The Admiral made some inquiries. He was quickly told to stop pursuing the matter. Admiral Deacons got back in touch with David and ordered the determined Captain not to continue looking into the matter. The Admiral seemed slightly unnerved, as though someone even more powerful had gotten to him. Admiral Deacons told David his inquiries were raising red flags all over the place. The Admiral didn't stay on the comm line very long. David got the feeling the Admiral was being monitored or at least he was worried about being monitored. David passed the information on to Brynna and Lexi. All three found the situation to be highly suspicious.

Brynna was getting frustrated. She tossed the data pad onto the table in front of her. "I don't understand. What's so important about a fifty- year-old file? No one who was in power then is still in power now. It couldn't possibly cause any problems for anyone, except possibly us, because we don't have it. How are we supposed to say in good conscience the Commonwealth is not a big bad monster?"

Lexi was almost as frustrated. "Maybe it could still be a source of embarrassment for someone who was young and naive then, but in a position of power now?"

David shook his head. "It's possible. In either case, we've been ordered to leave this alone. I suggest you plan for worst case scenarios. Imagine what might have happened and prepare a response."

Brynna wasn't overjoyed by this option. "I think I will have Cheyenne and Aulani research the local public databases for as much information as they can find. I just don't want to be blindsided."

"Let's just concentrate on what the Commonwealth is now and chalk the past up to a previous administration's bad choices. There's not really anything we can do about what's happened in the past anyway." Lexi pulled a lock of blond hair out of her face and tucked it behind her ear. It was her way putting things in their place metaphorically.

The morning of the debate and the crew loaded into vehicles sent by Moderator Tarmon. They were escorted by Colonel Bernt and his security detail to a building a few miles to the east. It was positioned on a cliff overlooking a spectacular pristine undeveloped beach front. The building was laid out as a do-decagon. Each of the twelve sides was surrounded by a shaded patio, a well-manicured lawn and gardens. There were benches and gazebos scattered throughout the gardens. The building itself had twelve supports stretching from the ground and twisting together upward into a spire. The walls appeared to be made of glass or clear crystal. The core of the building held the kitchen, maintenance closets, storage, and other building necessities. The buffet, debate floor, and seating were arranged around the outer ring, so they had the best view of the surrounding countryside and ocean.

The crew was dressed in their Class Two uniforms. They looked sharp in their business style uniforms. Their uniforms blended in nicely with the business clothing styles of the Dreans. The Dreans and the crew began their day by having a bountiful breakfast together and a fair amount of idle chatter. After a relaxed breakfast, Moderator Tarmon led Brynna and Lexi to the platform which had two tables on opposite sides each with table top podiums. She introduced them to the man who would be presiding over the debate. "Commander Alexander, this is Kato Navid, Arbiter of Taiomah. He will be overseeing our debate." Brynna and Lexi would be representing the Commonwealth while Irena Noe and Damarion Torrell would be representing Drea's position. The Moderator wanted to remain as neutral as possible. As the debate got underway, everyone took their seats and the guidelines were laid out for everyone. Each side would make an initial presentation starting with the Commonwealth. Once both sides made their opening presentations, the Arbitrator would present suppositions each side would address and be given opportunities to counter the others' statements.

The debate seemed to be stacked heavily in the Dreans favor, but Brynna was undaunted. She began the presentation cheerfully and confidently. She presented a brief overview of the development of the Commonwealth and its purpose to share resources equally among all members of the Commonwealth. Brynna emphasized the Commonwealth existed to do what was best for every one of its members. They didn't oppose wealth, but they did oppose wealth accumulated out of the detriment of others. It was a socialistic governmental approach. The government would basically rob from the rich and give to the poor. The rich learned ways to minimize the effects by stepping in and helping in a voluntary manner. This kept the government from getting too close. Brynna knew it was a volunteerism based out of greed, but she presented it positively as large corporations being gracious benefactors. She also assumed the Dreans would suppose the same thing.

Irena Noe made the initial presentation for the Dreans. She gave a brief history of their world as peaceful followers of the Ancient Texts. Their history mirrored most every world. They were working towards global unity and were nearly there. They still had primitive religious practices, but they didn't seem to be superstitious about them. When they reached the point of the Commonwealth's introduction, Damarion Torrell took over the presentation. He painted a very bleak picture of a peaceful race who tried to meet the expectations of the giant military force and when they could not, were violently punished. It caused numerous conflicts among the nations and nearly plunged them into a global war. The nations spent the next ten years cleaning up the mess and rededicating themselves to following the teaching of the Ancient Texts. They wanted to be prepared the next time the Commonwealth appeared, so they continued to teach Intergalactic Standard as a common language for two reasons. First, it was an easy language to learn and teach. Second, many of the ideas the Commonwealth taught fell right in line with their own Ancient Texts, so keeping the language of the Commonwealth seemed a prudent move. According to Damarion, the Commonwealth destroyed all planetary space programs, verbally forbid them to develop any other space craft and left the satellites in place to insure no space craft could ever leave the planet. Chancellor Torrell reported a few other attempts were made but met with disaster when they attempted to leave the planet's atmosphere.

Arbiter Navid was a wise man in planning his questions for the debate. His first question cut right to the heart of the matter. "Is the Commonwealth guilty of the atrocities occurring forty-seven years ago?" Brynna and Lexi had no documentation they could present to answer the question. They did notice Chancellor Torrell seemed overly eager and anxious to address their response. He was sitting forward in his seat leaning on the table in front of him. There were table cloths covering the tables, but it appeared the Chancellor was bouncing one of his legs in anticipation.

Brynna and Lexi discussed their options. Brynna stepped back up to her podium she took a sip of water and a deep breath of air. "This planet has obviously suffered at someone's hand. I was not here, nor was I even born then, so I cannot say one way or the other if the Commonwealth is guilty of these atrocities. It is entirely possible it is. It is also possible the Commonwealth had enemies who perpetrated these acts to make the Commonwealth appear guilty. I was not able to find anything in our historical database giving the extent of Commonwealth interaction with Drea III. We may well have done your planet a great wrong. I know the satellites above your world are Commonwealth satellites, but are they there because the Commonwealth wanted to stop your progress, or to protect itself from its enemies? You stated that as a result of contact with the Commonwealth your world suffered from a global war. This was not a war with the Commonwealth. Did the Commonwealth have enemies on this very world who caused destruction to put the blame on us? I have no proof, only supposition. If you were at war after we left, we were not the only ones who may have been to blame. What I can tell you is, those in command and in positions of authority are long gone. The crew of this ship are faultless." Brynna confidently sat down.

Chancellor Torrell looked like he had the wind taken out of his sails. He anticipated the crew would claim total innocence and he was thoroughly prepared to attack Brynna's denials, but her supposition of possible guilt left him little room to fight back. Damarion and Irena spoke briefly and in what appeared to be strained whispers. Damarion started to get up and Irena grabbed his arm and pulled him back down. She whispered something else to him. The man seemed to ease up a bit and this time Irena let him go to the podium. Damarion presented audiovisual records of attacks which were clearly from space, on several launch sites for Drean space crafts. Damarion emphasized the point that the attacks were clearly documented as coming from outer space not inner space.

The devastation left behind after the powerful blasts of energy from such a long distance was overwhelming. It was Brynna and Lexi's turn to gather their wits. Lexi asked Brynna to let her respond to this one. Lexi went to the podium. "This was truly a devastating experience, but may I ask if you have any audiovisual records of the ships firing these blasts? There are others out there who have weapons of this nature."

Damarion's eyes were cold and hard. He stared at Lexi as though he were trying to bore a hole through her. He answered simply and calmly. "Those blasts came from your satellites."

Lexi gave Brynna a shocked look. She had never heard of any such actions by the Commonwealth. Lexi didn't know what to say next. Brynna took Lexi's place at the podium. "Arbiter Navid, from the evidence put forth at this time, I must conclude and answer your question this way. It would appear from the evidence presented, the Commonwealth of fifty years ago, may very well have been guilty of great atrocities against your people. We concede to this one point." It was brief and to the point. Brynna knew if she said anymore right now, no one would hear her. She moved back to her seat. Angry murmurs ran through the crowd. The crowd wasn't very large. There were about twenty dignitaries present. In addition to the guests, the security staff were present along with those serving food and the custodial staff. Despite the fact, they were supposed to be occupied with their duties, they were extremely curious and paying more attention to the proceedings than they should have been.

The Arbiter gave the crowd a moment to calm down. He asked a less inflammatory question and one question clearly slanted the opposite direction. "What has the Commonwealth done since this time? Has it improved?"

This time the Arbiter let the Dreans go first. Chancellor Noe fielded this question. Her answer sounded remotely like Brynna's answer to the first question. Irena indicated the Dreans had no direct contact with the Commonwealth in the last fifty years. Their only recent contacts were from the ship's crew. She did comment the crew had been quite well behaved and polite in their dealings with the Dreans.

Brynna thanked the Chancellor for her kindness and proceeded to explain their current mission was to seek allies among lesser developed planets and offer a leg up in technology. She also made a point of telling them in their current agreement, they had agreed to leave the satellites dormant.

Chancellor Torrell countered with a very brief rebuttal. "That agreement was conditional on your beliefs and the results are yet to be seen."

After a couple more hard questions, the group took a break for lunch. The crew mingled as much as they could, considering the hard feelings present in the room. Moderator Tarmon also told them the Intercessor would be arriving soon. She sounded disappointed he had not gotten here before now.

After another leisurely meal, the deliberations started again. This time the questions were put to the Dreans. "Did the Dreans act inappropriately to the Commonwealth on their first encounter?"

Chancellor Torrell looked like a volcano about to blow. It wasn't their turn, but he hit the podium and started answering before the Arbiter had a chance to stop him. "What kind of ridiculous question is that? We had never even left our solar system. How could we have acted badly to them? They came to us. We aren't responsible for this." The man continued to rant until his time was up. Chancellor Noe finally managed to get him to calm down and return to his chair. The Arbiter chastised him firmly for jumping ahead and ignoring the guidelines. He warned the Chancellor not to repeat his error.

Brynna stood calmly and quietly and moved to the podium. She hoped the audience would see the humor in her next comments. "If all Dreans acted as calmly as Chancellor Torrell, there might be reason to believe Dreans did act inappropriately. However, I do not believe all Dreans have his… temperament." A ripple of snickers now filled the crowd as they enjoyed the irony of her comment. She then moved on to answer more suitably. "The Drean world was not united, which is one of the criteria for joining the Commonwealth. In that respect, they were inappropriate by Commonwealth standards. I can only assume the leaders of the day knew this before they approached your world and were prepared for it. It is possible certain factions on your world did act inappropriately, but…" Brynna saw angry looks and heard disgruntled comments from the audience again. "but, from the way we have been treated since we arrived and the things we have seen, I seriously doubt your people acted inappropriately. Your own Moderator Tarmon, while telling us we were not welcome here, also warned us away from the satellites. I have not seen anything indicating with any certainty the Dreans instigated such treatment."

Brynna received a round of applause after her comments. She felt almost like a traitor. She had to admit someone in power in the Commonwealth could have been guilty of war crimes. She couldn't blame the Commonwealth itself, so it had to be some isolated individuals. She hoped her honesty and willingness to accept some of the Commonwealth blame would buy her some goodwill. Sometimes she hated diplomacy. It made her feel less than respectable.

During one of their last breaks, Moderator Tarmon pulled the Arbiter aside and talked with him at length. Brynna and David took notice of it and wondered what was up. Jake was staying as vigilant as he could, but there seemed to be no cause for alarm here. He had his scanner programmed to monitor the area outside the building and made rounds throughout the building. David had Jake stand down for a while and put himself and Thane on security detail. Each one took about a two-hour shift at a time. In a relaxed environment, David knew it was hard to stay vigilant.

As the last round of debate started, the crew noticed its wording was rather odd. "Our people recognize your answers are favorable. However, a person's words and actions may not be the same. In light of that, our last question is this: What worlds can we go visit to see if the Commonwealth is doing all it has said?"

Brynna and Lexi gave each other puzzled looks. Brynna got up again and moved to the podium. "I'm afraid I don't understand your question. Do you want to know what worlds belong to the Commonwealth or are you asking what worlds we have visited on our current mission? Our mission has just begun, so our work may not be clearly visible although we would be glad to take a very small delegation there. Our ship only has room for a couple extra people on board."

The Arbiter clarified. "Name the worlds you have visited on this mission. We want to see what you have done on those worlds."

Brynna was still confused, but she tackled the question as best she could. "We went to Galat III and Medoris IV. Both worlds are primitive, and we've only just left them a short time ago, so I wouldn't expect the changes to be blatantly obvious. How is this a question to be debated?"

Moderator Tarmon stood up and went to stand by the Arbiter. "It can be debated once we have seen the changes you have made on those worlds."

Brynna's confusion was not abating. "Do you expect us to take you to those worlds?"

Moderator Tarmon shook her head. "That will not be necessary. We can get there on our own."

Brynna glanced at Lexi before asking, "How do you propose to do that?"

"When your Commonwealth destroyed our chances to travel through space, we pursued other means of traveling off world. We have learned to utilize a technology that punches a... umm... a sort of tunnel or hole through space. We can go from the surface of this planet directly to the surface of another in the blink of an eye."

As if on cue, Brynna blinked. Lazaro couldn't help himself and interrupted. "You've developed worm hole technology?"

Moderator Tarmon gave the engineer a blank stare. Their terminology was different, so the two weren't communicating well. "Our engineers can explain the basics of this technology to you." Chancellor Torrell looked like he was about to come flying out of his seat. The Moderator held her hand up to silence the man before he could object. "If we establish relations with the Commonwealth, we can consider sharing the technology with you, but a general explanation will have to do for now."

Lazaro looked like a kid in a candy store. "Can we go with you?" David was standing in a strategic point in the room. He took a step forward and caught Lazaro's eye. Lazaro slowly sat back down in his seat, although he looked like he would be up again in a second.

The Moderator paused after seeing David's reaction. "It is only fair you be allowed to send a party, along with our delegation. It is up to your leaders if they choose to send representatives. Tomorrow morning, we will send a vehicle for you and you may send a delegation or just watch if that is your desire. I would like to send out two teams one to Galat III and one to Medoris IV. We will need to see one of your star charts to know the locations of these worlds."

Brynna hesitated and looked towards David for guidance. David stepped to the edge of the platform. Brynna moved over to speak with him. After a moment she returned to her place at the podium. "We'll give you a copy of the star charts when we return to the ship this evening. We will have to discuss whether to send a delegation with you. You will have our decision in the morning."

The debate was concluded, at least for the day. The crew continued to mingle and visit. Most of the guests excused themselves shortly to go back to their offices. Moderator Tarmon encouraged the crew to enjoy the facilities as long as they liked and to eat their evening meal there as well. She left vehicles there for their return to the ship. The crew enjoyed themselves taking walks on the beach and through the gardens.

David and Brynna went for a walk on the beach themselves. Brynna thought her husband seemed unusually quiet and moody. "David, what's on your mind?"

The preoccupied Captain stopped, looked at the picturesque scenery and shook his head. He turned to see the wind blowing her long brown hair around her pleasant face. "You wanna know what's on my mind? Here I am, standing on a great beach with a gorgeous woman and all I can think about is work. I'm just thinking, I must be a total idiot." Knowing already what her next question was, he decided to go with his next instinct. He quickly wrapped his arms around her and kissed her passionately.

In a moment Brynna pulled back. She settled into his arms and quietly whispered in his ear, "You're not getting away with that."

David pulled back. "What?! I was just trying to correct my mistake and start enjoying the moment."

Brynna grinned. "Yeah, sure you were."

David realized he needed to put her concerns at least on hold if not to rest. They were, after all, not currently in crisis mode and should relax a little. "I was just hearing all the discussion that's about to happen in the conference room tonight. Here I am, in such a peaceful setting, and I'm working on work. I really do want to relax and just be your husband for a few minutes. I also wish I had brought a change of clothes and some swim wear. I haven't been swimming in ages."

Brynna knew it was all the information she was going to get at this point. He was keeping things to himself, but she knew better than to push right now. She did have the distinct feeling he thought he was fooling her. Sometimes she would let it go and other times she would let him know she was letting it go. It was surprising how quickly she had learned to read him. They had only been married for five months and only known each other a few months longer than that.

The atmosphere must have been influencing her generosity. She let it go and didn't bother to give him notice. The couple spent a few more minutes walking hand in hand talking about the scenery, their future, whether they would extend their marriage contract and have children. When David mentioned the possibility of the two of them staying together and having children, he saw the light in Brynna's eyes brighten. He loved that light in her eyes and never wanted to see it wane. He promised himself never to do anything to cause that light to go out. After a while longer, the couple decided it was time to head back to the ship. David linked his comm unit in to the entire crew and told them to rendezvous back at the meeting room they had been in all day. As promised an evening meal was waiting on them. There was considerably more food than they would eat, so Brynna invited Colonel Bernt and his men to join them. The Colonel declined politely stating he and his men were on duty. Brynna pushed a little harder and told the Colonel she and the crew would be offended if he and his men didn't join them. She even suggested half of his men eat first and then she and the crew and the other half of his men eat second, so someone was always on duty. After much cajoling, Colonel Bernt relented and they had a quiet dinner together. After dinner, the Colonel escorted the crew back to their ship.

Brynna sent Marissa and Aulani to the bridge to provide Colonel Bernt with the star charts the Moderator requested, right down to their precise landing points. David and Brynna headed immediately to the Captain's office and discussed the Moderator's offer to take them off world. The first thing they discussed was whose input to include. David didn't really want anyone's input.

He had already made the decision, but he knew it wouldn't be well received. Brynna wanted Jake, Lexi and Lazaro in on the discussion. David stared long and hard at Brynna. "You wanted to know what was on my mind at the beach?"

Brynna sat down next to David. "Yes, I do. I knew there was more than what you said, but I assumed you had your reasons for not telling me."

David's face softened. "It's getting harder for me to keep my secrets from you. I was already playing out in my head the entire conversation I would hear in the dining hall. Jake would be adamantly against going to Galat III. Lazaro would beg to go to either place, just so he could see the technology in action. Thane would be begging to go as well. Lexi would question my motives on going to Galat or on not going to Galat. It really wouldn't matter, she would question it either way. You know the routine. So, do I simply give the orders, or do I give everyone a chance to speak then do what I was going to in the first place?"

"What orders have you already decided on without consulting me?" Brynna was peeved. It wasn't like David to not consider her opinion on matters like these.

"I'm going to lead a four-person team to Galat. You're taking a four- person team to Medoris and four crew members will stay behind at the launch site."

"You know Jake's going to object to any contact with Galat."

David nodded. "That's why he's staying behind. If I come back acting inappropriately then he can shoot me."

Brynna felt her blood beginning to boil. "David, you are taking this situation far too lightly. This is no joke."

David was quick to come back. "I'm being quite serious. Do you see me laughing? I'm taking Lexi on my team and we will minimize our time there as much as possible, but we've already seen Arni go anywhere he wants. Does going back to Galat matter anymore? Besides, if we don't go to Galat, the Dreans will wonder what we're hiding. Are you ready to ask them about Arni?"

Brynna leaned back in her chair. David added one final comment. "That's what I thought."

Brynna headed for the door. She knew disagreeing with him would be pointless right now. She decided to change her approach and try anyway. "David, are you sure you should go back to Galat? What if it makes your dreams worse?"

David's tone softened again. "I have to see for myself. If everything is fine, then the dreams will stop. I know they will."

Brynna moved back over and sat down beside him again. "But what if everything isn't fine?"

David stood and moved away from her. He didn't want to see the look on her face when he answered. "I don't know."

Brynna walked over behind him and wrapped her arms around him. She laid her head on his shoulder and held him tightly. He turned around to face her and returned her hug. Yes, he was unable to hide much from her anymore. Brynna was clearly seeing the sorrow in his eyes. She suddenly pulled back. "David, do we need to resign from this mission?"

David smiled. One word in her question meant more than anything to him. Brynna said "we." Yes, they were married, but she had every right to divorce him and continue the mission without him. She was willing to drop out and stay with him. The one thing he seemed to fear the most these days was losing her. "You know we can't resign from this mission for two years. We'd be court martialed."

"We could claim Arni's interest in you was affecting the mission and request reassignment for the good of the mission."

David stroked her hair gently. "One way or the other, I'll be fine. If something has happened on Galat, I'll find out what and who's responsible. For better or worse, I'll handle it. Would you like to know who's on your team?"

Brynna took a deep breath. David's avoidance tactics had struck again. "Sure, who's on my team." She decided it was better just to go with it.

The next morning, David addressed the crew with their orders. He presented it in such a manner they knew not to question him. He assigned Thane, Laura and Lazaro to Brynna's team. Marissa, Lexi and Aulani were on his team and he left Jason, Braxton, Jake and Cheyenne to stay behind and watch the proceedings.

Since Captain Alexander had already spoken with the Commander the night before they were both prepared to handle any objections from the crew. David addressed the crew as though their arguments had already been made. "Although, I am not required to explain my decisions, before any of you object, I will give them to you anyway. We aren't supposed to have any further contact with known enemies, but here's my problem. We either need to visit both worlds equally or neither. If we go to Medoris and don't go to Galat, the Dreans may feel we're hiding something. We haven't told them about our enemy and we don't want to damage our relations with them further. It has also become apparent that Arni Liontari can travel wherever he desires, perhaps this is how. I expect to find answers and I am keeping our exposure to a minimum. Jake, it's your job to get the four crew members left behind back to the ship and into space if anything goes wrong. It's also your job to discreetly make sure all crew members coming back from Galat are not compromised. If you suspect anything is wrong with any of us, don't do anything in front of the Dreans. Wait until we've all returned to the ship. Are we understood?"

Jake was sitting in his usual corner with his chair leaned back on two legs, but this time he was sitting sideways in his chair paying close attention. It seemed as though the Captain's talks were getting through to him. He didn't appear to be as anxious about the Captain's risky decisions. He had a habit of cornering the Captain after meetings, but not this time. He simply walked away and made sure the crew was adequately armed. His silent cooperation was deafening.

The crew was ready to go when the vehicle arrived for them. The trip took them into a nearby town. It was the city where the UWC met. The vehicle drove them into an underground parking garage of a secured facility. The crew was let out along with Colonel Bernt and the security detail at an elevator. The elevator was large enough that one of the vehicles could have driven straight onto it. The crew and the security detail were all able to fit onto it comfortably. Jake had that "nervous cat" look again. He paid close attention to how Colonel Bernt accessed the doors and elevators. He wanted to know everything that had to be done to get out in a hurry if necessary. The elevator took them down what felt like quite a distance. Captain Alexander began to be somewhat concerned as well. This was obviously a very secure facility which made it difficult to get in and out of. The other thing concerning him was no one from the council had shown up to greet them. The elevator finally stopped and the crew found another vehicle waiting to take them down a long corridor. The crew was silent as they climbed onto the vehicle and rode down the long hallway until they reached a large set of doors. Colonel Bernt placed his hand on a scanner to open the doors. The doors opened to reveal a brief corridor leading to a room the size of an auditorium. There were two doors in the corridor, one on each side. The Colonel led the crew through one of the doors and up a half-dozen steps to what appeared to be an observation room. Moderator Tarmon, Chancellor Noe, Chancellor Torrell, and Arbiter Navid were all present along with several other delegates who had attended the debate. Moderator Tarmon welcomed the crew warmly.

Chancellor Torrell stood with Chancellor Noe on the opposite side of the room. When he saw how the Moderator welcomed the Commonwealth ambassadors, he looked like he was ready to vomit. He kept his voice down yet made his complaints clear to Chancellor Noe. "How can Saundra be so friendly with our sworn enemies? It's revolting. It makes me sick to my stomach to watch her."

Chancellor Noe glanced down at his half-eaten plate of finger foods. "I can see that. You've hardly been able to eat a bite since we got here." She allowed her words, heavily laced with sarcasm, to sink in before walking over to join Saundra in greeting their guests. These people seemed like normal people to her, not the monsters Chancellor Torrell made them out to be. They had not been pushy or forceful, nor did they appear to have a condescending attitude towards their planet. The crew seemed to genuinely care about people.

Moderator Tarmon took the group on a tour of the facility. The room on the opposite side of the corridor was the control room. There seemed to be a very sparse amount of equipment in this room. Lazaro inquired about the emptiness. The two engineers who had helped with the ship's repairs were present. The young woman known as Robin was more than happy to explain. "You see the modules out there?"

Lazaro looked out into the cavernous room beyond the glass window of the control room. "Yes, you've got what, four of them?"

Robin nodded. "Each of the modules have self-contained power sources and operate without external sources of energy. Basically, this control room serves as a safety mechanism. We communicate with the modules or pods and tell them when it is safe to depart and return. We monitor for a buildup of tachyons to know when a pod is returning and clear the room of people. The pads they launch from also generate a tachyon field to aid in launch and return. It works kind of like a magnet to keep the pods from landing in the wrong place. It creates a tachyon pocket which pulls the pod into its proper place. We also monitor the pod systems during power up and shut down for any kind of anomalies indicating a malfunction."

Lazaro looked like his eyes were about to pop out of his head. Cheyenne had never seen her husband this fascinated. She expected him to start drooling at any moment. Robin escorted the crew out to the pods and gave them a basic explanation of how they worked. She had been warned earlier not to divulge the particulars about the technology. She did her best to keep her explanations as generic as possible, but Lt. Commander Dominick asked such in-depth questions. It wasn't easy.

An hour or so later, they were ready to start the launches. David explained who of his people were going where. Moderator Tarmon planned to send two of her own people and four security guards in each pod. Just as a demonstration of how the pods worked and their safety, she sent one pod ahead to Galat III. Its intent was to come straight back. After it arrived, a communication was received from the pod indicating some unusual readings in the planet's atmosphere. The pod's crew indicated they were going to check it out before returning.

Moderator Tarmon seemed slightly embarrassed by the flaw in her flawless demonstration. Brynna asked if they needed to wait for the pod's return before their departure. "No, the only reason I sent the first team was to demonstrate the safety of this type of travel. Your team can depart whenever you are ready."

To Lazaro's delight, Brynna said, "Well, let's go then. Your other party has communicated they arrived safely, so I see no problem."

Moderator Tarmon smiled. She could see Brynna understood her situation and was grateful to her for taking the pressure off.

Chancellor Torrell and Arbiter Navid boarded the pod bound for Medoris along with Brynna's team and the security detail. Lazaro was excited and chose a seat closest to the pilot. He watched her every move closely. Each pod launch was preceded by the launch of a buoy. The buoy was very small, about the size of a man's shoe, and contained a sensor to scan the immediate area to be sure the area was clear enough for a landing then it would signal the pod. It would also emit a very small tachyon field to guide the pod to its landing site. Lazaro and the others watched out the ports or windows to see the launch of the buoy. The pod powered up as soon as the buoy launched. In a swell of power and bright light the pod shimmered then vanished.

In a couple moments, the pod crew made contact. David heard Brynna's voice come across the comm line. "Captain we've arrived safely. We appear to be at the exact location of our previous landing on Medoris. We are going to head east to talk to the Kimbra first. We will be out of touch for several hours unless they see fit to offer us a carriage and some horses to speed things up."

David stepped to the control panel. "Acknowledged, Commander."

He then looked at the Moderator. "Should we wait for the other team to return before we depart for Galat?"

As if on cue the monitors began to react. Engineer Kelly scowled. "The Galat team is returning without any communication."

Moderator Tarmon reacted, "What?!"

Judging from the serious nature of their faces and the tone of their voices, David assumed this was a breach in protocol. He moved back out of their way. He got a familiar sick feeling in his gut. As soon as the pod appeared and shut down, a man emerged and raced towards the control booth. As soon as he reached it, he headed straight for the Moderator. He spoke in breathless, hushed tones. The Captain couldn't make out what he was saying, but he knew when Moderator Tarmon's face went pale it wasn't anything good. She appeared shaken. She looked up at the Captain. "I need the room."

David moved the rest of the crew from the Control Room to the observation room. Jake immediately let the Captain know he didn't like the situation. David curtly acknowledged him while watching the empty spot on the floor where Brynna and the others had disappeared.

Minutes later, the Moderator came to talk to David. "Captain, I don't think we will be able to take you to Galat III. There appears to have been some sort of major catastrophe there. We will send a team back to investigate, but I can't send you right now. Are you sure everything was fine when you left there?"

David's breath had gotten shallow. "Yes, everything was fine when we left. There were a thousand people sitting around on a hill listening to one of the locals speak. Please tell me what's happened. These are very intelligent, peaceful people. My crew and I enjoyed working with them. Moderator Tarmon, I need to know what happened."

The Moderator studied his face. "Most of the town has been leveled and is nothing, but ash. There are bodies everywhere. Even homes outside the town have been destroyed. We'll send a team of our own to investigate what happened."

"Moderator Tarmon, let my people go in. We spent weeks working with these people. We knew them by name. We can help find out what happened."

The crew's faces were pale and serious. The Moderator wasn't about to give in despite seeing the shocked looks on the crew's faces. "Captain, we know the Galatans as well. We have visited their world many times. I'm sorry, but their world was fine until it was touched by the Commonwealth. I can't allow you to go until we know what happened."

David seemed almost desperate by now. "I understand, but we didn't do this. Moderator, we taught them how to make glass, got them to teach women how to read and write, and we improved the ventilation in their town hall. We did not do this. I didn't do this."

The Moderator was nearing anger. "You didn't do this. Exactly what does that mean? Who are you trying to convince, Captain? Never mind, it doesn't matter. I can't let your people in there. After..."

"Let them go." A male voice from behind the Moderator spoke with authority.

The Moderator gasped. She turned towards the voice and bowed her head. "Intercessor, I did not know you were here." The Dreans in the room bowed their heads.

David and the crew immediately recognized the voice. Before them stood Arni Liontari. "Arni, why am I not surprised." Arni stood there wearing simplistic Drean attire. His face was now clean shaven. David stared at Arni, but Arni paid no attention to him.

Arni looked around the room at the bowed heads. "Be at ease, everyone."

The Moderator took Arni's hand in her own and kissed it. "Intercessor, he calls you by your name?"

Arni smiled at the woman. "He always has. I have asked you to do the same, but you cannot bring yourself to do so."

"Forgive me Intercessor, but you are too important for me to treat so casually. May I ask, why you want me to allow them to go to Galat III?"

Arni looked at David and the crew. "They need to see what has happened for themselves."

The Moderator nodded. "I will do as you wish... Lord Liontari."

Arni smiled at her attempt to call him by name. As David walked over to speak to his crew, the Moderator had one more question for Arni. "Lord Liontari, what will we find on Galat?"

Arni's smile faded, "Cold, hard truth."

David made one adjustment to the team heading to Galat. Moderator Tarmon informed David they would be sending two pods to Galat to cover more territory. In light of this new information, David decided to take the remaining members of his crew and split them between the two pods.

David and his team were on the first pod along with Chancellor Noe, Arni, the pod crew which consisted of a pilot and co-pilot and eight security personnel. Jake's team was on the second pod with a similar complement only Moderator Tarmon was on board the second pod as well as Engineer Kelly.

David ended up sitting directly across from Arni. He remembered his orders now included the option of asking Arni as many questions as he thought he could get away with, so David started to work. "What are we going to find on Galat? Really?"

Arni's face seemed sad. "Your master's handiwork."

David didn't like cryptic answers. "Exactly what is that supposed to mean?"

"Do you really want me to tell you or would you rather figure it out for yourself? You've already seen it."

David felt his heart begin to pound. It felt strangely heavy. Feeling an unexplained emotional pain, David looked Arni in the eye. Calmly and quietly he beseeched, "Please tell me."

"Today you will see what it means to be a part of the Commonwealth and exactly what Luciano Hale is capable of." Arni wasn't mincing words this time. "Every human life on Galat III has been eliminated by the Commonwealth."

Lexi, Marissa, and Aulani were sitting near David hearing the conversation. No one else heard it. The four of them sat there in disbelief.

David glanced at Lexi then realized he had stopped breathing. The sick feeling in the pit of his stomach was back again, or had it ever left? He looked back at Arni and took a deep breath. "I see." Maybe asking Arni questions was not such a good idea after all. In either case, he needed a break before trying again.

Seconds later the pod powered up. The lights flickered and the hum of the engines began to power down again. The Captain glanced up at the pilots. Their positioning was rather odd. Since this wasn't a vehicle that traveled along the ground, they faced the inside of the pod instead of the front. The pilots were shutting things off. There was no sign of concern on their faces. David glanced out the nearest port. They were no longer in the hangar. He could see sunshine and trees.

Once the pilots allowed the passengers to disembark, the crew stepped out on familiar ground. It was Fall on Galat III. The leaves were a beautiful array of colors. For all the trepidation they had felt earlier, the serenity of their current surroundings seemed to relax the crew slightly. The group began the short trek towards the town. The passengers from both pods walked quietly and said little. The Captain's stomach relaxed. His heart stopped beating as thunderously as it had a few minutes ago. As they rounded the last curve in the dirt road, what remained of the town came into view. The bulk of the town had burned to the ground and bodies littered the streets. David heard several gasps. Some were from his crew and others from the Drean complement.

Moderator Tarmon approached Arni. Her face was pale and drawn. "Intercessor... your mother was here. Is she... did she...?"

David looked at Arni, there were tears in his eyes. Arni spoke calmly and quietly. "She was here. She is now with my Father."

Cheyenne wasn't one to speak up very often, but this time she had a question burning in her mind. "Arni, we've seen you bring others back from the dead. Can't you bring her, and the others, back?"

Arni saw both compassion and confusion in Cheyenne's question. He smiled weakly at her. "I could, but to bring them back now would do more harm than good. It would be cruel to bring them back. At least they died quickly."

Cheyenne's confidence was waning, but she pushed through it. "I don't understand. How would it be cruel to heal a person's injuries and bring them back from the dead?" Cheyenne's skills in translation and communications gave her insight into other people's thinking, but she wasn't as good at conveying her own thoughts.

Arni smiled again. "Once a person has eaten at my Father's table, no other food satisfies." Cheyenne gave him another confused look. She wasn't sure asking again would make anything any clearer. David started to get annoyed at the cryptic response. Arni attempted to help her understand. "Imagine you were born into a life where you had nothing, people despised you, finding food was a daily struggle, a life similar to the Akamu. Then one day you wake up into a warm environment filled with light. Everyone around you loved you instantly and you never had to wonder where your next meal was coming from. Would you want to wake up again and find yourself back in your first life?"

Now Cheyenne looked vexed. "But life isn't like that. These people cared about each other. Despite their primitive situation, they had good lives."

"True, they did have good lives, but someone hated them enough to kill them. Imagine they are now living a life a thousand times better than this one. How dissatisfied would they be to return here? The example is very crude and basic, unfortunately the only way you can truly understand is to see it for yourselves. I doubt any of you would volunteer to die today, would you?" Arni looked at Marissa, who winced noticeably, then at David. Captain Alexander decided it was time to change the subject.

The Captain gathered the crew around and made assignments. He divided them up into teams of two and sent them north, east, and west of the town. The pods were to the south, so there was really no point in sending a team back the way they had just come. The Captain instructed them to do extensive scans of the area to look for survivors and to find out whatever they could about the devastation. David and Aulani would be team one and they were going to stay in the town itself. Jake and Marissa were team two. Marissa quickly volunteered to head north. David started to deny her request because it was obvious something or someone was on her mind. He didn't want her to be too emotionally involved. Ultimately, he realized he had insisted on coming to Galat for the very same reasons. He granted her request. Braxton and Lexi were team three and headed to the east. Jason and Cheyenne headed west. The Moderator split her security personnel up and sent them out with each of the teams to run their own scans.

Marissa headed off so fast in a specific direction Jake had trouble keeping up with her. As soon as she saw the house she was looking for, she took off running towards it. This house was still intact although the nearby barn was burned to the ground. Inside the barn were the bodies of what appeared to be a man as well as a dog and two horses. It looked like the man had been leading the horses out of the barn because they were not in stalls and their bodies were laying adjacent to each other. Marissa paused to look in the barn then ran for the house. She turned her scanner on and detected more bodies under the floor in the house.

By this time, Jake had caught up to her. "Marissa, what's going on? What are you looking for? Who are you looking for?" Marissa was looking around the room to find out how to get in the structure below the house. She ignored Jake and kept her eyes fixed on her scanner display. Jake finally grabbed her arm. "Marissa, what's going on?"

Marissa seemed close to tears. "Jake, there are three bodies beneath the floor in some kind of basement or cellar. I have to see them. Help me find a way to get down there."

Jake knew she would not give him an explanation until she found whatever she was looking for. "Okay, I'll help you look."

The two security personnel finally caught up to them and found them wandering around looking at the floor and under furniture. Jake told them what they were looking for. The two men went outside to search. One returned shortly saying he located a door leading under the house. The three walked outside and around to the door. The second security guard was already under the home with a light, taking scans. Marissa went cautiously down the stairs and found three bodies huddled in the farthest corner. It was a mother and two children. One appeared to be a boy about ten years of age and the other was a little girl about four years of age with long curly brown hair. Marissa knelt beside the boy. He was clutching a small glider made from sticks and fabric from the ship. The little girl held a doll Marissa had seen before. It was the same doll the little girl who sat in her lap during the shuttle ride had been clutching. Tears began to roll down Marissa's cheeks. She couldn't look at the three any longer. The young lieutenant raced up the stairs from the cellar and ran several yards away to a nearby fruit tree laden with rotting fruit. She knelt on the ground and began to sob uncontrollably. Jake chased after her again. He caught up to her and knelt in front of her. Gently wrapping his arms around her, Jake held her tightly until her sobs began to ease.

After Marissa calmed down, the two sat down under the tree and talked for a while. Marissa told Jake about the beautiful brown-eyed girl who had sat in her lap and chattered happily during the shuttle ride Thane gave for the children in the area. She told him about the interest her older brother had shown in flying. Thane had taught him to make gliders and kites. The children had been so alive and now were just gone. Marissa took the opportunity to tell Jake how much she had been concealing her desires to adopt children after the mission. Jake continued to comfort her for a few more minutes and promised they would talk about children as soon as this current crisis was over.

The Drean Security Officers finished their scans and were running out of ways to "appear" busy. Jake finally told Marissa he needed to complete a set of scans for himself and they should move on to see if there were survivors further out. Marissa stayed where she was for a few more minutes to pull herself together while he ran his scan. Jake and the two security officers moved the body of the man from the barn and laid him beside his wife and children in the cellar. After securing the cellar again, the four headed further north. They spent another two hours searching. No one was found left alive.

The teams headed east and west found the same things. The people had been killed about a month earlier. David, Aulani, the Moderator, and Arni searched the town for clues as to what happened. They ended up splitting up to cover more ground. David heard a noise inside one of the buildings still standing on the outer edge of town. He went to investigate. He opened the door to the building and walked in, carefully stepping over pieces of furniture turned over on the floor. Behind a counter, he found a wild dog gnawing on the body of one of the townspeople. As soon as the animal saw him it began to growl and snarl at him. David started to slowly back away. The dog advanced towards him. The beast continued to snarl and growl. It crouched down on his haunches. David knew it was preparing to attack. He reached for his weapon. He wasn't fast enough. The dog leaped at him and knocked him to the ground sending his Tri- Emp flying across the room. David grabbed the dog's snout with both hands and tried to hold his jaw closed. The dog's face was right in David's face. He could smell the foul odor from his breath and the dog's saliva was beginning to run down his arm and dripped onto his shirt. The saliva caused his hands to start slipping. Just as David was about to call for help, a voice spoke from behind him. "Get out and never return to this city."

The dog pulled away from David and ran yelping out the back door he had entered through. David relaxed then looked to see who had spoken. It was Arni. Arni reached down and helped the Captain to his feet. While the Captain retrieved his weapon, Arni drew water from the well in the building. He poured the water into a bowl and handed it to the Captain along with a dusty towel, so he could clean up. It took a minute for them speak to each other.

The Captain spoke first. "You seem to be getting in the habit of saving me."

Arni was leaning against a table with his arms folded waiting on the Captain. He smiled an odd smile. "You have no idea."

David took a deep breath. Arni was being cryptic again. He decided to let this one pass considering the man had just saved his hide again. "Thank you."

David paused then said. "That was a strange thing to say to a wild dog though. It's not like he could understand and obey you."

Arni had been looking casually around the room. He looked directly at the Captain to respond. "He understood me, and he will obey."

"Did he belong to you?"

"No more so than any other dog."

David finished cleaning up and laid the towel down beside the bowl of water. He stood there deep in thought for a moment. "Is this what you meant when you said I had seen it already?"

Arni nodded. "Yes."

David continued. "You warned me about this and I didn't listen. This is my fault, isn't it?"

Arni walked over closer to the young Captain. "When Marissa died, even though I repaired the damage, you were upset with me when you found out I could have prevented the tornado and didn't. I didn't start the tornado, although I could have, and I didn't stop it either. You didn't do this, but you could have prevented it. Luciano Hale did this."

David looked up and saw the Moderator and one of the security guards standing in the doorway. He wondered how much she had heard. She lowered her head. "I'm sorry Intercessor, we did not mean to interrupt. We heard a commotion and came to investigate."

Arni looked casually over at the pair. "It's alright. It seems the Captain learns better when faced with a hungry, wild dog than a casual conversation." Arni walked out the door, past the Moderator, and headed up the street.

David called out after him. "Thanks for the vote of confidence." David heard a distant returned, "You're welcome."

The Moderator looked confused. "A wild dog attacked you? Are you hurt?"

David shook his head. "No, I'm fine. Arni took care of it, and me, again."

"Were you injured? Did the Intercessor heal you?"

Again, David shook his head. "Not this time. He has healed me before. He did hand me some water and a towel to clean myself up."

The Moderator was in awe. "The Intercessor can heal all of Drea's illnesses with a single word, but he has insisted we continue to pursue medicine and treat ourselves. It's a rare thing to be healed by the Intercessor. You must be important to him."

David stepped out into the sunlight, but then turned back around to respond to her flattering comment. "He seems to think so, but I don't understand why."

The Moderator smiled. "There are several things he says... or does, that no one understands. He is as clear as the Ancient Texts sometimes." She laughed. "Sometimes the Ancient Texts are easier to understand."

David hit his comm link. He warned the other teams about the wild dogs and checked each team's status. Each team believed they had collected sufficient information for a preliminary evaluation. David ordered his people to rendezvous back at the pods. David and the Moderator discussed what to do about the bodies. David wasn't comfortable leaving the bodies to be devoured by wild dogs or other animals. The Moderator agreed. "Captain, as soon as we get back, I am going to send all four pods back here with men and equipment to begin retrieving bodies and giving them a proper interment. Do you know if they buried their bodies or cremated them?"

David didn't know. He didn't remember grave sites or cremation facilities, but he hadn't been looking for them either.

"Perhaps Arni is the best one to ask. Since he grew up here, he should know."

After hearing the Moderator refer to Arni as "The Intercessor," he was tempted to address Arni the same way. He thought perhaps it was making Moderator Tarmon uncomfortable, but since he had gotten to know him on a first name basis, he found change awkward. He also remembered Arni asking the woman to change her method of addressing him.

The teams met back at the pods where the Moderator caught up with Arni. She asked what he preferred. Arni didn't seem overly concerned. He advised her to do whatever was fastest and easiest. His remarks weren't based on a lack of caring, but more on how much he cared. All family members were dead. No one would be by to visit the graves, so keeping them on their own property was unnecessary. His concern was in getting it done in the simplest way possible.

Jason, overhearing the conversation, volunteered some information. He had done numerous scans on the sick and could identify a great number of individuals as well as had access to a map of the area and who resided where. He couldn't account for everyone, although he could account for a reasonable number of residents. The Moderator thought for a moment and decided to make one mass grave and one massive monument with the names of the known deceased inscribed on it with one exception. She wanted to locate the homestead of Slaina the Healer and create a separate grave and monument for the mother of the Intercessor. As soon as the pods returned to Drea, Jason interfaced remotely with the ship's computer and pulled the information from Galat

III. He downloaded a copy into the Drean database. The Moderator gave the data a brief glance, and then gave Jason a puzzled look. Jason moved over beside her to see what she was looking at. "What is it? What's wrong?"

The Moderator looked at Jason and at Cheyenne. "This data can't be right. These are your names, not Galatan names."

Jason looked down the list and under Taldor and Essa's names were the names of their children including their infant namesake twins, Jason and Cheyenne. Cheyenne's eyes met the Moderator's and tears began to roll down her face. She and Jason had specifically gone to Essa's home. They hoped to find they had left town or taken a journey and weren't home when the catastrophe struck. To their dismay, they found Essa's body in her kitchen and a cradle near her holding the bodies of the two infants still snuggled close together. The twin's arms were wrapped around each other as if to protect and comfort each other from the disaster.

Jason and Cheyenne were thankful the wild dogs or animals had not found their way into the house to disturb the precious bodies. They made sure to secure the doors and windows carefully before they left. Cheyenne was so disturbed by the sight she ran outside quickly and threw up. One of the security officers was equally upset and threw up near her. The security officer apologized and explained his weakness. He and his wife had a little boy about to turn three and were now expecting a baby girl. It was just too close to home for him.

Brynna's team was not expected back for several more hours, so David made a request of the Moderator. "May I leave two of my people here and take the rest of the crew back to our ship?"

The Moderator had her mind running several different directions and was having trouble processing his request. "You want to leave two people here instead of taking all of them back with you? Are you concerned about your people on Medoris?"

A part of him was a little concerned, but he felt sure Arni would have warned him if Medoris was in danger. At least he hoped that was true. "If I go back to the ship, when the others return from Medoris, they are going to know something is wrong. I would rather the explanation come from Lexi or myself. I don't want them to worry all the way back to the ship. I would also like to start looking over the scans to see what I can find out about who did this. The Commonwealth may be the ruling power in this galaxy, but there are still renegades and criminals out there. I will find out who's responsible, Moderator. You have my word."

The Moderator nodded. She called to have their vehicle brought back to the elevator. Colonel Bernt escorted the group back out of the large underground facility. The entire group was silent on the trip back. Colonel Bernt could stand the silence no longer. He changed seats, so he could sit near the Captain who was staring blankly out the tinted window. "Captain, if this is not my concern please tell me, what happened on Galat?"

David turned his head slowly to focus on the Colonel's face. The young captain had been wringing his hands as if he could subconsciously wash away the sights he had just seen. He leaned forward in his seat and rested his elbows on his knees. He cleared his throat. "I don't know whether your government cares or not, but I think you'll know soon enough. All the inhabitants of Galat III, at least on the part of the planet we went to, are dead. Men, women, and children- there were no survivors. The town was mostly burned to the ground, as well as some dwellings outside of town."

The Colonel's face was now as solemn as all the crew's faces. In a moment, he managed to ask another question. "Can you tell what happened?"

David continued to wash his hands. "That's what I'm going to work on when I get back to the ship. We took numerous scans and we're going to get started studying them."

The rest of the ride was in silence except for the occasional sniffle as a crew member teared up again. As soon as the crew boarded the ship, David started giving orders. He sent Aulani to contact CIF headquarters to find Admiral Deacons or any other Admiral if he wasn't available. He told her to report only that they had information regarding the inhabitants of Galat III. He sent Braxton and Marissa to start studying the scans of the structures and Jason to study the scans from the bodies.

Cheyenne stood there trembling and looking at David. Fighting back tears she pleaded, "Captain, I need a job. Give me something to do."

David was still not comfortable with showing affection to female crew members, but Cheyenne needed something. He reached up and pulled her head gently to his shoulder and gave her a gentle hug. In a moment, he felt her relax. He waited another moment then released her from his grasp. "Go help Jason." He said it in such a soft gentle tone, she almost didn't realize it was the order she had asked for. She wiped the tears from her eyes and headed down the corridor towards the med bay that doubled as Jason's office and workstation.

David headed to the bridge. Aulani quickly informed him that their schedule and the Admiral's schedule was out of sync again. It was about six in the morning back home. The Admiral was probably in the shower. David had mixed emotions about Aulani's update. He wanted answers, and he wanted them now, but he really wanted the results of the scans available before he spoke to anyone. He paced back and forth for a moment then hit the comm line at his duty station. "Lt. Commander Flint, do you have anything for me yet?"

Braxton looked at Marissa and blinked. "Uh... not much yet sir. It appears to be an energy weapon like those used in the Pacification Fleet. "Those weapons don't cause fires. There were numerous fires. How do you explain those?" David snapped.

Braxton knew the Captain was not upset with him, so he didn't take it personally. "Captain, I do have an explanation for the fires. The inhabitants of Galat caused the fires, not the energy weapon. Those fires were caused by dropped lanterns and candles knocked over when the energy weapon was discharged. If the residents used something other than open flames, there wouldn't have been any fires except maybe for kitchen fires."

"Understood. Lt. Commander, I need you to compare the energy signature against the Pacification Fleet before you make any other comparisons."

Braxton glanced at Marissa. "Yes, Captain." He really wanted to ask why, but he knew this wasn't the time.

David cut off the connection to Engineering and hailed Jason. Jason had no more to report than Braxton.

The Captain paced back and forth on the bridge. He tried again to sit down in his chair. He knew his crew just needed time. Time was the one thing he was having difficulty giving them. He already knew the answers to his questions, but he needed proof. Finally, he came to a command decision benefiting himself and the crew. He jumped out of his chair and went down to the dining hall and made coffee for everyone. He knew making coffee wouldn't take very long, but it kept him busy enough not to drive himself crazy. Hopefully it would keep him from driving everyone else crazy as well. After taking coffee to each of the crew members, David told Aulani he was going to take a shower and change into a clean uniform. He could still smell the scent of the wild dog on himself. If it was bothering him, surely the smell was bothering the others as well. It would also give the crew more time to work without him breathing down their necks.

<hr>

By the time the Captain returned to the bridge, both teams were ready to report to him. They were all waiting on the bridge for him with somber looks. The Captain took his seat on the bridge. "Alright, Lt. Commander, let's hear it."

Braxton touched a couple controls on the duty station where he was sitting. The technical readout for four energy signatures popped up on the main bridge display screen. "Well, Captain, the first signature on the screen is the scan taken on Galat. The second is the energy signature for the weapons used on the Pacification Fleet. As you can see they are nearly identical." Braxton manipulated the controls until the two signatures overlapped. The third is an energy signature from a commercial grade energy blaster used by asteroid miners. As you can see the pattern is similar, but not a match to the one from Galat. The fourth..."

The Captain leaned forward in his seat and scowled at the images. "That fourth one is identical to the Galat energy signature."

Braxton swallowed hard. He looked at the images, and then looked back at the Captain. "Yes sir. That's what I was about to tell you. The last one is an identical match. It's an energy signature I found on file from a Pacification Fleet ship known as the SS Restitution."

Aulani's eyes widened. "We did this? I mean, the Commonwealth did this? I don't understand. Who's responsible for such a thing? Surely the Supreme Executor wouldn't sanction the eradication of an entire planet? He's done nothing but try to keep the peace. He practically did away with death penalties in the entire galaxy. He promotes human life. He doesn't destroy it."

David allowed her to vent before moving on. "Ensign, I'm going to see what I can find out, but we need to stay calm about this. It's possible the Supreme Executor doesn't even know this has happened. This is a big galaxy, and Galat is barely on the radar. If any of you hear from any of the Commonwealth authorities, listen closely to what they say and don't say. Don't volunteer information and definitely don't volunteer your opinions. If you are asked for an opinion, I suggest you keep it brief and put it in broad terms."

Braxton gave a wry look to the Captain, "Do you mean something like, it was an unfortunate situation?"

The Captain gave Braxton a similar look in return. "As long as they aren't reading your face because it definitely was not in agreement with what you said."

Braxton's face sobered. "Yes sir."

Jason had been quietly waiting for his turn although there wasn't much point in his report this time. "Captain, just so you know, my findings concur with Braxton's. I didn't pinpoint the energy signature to an exact ship, but it was clearly a Commonwealth weapon that killed these people."

Cheyenne was standing near Jason and quietly taking in all the information. She occasionally wiped away a silent tear. "Captain, where do we go from here?"

The Captain looked down at the floor for a moment. "Ensign, get those satellite codes and change them. If we let the Commonwealth know Arni's here, they may come and destroy an even larger planet's population. We agreed to go and leave this world in peace. I intend to honor that agreement. I'm giving them the new satellite codes, so they have the option of protecting themselves."

The crew got quiet and looked back and forth at each other. Braxton finally spoke up. "Captain, that's treason."

The Captain sat back in his chair. He finally spoke softly. "I know, but I won't be responsible for another genocide. These people saved our lives."

Aulani suddenly looked guilty. "The Commonwealth knows we were here. What do we put on our reports?" She couldn't believe she was agreeing to commit treason with the Captain.

"We could report everything as it happened up until we did the wormhole jump to Galat and Medoris. We don't need to mention Arni by name. He could be known as a religious leader known as the Intercessor. I would say we lost the debate and the inhabitants will be asking us to leave. It's an omission of information more than falsification of information. We could advise the Commonwealth to check back with them in another fifty years after this generation is long gone."

Braxton frowned. "You have a way of making it sound better than it is."

Marissa had said nothing up until this point which had the Captain concerned. He finally looked at Marissa who was staring at the floor. "Lt. Holden?"

The Lieutenant slowly looked up. All she said was, "Convincing Jake may be a problem."

David nodded then addressed the entire group. "She's right. We can't be on both sides. Fill out your reports as you see fit. If anyone commits treason, it will be me and me alone. I don't want this crew divided. I'll take the heat if anything goes wrong here. As far as you know, you submitted your reports accurately and if this does come back to bite us, it will fall on me, not any of you."

Aulani's face contorted. "Is this a conspiracy not to commit treason?"

David looked at her with a serious look on his face. "I said if. No one is confessing to treason. This was just a casual conversation. We were venting our frustrations. We're over it now. We will leave this planet as discussed because we've lost the debate for certain, and we will file our usual reports. Let's start getting this ship prepared to leave. We told them we would leave under cover of darkness, so we'll either leave late tonight or tomorrow night at the latest. Any questions?"

The crew still were in shock over the day's events. No one had any questions. They all knew their reports were going to be altered after they were submitted. Most decided to submit their reports, so they wouldn't need to be altered yet still be accurate, although maybe not quite complete. After a minute of silence, the Captain dismissed them to return to their duties.

A couple minutes later, Cheyenne walked up to the Captain with a data crystal in her hand. "Captain, the codes we used to shut down the satellites were broadcast on an open channel. They were also fifty-year- old codes, so I updated them. This data crystal has the new codes and the transmission frequency. It also contains the programming protocols from fifty years ago in case you need to do some reprogramming of the satellites. I ran a diagnostic on the damaged satellite. When we hit it with that last blast, it suffered a system overload. Once it comes back online it should be fully functional."

David looked incredulous. "Are you telling me we just stunned it?" Cheyenne nodded. "If the commander hadn't gotten the shutdown sequence when she did, it would have rebooted and started firing again." David got that all too familiar knot in the pit of his stomach again.

He started thinking the knot was going to be his daily companion. He rubbed his face with his hands and sighed. Someone was definitely watching out for them. Those satellites should have destroyed them. He finally addressed the young Ensign again. "Thank you, Ensign. Did you keep a copy?"

Cheyenne glanced at Aulani who was busy on communications. "Yes sir. I also programmed a back door several layers deep in the programming, so we can get back in if we need to." She had kept her voice low during the entire conversation. Even though the Captain said they were to keep things above board, she knew his intention was more in line with his earlier train of thought. "And Captain, the new codes are not standard CIF codes. The funny thing is they look a lot like the Moderator's personal communication codes. I think the transmission frequency also matched Drean frequencies. Perhaps the Dreans picked up the codes from the open channel when we shut the satellites down. I'm not sure how that happened sir." She grinned slyly.

David smiled. "Thank you again Ensign. He slipped the crystal into a pouch on his utility belt."

Later that afternoon, Brynna's team returned from Medoris in an unusually good mood. The work they had done on Medoris had stayed intact. Brynna was afraid the inhabitants might revert to their old ways as soon as the crew was gone, but everything seemed to be going well. Chancellor Torrell and Arbiter Navid were treated as honored guests and were in good moods until they noticed the demeanor of those who had gone to Galat. Brynna was surprised to find David had already returned from Galat and gone back to the ship. When they boarded the vehicle taking them back to the Evangeline, she finally asked Lexi what was wrong. Lexi and Jake had been given explicit instructions to keep discussion to a minimum until the group was back on the ship. Lexi gave Brynna as much information as discreetly as she could. "Commander, the Captain said he would give you the details when you reach the ship, but…"

Lexi was clearly rattled. "Lexi, what is it? What happened on Galat?" Brynna entreated.

Lexi gave Brynna a purposeful stare. "Let's just say the Captain's dreams… or nightmares… came true."

Brynna didn't make the connection immediately. Lexi watched Brynna's face change as the reality hit her. She finally gasped quietly. The other crewmen looked at her quizzically. They instinctively knew better than to ask any questions. They knew they would learn whatever they needed to know soon enough.

It was a long quiet trip back to the ship. Jake and Lexi's moods quickly set the tone for the trip back. Jake tried to make some small talk by asking about the group's visit to Medoris, but the conversation felt forced by all and fell short. As soon as the vehicle reached the ship, the crew quickly got out and climbed aboard. Brynna sent them to clean up with the warning of a potential briefing shortly.

Brynna went immediately to find David. She found him in his office and sat down across from him. She didn't care for the look on his face. She couldn't get a reading of any emotion at all from him. "David, what's happened? Lexi mentioned something about your nightmare coming true, but she was very vague."

David stretched and stood up to walk around. He had been too still for too long. He took a deep breath then turned around to face her again. "As far as we can tell every human life on Galat III has been eliminated. The planet was attacked from space by an energy weapon. The energy signature is an exact match to the Pacification Fleet ship known as the Restitution. I've put in a call to the Admiral to see if I can find out who's responsible. I've told the crew to turn in their reports as they see fit, but we aren't going to put them through the proofing loop this time. We made a deal to leave these people in peace and that's what I intend to do. Do you have a problem with that?" He leaned over and placed his hands down on the table in front of her.

Brynna was having trouble processing everything David had said. "David, have you changed loyalties?"

David stood up. "I suppose it depends on what I hear from the Admiral. I can't be loyal to anyone who supports mass murder. Cheyenne and Jason found the bodies of their namesake twins lying peacefully in their crib, dead. DEAD!" David slammed his fist on the tabletop as he continued his tirade. "Killed from space! None of these people ever saw the faces of their enemies! Arni seems to think the order was given by Executor Hale. If he's right, then maybe I am changing my loyalties. If it was someone else, then I will pursue prosecution of whoever did this."

Brynna had stopped breathing when she asked David about his loyalties. She realized at the end of his tirade she still had not taken another breath. She forced herself to relax and take a breath. David continued his rant. "There were wild dogs roaming the countryside eating the flesh from the dead bodies lying on the ground. One of them attacked me. Marissa found the bodies of two of the children they taught to make gliders after giving them a shuttle ride. They were huddled in fear under their house with their mother's arms wrapped around them. We did this! I did! I could have prevented it, but I didn't. This is my fault! I need to know. Do I need to plan to stay behind while you take the ship and leave? I would rather stay behind than get spaced in a couple days."

Brynna's hands began to shake. She had trouble looking him in the eye. "You're right. We made a deal with these people, and I wouldn't have made it if I didn't intend to follow through on it. Captain, I need to know. Do you serve the Commonwealth, or do you serve the House of Liontari?"

David jerked a chair out from under the table and sat down. "I do not serve the House of Liontari. I still serve the Commonwealth, but this can't happen again, ever. I may skirt around the edges of our mandate, and it's possible I may commit treason before we're done here on Drea, but it won't be because of any loyalty to Arni."

Brynna breathed easier. She didn't want to execute her own husband. She wasn't sure how she felt about reporting him for committing treason. At least there was no death penalty for treason although the re-education included a total erasure of his memories, so it would be like he had never existed. "David, you mentioned Arni. Was Arni on Galat?"

David was momentarily distracted from his rant by her question. "Nooo. He's their precious Intercessor." He replied emphatically and slammed his fist on the table again.

Brynna seemed stunned for a moment. "The Intercessor? So, what do we do now? Our oath to the Commonwealth is in direct conflict with our promise to leave these people in peace."

David displayed the recently acquired data on the computer screen for her. "Here's everything we got from Galat. I plan on conducting a briefing in an hour. The ship is prepped for departure. We can leave tonight, or we can stick around and say an appropriate farewell to the Moderator and her companions. I would like the chance to give her an explanation rather than just disappear into the night."

David started the material running, then abruptly left the room. The Captain had put together several of the audiovisual recordings of what they encountered on Galat. He put the more graphic sections together for maximum effect. He was recording when the wild dog attacked, so that footage was also available. He felt a small twinge of guilt about trying to manipulate the crew's emotions, but if they weren't there in person, they wouldn't be affected the same way as those who were. David wanted everyone on the same page. He also knew hiding his feelings or actions from Brynna would be extremely difficult, so it was better to get his feelings and attitudes out in the open.

Forty minutes later, Brynna walked out of the Captain's office feeling stunned and sick. The manner of death wasn't particularly gruesome. There was no visible damage to the bodies although many appeared to have convulsed as they died. It was simply the cold detached manner. They were slaughtered and left lying in the streets and on the floors. No one even attempted to give them a proper burial. Seeing the wild dogs almost did Brynna in. Brynna went to her quarters, splashed some water on her face and tried to get her mind off what she had seen, so she would be ready for the briefing.

The crew was already beginning to assemble in the dining hall. David had prepared plenty of coffee. The crew helped themselves but said very little to each other. At the staff meetings, David and Brynna usually remained seated, but this time David stood. Cheyenne was on the bridge monitoring communications and scanners. She connected to the meeting via one of the computer monitors in the dining hall. Everyone was assembled earlier than the scheduled, so David got started.

"Since everyone's here, I'm going to go ahead and get this over with. Some of you are already aware of this information. Some of you don't know any of it. I want us all on the same page. Forgive me if this is a repeat for some of you, but it needs to be done. Look away if you need to." The three other crew members who returned to Medoris gave each other concerned looks. David continued. "Galat III was attacked from space by an energy weapon. As near as we can tell, all human life on the planet has been destroyed." David paused to give them a chance to comprehend what he said.

Thane took the moment of silence to be an opening for questions. "Captain, do we know who...?"

The Captain held up his hand to stop Thane. "Before we get to that, you need to see this for yourselves." The Captain nodded and Brynna hit the controls to start the same footage she had just viewed in the captain's office. She did lower the volume until it was barely audible. She wanted very badly to fast forward through it but knew not to. Fortunately, David did not let it continue through the entire footage. Once he saw they were all been deeply affected, he stopped it. "There's more if any of you want to see it later. I think we've all seen more than we wanted. The Dreans are organizing teams to go back and create mass grave sites with markers listing any known names. The Moderator is also creating one separate grave site with its own marker for Arni's mother, Slaina."

Jake jumped in. "Captain, I know you weren't wanting questions now, but we may have ticked off the most powerful beings in the galaxy.

Is Arni gunning for us now?"

David knew it was a worthwhile interruption. "No, Arni isn't gunning for us. He's saddened by what happened, but he seems to have accepted it. After we returned to the ship, we examined the energy signature. Braxton, show them what you found."

Braxton repeated his earlier demonstration showing the energy signature was an identical match to the Commonwealth ship known as the Restitution. Jason added his results confirming Braxton's findings.

Before anyone could start asking questions again, David quickly took control. "We told this world we would go away and leave them in peace if they could prove to us the Commonwealth was still not trustworthy. It appears they have won their argument."

Jake jumped in again. "Captain, you aren't suggesting..."

The Captain again held his hand up to stop him. "I'm about to tell you what I'm suggesting, Chief, if you'll let me finish. Someone needs to be held accountable for this travesty of justice. The Commonwealth represents itself as an instrument of peace. I intend to find out who authorized this attack and see they are prosecuted to the fullest extent of the law. I also, do not intend to allow them to do this to another planet. We will file partial reports to the Commonwealth, while this is being investigated. I will report directly to the Admirals' board what has happened. We need to keep the list of people who know about this as small as possible if we intend to find the guilty party. I feel certain the Supreme Executor would not want the Commonwealth's name to be sullied. He's worked so hard to make this galaxy good for everyone concerned. Yes, this will mean pushing the regulations all the way to the edge. I am going to utilize the Captain's prerogative, so if it blows back in anyone's face it will be mine."

Brynna jumped in to play devil's advocate because despite the fact everyone appeared to love and trust their Captain, she knew they were going to be thinking what she was about to say. "Captain, you know there is no such thing as Captain's prerogative. That won't stand up in a court of law, or should I say a Court Martial?"

David looked at her. Her demeanor suggested she was deadly serious, but something in her eyes said this was for his benefit. "I know, which is why you are submitting your full complete and accurate reports to me and I will submit those reports through official channels, although they may not be entirely complete… for now. I will update the full reports once my investigation is complete. This will keep all of you out of harm's way."

Brynna pushed just one more time. "What happens if this gets found out while you're conducting your investigation? Won't we get into trouble for not reporting you?"

Brynna's body language was less serious this time and slightly more relaxed. David thought maybe she wasn't sure how her first question would be perceived, so she was more on guard. Finally, David responded cautiously and quietly. He didn't want his tone or attitude to be misunderstood. "In answer to your first question, all you know is you turned in a full accurate report to me as ordered. There are no broken regulations there. You won't be held accountable for that. This meeting is somewhat off the record. The fact that I'm telling you what I may do does put me, as well as all of you, at risk for conspiracy charges. Every one of you does have the right and responsibility to report me if you believe this goes against the good of the Commonwealth. I won't stop you. Before you do, I am putting you on notice, I will not be responsible for the extinction of another civilization. If you report me and these people die, that's on you. I'm not doing this just for an Adrenalin rush. A genuine travesty of justice has occurred. I intend to find out who's responsible and report it to the Supreme Executor." David paused to let his words sink in. "Any more questions?"

David looked at Brynna to see if she had any more questions to offer. She stood there silently. The Captain then looked around the room. He made eye contact with every individual and each person's eyes seemed to indicate consent to move forward with his plan. Jake was leaned back in his chair again and didn't appear ready to come out of it. That was a good thing as far as David could tell.

The last person to make eye contact with the Captain was Marissa. She slowly looked up at him. "Captain, I want to know who did this too. Even if this was the home of our enemy, these people didn't deserve this. I'm behind you all the way on this."

Jake glanced over at his wife expecting to see tears again. This time her eyes were full of anger. Thane worked with Marissa regularly and had never seen such strong emotion in her eyes. He loved to irritate her just to try and get her riled up, but even when she was at her angriest, it never looked like this. Thane looked over at his own wife's face and saw a similar expression. Aulani was nodding. "Captain, Aulani and I are with you too." Several other voices chimed in.

David breathed a little easier knowing his crew supported him on this. Braxton brought the focus back around again. "Captain, what's our next step? What about the Dreans? Are we leaving tonight, or do we tell them what we know?"

David glanced over at Brynna who gave him a slight shrug. The Captain didn't want to back down at this point. "I think we need to be completely honest with them. It's their lives we're gambling with. I say we go to the debate tomorrow and tell them everything. We'll probably get thrown off the planet for sure, but we were leaving anyway. It also gives them the chance to reconsider their relationship with their intercessor if they know the risks of remaining in league with him." The Captain got several nods of approval from around the room. The only one not approving was Jake. David looked directly at him. "Any concerns?" Jake set his chair back upright. "Captain, they may not take this information very well. They already have a grudge against the Commonwealth. What if they decide to take some sort of revenge out on us?"

David nodded. "I suppose that is a concern, but we've already told them the Commonwealth knows where we are, and this is where they will look for us if something happens. They also have what happened on Galat as motivation to let us leave. Do you think that's enough to counter any such desire?" The Captain wanted to win Jake on the merits of his arguments alone instead of bullying him into agreement. "Do you have any other suggestions?"

Jake leaned forward in his seat. "I do have one. Program a distress call to go out if we aren't back to the ship within say four hours?"

The Captain nodded. "I like that idea. Aulani and I will get it set up.

Anything else?"

Jake still looked concerned. "Do we need to take the entire crew? Can't we send a small representation and leave everyone else on the ship?"

The Captain thought about it for a moment. "I'd like to take everyone to let them know we are all upset about this. I don't want them to feel like we are up to something or hiding something by keeping the bulk of the crew sequestered. It could put us in more danger. Yes, it will make us more vulnerable, but it also shows our willingness to be vulnerable and trust the Dreans."

Jake shook his head. "I hate these stupid mind games."

David nodded in agreement. "I'm not fond of them either.

Commander, are you alright with this?"

Brynna was now leaning against the wall. When the attention focused on her, she stood erect again. In a moment, she nodded. "Yes, I am. These people saved our lives and despite their hatred of us, helped us repair our ship. They could have destroyed us several times over if they wanted to, but they haven't. We owe it to them."

Jake quipped. "Maybe they haven't had sufficient reason until now." "Captain, I have Admiral Deacons for you on a secure channel, priority one." Cheyenne interrupted from the bridge. David moved hastily towards the door and responded over his shoulder. "I'll take it in my office."

David got to his office and signaled Cheyenne to connect the transmission. He stood at attention as she put the call through. Admiral Deacons voice spoke immediately. "At ease, Captain. You might want to sit down for this." David sat down quickly. The Admiral was talking quickly and quietly. "I understand you found out about Galat III. Is that correct?"

David nodded, "Found out . . .? So, you knew about this?"

The Admiral cut him off. "David, how did you find out about it? You had orders not to return to Galat. I thought your ship was still on Drea III?"

"We are on Drea III, sir. We... uh... got the information from a third party." David wasn't sure how to explain his trip to Galat III, or even if he should.

The Admiral decided maybe it was best he didn't know either, so he interrupted David's attempt to explain. "Never mind, that's not important. What is important is that you stop asking these questions immediately."

"Admiral, my crew have seen the images of a slaughtered population. They're quite upset. Is the Supreme Executor aware of this? I know he would not sanction such a thing, but the energy signature has been positively identified as coming from the Pacification Fleet."

The Admiral cussed under his breath. David was startled. He had never heard his uncle cuss before. Admiral Deacons believed in maintaining the highest level of professionalism and felt foul language showed a lack of moral fortitude. David waited silently. If something had his uncle this rattled, it was probably best to wait until he was ready to speak. Finally, the Admiral looked back at David. "David, that decision came down from the Admiral's board. Admiral Garcia pushed it through despite my objections. I thought your suggestion to quarantine the planet was appropriate. Admiral Garcia wanted to set the standard for all enemies of the Commonwealth." The Admiral paused for a moment. "Captain Alexander, I looked at the history of Drea III. No one gets near that planet without being shot down. How did you get in there?"

David was starting to weigh his answers carefully. "We were nearly shot down, sir, but Commander Alexander was able to retrieve the shutdown codes from the archives just in time. The ship was damaged, but we have completed our repairs. We are preparing to leave here in the next day or two."

The Admiral noticed David wasn't volunteering too much information and smiled to himself. His nephew was a discerning young man. The Admiral decided to do whatever he could to help his nephew without saying more than he should. "Captain, from this point on, I feel it would be safe for you to assume all enemies of the Commonwealth will be treated in a similar fashion, so make sure your reports are accurate and complete. I would hate to see an entire planetary population be wiped out due to a minor misrepresentation. Do you understand what I am saying?"

David saw fear in his uncle's eyes. Now there were two things he had never seen his uncle display before. "Yes Admiral, I understand. Is there anything else I should know?"

The Admiral thought for a moment. "Be careful who you trust. It feels like some things are coming to a head. I wouldn't want you to end up as somebody's fall guy. Don't forget, even though this is a secure channel, anyone with the right decoding equipment can still pick it up."

David was starting to feel cut off from his support system. His uncle was clearly telling him it wasn't safe for the two of them to speak freely. "Understood sir." David paused a second then changed the tone of the conversation. "May I ask a personal question, sir?"

The Admiral looked at him sternly thinking his message had not been received. "It depends on the question."

"I was wondering if you've heard from my sister. She was expecting her first child when we left home."

The Admiral breathed a sigh of relief. Perhaps he had understood. David could see the relief in the Admiral's face. "Yes David, your mother contacted me. I almost forgot. Abigail had a boy right after the last time I talked to you. She named him Joshua Aiden Williams. He's a fine healthy boy. She sent some pictures which I am sending to you now. Your mother also sends you her love. You really need to try to contact her more often."

"Yes sir. If you talk to her before I do, please pass on my congratulations and my love to the family. I'll try to use a personal channel next time instead of a secured channel. I wouldn't want to get either of us in trouble."

"I'll use Admiral's prerogative and let it go this time." The Admiral told David to give his best to Brynna and to let the crew know he thought they were doing a good job as well. As soon as he closed the connection, David leaned back in his seat and tried to process what he had heard and not heard. Before he could return to the briefing Cheyenne was hailing him again.

"Captain, I have Admiral Garcia for you on a priority one secure channel."

David wasn't sure he liked having the attention of this many high- ranking officials. "Put it through Ensign and let the crew know it'll be another few minutes until I get back."

Cheyenne acknowledged his order and connected the call from the Admiral.

David stood again. "Admiral Garcia, Captain Alexander here."

The Admiral had David sit down as well. "Captain, you've been asking about Galat III. Is that right?"

"Yes sir. We received reports from a party who had visited Galat III recently. The entire population had been wiped out. I was wondering if we had any ships in the area to investigate or if we should go investigate since we are ready to leave our current assignment."

The Admiral's face revealed no emotion. "That won't be necessary.

We have it handled."

David decided to bombard Admiral Garcia with questions to keep him from asking questions David didn't want to answer. "Admiral, does the Supreme Executor know about this? He has always been so proactive in the promotion of peace. I would think this could be a problem for him."

The Admiral scowled at him. "Why would this be a problem for the Supreme Executor?"

"Well sir, if he isn't aware of it or doesn't know who's responsible for it, they could use it to attack him politically. We are talking genocide, sir." David was hoping the Admiral would interpret David's youthful appearance as naivety.

The Admiral wasn't sure how to take the young Captain. "They were followers of the House of Liontari, our enemy."

"Yes sir, I know sir, but if word got out a peaceful planet filled with women and children were slaughtered and the Supreme Executor didn't do something about it. Well sir, it just wouldn't look good. I feel certain the Supreme Executor would not appreciate anyone trying to discredit him and the Commonwealth, don't you?"

"Captain, I appreciate your enthusiasm, but the Supreme Executor is fully aware of the situation on Galat III. I hope you understand, given the insidious nature of our enemy, the Commonwealth has but one alternative in dealing with him. All those not loyal to the Commonwealth are going to be destroyed. This initiative supports the Supreme Executor's peace agenda."

David sat back in his chair. He appeared to be considering the Admiral's words. He leaned forward when he was ready to respond. "That's an aggressive strategy, sir. I never would have expected that from the Supreme Executor given my last conversation with him."

This time the Admiral's face was readable. He was clearly shocked the Supreme Executor had spoken to the brand-new Captain of such a small insignificant ship. "When did you speak to him?" The Admiral was trying not to sound too demanding.

"He contacted me before we entered the Drean system. Is there a problem, Admiral Garcia?"

The Admiral still appeared flustered. "No, there's no problem. Listen, Captain, the Supreme Executor authorized the destruction of the Galatan population. You just keep doing your job of pointing out the weeds in our garden and we'll take care of pulling them. Is that understood?"

David gave an almost cheerful, "Yes sir. Is there anything else sir?"

The Admiral stared at David closely. "Do you have a problem with this, Captain? If so, let me know now."

David shook his head. "No sir, it isn't a problem. I just didn't want the Supreme Executor to be caught off-guard, but since this is his plan then I'm good. I was just not aware and thought he should know before it caused any… embarrassment."

The Admiral seemed to be satisfied with David's responses. He cautioned David not to let the information out to the public. The Supreme Executor planned to make a formal statement before that happened.

When David was finally alone with his thoughts again, he allowed himself the luxury of being both shocked, then angry. He wanted to punch something very badly, but there was nothing in his office he was willing to risk breaking. He knew he needed to pull himself together, quickly. There was a room full of people waiting on him. The door to his office chimed. David looked towards the door and hollered, "Enter." He saw Brynna walk in, take one look at him, and her expression changed. David gave a barbed response, "I look that bad, huh?"

"Uh... yeah. Do I want to know? Forget that. Do I need to know?" Brynna stopped shortly inside the door because David was pacing back and forth leaving her little room to maneuver in the small office.

"I'll tell you after we leave Drea. If I tell you now, it will affect both of us. Let's continue with our original plan, then we'll have to talk to the entire crew because this affects all of us. I do want to make one change though. I want you to address the Dreans. I'm not sure I can right now."

Brynna fought the urge to ask what he was keeping from her. "I can do that. David, you still have the crew waiting on you and they don't need to see you like this. You need to think about something totally unrelated." David had trouble for a moment coming up with anything to think about. Brynna tried to distract him by moving up close to him and wrapping her arms around him. He instinctively wrapped his arms around her as well, but the look on his face didn't change. Suddenly he remembered the last couple minutes of his conversation with Admiral Deacons. He grabbed Brynna's arms and pushed her away from him. "Hey! I'm an uncle. You're an aunt. Abigail had a boy. His name is Joshua Aiden."

Brynna gave him a wry smile. "Well, Uncle David, I will try not to take that affront to my affection personally, this time."

David pulled her closer and gave her a quick kiss on the forehead. "Thanks for everything. I don't know what I would do without you. We need to get back to the crew. Maybe they'll forgive me for keeping them waiting when they hear about my nephew."

David and Brynna walked back into the dining hall in better spirits than the previous minutes. David instructed the crew to carry their standard sidearms per protocol. He informed them, per the Admirals, not to discuss any of this with anyone not part of the crew. He didn't want it going out in personal messages or to the Dreans. Brynna would make a concession and farewell speech at the next meeting with the Dreans. Lastly, he apologized for taking so long to get back to them. He casually mentioned it was in relation to his investigation and would have more information for them as soon as it was available. He also announced proudly the birth of his new nephew. He hated using a newborn baby he had never even met as a way of avoiding a nasty issue. The meeting adjourned, and everyone went their separate ways. David and Aulani headed to the bridge to work out the automated distress call details. After they finished, Brynna invited David to go running with her outside the ship. Jake took Marissa up on top of the ship for guard duty while watching the sunset. Tomorrow was going to be a difficult day, so they might as well have a little peace and quiet.

David and Brynna pushed themselves to the point of exhaustion on their run. It gave them time to think and plan for the next day as well as take out some of their frustrations. After their run, Brynna worked on her notes for her impending speech while David got a shower. The two got to bed late, but they slept hard.

The rest of the crew did not fare as well. When David and Brynna headed into the dining room for breakfast the next morning, they found Thane and Aulani were having breakfast with Braxton and Lexi. Both couples looked tired and their conversations were noticeably shallow and sparse. Marissa came in and grabbed a piece of fruit, a pastry, and a stout cup of coffee. Jake had already come and gone. He was going over weapons in the armory. The rest of the crew filtered in little by little. Each one wore a haggard expression on their faces. The knowledge of what they learned last night weighed heavily on them all. Looking at each face, he knew he had done the right thing by waiting to tell them the rest of the story. No one would have gotten any sleep if they knew what Admiral Garcia had said. David did have to consider one possibility. What if the Admiral lied? What if the Supreme Executor didn't know what happened? He would have to bide his time and wait for the right way and the right time to find out.

When it was time to leave for the debate, David solemnly lead the crew to their transportation. The ride was just as quiet as breakfast. The group didn't touch the buffet prepared for them this morning but milled around quietly. Moderator Tarmon noticed the crew's subdued behavior. She was silently impressed the tragedy on Galat III had so deeply affected the Commonwealth diplomats. She thought perhaps she had been wrong about the Commonwealth. The Dreans seemed to be equally as dazed by the situation on Galat.

The Intercessor, in an attempt to avoid the inevitable pomp and circumstance, arrived early. He made the rounds talking to everyone as they arrived. When the crew arrived Arni didn't make any particular effort to speak to them. Just before David and Brynna headed to the platform, Arni finally approached the two of them. "Captain, Commander, I know you aren't going to listen to me, but you need to simply walk away. Don't take responsibility for what happened on Galat unless you plan to also accept the consequences. You were right. You didn't cause this. Luciano Hale did. He's the one who needs to pay for this."

David and Brynna looked at each other. David listened and mulled his plea over carefully. "Arni, I appreciate your concern. I don't understand why you care what happens to us, but I do appreciate all the help you've given us. Perhaps we need to talk more later, but I'm not about to sit back and let this planet suffer the same fate as Galat III. They need to know what they're up against."

Arni smiled. "I'm glad you are starting to see things more clearly. I still wish you would walk away."

Brynna looked back and forth at David and Arni. "Wait a minute. Are you saying the Supreme Executor is responsible for what happened on Galat?" She was doubly shocked; first by learning that the Supreme Executor was directly responsible for the attack and second because David wasn't surprised. It was apparent this was the piece of information he had been withholding from her. "David, why would he do such a horrible thing? Who told you? Are you sure your information is accurate?"

David grabbed Brynna's elbow. "I didn't want to tell you because I didn't think I had enough information yet. I also wanted to wait until we left Drea before dealing with this. Let's finish this and then we'll cross that bridge."

The Captain knew he needed to get her focused on the speech. "Arni, would you consider spending some time with us later. I have some questions that need answers."

"I will spend as much time with you as you like. Call my name at any time and even if you do not hear or see me. I will still be there." Arni moved away from the couple. The couple saw him walk past the Moderator and whisper something to her quietly then he moved on. David and Brynna moved to the platform and took their places.

The Moderator approached David and Brynna while the other representatives took their places. "Captain, Commander, I'm sorry, but we would like to cut this short today. I've declared the next seven days as a time of mourning for the Intercessor's loss and the loss of life on Galat."

Brynna stood up in deference to the Moderator's position and situation. "Moderator Tarmon, we understand and are in complete agreement. Our entire crew has been hit equally as hard by this tragedy. We have closing remarks and then we plan on leaving your world after dark tonight."

"I'm not sure I understand. You no longer want to present your proposal to the Council?"

"Moderator, I will explain it all in closing remarks." Brynna assured her. The Moderator moved to take her seat still looking confused.

As the meeting got under way, the Arbiter offered both sides a chance to ask any last questions of the other side. Neither side had any questions. The Arbiter then offered each side the opportunity to make closing remarks.

Brynna stood up and moved to her podium. She took a sip of water and took a deep breath. "Moderator Tarmon, Arbiter Navid, Chancellor Noe, Chancellor Torrell, United World Council Members, we wish to extend our deepest apologies. Our agreement was to present evidence that we represented a peace-loving society that was no longer the monster you once knew. If we were unable to convince you, as per our agreement, then we would leave your planet and leave the satellites surrounding it dormant. We have failed and are prepared to do just that. Tonight, after nightfall, our ship will depart."

A low murmur ran through the room as questions and comments were whispered back and forth. The Moderator stood up and interrupted the proceedings. "Commander, shouldn't we be the ones to decide that for ourselves?"

The Commander glanced at Arni who shook his head and then at David who nodded at her. Strangely enough she wanted to trust Arni, but her husband was her commanding officer. "Moderator, I know you will be convinced we aren't to be trusted when you hear the rest of our statement. I was waiting to share at least one piece of information when we made our proposal to the United World Council. The Commonwealth sent us out as goodwill ambassadors to seek new allies and to search for a declared enemy of the Commonwealth. We didn't know it would be an issue until yesterday. We didn't know what plans the Commonwealth had for its enemies until yesterday. You have won this debate. You have convinced us the Commonwealth is not to be trusted. We will leave here and do whatever we can to keep the Commonwealth from ever returning here."

The answer was staring her in the face, but the Moderator couldn't quite make the pieces of the puzzle fit together. "Commander, I'm afraid I don't understand. You knew before you landed here the Commonwealth was our declared enemy. Can you please explain yourselves?"

Brynna saw Arni again slowly shake his head. Every time she saw him do it, she became more unnerved. She wanted to look away from him, but he was sitting beside the Moderator. This time she noticed a tear slowly rolling down his cheek. Now, she was really unnerved. She decided to just say the rest of it quickly and get it over with. "The Commonwealth's enemies are those who side with the House of Liontari. The Commonwealth destroyed Galat III because we reported the presence of Arni Liontari and his mother."

For a moment, you could have heard a pin drop as the shock of her statements hit. In a second, tempers began to flare. Angry comments and insults were hurled at the crew. Brynna saw fists being shaken in the air at her and the crew. Jake and Thane were sitting on the edge of their chairs ready to protect their commanders if necessary. The Arbiter and the Moderator tried to get everyone to settle down. They were flatly ignored. Finally, Arni stood up and raised his hands to quiet the crowd. As soon as they began to see his gesture, the angry mob grew quiet. Once settled, the Moderator ordered Colonel Bernt to escort the representatives from the room except for the Arbiter and the two Chancellors. The Moderator approached the crew and advised them to stay put for their own safety. She then excused herself to see to the evacuation of the other delegates. It was clear she was just as angry as those she sent away. Being an excellent leader of the people, she did not allow it to hinder her judgment. David and Brynna left the platform and joined the crew at the tables on the floor of the assembly hall. They made no attempts to leave the room. As things started to settle down, David saw Moderator

Tarmon give Colonel Bernt one final set of instructions. Moments later numerous security officers entered the room and positioned themselves along the perimeter. David glanced at Jake and said the only thing he could. "Uh- oh."

Moderator Tarmon approached the crew but kept a discreet distance. She paced back and forth in front of them for a moment. Finally, full of anger she spoke. "Do you understand what you've done? You brought the Commonwealth back to our doorsteps and with it more death and destruction. My people are now out for blood. No one ever paid the price for what happened here fifty years ago, and what happened on Galat III goes way beyond that. It would have been better if you had just left and said nothing! I do need to ask one thing. Why? Why did you stay last night, and why did you feel the need to tell us what you had done?"

Brynna stepped forward to answer her, but David pulled her back and took her place. "Moderator Tarmon, we didn't want to be responsible for the extermination of another planet's inhabitants. We wanted you to know what the Commonwealth is capable of. When we leave here, our reports will not include the identity of your Intercessor, nor how we found out about what happened on Galat." The crew seemed to all be supportive of the Captain's statements except Jake. Something about the way the Captain had worded his statements felt wrong to him. They agreed to turn in incomplete reports while the Captain conducted his investigation, but this time it sounded like the Captain never intended to correct the reports. Jake thought maybe the Captain was just trying to placate the Dreans.

The Moderator turned and walked over to Colonel Bernt. "Did you get the extra troops in place?"

The Colonel nodded. "I have extra troops and vehicles for the convoy. I sent additional troops to safeguard their ship."

The Moderator turned to face the crew to be sure they and everyone remaining in the room could hear her. "Place them under arrest. The charges are murder, conspiracy to commit genocide, espionage, fraud, bribery and whatever else I can come up with."

Brynna spoke out, "What?! We were trying to protect you. We haven't meant anyone any harm. This wasn't our fault! You have no jurisdiction over Galat!" As she spoke, she and the others drew their weapons to protect themselves.

Moderator Tarmon looked at Brynna coldly. "And who is there left on Galat to prosecute you? Jurisdiction doesn't play into crimes of this nature."

Colonel Bernt's men drew their weapons and started moving to subdue the crew. They were surrounded and outnumbered two to one. This didn't account for an unknown number of troops waiting for them outside.

The Moderator and her companions were quickly ushered away from the impending firefight. Arni would not allow himself to be escorted away despite the pleas of two frustrated security guards. Arni placed himself strategically between the crew and the advancing troops who froze as soon as it was clear the Intercessor was in danger. Arni raised his hands. "Captain Alexander, please, may I speak to you?"

The Captain stepped forward cautiously. "Arni, you know a lot of things. I don't know how you know them, but you know I mean these people no harm. You also know my crew will fight to protect themselves. Let us leave peacefully and we will keep our word. We'll leave you out of our reports."

Arni stepped closer and to the Captain and spoke softly. "Captain, I asked you to walk away. You still don't want to trust me. I've shown you nothing, but the truth in every case. Luciano told you I would take over your minds. Have I done that? In every situation, I have advised you, offered to help you, but I have never forced myself on any of you. Please trust me this one time. Put your weapons down and don't resist. I will keep your crew from being harmed. In a few days, they will be set free and allowed to return to space."

David glanced behind him at his crew. They were focused as trained, but still showed glimmers of fear. "The crew will be set free and won't be harmed. What about me?"

Something flickered across Arni's face. It was so quick David couldn't identify it. "They will be arrested and charged, but will be freed in a few days. Your story is not so simple. If they resist at any time, injuries will result. I know your crew. They are capable of putting up a good fight, so it will take a good fight to put them down." Arni looked over at Lexi. "Lexi, I told you when Manton and Vesta were holding you prisoner in the caves I would protect you. I warned you not to resist, did I not?" Lexi stared at

Arni. She wasn't sure what to make of his questions. Was he really the man who helped her? Arni persisted. "I warned you not to resist. What happened when you disobeyed my instructions? Manton would not have harmed you if you hadn't fought him."

Lexi cocked her head. "That was you? You were Gabe? You were the one who helped me?" Lexi bit down on her lip. "I'm sorry. I should have listened to you."

Arni looked back at David. His eyes pleaded with the young Captain. "David, please trust me at least this one time. Put your weapons down and do this one, my way. You don't have the resources to get out of here unscathed. You will be taken into custody regardless."

David looked around the room at the number of men surrounding them. He reached for the control on his comm link to send the automated distress signal he and Aulani had set up. Arni was now within reach which thoroughly exasperated the security forces. He reached down and stopped David from touching the control. "David, trust me."

David wasn't sure why he did it. He dropped his hand away from the control. He turned around to the crew. "Put your weapons down. We're outnumbered and outgunned. We won't make it out of here. We agreed we didn't want to be responsible for the death of another civilization. I don't want to be accountable for even one death on this planet."

Jake looked at the men surrounding them and back at the Captain. He knew the Captain was right about being outnumbered, but he preferred to go down fighting. He gripped his weapons even tighter. The crew could see Jake was determined not to let this fight go. David laid his weapon on the table nearest him. Brynna followed David's example. The others lowered their weapons, but they weren't quite ready to release their grip on them yet. David moved towards Jake. "Chief, put your weapon down. We can't win like this, we'll just get hurt for no good reason. We've been charged with numerous crimes. We need to face these charges with honor. There's a chance we can win our case if we act appropriately now."

Jake looked at David then at the rest of the crew. The chief moved his weapon until it pointed at David's head. "He turned you, didn't he?"

David shook his head. "I am not serving the House of Liontari. I put my weapon down because I can't win this scenario. This isn't the fight I signed on for. The Commonwealth hasn't asked this of me. I would have given my life in the fire ring or given it to save Marissa from the tornado. I'm not willing to hurt these people for defending the lives of others. I'll take my day in court and then if it is necessary, I will give up my life, but only then."

David paused and watched Jake process. He tried hard not to look at the weapon aimed at his head. Maybe this is what Arni meant by his story not being so simple. David stepped closer to Jake until the weapon was in point blank range. He held his hands out to his sides, so Jake could keep track of them. David spoke softly to Jake. "Jake, I'm going to need you. Arni says the crew will be released in a few days. I need you to get Brynna and the rest of the crew safely off this planet. I got the feeling I won't be leaving here. I need you, Jake. Please put your weapons down." Jake slowly lowered his Tri-EMP. A chill ran down David's spine as he caught sight of the weapon's setting. The Tri-EMP was set to kill. Jake reset the weapon to its lowest setting and turned the safety on. As soon as it was secured, he tossed it onto a nearby table along with his shield and the knives he had squirreled away in his uniform.

The rest of the crew followed Jake and the Captain's examples. The security forces quickly moved in and forced the crew to their knees with their hands on their heads. They placed security binders on each one with their hands bound behind them. The security detail escorted the crew back out to a vehicle that was very different from the one that had brought them in earlier. The men and women were split up in separate vehicles. The vehicles were designed for the transportation of prisoners. Each seat had a "V" shaped harness or safety bar that pulled down from overhead and fastened into a latch between their legs. It appeared to have the dual purpose of keeping prisoners safe in the event of a vehicle accident and preventing them from escaping.

PART FIVE

DEATH & DEALS

THE DEAL TO END ALL DEALS

The crew was transported to an underground facility beneath the assembly hall for the United World Council. They were given solid white, form-fitting prison uniforms. The fabric was a knit material that stretched to fit the body. The collar was a mock turtle neck style and the sleeves were three quarter length. The tunic extended down to the top of the thighs. The pants were also of a fitted knit material that went down to the ankles. Their shoes were like socks with a thin padded bottom. The uniforms were designed to keep prisoners from concealing contraband and to keep them from hurting each other. The uniforms felt more like something you might lounge around in. Perhaps it was intended to affect one's mindset.

The crew had to turn in every piece of equipment they carried including their comm units and scanners. David paused for a second before removing his comm unit. He was toying again with the idea of sending out the distress call, but he knew if the Commonwealth came, they would only bring death to these people. It wasn't as much about trusting Arni this time, as trusting what he now knew about the Commonwealth. The men and women were still separated, but as they were scanned and assigned to cells they were divided even further. Two crew members were assigned to each cell. Jake stayed close to the Captain. Despite his concerns about him, it was still his job to protect the Captain.

The cells below the UWC were reserved for the highest profile cases. The crew was not yet fully aware of the seriousness of their situation. Such high-profile cases were ones destined for the death penalty. Drea had very few cases reaching this point. The Commonwealth still had the death penalty as a possible end to a life of crime, but it was rarely utilized because of the availability of so many more options. The crew was not expecting the possibility of a death penalty.

The cells were very basic. The walls, ceilings, and floors were all as white as the uniforms. The front of the cell consisted of a clear polymer. The door slid open to one side then slid back into position and sealed shut. As Jake and the Captain walked into their cell they saw a bunk on each side which was a little more than a padded shelf. The back wall consisted of small square distorted glass cubes with bathroom facilities behind it. Directly in front of the back wall was a table and two chairs. All the furniture was permanently fixed to the floor. After both men were inside the cell, they heard the door slide shut and hiss as the seal was re-established. Instinctively the two looked around for air vents after hearing the door seal. There were several small air vents in the ceiling. It took about fifteen seconds for them to explore their new surroundings and fifteen minutes for boredom to set in.

Jake and the Captain stood there looking at their new home. The Captain finally looked at Jake. "So, which bunk do you want?"

Jake looked at both bunks, but his eyes seemed to gravitate towards the one on the left. "You're the Captain, you choose one and I'll take the other."

The Captain shook his head. "I don't think I'm quite a Captain at the moment. I seem to be prisoner number twelve."

The Captain walked back over to the door and looked out into the hallway. Jason and Thane were in the cell directly across from them. The Captain saw Braxton and Lazaro disappear into the cell next to them. David wondered if the cells were sound proof when he heard the door seal. "Jason, Thane, can you hear me?"

Jason and Thane were still standing at the front of their cells keeping track of the other crew members. The two looked at the Captain the instant he spoke. Thane answered for the two of them. "Yes sir, we can hear you."

The Captain continued to survey the surroundings while responding to his crew. "Okay good."

Thane followed the Captain's lead. "Your orders, sir?"

The Captain stopped looking around and focused on the two men in front of him. "Cooperate, for now. Don't cause any problems. Understood?" Both men he could see accepted the orders as well as the two he couldn't see.

When the Captain turned back around, Jake had moved to his preferred bunk on the left and sat down on it. David smiled. He knew Jake would defer to him no matter how badly he wanted something. He also knew by turning his back on Jake, the chief would go ahead and make a choice. The Captain moved to sit on the opposite bunk. Jake scooted forward. "Captain, are you sure you don't want this one?"

The Captain just waved at him to keep his place and then he laid down on the opposite bunk. In a minute the Captain sat up and announced loudly for all his men to hear him. "Gentlemen, our goals are to be on our best behavior, concentrate on staying physically fit and get plenty of rest. I know none of you slept well last night. Try to get some sleep and when we are given legal counsel, we'll reassess our options. Any questions?" Each man gave an appropriate affirmation of their orders. It was the middle of the day, but David was glad to lie down and relax. He was trapped in a situation where he had no control. It was disconcerting, but also liberating.

As the two lay there resting, Jake rolled over and raised up for a moment. "Captain, why didn't you want us to fight back this morning?"

The Captain rolled over to look at him. "I had several reasons. Do you want them all?"

Jake nodded. "At least the major reasons."

The Captain laid back down on his back and tucked his hands behind his head. "First, like I told you this morning, we couldn't win. Someone would have gotten hurt and I'm responsible for this crew. I didn't want that to happen to any of you. Second, we might have a chance to win in a court of law. Third, if the Commonwealth came here it would only bring a lot of death and destruction. Fourth, well you won't like this reason, but Arni asked me to surrender peacefully."

"Captain, why did that have any bearing on your decision? He's our enemy."

David didn't have to look at Jake to know his hatred for Arni was clearly displayed on his face. The venom could be heard clearly in his voice. "Jake, Arni hasn't made many requests or suggestions. The few times he has, and we didn't listen, bad things happened. Arni is in a position of power and the Dreans listen to him. He was in a position to help us or hurt us. We were already in a no-win situation. What harm would it do to cooperate with him? Would you really have risked the crew's lives on such a long shot?"

David rolled over and looked at Jake. There it was, a twinge of doubt. That's all David needed to see. Jake didn't seem ready to admit he was wrong to resist, but he could go along with the idea it was David's call, right or wrong. Before rolling back over to face the wall, he gave Jake one last piece of advice. "Just keep your eyes open for options." David wasn't really expecting any options, but it gave Jake purpose and kept him out of trouble. David relaxed and took a substantial nap.

A couple hours later he was awake and hungry. A guard walked past their cells. David called out to him and asked about food. The guard gave him an angry look and muttered, "Shut up!" The man kept right on walking. David wasn't sure what time it was, but they had not eaten since breakfast and it had to be late afternoon if not early evening. Another guard walked by and David asked again. "Excuse me, sir? We haven't eaten since breakfast. Are you planning on feeding us anytime soon?"

This guard also gave the Captain an angry look and kept going. He shouted over his shoulder. "You're a big boy, I think you can feed yourself." The Captain gave Jake a curious look.

Five minutes later the corridor filled with guards. The crew watched to see what was about to happen. Lazaro and Braxton were cuffed and removed from their cell. David called out. "Hey! Where are you taking them? Guard! Where are you taking them?" The guards just ignored him. A couple minutes later Jason and Thane were also cuffed and taken from their cells.

Jake looked at David. "Maybe we'll find out where they were taken in a minute."

David watched the hallway as best he could. "I hope so." Moments later, guards pulled David and Jake cuffed from their cells. The two were ushered up several floors, and into a large conference room where the other men were seated. He and Jake were roughly shoved into two more chairs on the same side of the table as the other men.

The room was sparsely decorated. The head of the table was a few short steps inside the door. On the other end of the table was a wall of windows. There was a door on the left and right walls near the windows. A credenza lined the left and right walls. One contained some decorative artwork and the other held a pitcher of water and some glasses.

Seconds later the door opened. Laura and Cheyenne were ushered in. As soon as Cheyenne saw Lazaro she bolted towards him. "Lazaro!" Lazaro stood up to meet her.

One of the guards instantly ordered him to stay in his seat. "Sit down! Your days of ship board romances are over!"

One of the guards who was escorting the women in went after Cheyenne. He grabbed her arm and jerked her back around to face him. "Don't you ever run from me again!" He slapped her hard across the face knocking her to the floor.

This time Lazaro didn't keep his seat. He stood up with such force his chair flew several feet behind him and fell over. Jason stood more cautiously, keeping his eyes on Laura who was held firmly by the arm near the door and away from the scuffle by another guard. Lazaro was around the end of the table in no time, but another guard was faster and collided with him to stop his advance. He pulled a small thin instrument from his belt and shoved one end of it into Lazaro's chest. Lazaro convulsed and cried out in pain.

The guard who slapped Cheyenne glared down at her and ordered her to get up off the floor. Seeing her husband's treatment, Cheyenne wasn't inclined to want to cooperate. She rolled over onto her back and firmly planted both her feet into her guard's abdomen. After recovering from the blow, he reached for his own weapon of pain and started towards Cheyenne. By this time the other men were on their feet. David and Jake, with their hands still bound behind them, came across the top of the table. David plowed into the man about to attack Cheyenne while Jake did the same to the man standing over Lazaro.

While the guards began to rethink their situation, David took advantage of the brief lull. "Stop! I am the Captain of this crew. I am responsible for them. If you have a problem with them, you bring it to me!"

David looked at his crew. "Take your seats. Arni asked us not to resist and that's what we need to do." Most of the guards backed down at the mention of the Intercessor's name except the one who had slapped Cheyenne. He wasn't about to be made a fool of. The guard pulled Cheyenne off the floor and shoved her towards a chair then approached David. Jake was still standing close to the Captain, but was moving slowly towards his seat, giving the appearance of compliance without leaving his Captain vulnerable. David kept his eye on the guard in front of him but spoke to Jake. "Chief, go back to your seat and stay there, no matter what."

The guard who stood in front of David, waited until everyone was back in their seats. Two of the guards pulled Lazaro off the floor and dropped him back into his seat. David kept his eyes locked on the bully. "So, can I go back to my seat? Or do you need to teach me a lesson and show off for your buddies first?"

The guard slowly reached for his disciplinary rod. David didn't blink. He addressed the crew again. "Everyone keep your seats... please." As soon as he uttered the last word of his sentence the guard shoved the rod into David's abdomen. David gritted his teeth. A blast of pain and electricity rushed through his body causing his muscles to contract and convulse in rapid waves. Although he tried not to make a sound a forceful groan still escaped from his throat. David dropped to the ground. The man released him then jabbed him again. He pulled his rod back and was about to hit him a third time when three people entered the room.

"What's going on here? Sergeant, what are you doing?" The voice belonged to Moderator Tarmon. Her companions were the Intercessor and another woman the crew had not met.

The Sergeant stepped back and holstered the rod. "My apologies, Moderator Tarmon. I'm sorry you had to see that. This one wasn't wanting to cooperate."

Cheyenne jumped to her feet. "He's lying! The Captain was protecting me from him!"

David continued to roll around on the floor. Arni stepped around the Moderator and her guest. He helped David up and into the closest chair. David's muscles continued to twitch, and he was quite weak. The Moderator knew from experience David would have trouble answering questions for a few minutes. She looked at Cheyenne's red, bruising face, Lazaro's pale, shaken physique and the ongoing glares at the Sergeant. She put the pieces together rather quickly. "Sergeant, why do they still have their binders on? Standard operating procedure is to remove them when prisoners reach this room. You seem to be having difficulty doing your job. Explain yourself."

The Sergeant tried to look as innocent as he could. "These are extremely dangerous people. They obviously have no value for human life. They killed the Intercessor's friends and family. They flaunt their Commonwealth lifestyle like they own the galaxy. They had to be shown we have standards here. We..."

The Moderator scowled at him. "That's enough. Yes, we have standards which you obviously don't care to adhere to. We do not punish the innocent, and until they have gone to trial, that's what they are. We have only suspicion of guilt, not proof. It would appear you don't value human lives either, Sergeant. You might try talking to them if you want them to change something they're doing."

Lazaro had recovered his wits enough by this point to speak again. "If - If he t-touches m - my wife again, th - there won't be a planet b - big enough for him to hide on."

The Sergeant had assumed the two were merely lovers. He swallowed hard and looked back at his victim. Cheyenne was giving loving and appreciative looks to her husband for trying to defend her. "Moderator, I'm sorry. I didn't know those two were married. I just thought it was some cheap shipboard romance."

"Then I hope you won't be too surprised to find out the entire crew are married couples who were separated from their spouses without warning. How would you react if you were suddenly yanked away and placed in cell away from your wife, Sergeant? The parameters of your job do not include making people pay for their crimes. I'm putting you on a three-day suspension after which you will be assigned to a new facility. Clean out your personal items and return on the fourth day to pick up your new assignment. Maybe you'll be fortunate enough to be assigned to a post-judgment facility."

The Sergeant glared at David even harder. He gave a slight bow to the Intercessor and the Moderator. "Yes, Moderator Tarmon. I'm sorry ma'am." He quickly stomped out of the room nearly running over the guards bringing Lexi and Aulani into the room. The Sergeant was heard muttering under his breath as he moved down the hall. The guards began releasing the binders from the crew's wrists. They didn't want to find themselves being reassigned with their colleague.

While they waited for the last two women to be brought in Arni sat down next to David. He leaned in, so they could talk quietly. "David, just because I said your situation was more complicated didn't mean you should look for trouble."

David leaned forward as a guard removed his binders cautiously. David didn't even look at the guard. His eyes were still having trouble focusing. He merely rubbed his wrists and continued his discussion with Arni. "I – I wasn't looking for tr-trouble, it just f - found me. It's my job to protect these people, they depend on m-me. Why do you r-really care about what happens to me? It's not j-just a j-job because anybody can do a job. What is it?"

Arni gave David a pensive look. "My Father will explain it to you... soon."

"So, I'm going to die th - then. Is that what was so complicated?" "Someone has to right all the wrongs that have been done. I can fix

this, but not the way you think. You don't have to die and neither does your crew."

The last two guards ushered in Brynna and Marissa. Arni stood up to give Brynna his seat. After moving aside for her, he walked past David towards the far end of the table. As he passed David's seat he touched him lightly on the shoulder. David felt the twitching and tingling sensations dissipate and his strength return. He turned in time to see Arni reach out and take Cheyenne's hand and whisper something to her. He saw her reach up and touch the side of her face that had been hot from the blood rushing to her skin. When she turned to look at Lazaro, David could see the swelling and bruising were gone. He released her hand and nodded at Lazaro. Lazaro held his hands out in front of him. He opened and closed them as though he couldn't believe they still worked.

Lazaro looked up at Arni. "The tingling's gone!" David was equally surprised. He knew Arni had just healed him and Cheyenne, but he hadn't touched Lazaro. This was a new piece of information. Touching was not a requirement for transference of Arni's power.

Arni walked to the window and stared outside. The woman who came in with Arni and the Moderator sat down at the head of the table. The Moderator remained standing near the head of the table. "Captain, Commander, this is Rachel Johan. She is to be your legal counsel."

David glanced at the crew then back at the two women at the head of the table. "Counselor Johan, I actually have a lot of questions, but let's start with this. Just how much trouble are we in?"

The moderator started to take her leave. David needed to speak to her for a moment. "Moderator, before you leave, I wanted to say two things. First, we appreciate your professionalism and restraint despite the fact you probably wanted to execute us on the spot. I appreciate the fact that you demanded the same professionalism from the security guards.

Thank you for whatever you had to go through to get us legal counsel. The second thing is... well, I don't mean to complain, but, my crew hasn't been fed since we've been in custody."

The moderator looked confused for a moment. She glanced at Rachel. David saw her confused look give way to anger. "Rachel, please conduct your meeting. I will see to getting food delivered here immediately and I may just make more heads roll for this. I told the warden these prisoners required extra special attention. He's about to get an earful from me. Please orient them, so that when they go back they will have a knowledge base. Captain, Commander, I apologize to you and to your crew. This is not how a civilized world should treat anyone, no matter what they may be guilty of." The moderator promptly left the room.

Everyone's attention turned back to their legal representative. "Captain, I've just started familiarizing myself with you, your crew, and all the aspects of your case. Let me give it to you in general terms. You have been charged with numerous crimes most of which are capital offenses. In other words, if you are found guilty of any one of those offenses, you and your crew could be executed. That's the worst-case scenario."

Cheyenne let out a gasp and turned visibly pale. The crew was already in a serious frame of mind when they were brought into the room. With this new information, a heaviness settled in. Aulani looked down at her hands, realized they were shaking, and promptly tucked them under her thighs. Everyone was trying hard not to show weakness or at least trying not to lose their military bearing. David knew the crew needed to hear it for themselves. He had the distinct feeling they were feeling annoyed and inconvenienced without grasping how much trouble they were in. Neither David nor Jake flinched when their counselor explained the gravity of their situation. His lack of surprise was obvious to Rachel. Brynna and Lexi looked as though their suspicions were merely being confirmed.

Rachel went on to explain the basics of Drean judiciary procedures. The crew would be brought before a board similar to a military tribunal. The board would decide their fate. "Captain, I have files on you and your people, but it's going to take some time for me to review them. Can you just give me a basic run through, so I can see what your side of this case is?"

David glanced at Brynna. "Forgive me Counselor Johan . . ."

Counselor Johan interrupted. "Captain, please... when we are talking in here, call me Rachel. I'm not one to stand on formality."

David eyed the woman cautiously. "As you wish. Rachel, I need to ask you a couple things first. Why did you take this case?"

Rachel thought his question to be rather enigmatic. "Captain, why is this such an important question? I would think you would be glad to have anyone at all willing to take your case. We really don't have a lot of time to prepare for your trial. Word has spread quickly, and people are out for blood. Guilty or not, yours will suffice. We must get this trial started quickly. We only have days to be prepared. Can we please move on?"

David got up to move around which obviously made the guards nervous. Arni waved the remaining four armed guards out of the room which didn't do much to relieve their angst. David felt better though. He turned back to face the vexed lawyer. "Rachel, the second question I had is closely related to the first. Is the information I give to you protected or can you use it against us in any way? Here's the thing. We don't know your justice system. We don't know you. All we know is we tried to be honest with you, and now we've been incarcerated for it. The only reason I might have to trust you is desperation and to be perfectly honest, I may be at your mercy, but I'm not desperate yet."

Rachel gave the Intercessor a frustrated look. Arni nodded for her to proceed. She looked back at the Captain. "I am doing this because the Intercessor asked me to. I am a good legal counselor, but I tend to take cases no one else wants. I usually take cases I believe in, but the party may not have the financial means to pursue justice or they are up against overwhelming odds. No, I didn't want this case, but if the Intercessor asks you to do something, you do it. If he values you and your case, then so do I."

The woman paused to let her words sink in. "Captain, I don't know if you are guilty or not, but I intend to give you my absolute best. No one else on this entire planet wants anything to do with you and I may never get another case again after defending you, but . . ." Her sentence trailed off leaving only an implication. "Captain, I can only help you if you trust me and talk to me. I can't do my best work if I don't have all the pieces. The information you give me is protected. The only thing not protected would be any knowledge you give me of future crimes. If you decide to bust out of jail, don't tell me about it. That's not protected."

David studied her for a moment then turned to look at Arni. Arni gave him no help whatsoever. His back was turned, and he stood staring out the window. David looked back at her. "Just one more question then I'll tell you everything you want to know. Isn't it a conflict to have him in here?" David nodded in the direction of Arni. David saw the reflection of Arni's face in the window. He was clearly amused by David's question. Rachel wasn't quite sure how to answer. For someone who made their living through verbal arguments, Rachel was nearly at a loss for words. Finally, she found a way to answer. "Captain, if he were an ordinary human then yes, it would be a conflict, but to be honest, his presence is the best thing for you. He is the only surviving party of the Galatan massacre. His support for you may be the only thing keeping you alive. And before you ask, yes, it is possible he could be called on to testify. If he is, he will speak the exact truth, right down to the very thoughts behind the actions. If he is called on to testify, it won't matter whether he was present or not. Present is better than not."

Arni chose this moment to inject his words of wisdom. "Captain, you and your crew must testify honestly, even if it would seem to be to your own detriment. I have the situation well in hand. If I choose to do so, I can allow you to be executed then resurrect you afterwards. That isn't what I have planned, but you have to trust me with your lives. I do not control your minds, you must make your own choices. I will never control your minds – ever."

"If we lie to protect our own skins, would it mess up your plans?" Jake interjected sarcastically.

The Captain scowled, "Jake!"

Arni folded his arms across his chest and leaned back against the window. "Overall? No. The finer points will be made more difficult. You will only harm yourselves by lying. I intend to ask for mercy on your behalf. If you are caught lying, it will be harder to convince the Judicial Board to grant my request. My requests carry a lot of weight, but many would consider me to be too kindhearted for my own good and would deny my request on that basis alone. I do not control the minds of the Judicial Board any more than I control your minds. They can choose to deny or even defy me if that's what they want."

The Captain sat back down in his seat for a moment contemplating Arni's words. There was a lot of wisdom in what he said. Brynna turned her chair to face David. "Captain, there are twelve people in this room and twelve different versions of the same truths. We got ourselves into this situation by trying to warn them about the Commonwealth. We can't start hiding the truth or lying to cover anything up. It'll just make things harder."

Lexi chimed in. "She's right, Captain. I would advise we all be as honest and straightforward as possible."

The Captain leaned forward and put his elbows on the table. "Tell the truth to the best of your abilities. There's nothing to be gained by lying. Are we clear on this?"

Jake looked like he swallowed something rotten. "But Captain..." The Captain gave Jake a firm look. "That's an order, Mr. Holden.

The Commander and the ship's sociologist have agreed this is the best course of action."

Jake sat back sullenly in his chair. "Yes, Captain."

The Captain turned back to Counselor Johan. "My name is David. I am the Captain of a small Commonwealth ship known as the Evangeline. We were commissioned by the Commonwealth to make allies of the lesser developed worlds who aren't considered part of the Commonwealth. We were authorized to give advances in technology as a demonstration of goodwill. We were to unite these worlds against our enemy known as Pateras El Liontari. Galat III was our first stop. We gave them access to small technological advances. We told them upfront we were seeking information on the House of Liontari. We didn't tell them he was our enemy."

Rachel gave Arni a distraught look. "Intercessor, how can you ask me to do this?"

Arni gave Rachel an understanding look. "I have my reasons, Rachel. Trust me, it will be a long time before you understand it, but it will work out for the best. It will get even darker before the light returns, but it will return."

Rachel seemed to shudder then collected herself. "Yes, Intercessor.

Captain, please continue."

"We spent around three weeks on Galat. We left, filed our reports with the Commonwealth and were on Medoris for several weeks. After we left Medoris, we came straight here. It took four days to get here and we sat on one of your moons for four days to study your planet. Since then we have been here. When we left Galat, the people were alive and well. We did not go back there, until yesterday."

Rachel made some notes in her files. Then looked back at the Captain and asked. "You said you filed your reports. Who did you file your reports with and did you know what would happen when you filed them?"

David sat there looking down, contemplating his answer. Brynna jumped in when he didn't answer. "Of course we didn't know what would happen."

David glanced at Arni and felt a wave of guilt wash over him. "Counselor, could I speak to you alone?"

Rachel glanced up at Arni who nodded. "There's another conference room next door."

Brynna jumped in to object. "Captain, this affects us all. You can't..."

David stood up and harshly addressed Brynna and the crew. "Commander, are you questioning my command decisions?"

Hearing his tone, Brynna hesitated. "No sir." There was a pained look in her eyes as she looked at him.

David looked around the table at the faces looking back at him. Her concerns, though not fully voiced, made their point. He knew the crew needed some reassurance. "Listen, everyone, I need you to trust me. I told you this would fall back on me. I'm taking full responsibility for this. Arni has given me his assurance he has things well in hand. He has a great deal of pull on this planet, so I think we can give him a certain amount of trust. I will report back to you shortly."

David followed Rachel towards the door with Arni following behind the two. Rachel turned back to the crew. "Just in case you had any thoughts about leaving, your guards are waiting in the hall."

The three went into a room nearly identical to the one they just left. The group sat down at the head of the table. Rachel laid out her files again. "Alright, Captain, what didn't you want to say in front of your crew?"

From the tone of her voice, David gathered she deeply resented this whole situation. "Rachel, you asked if we knew what would happen when we filed our reports. My crew may have had reason to have doubts and questions, but it was not something they would really expect. The Commonwealth has all but eliminated the death penalty in favor of re- education. My crew have not known of any such actions taken by the Commonwealth until this mission and even then, it was regarded as a last resort when re-education was unsuccessful, and incarceration wasn't a viable option. We learned just before we left of some executions recently done, but it was presented as something closer to a 'mercy killing.' We were sent to establish new allies and report any contact with allies of Pateras Liontari, not to harm anyone. We were goodwill ambassadors as far as we knew. And before you ask, yes, it could be viewed as spying. It was a multifaceted mission. Now, knowing this information, what are our chances of beating these charges?"

As if her face were not serious enough, she now displayed a far more grave appearance. She pondered his question briefly. "Captain, our justice system no longer protects anyone from self-incrimination. You would have to testify. We believe in getting everything out in the open to fully understand the nature of a crime. If you testify to this, and it will come out, you and your crew will be found guilty of being Commonwealth spies. Spies aren't entitled to a trial. They can be executed, no questions asked. Here's the crux of the matter, the prosecutor would have to know what questions to ask to get at the truth, but I can't see him missing this information."

"Counselor, what if I refuse to answer questions?"

"You will be sentenced on what information we already know and there will be no chance for mercy. You will automatically be viewed as hiding something which translates to guilt. Between our previous interactions with the Commonwealth and your previous admissions, your chances are pretty much zero." She looked at the handsome young Captain. It was clear he carried the weight of several worlds on his shoulders. Maybe he didn't know what his people had done and were capable of. She suddenly had compassion on him. "There's something else you need to know, Captain. Each witness will be connected to a computer which determines the accuracy of your answers. You are also subjected to a medication which isn't foolproof, but it makes it harder to lie and easier for the machine to detect lies."

David sat back in his seat and stared at the table. He finally leaned forward with a determined look on his face. "I have two possible propositions. The first is, you put us on our ship and banish the Commonwealth from this world forever. We file a report saying this world is in a hopeless disarray with no chance of being an asset to the Commonwealth. We don't mention Arni in our reports, so the Commonwealth doesn't come here looking for him. We also give you the access codes to the satellites surrounding this world, so you can reprogram them to protect your planet."

The young counselor shook her head. "I can guarantee the answer will be no. There are a lot of powerful people who want your people's blood. They didn't even want to wait for a proper trial. They aren't going to let you walk out of here unscathed."

David sighed. "I pretty much knew that, but I had to ask. I liked that idea better than the other one."

"Captain Alexander, your plans and propositions really aren't going to help. Your trial is little more than a formality. I'm sorry to have to be the bearer of such bad news, but that's what your situation is."

The Captain looked at the young woman. She was definitely uncomfortable with her own position. "Rachel, there's one thing your people need to know. The Commonwealth knows where we are and if we don't report in, they will come looking for us. If my people don't leave here, they'll come here in greater force than your people can imagine. Their weapons can destroy your people from space. You won't even see the faces of your enemies. You'll die just like the inhabitants of Galat. We stayed here last night to warn you what we discovered. We wanted you to know what kind of enemy you were facing. We basically committed treason by staying here. Doesn't that count for anything?"

Rachel glanced at the Intercessor again before answering. "I can't predict the future, Captain. It could make a difference. You could be eligible for mercy. If your people confess their crimes and what you did to try and save us from the Commonwealth. Your death sentence could be commuted to life in prison."

David scowled. "That isn't going to help your people. If we don't leave here or give them a reason to look for us elsewhere, they will come here and what happened fifty years ago will seem like a walk in the park. My people, and yours, will die. I don't want to be responsible for the death of another civilization." He slammed his fist on the table and abruptly got up and walked over to the window.

Rachel seemed stunned. She sat there staring at the back of David's head with her mouth hanging open. She wanted to respond to him but wasn't sure how. She finally found something to say. As she took a breath to speak, Arni placed his hand on hers to stop her. It gave David another minute to think.

David continued to stare out the window when he began again.

"Here's my last offer. I will confess to these crimes freely if my crew can return to our ship and the ship is allowed to leave. I will stay and face whatever judgment your courts see fit. We will still give you the satellite codes when my crew reaches space."

"That is an honorable action Captain, but you and your crew would have to testify truthfully you were the only guilty party. I don't think -"

David turned away from the window and interrupted her. "My situation is a little bit different. You wanted to know what I didn't want my crew to hear, well here it is. I was told if I reported Arni's presence on Galat, I would get them killed. My crew didn't have that information, only I did. They were following my orders as any good soldier would. My crew found out about it afterwards, not before."

Rachel sat there with her mind racing. She was angry she had to represent a man she now despised. She was thinking about the legal possibilities and ramifications of David's proposal. She glanced at Arni who nodded again. She swallowed hard. "I can talk to the prosecutor to see if he may accept such an arrangement. Why would you suggest such a thing?"

David glanced at Arni. "The Commonwealth didn't tell me for certain what they had planned for worlds infiltrated by the Liontaris. I did know they had plans, but I didn't know the specifics. I'm the one responsible, not my crew. I knew deep down, and I did it anyway. I got those people killed. I don't want to be guilty of another civilization's extinction. You take this deal, and I will send my people away with orders to protect this world from the Commonwealth."

Rachel wanted to vomit. She walked over to the credenza and poured herself a glass of water. She blinked back tears for the Intercessor's people and the pain she knew he must be feeling. She wondered why he defended these monsters. She returned to her seat and sat the glass down on it more forcefully than she intended causing the water to splash out of the glass and the glass made a loud bang as it hit the table. "I will make the offer, but here's what you need to know. This would be a sentencing agreement only. It would have to be approved under the Mercy Clause of the Judicial Code. What that means is, the prosecutor, the judge, and the one who brought the charges would all have to agree to it. In this case, it would be the Moderator. You and your entire crew would still go to trial and be sentenced, but only you would face the sentence."

David looked puzzled. "I'm not sure I understand. My crew would stand trial, but not be found guilty?"

Arni knew that Rachel was struggling, so he volunteered to expound on her explanation. "No, David, they would be found guilty, but under a mercy agreement, one person takes the punishment for another. You would have to die a death eleven times more painful than one death, and your crew would have to watch. The idea behind the mercy clause is when one is guilty, and another takes his place, he would owe the one who died. It is a debt so great, the one who lives would live a life twice as fulfilling as either would have lived to begin with. It is called a 'love debt' because there is no greater debt. If such a person didn't fulfill his obligation to the one who died and were to face additional criminal charges, he would not be eligible for mercy again, and he would have to pay for the original crime."

Rachel looked at David. "Are you sure this is what you want to do? It is by design a longer, slower, and more painful death, so those who survive you will never forget what you did for them. Don't misunderstand me though. It isn't a death that will take hours. It just won't be instantaneous. It will also have to be similar to the death used on the Galatans. We believe in making the punishment fit the crime."

David walked over to the credenza and poured himself a glass of water. He took a hard swallow. He looked down at the glass. He felt like he was shaking, but his hand was steady. He turned to face them. "There's no way my crew can leave before my execution?"

Arni and Rachel both shook their heads. Rachel explained, "They have to watch you take their punishment."

"Fine. Let's do this, but I want the agreement in place tonight. I don't want my people wondering if they're going to die. I want to put them at ease." David moved back to his seat to await the decision.

Rachel nodded then touched the tabletop which activated several screens built into the walls of the room. In a moment, the face of a man, who appeared to be in his forties appeared. He had dark hair with a small amount of gray near his temples. He wore what David now recognized as a Drean business suit. It was dark gray in color and seemed to complement his hair. From the tone of the conversation, David gathered he was the prosecutor. His name was Gunter Finley. At first the man was adamantly opposed to even entertaining the thought of a mercy agreement. Rachel persisted. "Counselor Finley, I would like to get all the involved parties together on a conference call, so I only have to go over this one time. If everyone is so fiercely opposed, it's going to make for a long night for me. Just hear us out, I have reason to believe these twelve people are not as guilty as we seem to want them to be."

"Want them to be? I've seen the evidence. I have no doubts about their guilt. I'm not just hoping they're guilty." Counselor Finely was genuinely offended at her suggestion.

Rachel jumped in quickly to keep his attention. "Counselor, the Intercessor has given this case special attention."

Gunter leaned forward into the screen. "Well, I would think so. It was his home and family that were destroyed. I can see why he would be out for blood."

Rachel gave the Intercessor a frustrated look. She wasn't sure how to explain his involvement. Arni moved around to place himself into view. "Counselor Finley, I would appreciate it if you would consider what Counselor Johan is requesting. I am not out for these people's blood. I would consider it to be a personal favor."

The man stared at the Intercessor as though he had lost his mind. When he recovered from Arni's shocking request, he wet his lips before speaking. "Intercessor, I don't understand this, but I will do as you requested. Get the others on for a joint conference and I will listen. I'll even try hard to keep an open mind."

Rachel quickly got the other two connected. This time she started the conversation differently. She started with the words, "The Intercessor would like . . ." Her conversations went much smoother.

The moderator re-entered the building with food for the crew, so she informed Rachel she would join them personally in a moment. Moments later she entered the room with food for the Captain. Rachel had the judge and the prosecutor on two of the monitors in the room. She widened the angle, so all four people in the room were visible to the two men on their screens.

Rachel's presentation to the group was short, sweet, and to the point. She gave them David's proposal and his warning about what could happen if his crew simply disappeared on Drea. Once she was done no one spoke for a several seconds. Arni took the liberty of speaking first. "Ladies and gentlemen, I would like to ask that the mercy clause be applied to myself. I will accept their sentence as my own." It wasn't his intention to merely get the conversation started, but it did just that. Everyone began to talk at once. Each one offered adamant denials of the Intercessor's request. David stared at Arni.

Arbiter Navid was a judge by trade. Since he was already familiar with the case, he was assigned to be the lead judge for the crew's trial. Judge Navid's voice finally overpowered the other voices. "Intercessor, you know we would do anything you ask, but this cannot happen. You are too important for us to lose. You are the victim here. You aren't connected to this crime in any way. Our people would not sit still for such a thing. I cannot grant your request to take this man's place."

David could hold his questions in no longer. "Intercessor, I offered my life to pay for what was done to your people. Why would you ask to take my place? What's so important that you need me alive?"

"It's not just that I need you alive. It's that I don't want you to die. There is a difference. There is much more to this than just your crimes. Only my death can protect you from the coming destruction. My death is foretold in the Ancient Texts. This cannot be stopped. It should not be stopped. Judge Navid, Moderator Tarmon, Counselor Finley, will you please accept the Captain's offer?"

The three again got quiet. Moderator Tarmon spoke first. "Intercessor, I will do as you ask. The Captain can pay the price for his crew. I will grant mercy to the crew of the Evangeline. Once the execution is complete and the price has been paid, I will agree to allow the crew to leave after the standard waiting period."

Judge Navid addressed the prosecutor. "Counselor, I will agree to this if you will." Counselor Finley shifted uneasily in his chair. "Before I make my decision, I have a question. Intercessor, I heard your answer to the Captain, but why would you offer yourself for him? I know what the Ancient Texts say, but why here and now, and for the likes of him?"

Arni offered little in terms of any further explanation. "Because I have seen what is in his heart."

Counselor Finley stared at the faces on the screen. Finally, he leaned forward. "Captain Alexander, I want to be sure we are clear on this matter."

David leaned forward as well. "Yes, Counselor?"

The prosecutor's eyes became cold and hard. "You understand you will plead guilty on behalf of yourself and your crew?"

David swallowed hard again. "Yes sir."

"You also understand the sentence for this crime is death? The manner of execution is yet to be determined, but it will be a death commensurate with the death of those on Galat. You also understand by accepting the penalty for your crew, it will be twelve times the pain and last twelve times longer than a single death should take? Your crew must be present and watch your execution and on the third day they will be escorted back to your ship and will be permitted to leave. They may take your remains with them, if that is your desire, to inter however you choose. It is also understood when you leave, your crew will give us the access codes for the satellites and they will file false reports to keep the Commonwealth at bay. Is this the agreement as you understand it?"

David didn't even blink. "Yes, Counselor Finley. I understand what I am agreeing to."

The Counselor had another question. "How do we know your crew will keep their end of this arrangement?"

David tried not to hesitate because he knew it was going to take a small amount of trust on their part. "I will need some time with my crew prior to my execution to give them final orders. I suppose I can't guarantee that days later they might disobey my last orders, but I would hope they would honor this as a last request. I think they understand what is at stake. They are as upset about Galat III as you are. They don't want it to happen to your world."

Arbiter Navid was equally concerned about releasing the crew. "Who is your second in command?"

David didn't like where this was headed. "Commander Brynna Alexander, my wife."

"Oh, yes, your wife. That's perfect. She will never agree to this. As soon as she gets off this planet she will send the Commonwealth here as fast as she can to get revenge." Arbiter Navid snapped.

David didn't hesitate. "My wife is a good soldier. She'll follow my orders."

The Arbiter studied David for a moment. "Bring her in here and tell her now. I want to see her reaction. If I am convinced, then I will agree to your proposal. Counselor Finley?"

Counselor Finley wasn't enthused but gave his affirmation to the Judge's condition. Rachel stepped to the door and asked one of the guards to escort the commander from the other room. Brynna was surprised to see such an array of people in the room and on the video screens. Rachel waved her over to the empty seat next to David. David tried to wipe the distant look from his face before he turned to face her. It didn't work.

Brynna took one look at him and got scared. It wasn't overtly obvious, but as soon as David took her hands in his, he knew. "Captain, what's wrong?"

He smiled weakly at her. He glanced at the untouched tray of food sitting on the table in front of him. "Low blood sugar."

She had the urge to laugh at him and call him a liar, but the seriousness of the situation quickly suppressed the thought.

David struggled to find the right words. He decided to give her the good news first. "Commander..." Brynna's hands went cold. This was not going to be good news and she knew it. David felt her flinch and started again. "Commander, I have a way to get the crew safely to the ship and off this planet, but you must follow my orders because I won't be able to come with you. Can you follow my orders?"

Brynna eyed him carefully. She hesitated. "Yes sir. What are your orders?"

David looked down at her hands and gently squeezed them. "You are to send reports to the Commonwealth concealing the Intercessor's identity and give the Commonwealth no reason to come here."

Brynna looked puzzled. "Captain, we already agreed on that. Why are you telling me this?"

David patted her hands. "I'm getting to that. You will go to the ship and once you are in space send the satellite access codes to the Moderator as we also already agreed then send those reports. You will need to also send a falsified report to the Commonwealth to explain... my death."

David felt Brynna's hands break out into a cold sweat. Her face went white. "David... No." He saw tears start to well up in her eyes. She grasped his hands tightly.

David mentally took off his "Captain's hat" and put on his husband's hat for a moment. "Brynna, listen to me. It has to be this way. I can't have this planet's blood on my hands and I don't want it on yours either. No one can know what really happened here. Promise me you will follow my orders. It's the only way you and the others will be safe." He squeezed her hands again and looked emphatically into her eyes. "Brynna, give me your word you will do this my way. Commander, can you follow my orders? Commander?!?"

Brynna pulled herself out of her fear and anguish enough to answer. "Yes, Captain." It was all she could manage.

Arbiter Navid had one last question. "Forgive me, Intercessor, but I must ask. Will the Commander keep her word? Will our people be safe? You asked for our cooperation. What assurances can you offer us?"

Arni looked at the man with fire in his eyes. "It should be enough for you that I have asked. Nothing else should be required. I gave you everything you have, and I can take it away. I am not giving you any assurances save this one. My Father is in control. Whether he chooses to prolong your lives or take you to be with him, it is by his design. He knows what he is doing."

The Arbiter, along with everyone else in the room, was clearly rattled. He swallowed. "Forgive my impertinence, Intercessor. Captain, I accept your proposal." The prosecutor gave his approval as well.

Judge Navid was quite ready to take his leave of the conversation. "Counselor Johan, have the agreement drawn up and signed tomorrow. We will complete the process in court day after tomorrow."

Rachel breathed a sigh of relief. "Yes, your honor."

The judge quickly disconnected from the video conference. He had shamed himself to the Intercessor in front of others. He sat back in his chair and stared at the blank screen, mentally kicking himself for challenging the Intercessor. As he sat there he heard the Intercessor's voice. "Don't be too angry at yourself. You weren't the only one asking those same questions." Kato sat up straight in his chair and looked around. He was alone in the room. He decided it was time to get some fresh air and headed outside.

The Prosecutor closed his side of the conference out in similar fashion. The fact the Intercessor had not given them any assurance of their own safety was disconcerting. It was not a guarantee something bad would happen, nor that it wouldn't. There was nothing like one of life's uncertainties to set one's priorities in their proper order. He quickly left his office to get home to his wife and children.

As soon as the two men were gone Brynna looked up at David. Quiet tears still lingered on her face. "David, I don't understand. This wasn't a done deal? Am I the reason you reached an agreement like this? What just happened?"

While David quietly explained the situation to her, Arni and the two women moved over to the window to give the couple a small amount of privacy. The Moderator looked at Arni. She clearly had an abundance of questions and doubts, but she didn't voice any of them. Arni placed his hand on her shoulder. "I need your assurance that once the sentence has been carried out, the agreement will be honored and no one else will die. Only one life is needed no matter whose life it is. Hold the others to it no matter what."

The Moderator's puzzled look only got worse. "Of course, Lord Liontari."

Rachel was shocked to hear the Moderator call the Intercessor by his name. She had heard the Captain call him by his first name and it always felt wrong when she heard it. Arni looked over at Rachel. Knowing her thoughts, he smiled. "Rachel, it's just my name. It was meant to be called any time you want my attention. I want you to use it."

In a few minutes, it appeared the explanation was complete. David and Brynna were standing in a quiet embrace. The three moved back to their seats and began to discuss a few details. David wanted to know why Arbiter Navid was to be the lead judge for these proceedings. Moderator Tarmon explained that unless a judge was considered a victim or emotionally involved in some way, simple previous exposure to a case did not constitute a bias. It was considered an advantage to getting at the truth. Rachel assured David it would not adversely affect his case. She also told him the other judges on the judge's panel were Chancellors they had already met.

The three also discussed the lack of food for prisoners. David finally started to eat the food in front of him while the moderator asked Brynna a few questions. "Commander, why is it your people haven't eaten?"

Brynna shrugged. "No one brought us any food or took us to a dining hall. We tried to ask about food, but the guards were very definitely ignoring us."

The moderator was torn between anger and laughter. She decided anger was the better choice. "No one oriented you to your cells?"

Brynna slowly shook her head. "We were shoved into our cells, our binders removed and left without so much as a word. When we tried to ask about food later we were told to shut up and called some rather impolite names." David mirrored her story with a matching story of his own.

The Moderator continued to glower. After listening to them she got up and paced the floor for a moment. "Captain, Commander, I apologize for the way you were treated. We don't treat our prisoners like this. At least we didn't before now. There are food dispensers in every cell as well as an audiovisual feed to watch news reports, entertainment broadcasts or learning feeds. We've learned boredom can cause problems among prisoners, so that's the one thing we can offer. Bringing in reading materials proved to be problematic because of the types of things being smuggled in. Your cells are not resorts, but so long as you behave, you have at least the one positive stimulus."

David ate as much as he could of his meal, but his appetite had greatly diminished over the last hour. He and Brynna felt a little sheepish after finding out about the food dispensers being right there in the cell with them. The Moderator told them she would see to their cell orientation personally and then have a long hard talk with the Captain of the prison guard about their treatment.

As soon as David finished eating, the group walked back to the other conference room. David quietly told Brynna to keep her eyes fixed on him. He wasn't ready to tell the crew the whole arrangement, but he did want to tell them enough to put their minds at ease. Before David entered the crew's conference room, he changed his entire demeanor. He presented himself as a picture of confidence.

Jake was judiciously watching the door while standing near the window. When the Captain walked in, Jake called the room to attention. The Captain had previously dispensed with this formality on the ship. Jake thought perhaps a reminder of the Captain's authority would be in order this one time. Rachel and Moderator Tarmon were startled by the display. They hesitated then continued to the table to take their seats. The Captain and Commander continued several steps into the room before releasing the crew from their stance. The Captain ordered everyone to their seats. Counselor Johan started to speak. "I apologize for taking so long. We've been in a conference call with the other court officials. We..." "Excuse me, Counselor, but do you mind if I tell them?" David interrupted. Rachel was not sure why this mattered. She assumed it was either a "military" thing or perhaps a "cultural" issue. She yielded the floor to him. David stood back up and began to move about the room while he spoke. "We have some good news and some bad news." David didn't take the time to ask them which they wanted first but made his own choice. The good news is we are working on a plea agreement taking the death penalty off the table. You aren't going to be executed." Several sighs of relief were heard around the table. David paused to let it sink in before continuing.

The crew's resident pessimist, Security Chief Jake Holden, jumped in. "What's the bad news?"

David grimaced. "Well it's a multifaceted issue. I had to agree to several things. We still have to participate in a trial of sorts where I will reveal our participation in the crimes we are charged with. We will be pronounced guilty and sentenced, but there is a "Mercy Clause" and Arni has asked for it to be granted to us. The sentence is still a death sentence, but it will be commuted. The crew will be held here for three days, then escorted to the ship and essentially be deported."

Jake's eyes narrowed. "And..."

David smiled. "And the part you aren't going to like is we have to give them the satellite access codes once we reach space. The Intercessor's name is never to be revealed. False reports will have to be filed to dissuade the Commonwealth from coming here again."

Rachel and the Moderator exchanged shocked looks when they realized the Captain had no intention of telling the crew the rest of the agreement.

Laura caught sight of the looks they exchanged. "Moderator?

Counselor? Is everything alright?"

Realizing, she was jeopardizing whatever the Captain was trying to do, Rachel attempted to cover. "I am just in shock. I still can't believe everyone agreed to this. You have a very skilled Captain." Her eyes cast fiery darts at the Captain.

The Captain smiled and winked at her. He put his hand gently on Brynna's shoulder to offer strength and support and offered an explanation. "Who wouldn't be persuaded by a potential attack by the Commonwealth if we disappeared here without a word?" The Captain thought maybe he was getting the hang of keeping his thoughts hidden. His eyes landed on Arni and catching his gaze. Arni discreetly shook his head.

As the group prepared to leave the room, Arni came and knelt in front of Brynna who was vacillating between anger, sorrow, and maintaining her command presence. He took her hands in his and spoke softly to her. "Brynna, please trust me. You aren't going to lose him. I won't let him die, but you have to trust me."

Brynna just sat there looking at the face in front of her. Who was this man? He was their enemy. How could she allow herself to trust him? Finally, she decided. "Arni, I'm not asking for your help, but if you do what you've said, you'll have earned some trust from me, but not until then."

He squeezed her hands. "Not one member of your crew will die on this planet. There will still be pain and suffering, but I won't let David take this punishment. This one's mine."

Brynna searched his face for more answers. "Arni, he won't let you take his place."

Arni smiled. "Then I won't ask his permission." Brynna managed a weak smile.

The guards came in to start placing binders on the crew. The Moderator looked at the Captain, "Do I have your word, your crew will behave?"

The Captain made quick eye contact with the entire crew before answering. "You have my word."

Moderator Tarmon waved the guards off. "We won't need to use those binders."

The lead guard objected strenuously. "Moderator, this is standard protocol and a security risk."

When the Moderator started to repeat herself, David jumped in. "Moderator, I'll go in binders. My crew won't do anything to endanger my life. I'll be the insurance policy."

The Moderator gave each couple a moment together while she started raking the current guards over the coals. She "informed" them they would go as a group to the women's cells then to the men's cells. The guards were appalled at the idea. This was a serious breach in protocol and a high security risk. The Moderator allowed them time to contact their superiors and give them notice of what was coming their way. The elevators weren't big enough to hold the entire group, so they had to go back to the prison complex in several small groups. The prison was such a high-level prison there were only a few others detained there. The Moderator took the women into one cell and showed them how to access the food dispensers, the audiovisual feeds, and how to access the communications network. She did caution them they would only have access to a few key people on the communications network. They could speak to each other, their own attorney, the prosecutor, the guard station, and the warden. Moderator Tarmon added herself to the list. Normally, prisoners had more freedom in who they could contact, but due to the nature of their situation, their access was severely restricted.

The Moderator finished her explanation of the facilities including the bathroom facilities and stepped out of the cell in time to have the Captain of the guard brusquely join the group. He pulled the dignitary aside. "Moderator Tarmon, what's going on? Why are you here? This isn't safe."

The Moderator glared at the man. "Captain Parker, did I not contact you and specifically tell you these prisoners were of the highest priority? I am quite sure I told you they were unfamiliar with our technology and would need to be handled with the utmost care."

The Captain gave her a blank stare. "I don't understand, Moderator. My people have steered clear of them and I made sure they were not harassed or harmed. I gave them the highest level of protection. What's happened?"

The Moderator rolled her eyes. "These people were not told what was expected of them. They have never been prisoners before. Your people didn't explain the prison facilities or routines. One of them treated one of the women inappropriately. None of them have had anything to eat for at least eight hours. I had to go and personally bring them food while they met with their legal counsel this evening."

The color drained momentarily from the man's face then it returned in full force. He turned beet red. He had no other recourse, but to apologize. "Moderator Tarmon, on behalf of myself and my staff, I apologize profusely. I didn't understand what you meant when you said they were unfamiliar with our technology."

The Moderator waved her hand towards the crew. "You owe them an apology more than you owe me one. I told Captain Alexander it isn't our policy to mistreat our prisoners."

Captain Parker quickly swallowed his pride. "Captain Alexander, I would like to offer my most sincere apology to you and your crew. I will talk to my staff again to help assure you are not mistreated again. Even prisoners accused of the most heinous crimes are to be treated humanely. This will not be repeated."

David didn't want to prolong the man's embarrassment. "Thank you, Captain. If you have any problems with my people, please don't hesitate to talk to me and I will do whatever it takes to make things right. I take full responsibility for the behavior of my people."

Captain Parker scowled. "I am in charge here, Captain Alexander." David nodded. "I understand, Captain Parker. I meant no disrespect.

Among my people, there is still a chain of command system among prisoners of war."

Captain Parker looked confused. "Prisoners of war?"

Moderator Tarmon frowned. She had not considered the ship's crew as prisoners of war, but it was now clear that's what the crew considered themselves. As she considered the Captain's situation, she had to admit he might be right about their status. They did consider the Commonwealth their enemy. "Captain Parker, as you can see this is an unusual situation. Please take a personal interest in their care."

The Captain gave the Moderator a firm salute. "Yes ma'am. You have my word."

The Moderator nodded her approval. She sent the rest of the guards and crew members on to their cells. "Captain Parker, I need to talk to you about the guard who struck one of the women. I took some liberty with his discipline." The two continued to talk as they walked back to the Captain's office.

The crew was more at ease now since the death penalty was no longer hanging over their heads. Each one went to their cell more easily. They spent the next hour combating boredom with their newfound audiovisual privileges. Lexi wanted to know what the general population was being told if anything. She and Aulani located a news station.

Brynna wasn't in any mood to watch anything. Sensing the Commander's mood, Marissa tried to make light conversation, but Brynna wasn't interested in talking. It was clear to Marissa, Brynna was hiding something. The lieutenant wasn't sure she should ask about it. Marissa walked over to Brynna's bed and sat down beside her. "Commander, I can see that something is bothering you. You are under no obligation to share, but if you need to talk, I know how to keep my mouth shut."

Brynna gave Marissa a weak smile. "I appreciate it Marissa, but it's not your mouth I'm worried about. If I told you what was on my mind, you'd end up feeling like I do or at least similarly."

The two women sat there not speaking for a moment then Brynna abruptly asked. "Can I ask you about the tornado?" Somehow saying, "Can I ask you about the time you were dead?" just didn't sound right.

Marissa shifted nervously, "What… uh… did you want to know?" Brynna wasn't sure what she wanted to know, so she started slowly.

"You don't have to answer if you don't want to, but I really need some answers. Do you remember it happening? I mean, do you remember… dying?"

Marissa looked down at her hands. She fidgeted nervously. "I don't really remember dying. I remember a warm bright light. It was really bright, but it didn't hurt my eyes like when the sun gets in your eyes. It didn't seem like I was there very long. Arni was there. I was so scared. Arni actually made me feel safe." Tears started to roll down her face. "I know I'm not supposed to feel safe in the presence of an enemy, but I did. I swear, I didn't commit treason."

Brynna had been sitting on her bunk with her back against the wall. When Marissa started to cry Brynna leaned forward and placed her left hand on Marissa's shoulder. "Marissa, it's okay. I understand how you feel. I really do. I feel like I have no choice right now, but to trust Arni. I'm starting to have doubts."

Marissa stopped crying. "What kind of doubts?"

Brynna eyed her cautiously. She expected to see suspicions on Marissa's face, but instead saw anxiety and anticipation. Brynna pulled one of her feet up onto the bed and wrapped her arms around her leg. She rested her chin on her knee. "I just haven't seen any evidence the followers of Arni are a threat to the Commonwealth. The Galatans were a peaceful people and the Commonwealth is the one who brought havoc and destruction. I just wonder why the Supreme Executor is so afraid of the Liontaris."

The two women were quiet for a moment. "Commander, Arni told me why."

Brynna put her foot down and twisted to face Marissa. "What did he tell you?"

Marissa bit her lip. "I'm not sure you're going to believe me if I tell you."

Brynna shook her head. "I'm not sure it matters whether I believe what you say or not. I just need something to hang on to."

Marissa winced at her own thoughts. She took a deep breath. "Do you remember how upset Cheyenne was when she found out that Arni wasn't human?"

Brynna nodded.

"Arni told me the Supreme Executor isn't exactly human. He said he's a non-corporeal being that can assume human form. He – He takes a human form and gets himself elected as Supreme Executor. Since the position is a lifetime position, he doesn't have to change shapes very often."

Brynna looked shocked. She started to get up and move around, but Marissa grabbed her arm. "There's more. He apparently used to work for Pateras Liontari and there are many more of them."

Brynna got up and paced back and forth in their confined space. She looked down at Marissa. "You aren't helping me get any sleep."

Marissa looked down at the floor for a moment. "I'm sorry Commander. I know you were upset already, and I shouldn't have said anything. I just needed someone to know. I haven't slept well since it happened."

Brynna's heart filled with compassion when she realized Marissa had been struggling with this knowledge for the last couple weeks. Brynna cocked her head sideways. "You haven't told Lexi or Jake, have you?"

Marissa shook her head. Brynna continued to pace for a minute. "This is crazy. There's been no scientific evidence or military intelligence indicating non-humanoid sentient life forms exist."

Marissa was now pale for fear of where Brynna was going with her statements. She tried to swallow, but her mouth was too dry. Her voice was barely audible when she finally responded. "I know it sounds crazy. It's why I haven't wanted to talk about it."

Brynna gave Marissa half a smile. "Marissa, I'm not calling you crazy. I was referring to myself. What I found to be crazy was; I'm not having trouble believing you, despite a lack of evidence. Is there anything else I should know? I doubt I'm going to get any sleep anyway. I might as well have the whole story."

Marissa saw the pain in Brynna's eyes. She wanted to ask Brynna again what was wrong but didn't want to push. Marissa got up and moved to the food dispenser and requested a glass of water. After taking a couple sips, she continued to recount her experience. "Arni told me Luciano Hale rebelled against Arni's Father and one third of his kind left with him. I don't know how many of those creatures there are, but apparently two thirds of them still serve Pateras."

"Why would they rebel? What happened to cause it? Did he say?" "Arni said Luciano was power hungry. He thought he could rule the universe better than Pateras. He also told me Luciano Hale is afraid of Pateras because he knows his days are numbered. He knows the Liontaris are coming for him."

Brynna felt herself start to relax a little bit. It was almost like listening to her father tell her bedtime stories as a child. She sat back down on her bunk and got comfortable. "Did you see Pateras?"

Marissa's face winced. "Not exactly. The warm bright light I mentioned was coming from Pateras, but I couldn't really see him. It was too bright, and there was a lot of sweet smelling smoke, like incense or something. I did hear him speak though."

Brynna felt herself get excited like she did when her father's stories reached a climax. "What did he say?"

Marissa sat back down on her own bed. She sensed the Commander's rising interest in her story. "He didn't say much, but he said it with such conviction... I don't know. It just seemed to say more than the actual words. He said Arni was his son, the most precious thing to him, and I should listen to him carefully." The two women sat there quietly pondering the message. Marissa suddenly laughed. "I feel like a giggly little girl telling ghost stories around a campfire in the wilderness."

Brynna joined her laughter. "I was just remembering the bedtime stories my father used to tell me."

Marissa stopped laughing and got serious again. "The Captain's not leaving with us, is he?"

Brynna was caught off guard and unable to hide her feelings. Her face displayed guilt, then sadness, before she could get her mask back up. "That wasn't fair, Marissa."

Marissa's heart sank. She was hoping Brynna would tell her she had it all wrong. "I'm sorry, Brynna. I wasn't trying to trick you. I was hoping I was wrong."

Brynna laid down and stared at the ceiling. "How did you figure it out?"

Marissa smiled. "Some newlyweds you just know aren't going to renew their marriage contracts. You and the Captain were meant to be together. He's the only thing I could see getting you this upset. I also noticed his wording was a little odd when he spoke to us. It was like he was avoiding certain words and his mood was just a little too good. I mean, we're in prison and he's smiling? He's smiling and you're frowning. That says he's hiding something and you don't like it."

Brynna looked over at her and wryly asked, "Are you trying to take over Lexi's job?"

Marissa blinked. "Um, no. That's not my area of expertise at all. I don't really get along with people that well. It's why I chose security and engineering as my secondary areas of focus. As a security officer, I don't have to get along with people, I can just bully them if they annoy me."

Brynna stared at Marissa for a moment. Marissa could not hold a straight face any longer and giggled again. Brynna relaxed and laughed. For a second, she thought Marissa was serious about bullying people. The two women finally settled in and began to doze off. Brynna listened closely to see if she could tell if the rest of the women were sleeping. She couldn't be certain, but she didn't hear any sounds of restlessness.

Moderator Tarmon and Captain Parker escorted the men back to their cells. After each one was secured, Counselor Johan excused herself to start drawing up the "Mercy Agreement." Arni left with her. Moderator Tarmon and the Captain of the Guard returned to his office to talk at greater length. The Moderator told the man about the Intercessor's request to offer the crew mercy. She also encouraged him to keep tight security on the crew because she knew the plea agreement would not be popular. The situation had already leaked to the public and the public was quickly crying out for justice. The Captain assured the moderator he would not take the situation lightly. Once she was satisfied he understood the stakes she excused herself. It had been a very long and very difficult day.

The Captain encouraged his men to get some exercise. The cells were large enough to give them room to move about without interfering with each other's movements. After a vigorous workout, David got a shower then laid down to get some sleep. He debated about trying to contact Brynna, but he was afraid if he did, the crew would find out the downside to the plea agreement. Some of the crew explored the new options in their cells for a little bit. Jake turned the news stations on and watched for a few minutes. Braxton and the others contacted their spouses one at a time. Jake was just getting off his call to Marissa when a voice came over the speakers. "Attention, inmates. Intracellular call privileges are closed for the night. Lights will be turned out in five minutes."

David looked at Jake. "Well, I guess I won't be calling Brynna after all."

Jake studied the Captain suspiciously. "I was starting to wonder if you were going to even try."

David looked down at the floor. "I'm just not comfortable putting my personal life on display. It destroys my command presence, and I can't afford to lose that just now."

Jake nodded his understanding, but his face didn't display the same conviction. The two men lay down on their bunks, and moments later the lights went out as promised.

The next morning the lights came on along with a shrill trilling, followed by an impersonal greeting, and a brief announcement regarding visitation to an exercise yard. There was a pause, and the voice came back on in the crew's cells informing them as to what time the guards would pick them up for their appointment with their legal representative. The crew got up, showered, changed into fresh prison uniforms, and ate breakfast. Their meeting with their legal counsel wasn't until after lunch, so the first part of the day was again met with boredom. The crew started investigating the Drean music and literature. Several of them would rather have looked at science or technology, but their access was denied. Braxton was able to access files on the historical development of the planet's architecture. It was a hobby he developed when he studied architectural engineering in his younger days.

David had heard enough references to the "Ancient Texts" he decided now might be the best time to see what he could find out about them. He found pictures of some of the original manuscripts, but only a few excerpts were translated into Intergalactic Standard. It appeared there were copies in the older Drean languages, but no one had gone to the trouble of updating them in the last fifty years. He did discover articles debating the virtues of translating the manuscripts into the language of their enemy. One article gave a comprehensive history of the language development, including the introduction of Intergalactic Standard fifty years ago. The introduction of the Commonwealth language had worked to help unite the planet. It gave each country a common thread and tied them to the Commonwealth. The Commonwealth had apparently worked on this world for ten years before their alliance fell apart. Because of the religious and political controversy, David was unable to use a translation program to read the texts. After numerous attempts, David became frustrated and shut off the viewer.

The guards came right on time to escort the crew back to the conference room. Rachel was waiting to give them an update on their situation. She didn't want to say the one thing the Captain avoided the night before. She stepped into the next room with him and Brynna to discuss her news before addressing the rest of the crew. When the three sat down at the table Brynna sat down opposite David instead of beside him. Rachel didn't notice the friction between them, but David was all too aware of it. Rachel moved on into her explanation. "Captain, Commander, the plea agreement has been approved and signed by everyone except the two of you. Commander, the others insisted you agree and sign off on it, since you will be representing the rest of the crew. Captain, if you would sign here." The Captain signed the document without hesitation.

Rachel handed the document to Brynna who sat there and just stared at it. She knew she was signing David's death warrant if she signed it. Rachel glanced nervously at the Captain who quietly asked her to give them a moment alone. Rachel nodded and stepped out into the corridor.

David moved over to the chair next to Brynna. He swiveled her chair around to face him. Brynna's gaze landed on the windows behind him. She couldn't bring herself to look him in the eye. David tried to put himself in her line of sight, but she looked away. "Brynna, I know you are upset, but this was the only thing I could do to protect you and the crew. If you don't sign this, then you'll be executed as well as the entire crew." Brynna turned and looked at the document. Without saying a word, she signed the agreement.

David reached over and gently turned her face to look at him. "Brynna, please don't spend my last few days being angry with me. I need your strength to get me through this." Brynna blinked back tears. She still couldn't look him in the eye.

"Brynna, I understand if you have to stay angry with me to cope with this, but I really hope you don't. I had to do this to save you. I put the Galatans' lives in danger and now I put you and the crew in danger. I didn't join CIF to destroy innocent civilizations. I joined to save lives, and it may be the last thing I do, but I will at least save you and the crew."

Brynna looked down at her shaking hands. David got up and moved to look out the window. He knew this was an incredibly heavy burden for her to bear. He only hoped she would get past it before the end. "David, you don't understand why this is so hard for me, do you?"

Without turning, David replied. "Maybe you should explain it to me." He was fairly certain he knew, but he wanted to hear her say it, for his sake and for hers.

There was a noise behind him and he felt a hand on his back. He turned to see Brynna looking up at him. "When we first got married, it was a convenience, a comfort measure for the mission. I got really comfortable. I admire you as a human being, as a man, and as a Captain. I don't just love you. I fell in love with you. I started picturing us together after the mission, renewing our marriage contract, and starting a family. That wasn't supposed to happen. David, you are a good man, and I would be a fool to let go of you. You don't deserve this. I always knew there was a chance any of us could die in the line of duty, but not you, and not like this. Please don't do this. Please don't leave me."

He wrapped his arms around her and held her tightly. She cried on his shoulder for a few minutes. He needed to be in her arms and much as she needed to be in his. They held each other for a long time without saying anything. Her sobs slowly subsided followed by her tremors. Brynna broke the silence by whispering into David's ear. "I'm sorry."

David pulled back and looked at her. "Sorry for what?"

Silent tears rolled down her face again. "I'm sorry for being angry at you and shutting you out. This isn't your fault. You're right. This is the right thing to do, but I just didn't want it to take you away from me. I would have done the same thing. What do you need from me to make this easier for you?"

David smiled. The consequences of his actions weren't real to him yet. His head knew, but his emotions were not fully involved yet. He gave her the only answer he could. "Just let me see your beautiful smiling face and tell me you love me as often as you can."

She swallowed hard and gave him a weak smile. "I'll try... I love you very much, David."

He gave her another firm hug and whispered in her ear. "Thank you.

I really needed to hear that."

Rachel came back into the room cautiously, trying not to look like she was interrupting them. David pulled back from Brynna and told her softly. "I love you more than anything."

The two walked back to the table and sat down side by side. Rachel picked up the document and saw Brynna's signature. She looked at the two. "Do either of you have any questions about this agreement?" David looked over at Brynna.

Brynna turned to Rachel. "Actually, I do. What happens if something about the agreement needs to be changed? What if David decides not to go through with it?"

Rachel frowned. "The Captain can change his mind right up until his execution, but that means the rest of you will be executed alongside him. Is that what you wanted to know, or is there a problem I need to know about? If you want to change your mind, now would be the better time."

The Captain shook his head. "I haven't changed my mind."

Brynna didn't have all the answers she wanted though. "What if someone were to offer to take the Captain's place though?"

Rachel stared at her for a moment trying to read her face. Was this just a question of desperation, or was she planning something? "Any changes, other than the Captain backing out, would have to go through the same approval process as the current agreement. This isn't something we take lightly. You've committed a heinous crime, and somebody has to be punished for it."

Brynna started to respond, but David put his hand gently on hers to stop her. "We understand. My wife doesn't want me to go down for this without a fight. She will abide by the agreement."

Rachel still didn't look happy. "This agreement means you don't fight. You accept your guilt."

David looked at Brynna but spoke to Rachel. "I'm the one who's guilty here. My crew didn't know the repercussions of filing their reports, and even though I didn't know the specifics, I knew something terrible was going to happen. I didn't know for certain, but the clues were there. I could have stopped it from happening, and I didn't."

Rachel seemed to relax a little. She started to gather her documents up and filed them into her briefcase. Once everything was put away, she stopped and stared at the table. David and Brynna waited for her say whatever was bothering her. "Captain, when do you plan on telling your crew what this agreement means? You can't keep this from them much longer."

"So, is this agreement final?"

Rachel nodded. "Unless you back out then we are back to the entire crew facing the death penalty."

"When is the trial?"

"The trial starts tomorrow morning at 9:00 a.m."

David leaned back in his seat for a moment. He looked over at Brynna. "What do you think? I don't want them to find out during the trial."

Brynna cleared her throat. "I think we should tell them now. I think they already suspect it, and you would be doing them a great disservice to not trust them with that knowledge. Marissa figured it out last night." "You're probably right. If I delay it any longer I'm just insulting their intelligence and their trust in me as their captain. Don't tell them I could revoke the agreement though. Is that understood?"

He looked at both Rachel and Brynna. Brynna gave him a curt, "Yes sir."

Rachel scowled at him. "Captain, I am not going to lie for you. I will agree not to volunteer the information, but I will be honest with all my clients. I am not your crewman. Are we understood?"

David took a deep breath. "Understood, Counselor. Let's get this over with then." The three stood up and moved to the other room.

The crew milled around in the conference room rather restlessly. Jake was the first to address the rest of the crew. "Why do they have to meet separately from the rest of us, then come in here long enough to fill us in on what they decide on our behalf?"

Marissa wanted to respond but was afraid if she spoke so quickly they would figure out she knew something. To her relief, Lexi jumped in first. "It's the Captain and Commander. It's their job to work on our behalf."

Thane spoke up. "I'm with Jake on this one. We shouldn't be kept out of the loop here. This involves all of us."

Lazaro walked up to Thane. He put his hand on Thane's shoulder. "Settle down, Lieutenant. That's bordering on insubordination at the least, mutiny at the worst." Lazaro then walked on around the table and sat down next to Cheyenne.

Thane gave Lazaro a baffled look. "Are you kidding me? We're facing a death penalty already, and you want to talk to me about mutiny and insubordination?"

Laura was a quiet optimist, but today she was more pragmatic. "I think the Captain must have a plan, but he may not want us to get our hopes up if it doesn't work. I would look at this as his way of taking care of us."

Jake came to the table and leaned over it placing his hands flat on it's cool surface. "How? What could he possibly have to offer them to let us go? The only thing I can think of is committing treason."

Marissa couldn't let him go any further. "Jake! That's not true! The Captain would never do that!"

Lexi saw the look on Marissa's face. "You know what's going on, don't you?"

Marissa suddenly had a guilty look on her face. Jake moved over and sat down beside her. He knew his pushy tone wouldn't work on his own wife. He had tried it before and she only pushed back harder than he thought possible. "Marissa, please, this affects us all. What are they doing?"

Marissa jumped up from her seat and moved away from the others. The room was silent waiting for her to say something, anything. Finally, she spoke. "I can't tell you, but he's not committing treason, and neither is the Commander."

The crew sat there hoping she would say more. Lexi pondered her words for a moment and the realization hit her. "Oh no..." Her eyes got wide. Everyone looked at her.

"Lexi, what is it?" Braxton asked.

Marissa wiped tears away and turned to face Lexi. "Lexi, you can't."

Cheyenne started getting scared about whatever it was that had Lexi wide-eyed and Marissa in tears.

The door opened. Rachel, the Commander, and the Captain entered the conference room. Lazaro immediately called the room to attention as Jake had done the previous night. This time Lazaro felt the crew needed a reminder of who the Captain was, and what kind of respect he deserved.

He had also figured out what Lexi had. The Captain was puzzled by the display and the fact Lazaro had done it, instead of Jake. The Captain made eye contact with Jake as he came through the door. Jake had made no move to call the room to attention. As David reached his seat, he called out "as you were."

Rachel was still uncomfortable with this display. This was her meeting, but for the first time in her career, she felt like she was at someone else's mercy. She didn't know whether to just start or let the Captain go first, so she split the difference. "Ladies and gentlemen, the plea agreement has been finalized. Captain, do you want me to give them the particulars about the trial or do you want to go first?"

David nodded to Rachel. "You go ahead. I'll do the heavy part last." Rachel went over the information they would need regarding the trial. The case would be presented. The devastation on Galat III would be recounted, then all evidence would be presented. The plea agreement would be entered into evidence and David would make his statements. If there were questions after that, they would be asked. The questions could be addressed to anyone by anyone and must be answered truthfully, or the plea agreement could be rejected. When she finished her discourse, she asked if anyone had any questions. Jake jumped in without reservation. "What aren't we being told?"

Rachel looked at David. "Captain, I believe this one is your question."

David nodded. "It certainly sounds like it." He got up and walked towards the windows. Brynna grabbed the arms of her chairs to brace herself. David's earlier request of what he needed to get through this echoed through her mind. She tried hard to keep from frowning or crying. She carefully pulled her wife hat off and put her commander's hat on. She managed a look of stoicism. Marissa looked back and forth from Brynna to the Captain. Sensing Brynna's struggle, she forced herself to concentrate on the Captain.

David braced himself for the heaviness of his own words and how his crew might react. "What aren't you being told? I wanted to be sure the crew's safety was guaranteed before I said anything. The plea agreement has been finalized and you will be allowed to leave on the third day after the sentence is carried out."

Thane was quicker than Jake this time. "Sentence? I thought you said it was going to be commuted."

David looked back out the window. Something about the bright warm sunlight gave him strength. "Your sentence is going to be commuted. It will be commuted to me." No one seemed to even breathe as his words slowly sank in. David looked at each of his crew members. Cheyenne, the youngest and most emotional of his crew, was pale and silent. Lexi looked like she had already moved past the shock and was now working on anger or sorrow.

He was having trouble interpreting the look on her face. Lazaro had a similar look.

Before anyone had a chance to respond the Captain continued. "There was no other way. It was either all of us or one of us. I'm responsible for the safety of the ship and its crew. I'm the one who filed those reports. This is my responsibility. You will be escorted back to the ship on the third day after my execution and you will be expected to leave immediately. You will send them the codes for the satellites as soon as you reach orbit. After you've left the system, you will file false reports to protect this world from the Commonwealth."

Jake stood up and started towards the Captain. "Captain..."

Marissa frantically grabbed at her husband's hand. "Jake! No!

Please don't do this!"

Jake gave her hand a gentle squeeze then pried her fingers loose and continued on his way. "Captain, I am the security officer. I am the one responsible for the crew's safety including your safety. I should be the one to do this."

A tiny piece of the Captain wanted to say, "Okay, sure Jake, go ahead and take this one", but he knew he would never be able to live with himself. "Jake, I appreciate the offer, but the only way this works is if they are sure the guiltiest party is the one who carries the punishment. I don't think you are the culpable one here. I do need you to get the crew safely back to the ship and get them out of this system. See to it the agreement is kept. I don't want the blood of another three billion lives on my hands. Consider this my last request."

Thane, now over the shock, asked, "Captain, why did you make this agreement without us? Why keep it a secret?"

Brynna knew she needed to show support for the Captain's decision. "He knew this would be upsetting and everyone was already upset by their own potential execution."

Lexi looked back and forth between the Captain, Brynna, and then Marissa. Marissa was not showing any signs of shock. She finally spoke her mind. "You knew about this last night. Why didn't you tell us then? I think we deserved to know. It's clear Brynna and Marissa knew. Why didn't you tell the rest of us?"

The Captain fought the desire to shut her down. "Not that I am obliged to explain my actions, Lt. Flint, but the deal wasn't complete last night. It is now. I wanted all of you to get at least one good night's sleep. Brynna knew because she had to know as part of the agreement. Marissa just figured it out. Are there any more burning questions?" Everyone got quiet. They were still too much in shock to ask any other questions.

Lazaro stood up and faced the Captain from his place at the table and called out. "Room! Attention!"

The room responded, except Rachel who looked lost again. Lazaro continued. "Face the Captain!" Everyone turned to face him as ordered. "Present Arms!" Rachel looked alarmed for a moment thinking they were somehow armed until she saw them all race a hand to salute and freeze in position. "Captain Alexander, your sacrifice for the lives of your crew in the line of duty will not be forgotten."

The Captain slowly returned the salute. He couldn't say anything more than, "Thank you. Thank you all."

The Lt. Commander called "Order Arms!" then released the crew to again take their seats.

David looked back at Rachel, "The floor is yours, Counselor."

Rachel developed an ache in her throat. She swallowed hard and did a quick recap of what to expect in the next few days. When she again asked if anyone had any questions, Jason had one. "What kind of execution can the Captain expect? Will it be humane?"

This was not a question she really wanted to field. "The punishment is as humane as we can make it, but it has to fit the crime. For instance, if you killed a man with a knife then you would have to die by a blade, but we would make it as quick and as direct as possible. In the Captain's case, since he is taking on twelve death sentences, the death will be slower and more painful."

Jason was persistent. "You still haven't said what the method of execution is."

Rachel hesitated. "I don't have the specific information yet."

Jason started to give her an angry retort, but David intervened. "Doctor, I know you are only concerned for my welfare, but dead is still dead. I would rather it be quick and painless, but I'll endure whatever I have to if it keeps the rest of you safe."

The Captain had one more question of a personal nature. "Will I be allowed any time alone with my wife before the end?"

Rachel seemed relieved to have the subject changed. "It is customary to allow husbands and wives to spend the night before the execution together if that is their desire. Neither is required to do so, or to spend the whole night together. It will need to be approved by the Judge, but it is our custom. One cell has been customized for this purpose." Brynna shifted in her seat. This wasn't the kind of topic she cared to have discussed in front of the crew.

Seeing there were no other questions for her, Rachel allowed the crew a few minutes to be with each other. The crew each expressed their personal sentiments to the Captain and Brynna. Jake was the only one who hung back. Marissa was puzzled by his detachment. "Jake, don't you have anything you want to say to the Captain and Commander?"

Jake shook his head. "I'm bunking with the Captain. I've got plenty of time to talk to him and plenty to say. I'm just giving the others their chance right now. I do want to talk to the Commander though."

Marissa was a little concerned Jake might take advantage of his bunking arrangement with the Captain and harass the poor man. "Well, I'd like to talk to him while you talk to Brynna."

The couple walked over to the Captain and Commander. Jake apologized profusely to Brynna for allowing this to happen. He asked her if there was any chance at all for him to take the Captain's place. Brynna appreciated his attempt, but she assured him it wasn't possible.

Marissa expressed both her appreciation and trepidation over the Captain's sacrifice. Despite his discomfort hugging female crew members, he seemed to have no problem hugging any of them today.

Once they all appeared to have their say, Rachel called for the guards to escort them back to their cells. The afternoon and evening seemed to drag on. Jake gave the Captain an ear full, which didn't do much to speed the evening up. David allowed him to vent to a degree, but when he got to the point of berating the him, David put a stop to it. The crew slept fitfully that night despite the Captain's orders to get in a vigorous workout. Everyone seemed rather groggy the next morning. David slept better than anyone else. The guards came bright and early to escort the group to their assigned courtroom.

The crew found themselves in a well-lit room. There were sky lights and windows along the upper edges of the walls. David assumed it was to allow sunlight in. The windows were too high to look out of. One could see an occasional bird fly by and clouds drifting past, but that was about it. Across the front of the room was a raised platform. It appeared to be a judge's bench with only five seats. On the right was what looked like a juror's box. It had a white wall that came up level with the back of the chairs. A transparent wall made of some type of Plexiglas alloy ran from the top of the wall to about eight feet in the air then across the top of the box. In the center of the floor was a chair surrounded by the same type of wall and Plexiglas as the juror's box. Opposite the judges' bench were two tables, presumably for the Prosecutor and the Defense Attorney. Behind those two tables were seats for spectators. A sizable balcony ran across the back of the room for an extensive number of spectators. Behind the Judges' bench was an expansive display screen for those who had trouble seeing. Rachel came in and put her things down on the table nearest the crew. She oriented them to the room. There would be a panel of judges who would determine if the agreement had been fulfilled.

David was disturbed by the thought that they could reject the plea agreement at this point. Rachel assured him if they answered truthfully, the judges were duty bound to honor the agreement or set him free completely if they determined the crew was not in fact guilty. Rachel emphasized the importance they all tell the truth as they knew it, and not try to hide anything. She pointed to the seat in the center of the room. She explained its purpose was to monitor their responses and would instantly notify everyone in the room if the individual were lying. Rachel also told them the proceedings would be broadcast worldwide. Once news had gotten out, it spread like wildfire and everyone insisted on knowing the results. Each person who took the stand to testify would be injected as soon as they entered with a truth inducing medication.

David and the crew were escorted to what he had thought was the jurors' box. They were locked in the compartment. Since this was a plea agreement proceeding, there would be no jury. The compartment David had identified as a juror's box was for him and the crew. It was a secure area to protect both the accused and those in the courtroom.

The room began to fill with people. Several prison guards remained on duty. The galleries filled with dignitaries from the United World Council, as well as other government officials. Once the room was full, the proceedings were called to order. The panel of Judges consisted of Arbiter Navid, Chancellor Torrell, Chancellor Noe and two other Chancellors the crew met briefly at the debate. Arbiter Navid was the presiding Judge. Judge Navid read the charges. "The Captain and crew of the Commonwealth ship known as the Evangeline are charged with conspiracy, conspiracy to commit genocide, genocide, espionage, and treason."

David glanced sharply at Rachel when the last charge was read. Rachel saw him but was confused by his obvious objection. The Judge addressed David directly. "Do you and your crew understand these charges?"

David glanced at Rachel again as he slowly stood up to answer. "Judge Navid, we understand all, but the last charge. How is it we are charged with treason?"

The Prosecutor stood to address the court. "Judge Navid, we intend to show multiple counts of treason. They have committed treason against the Intercessor, treason against the inhabitants of Galat III, and treason against their own Commonwealth." David wasn't sure if it made a difference, but he didn't understand how they could charge him with crimes against the Commonwealth.

Judge Navid scowled at Counselor Johan. "Did you not explain to your clients the nature of the crimes they are charged with?"

Counselor Johan stood and addressed the Judge with far more confidence than she felt. "Your Honor, I apologize. In light of the plea agreement, perhaps I did not go into sufficient detail with the Captain and his crew. All charges are covered by the agreement. I'm sure it will be made abundantly clear by the Prosecutor shortly."

Judge Navid turned back to David. "If you wish further explanation, I can delay these proceedings while your counselor discusses it with you, but I doubt it will change the outcome. Do you want to continue or take a break?"

David glanced at Rachel who slowly shook her head. The Captain looked back at the Judge. "I would prefer to continue and not delay this, but may we have a chance to speak with our counselor later if necessary?"

The Judge nodded. "You may. How do you and your crew plead?"

Rachel had already briefed David on the correct response. "On behalf of myself and my crew, we plead no contest."

Judge Navid continued. "The plea of no contest has been entered, and the plea agreement is also entered. Mr. Finley, please present your case." David and Rachel took their seats.

The prosecution began by displaying the images taken from Galat III. "This is the crime that was perpetrated. We do not know exactly how many people died on Galat, but we have not found one single living human being on Galat III. I have evidence from the forensic reports identifying the energy signature as one very much like the energy signatures from the Commonwealth attacks from forty-seven years ago. The signatures were not identical, but similar. I am also entering into evidence the information recorded from the debates including the closing remarks by their commander claiming responsibility for the deaths on Galat." The Prosecutor showed the court Brynna's speech and the immediately following uproar. He also included excerpts from the debate where Brynna mentioned the alliance between themselves and the Galatans. The Galatans had considered themselves allies with the Commonwealth. The Prosecutor pointed out this is where the charges of treason came in. The crew betrayed their alliance with Galat by not informing them of their war against the followers of Pateras El Liontari. Warning the Dreans about the

Commonwealth, although appreciated, was still considered treason. David and the crew quickly figured out the Dreans believed a crime was a crime and jurisdiction didn't matter.

Once the particulars of their crimes were laid out, Counselor Finley called David to the stand to confess. A guard released him from his box and escorted him to the witness chair. The guard secured him in the seat, gave him his injection and closed the door behind him. As soon as the door closed behind him, a privacy screen activated, and the glass clouded until no one could see in and David couldn't see out. Rachel told the crew it was there, so no one could influence his testimony while on the witness stand. His hands were closed around a metallic post and secured with cloth straps. Two small nodes were attached to his temples. Another cloth band was wrapped around his neck which had more nodes in it. He assumed they were for sensing changes in heart rate, blood pressure and sweat. He suspected they also measured neurological changes. The chair was calibrated with a few lead-in questions to determine a baseline. "What is your name, rank, and position for the record."

David answered, "I am David Liam Alexander, Captain of the Commonwealth Explorer Class Vessel known as the Evangeline." After a few more verifiable questions, the Prosecutor had him begin by making a comprehensive confession statement and informed him they would follow up with any questions needing to be clarified. David, Brynna, and Rachel had put together a basic statement, but the statement could not be read. It had to be in an impromptu presentation format. David took a deep breath and tried to relax, but he really felt like he was talking to himself since he couldn't see anyone. This was an awkward situation to say the least. He started back at the beginning. "I am David Alexander. I was assigned several months ago to Captain the Evangeline and its crew of eleven others to search for information on Pateras El Liontari and to recruit new allies for the Commonwealth among the less advanced civilizations. Our orders were to seek alliances and report back any information on our enemy. We were not to engage the enemy in any way. Our first stop was Galat III. We presented our offer of technological advances in exchange for an alliance and information on the Liontaris. We also requested a little fresh food and water. We helped them improve their irrigation techniques, building structures, introduced medical improvements, and education. We taught them how to make glass. The Doc helped their healer when a woman in labor was unable to deliver. He taught her how to deliver a baby surgically. The day we left we were introduced to your Intercessor, Arni Liontari. As soon as we knew of his presence we got out of there, as ordered. We prepared our reports. Arnnn- er- the Intercessor showed up on my ship. He warned me not to send the reports. He told me… if I sent the reports there would be blood on my hands, Galatan blood. I had no intentions of returning to Galat or harming anyone, so I didn't see how I could be responsible. I sent the reports. When we left Galat everything was fine, and we haven't been back until the day we went with your people. I fully expected to see the town and people just as alive as we left them. Our superiors never told us their plans, but if I had taken a clue from their treatment of others, I should have known better. I take full responsibility for what happened. My crew is not responsible for this, I am."

The prosecutor had numerous questions for David. "By your own testimony, you invited the Galatans into an alliance with Commonwealth. Is that correct?"

"Yes, sir."

"And they accepted did they not?" "Yes, sir."

"So, you betrayed their trust by reporting them to the Commonwealth instead of telling them their membership in the Commonwealth depended on allying against the Intercessor."

David sighed. "Yes sir, we were told to get out the second we found evidence of the Liontari influence. As soon as we felt we could safely evacuate, that's what we did. Personally, I assumed another team would be sent behind us to try to alter the loyalties of the population or the world would be quarantined."

Throughout the rest of the day, the crew was questioned to confirm the Captain's statements. Brynna's statements were the most damning of all since she had confessed in the debate to the Commonwealth's involvement in the Galatan deaths.

The Prosecutor demanded, "Am I to understand the diplomatic missions are led by you?"

Brynna answered truthfully. "Yes sir."

The Prosecutor then went a direction that put David into a tailspin. "So why is it the plea agreement is for the Captain and not for you? Aren't you the one responsible and not him?"

Brynna's heart rate spiked. David nearly came out of his chair, but Rachel signaled him to keep calm and stay seated. Brynna struggled with how to answer the question the best. "It's the Captain's job to see to the success of the mission and the protection of the crew. Every member has specific duties they are trained to do to help the mission succeed. I have been trained in the art of diplomacy. It's my job to plan our best approach when dealing with a particular society. On Galat, women were not accepted in roles of leadership, so David took the lead and I advised him. I took the lead here with his guidance. David made the decision for us to stay here to warn you about the Commonwealth. I followed his orders. He was too angry to address you himself, so he asked me to handle it. You should be thanking him, not trying to execute him."

An angry murmur ran through the gallery. After the Prosecutor was done with Brynna, Rachel called David back to the stand to affirm it was indeed his orders for them to stay and answer for their crimes. David didn't like her wording, but he was in no position to argue with his own lawyer.

Court was dismissed for the day after it appeared everyone's questions had been answered. Rachel met with them briefly to tell them what would happen next. Court would resume the next morning, and if any questions or concerns surfaced during the night, they would be addressed first thing then they would be sentenced. Rachel reminded them they would all be sentenced, then the sentence would be commuted by a vote of the judge's panel. David didn't like that there was a chance the agreement could fall through.

As the crew was taken back to their cells, it seemed the guards were colder and more distant than usual. David thought maybe it was just his imagination until he woke up briefly once during the night. He heard whispering and looked up to see two guards staring at him through the glass at the front of the cell. He stared back at the two shadowy figures for a moment then engaged the privacy screen. The guards had the authority to take the screen back down, but David knew he had made his point. The two moved on without incident.

The next morning the crew expected to be taken to court bright and early, but it was mid-morning before they were escorted to the courtroom. They solemnly took their places. The room was already full by the time they arrived. The court was called to order. Judge Navid asked both counselors if they had any further questions or evidence to present. Neither one needed any additional time. He then asked the other judges if they were satisfied. They were also ready to proceed. Judge Navid asked the crew to stand for their verdict and sentencing. The crew stood up as ordered, and David called them to attention. He wanted them to withhold any emotional response and the best way to control it was to put them at attention. Their military decorum was ingrained in them from day one.

The judge continued. "Crew of the Evangeline, you have plead no contest to the charges levied against you. This court finds you are indeed guilty of the charges presented with the exception of the charge of genocide. You are not guilty of the charge of genocide. You are guilty on all other counts. Although your culpability is less than that of your superiors, if the opportunity ever presents itself, your superiors will also be placed on trial as your co-conspirators. The sentence for your crimes is death. The manner of execution is yet to be determined."

The reaction in the gallery was one of elation. Everyone seemed to want the crew dead. In a moment, the Captain called, "At ease." Everyone took a deep breath and waited for the rest.

The Judge acted as though he couldn't stomach the rest. When he hesitated too long, Rachel stood up and started to address him. The Judge waved her off and spoke again. "A plea agreement has been put in place to grant mercy to the crew of the Evangeline and place the penalty on the Captain alone."

The crowd began to get angry and shouted out their numerous objections. The judge threatened to clear the room if the crowd could not contain their outbursts. Once they calmed down, Judge Navid poled the four judges to determine if the criteria of the plea agreement had been met and if they intended to honor the agreement. He received two votes in favor and two against. Judge Navid would now have to cast the deciding vote. He hadn't liked the agreement to start with and considering the outbursts in the courtroom, he didn't want to be in that position. He looked around the room. His eyes landed on the Intercessor, the only person that the crowd would acquiesce to. "Intercessor would you care to make a statement to the court since you are the only remaining survivor of Galat III?"

Arni knew Kato wanted someone to take some of the pressure off him. Arni walked to a point between the prosecution and the defense tables. "Ladies and Gentlemen. I have spoken of a day when the price for the crimes of all of humanity must be paid. That day is drawing near. I asked you, Moderator Tarmon, and Counselor Finley to allow me to pay for the crimes of the Captain and his crew."

The room had been deathly quiet when he started to speak, but a murmur began to ripple through the crowd. He looked around sternly and the voices got quiet. "You denied my request, so I asked you to allow the crew to leave this world and grant them mercy. You agreed to this and I am grateful. My mother and my friends are with my father. I am sorry they had to experience death, but I have come to stop the sting of death and grant a new life unlike any other. It is my desire for you grant them the same mercy I grant to you. Their lives are already changed by this experience and will continue to change. Honor my request and your agreement." Arni continued to stand there with his feet apart and his hands clasped behind his back, giving Kato his support.

Judge Navid looked down at his desk for a moment and weighed his options and his words. He already knew which way he was going to vote, but how to break the news to the rest of the world. He finally gathered his wits and his words. "Intercessor, we often do not understand your wisdom or your ways, but our mistakes happen when we choose to disobey your requests. I will honor your request and commute the crew's sentence to their Captain. The crew will be exiled from this planet on the third day after the Captain's execution. Execution will take place in three days. Court is adjourned!" The Judges made a hasty exit. Arni turned to face the audience who made a ghostly quiet exit.

David breathed a sigh of relief then scoffed at the irony of being relieved he was about to be executed. He and the crew were moved back to the conference room. They sat there stunned for a few minutes while waiting on Rachel to join them. Everyone knew when they joined the Commonwealth Interstellar Force they could die in the line of duty, but this boggled the mind.

Jake began to pace. He finally could take the silence no longer. "Captain, there has to be some other way."

David shook his head. He was unable to even force a smile and lighthearted reply this time. "There's not, chief. We all knew our lives could be required of us on this mission."

Jake leaned over the table and banged his fist on it. "This isn't right!" Several around him were startled by the outburst. Jake continued his rant. "Captain, this isn't dying in the line of duty. Marissa died in the line of duty! If Lexi had fallen into that pool of lava in the caves, that would be dying in the line of duty. If the Commander had died when the horse threw her, that would be dying in the line of duty. If you had died in the fire ring, it would be dying in the line of duty. This isn't. We should have contacted the Commonwealth for a full diplomatic envoy of lawyers to argue this case. It shouldn't have been up to us to stand alone. We could have left and told them from space or we could have…"

"Chief! That's enough!" Lazaro barked. "The Captain did what he thought was best for everyone concerned. He has acted admirably. He's saving our lives and the lives of everyone on this planet. The Captain is a hero by all rights. We are not going to belittle his sacrifice by second guessing his choices."

The chief looked sullen. "Captain, I'm sorry. I didn't mean to. I just meant…"

The Captain managed a halfhearted smile this time. "It's okay, Jake. I know what you meant, and I appreciate it. Laz, thank you too. I appreciate each one of you. You've all done your jobs and done them well. I couldn't have asked for a better crew. If I had to die to save a crew's lives, I'm glad it was this crew. You are worth dying for."

Cheyenne started to cry again. Lazaro put his arm around her to comfort her. He looked like he was nearly in tears as well. The Captain looked around the room. "I need everyone to promise me the Intercessor's name will remain a secret. Your reports can honestly say the people here refer to him as that out of either fear or respect. You can say he has a great amount of influence among the people on this world and is a very public figure. The Commonwealth is looking for a man who hides and travels a lot. They won't look for Arni as such a public figure. It will protect them from the Commonwealth. Promise me you'll keep this quiet, no matter what." The Captain made eye contact with each crewman one at a time around the table getting either a nod or a yes sir from each one. He looked at Jake last.

Jake hesitated then gave a disgruntled "Yes sir! But they don't deserve to be spared considering what you're doing for them." Jake turned and went to stare out the window. It seemed the window had a very calming effect. There was nothing special outside, just occasional birds flying by, a skyline of buildings, the streets below with vehicles and pedestrians passing by, but somehow it managed to relax his mind and ease Jake's mood.

Rachel walked in a moment later. She sat down at the head of the table. "I have news for you. Judge Navid had not officially commuted your sentence until a few seconds ago. He wasn't convinced your crew would keep their word until he watched your conversation in the last few minutes. He's convinced, so it is now official."

The crew was startled, and some were angry. Brynna was the first to address Rachel. "Are you serious? You were watching us? We've done nothing, but try to be honest with you, and even though it is costing us dearly, you still doubt us?"

Rachel's guilty look spoke volumes. "This wasn't my idea. I could have come in here and said nothing, which is probably what I should have done, but I thought you deserved to know the truth. I'm just trying to be honest with you."

David looked at the crew. "Don't be angry with Rachel. She's just doing her job, which is to help us. Rachel, what happens next?"

"You have tonight and tomorrow night to put your affairs in order. Give your crew whatever orders you feel the need to give. They will decide the manner of execution, and I will get the information to you tomorrow some time unless you would rather not know. The day after tomorrow, you will be moved to a special cell where you will have twenty-four hours alone with your wife if that's what you want. The third morning she will be moved back to her own cell until time for your execution which is scheduled for early afternoon. Do you have any questions?"

"I don't suppose asking for more than twenty-four hours with my wife would be possible, say something in the neighborhood of fifty or sixty years?"

Rachel gave a curt, "No. I'm afraid not."

David gave her a weak smile. "Then I guess I just have one question."

Rachel was trying not to get emotionally involved. She kept a professional distance from them until David asked her his next question.

"Do you have any regrets about taking this case?"

Rachel was caught off guard. She expected a question on procedures or legalities. She stammered and hesitated. "Uh, what?... Do I have regrets? I – I don't regret taking this case. The Intercessor was right to ask me to. I suppose my biggest regret was that I couldn't find a way to free you along with your crew. Captain, I..."

"It's David."

Rachel looked confused. "What?" "My name is David."

Rachel began again. "David, I've come to respect you and your crew. I'm sorry it's going to end like this." Her professional mask slipped, and her disappointment began to show through.

David reached over and placed one hand on top of Rachel's. "Thank you for everything you've done. My crew owes you their lives."

Rachel pulled her hand away from David's and brusquely gathered her things. She stood up to leave. "You can still contact me if you need me. I'll make sure the crew are released at the appointed time. I'll contact you tomorrow when I have more information for you." She whisked around and headed for the door. Stopping a couple steps from the table, she turned halfway around. "Captain – uh David, you're welcome, and again, I'm sorry I couldn't do more." She exited the room quickly.

Brynna redirected the crew's attention. "Captain, what are your orders?"

The Captain seemed to have lost his drive. After contemplating the question, his answer was simple. "Follow my orders to protect this planet. While we're here, don't resist. Respect their authority over us."

"What about after we leave here?" Brynna persisted.

David shook his head. "That won't be my decision. I can make recommendations, but Commander, that decision is up to you. Just please, protect this planet." There was an awkward silence for a moment which David himself broke. "I think we best say our farewells now. I don't know that we'll have much of a chance later.

The Captain spent a moment with each couple thanking them for their service. Again, he wasn't nervous about hugging his female crew members. All barriers seemed to have vanished as David hugged every crew member alike. David was just saying his last goodbyes as the guards showed up to start escorting the crew back to their cells. David stayed with Brynna until the last four guards arrived to take them along with Jake and Marissa back to their cells. David and Jake walked back to their cell in silence. The two said very little that night.

VENGEANCE

David had trouble sleeping, so he spent the next several hours recording messages for his family. He doubted they would ever get to see them, but he felt better having done them. He recorded a message for Brynna as well. He knew they would have some time together, but he wasn't sure if he would be able to say everything he wanted to. David finally felt like he was exhausted enough to sleep, so he started to lie down in his bunk when several guards approached the cell. David sat up. There were six guards. Anytime they had come to get them before there had only been two or three. Realization set in quickly. An over-abundance of guards in the middle of the night meant only one thing – trouble. David tried to activate the computer in the cell to contact Rachel, then the Moderator. The computer wouldn't activate. The guards opened the door. David moved over and gave Jake an abrupt shake to wake him up. It took him a couple seconds to process what was happening, but as soon as it made sense he was wide awake and ready to defend himself. The guards entered the cell but kept their distance. One of the guards moved a couple steps closer to the two men.

The two men assumed a defensive posture. The guard who had stepped closer finally spoke. "The prisoner known as Jacob Holden is to be moved to another cell. He has been reclassified as a detainee, instead of a prisoner. Don't resist and you won't be harmed."

Jake didn't alter his bearing. "That's okay. I'm good here. I don't mind being housed with a prisoner." His tone was clearly sarcastic.

The man turned to the Captain. "Captain, order your man to stand down and he will be moved to another cell unharmed."

Jake glanced at the Captain who was weighing his options. Jake took advantage of the opportunity to clarify their predicament. "What about the Captain? What's going to happen to him?"

The man turned his cold stare to Jake. "That's no longer your concern."

David heard Arni's words echo through his mind as though Arni had just said them. "Don't resist. I will keep your crew from being harmed. If they resist at any time injuries will result."

David relaxed his stance. "Jake, do as they say, and don't resist."

Jake had his feet spread shoulder width apart, his knees were bent slightly and his fists up in front of him. Without altering his posture, he gave the Captain a sideways glance. "I'm not going to leave you unprotected, Captain."

"Chief, that's an order. He's right. This isn't your job anymore. Do as they say, and don't resist."

"But, Captain!"

The Captain moved around in front of Jake and turned his back on the guards. He emphasized certain key phrases to discreetly give Jake a message. "Jake, please, whether it's today or three days from now, I'm not making it out of here alive. They want me, not you. Arni said you would be safe if you don't resist. I tried to call out for help, but they're smart. They cut off the communication in this cell. Jake, I guess this is your call now, but I need you alive and well to get the crew safely back into space. Please go." Jake realized what the Captain was trying to say and relaxed his stance. He didn't want to seem too eager to the men in front of him, so he slowly relented. "Are you sure this is how you want it, sir?"

David nodded. "Yes, Chief. I'm not the one you need to protect anymore."

David moved towards the back of the cell. Jake relaxed his stance and responded. "You know I'd stay with you to the end."

David nodded. "You're a good man, Chief, now go."

Two of the guards grabbed Jake and hustled him into the next cell over. The one guard who had been talking to David smiled sarcastically. "You know the communications net is out on the whole floor for some strange reason."

David smiled back at the man. "I know, but it got him to leave peacefully, didn't it?"

The man's smile faded. This prisoner was smarter than the guard expected.

David wasn't sure whether to fight back or not. He knew he was going to take a beating no matter what, but would he be better off resisting? Arni hadn't told him what to do. He decided these men had to be limited on time, so slowing them down, by whatever means necessary, was probably a good thing. Once the other two returned from securing Jake, they all moved into the cell and closed the door. The men engaged the privacy screen and turned up the lights. David assumed a defensive stance.

The leader of the group smiled again. "I was hoping you would resist."

David showed no fear. He simply smiled back at the man. "If I have to go down then I'm taking as many of you with me as I can. I do have one quick question though. Why? I'm going to be executed in three days anyway, and from what I've been told it's not going to be pleasant."

The man's eyes became very cold and hard. "The Intercessor is the greatest man to ever live. He's brought us so much since he first came here. Our world was in turmoil after your people left. He's far too quick to forgive. If it were me, I would make everyone on your crew suffer death then bring you back to life and kill you again and again for every life taken on Galat. Since we can't touch your crew now, then we'll make sure you pay, and pay dearly for what you did to the Intercessor's home."

David decided it was time to make them careless and the only way to do that was to make them mad. "So, you believe your Intercessor is ignorant and weak."

One of the men got angry immediately and took a swing at David. David easily dodged the man and threw him into a wall. Their leader was not so young and naive. David heard him mutter, "idiot" under his breath. The man looked at three of the others. "You, three, grab him!" The Captain used his combat training to throw one of the three into the other two. His actions only slowed them down. He managed to get in some punches and kicks before three coming at him simultaneously took him to the ground. They picked David up and held his arms, so he couldn't fight back. The young captain still managed to get in a few kicks. As the blows began to land increasingly faster, he could hear Jake yelling. Moments later he heard the other male crew members yelling then silence as he passed out from the blows.

Once Jake was moved to a separate cell, he tried immediately to get on the communication net, but discovered it wasn't working in his new cell either. Mentally he kicked himself for gambling with the Captain's safety, then did the only other thing that he could. He tried to yell for help. He thought perhaps there was another guard nearby who might not be sympathetic to the goons in the next cell. It was a long shot, but it was all he had.

The other crewmen heard Jake yelling and then heard the raucous coming from the Captain's cell. Jason yelled to Jake. "Jake! Why are you over there? What's happening to the Captain?"

Jake gave them a quick update. "They moved me over here, so they could get at the Captain. They're beating the life out of him! I can't get the communications network to let me call for help. Try yours to see if it works."

Thane moved quickly, but his wasn't working either. Hearing the conversation Braxton and Lazaro also tried. They yelled to the men in the Captain's cell and to anyone who might hear them. Minutes later the lights went out and the privacy shield opened followed by the cell door. The men slipped out in the darkness and left. A couple of them were limping slightly. The crew felt a small amount of satisfaction seeing the Captain had done some damage to these ruffians. After the men were gone and the hall lights came back up to normal, the crew again tried their comm units. The units remained inoperable. It seemed they intended for the Captain to suffer as long as possible.

Jake yelled to Jason. "Can you see the Captain?"

Jason yelled back, "I can see him. He isn't moving. I can't tell if he's breathing."

Braxton and Lazaro were standing at the front of their cells feeling helpless. When they heard Jason's report Lazaro walked back to the comm unit. He tried again to activate it. When it failed, he punched it. Then mindlessly he muttered "C'mon Arni help us out here." The comm unit booted up.

Braxton looked at Lazaro. "What did you just do?" Lazaro blinked then immediately contacted Rachel. Rachel promised them she would get help to them as fast as possible.

Rachel contacted Captain Parker at his home. It was clear to her he had been asleep in bed and knew nothing about what was going on in his own prison. Captain Parker called the prison medical unit to get to the Captain's cell immediately. He hastily got dressed and headed back to work. Rachel contacted the Moderator to let her know what happened, then got herself dressed to head to the prison. The Moderator sat there stunned for a moment. She decided she needed to see the situation for herself and promptly got dressed. Her husband, knowing she had been more upset in recent days, decided to go with her.

Lazaro told Jason and the others he had gotten through to Rachel and she was getting help. Jason slammed his hand against the door to his cell in frustration. Minutes later a medical team arrived along with several guards. The guards were all obviously nervous. The medical team consisted of two men who appeared to be rated as field medics rather than doctors. Jason overheard them saying that if the doctor didn't arrive soon there would be nothing left of the Captain for him to work on. Jason banged on his cell door repeatedly. "Hey! Hey! I'm that man's personal physician! Let me help him!"

The guards and the medics looked at each other and at Jason. The medics told the guards, "If we don't get a doc and fast, he's not going to make it. We would have to call for the Intercessor." The guards had already gotten an earful from Captain Parker. They knew their boss was on his way and not happy.

Jake heard part of their debate and jumped in. "Hey guys, I was told we're no longer prisoners, but detainees. Does that make a difference?" The guards shrugged and decided quickly the only way things could get worse was if their prisoner died. One of them stepped over and opened the doctor's cell long enough to let Jason out. Thane stepped away from the door to keep the guards from getting any edgier. Once the cell door closed, he moved back to the front of the cell.

Jason quickly assessed the Captain and determined he had a collapsed lung and internal bleeding, along with other possible injuries. He did what he could with the basic equipment the medics brought with them then demanded they get the Captain to a medical facility. The guards started to put Jason back in his own cell. Jason quickly set them straight. "Are you going to assume responsibility for this man's life, or should I say death? If you think this is his elaborate plan to escape, or mine, think again. I am not leaving this man's side until he is stable! Now step aside and let us do our jobs!" The guards grudgingly allowed the doctor to accompany the Captain to the infirmary.

Once the men disappeared down the hall Thane looked back at the Captain's empty cell. There were smears and drips of blood on the floor, the walls, and the furniture. He hoped some of it belonged to the Captain's attackers. In anger, he hit the door of his cell again then sat down dejected on his bunk. Jake moved away from the front of his cell and laid down on his bunk, although sleep was not in his plans.

Braxton and Lazaro moved away from the front of their cells. Braxton wasn't ready to settle down yet. "Laz, so tell me what you did."

Lazaro gave Braxton an odd look, "What are you talking about?"

Braxton stepped closer to Lazaro and spoke quietly. "To get the comm unit to work, what did you do?"

Lazaro shook his head. "Nothing, it just came on."

Braxton shook his head. "No way, buddy. That's not what happened."

Lazaro looked annoyed. "If you know what happened, then why are you asking me about it? I got mad, punched it, and it came on. We joke about stuff working because we hit it, but it's a coincidence or a loose connection. I didn't do anything."

Braxton glanced at Thane's cell. Thane wasn't within his line of sight. Braxton stepped uncomfortably close to Lazaro and whispered. "You called on Arni to help."

Lazaro stepped back looking startled. "No, I didn't. I didn't... I just said..." Braxton raised his eyebrows making his implication apparent without saying it out loud. Lazaro re-thought the incident, shaking his head. "I wasn't trying to – to ask for his help, not exactly. I mean I just wanted anybody's help right then and he seemed to be the one in charge. It had to be a coincidence." Lazaro got quiet for a minute. When he composed himself, he looked at Braxton. "I really wasn't trying to ask for his help. I was just frustrated. I wasn't thinking. You aren't going to tell anybody, are you?"

Braxton looked at Lazaro. He could see the worry in his eyes and knew most of it was for the Captain, not for himself. "No, we can't really say for sure what happened. As far as I'm concerned you punched the console, and it rebooted. Just be careful with your frustrations next time. Okay?"

Lazaro nodded. "Okay." The two sat there in silence waiting to hear about the Captain.

Thane hopped up and went to the front of his cell. "Hey guys! Should somebody contact Brynna?" The others came to the front of their cells as well. There were no quick easy answers.

Jake responded first. "I'm not sure we should tell her until we know how he's doing. Let her sleep if she can."

Braxton wasn't so sure. "If it were me, I'd want to know, even if I couldn't do anything about it."

Jake conceded. "Maybe you're right. I doubt she's getting much sleep anyway. Do you want me to tell her?"

The group agreed to let Jake talk to the Commander, but his comm unit was still not working. Thane's wasn't either, so Lazaro tried his. His face went white when he tried his unit and it was no longer functional. He tried hitting it again, but nothing happened. The men moved about restlessly in their cells. After a time, they decided no news was good news.

As soon as Jason got the Captain on an exam table in the infirmary, he told the medics he would need a great deal of help from them. "Gentlemen, I am a qualified physician, but I am unfamiliar with your medical technology. You'll have to help me out. I can handle the surgery aspect, but it's the on and off switches I may struggle with. Understand?" The two men looked at each other for a second. "Yes sir." They promptly started turning on necessary equipment and rattling off what it was used for. Jason ran a scan over the Captain to determine which injuries were the most life threatening. The Captain had several broken ribs. The broken ribs had wreaked havoc on his internal organs. One rib had punctured a lung and made a small hole in the pericardial sac. The sac surrounding his heart was filling with blood making it harder for his heart to push blood to the rest of his body. The ribs had caused lacerations to several other major organs. He also appeared to have several small internal injuries causing bleeding into his abdomen, a concussion, a dislocated shoulder, and numerous fractures and bruises. Jason ordered one of the medics to get a blood transfusion and fluids going. He ordered the other medic to hook his patient up to a high concentration of oxygen help him prepare for surgery. Jason changed his clothes and scrubbed almost as quickly as he did the day of Tharen's emergency surgery on Medoris. He wasn't happy about having to learn new equipment on the fly. Jason was working quickly to get the bleeding under control when the on-call physician walked in the door of the observation room.

The observation room was designed for guards to keep an eye on prisoners who might try to use their time in the infirmary as a chance to escape. Today, the observation room held more than the standard two guards. Tonight, the room was populated with the Captain of the Guard, Counselor Johan, Moderator Tarmon, and her husband. The doctor walked over to the window and saw Jason and the two medics doing major surgery. "What in heaven's name is going on here? Who's operating in there and who's being operated on?"

Captain Parker turned and walked over to the doctor quickly. "Oh good, you're here. Moderator Tarmon, this is Dr. Evans, the facility physician."

The Moderator was in no mood for chit chat. She moved abruptly over to the doctor and gave him a quick rundown on what was going on and what she expected of the man. "Dr. Evans, the man being operated on in there is scheduled to be executed in two days. It is of paramount importance that he makes it to his execution. The man operating is Dr. Adams. You will give Dr. Adams whatever assistance he needs. I do not have time for a turf war here. Are we clear?"

Dr. Evans nodded. "Yes ma'am." He moved on into the infirmary and scrubbed quickly. He approached Jason, introduced himself, and asked what he could do to help. Jason gave him a quick report of David's injuries and what sort of progress he had made. Doctor Evans followed Jason's lead and got started. The two worked feverishly.

After Dr. Evans joined Jason, Rachel realized the rest of the crew was probably worried about their Captain. She punched the button on the intercom to address the two doctors. "Gentlemen, I need a report on the Captain's condition, so I can let his crew know."

The two doctors were working so hard and fast they barely heard her question. Dr. Evans finally spoke up. "It's a little too soon to tell if he's going to make it or not."

Jason hearing his colleague's bleak assessment snapped out of his fervent concentration. "He'll make it! He's not a quitter!"

Rachel drew her own conclusions from somewhere in between the two men's professional opinions. She turned to Captain Parker. "Captain, I need to know several things. First, what is being done to protect his safety from this point on and to protect the other members of his crew? Second, what are you doing to find out who did this? Third, can you provide me with an escort to go talk to his crew?" The Moderator echoed the Counselor's questions. The Captain had been more concerned with David's health up to this point and hadn't considered any other aspects of his job.

Captain Parker knew what needed to be done. "Moderator Tarmon, Counselor Johan, I will do everything in my power to make sure the Captain and his crew are protected. I will get two guards in here momentarily to escort you to both sections of the prison. I'll contact a nearby base to pull in additional troops then brief every shift personally on their duties and what I expect of them. I'll bring in an external forensics crew to go over the Captain's cell and work on the surveillance footage immediately. After the crew is released back to their ship, I'll turn in my resignation. There's no excuse for me to allow two such incidents on my watch. Please forgive me." Without waiting for a reply, the man moved to the intercom and punched it. "Gentlemen, once the Captain is out of danger, I need you to collect any forensic evidence that may help convict his attackers, please."

Dr. Evans, who was well acquainted with such requests, gave a quick acknowledgment and kept working. Captain Parker moved to a computer station in the observation room and contacted a nearby military base requesting additional emergency troops. He contacted the local forensics department for an investigation team to be dispatched immediately. In minutes, he had half the city awake and moving, or so it seemed. He put the prison on lock down, so no one would be allowed in or out without his express permission. He also issued a list of who could move about freely. No one was allowed to leave their stations until properly relieved of duty. Moderator Tarmon could see Captain Parker now had a lot to do, so she volunteered to stay and watch the Captain's surgery. She promised to notify him immediately of any changes. Two guards arrived to escort Rachel to talk to the crew.

When the order went out to lock down the prison, an alarm went off, and lights began flashing in the corridors. The alarms weren't obnoxiously loud, and the lights weren't a drastic change, but it was enough to wake the light sleepers. Brynna and Marissa hadn't been sleeping well to begin with. It didn't take much to get their attention. They saw guards running past their cell with intense looks on their faces.

Marissa looked over and saw that Brynna was awake. "I wonder what's going on."

Brynna got up and moved over to the door to see if she could see anything. "I can't see anything from here, but I don't like it, whatever it is." The other women began peering out to see if they could see anything. They were too far away. Brynna attempted to get a news report. Her computer panel was dead. The others found theirs was inaccessible as well. Brynna shook her head. "I really don't like this." In a few minutes, they got bored and headed back to bed, despite the noise and lights.

Rachel took her escort and headed to the men's section of the prison. As soon as Lazaro saw her, he called out. "Rachel! How's the Captain? Is he alive? Is he going to be okay?"

Rachel asked the guards to move all four men into one cell. Initially they refused, but she quickly and firmly reminded them of their instructions to cooperate with her fully. She thought it would be easier to talk to them if they were all together. The guards moved Jake and Thane into the cell with Braxton and Lazaro. Rachel stepped into the cell with them and left her guards in the hallway. She sat down on the end of Braxton's bunk to talk to the men. "Gentlemen, David is alive. He's still in surgery, but he's in bad shape. Both your doctor and the prison doctor are working frantically to save him. Captain Parker is bringing in new guards from outside to protect him, and you, from any further attacks. He's also bringing in a forensics team to help identify the men who did this. Can you gentlemen help us with this in any way?"

Jake was quick to volunteer information. He was sure he could identify some of the men. Jake was also happy to report the men had various injuries the Captain had inflicted on them. The men gave as many clues as they could to identify the attackers.

As soon as Rachel had as much information as she could, she prepared to leave. She promised to keep them apprised of the Captain's condition. Rachel also assured them she was on her way to talk to Brynna and the other women. The guards returned the men to their cells before escorting Rachel out of the men's area of the prison. She stopped at the guard station near the women's cells to check on David's progress. There had been no changes.

She decided to tell Brynna somewhat privately. She told her escorts to get her into Brynna's cell as quickly and quietly as possible then to engage the privacy screen. The guards did as instructed. It wasn't fast enough to avoid being spotted by Lexi and Aulani. They didn't get a chance to ask any questions before Rachel disappeared into Brynna's cell. Their concern activated with the privacy screen.

Brynna had nodded off but wasn't sleeping very deeply when Rachel entered her cell. Marissa raised up when she saw Rachel and the guards enter as well. "Brynna, may I sit down?"

Brynna sat up and made room for Rachel to sit on her bed. "Rachel, what's happened?"

Rachel took a deep breath. Brynna had already figured out it had something to do with David. "Brynna, some of the guards were apparently unhappy with the court's verdict and they decided to take matters into their own hands." Brynna felt her heart racing. She gripped her blanket tightly and tried to stay calm. Rachel saw her begin to react and got to the point as quickly she could. "David's been badly hurt. He's in surgery right now. The prison doctor and your doctor are both working on him. Captain Parker has taken additional steps to protect him and the rest of the crew. He's alive, but it's touch and go."

Brynna stared at nothing for a moment. Arni's words echoed in her thoughts, "You aren't going to lose him. I won't let him die, but you have to trust me. Not one member of your crew will die on this planet. There will still be pain and suffering, but I won't let David take this punishment. This one's mine."

Rachel reached over and touched Brynna's arm. "Commander, are you with me? Did you hear what I said?"

Brynna turned her head and forced her eyes to focus on Rachel's face. "Has the Intercessor ever been wrong?"

Rachel was taken aback by her question. "What?"

Brynna repeated her question. Marissa sat there silently watching and listening. Rachel glanced over at Marissa before answering. "No, he's never been wrong. Sometimes we misunderstood what he has tried to say to us, but he's never been wrong."

Marissa pulled herself out of her own stupor. "He can't be wrong, ever. He knows all that can be known."

Brynna added up all the pieces of the puzzle mentally. Rachel saw her relax her grip on the blanket and her face seemed to be calm and peaceful. "May I see him?"

Rachel was a little confused, "David or the Intercessor?" Brynna calmly replied, "David."

Rachel thought about it for a moment. "I think that can be arranged. I've already given a report to the men and gotten some evidence on the men who did this to your husband. If it's alright with you, I'll have the guards take you to the observation room while I bring the rest of your crew up to speed."

Brynna pondered her plan for a moment. "When you tell them, also tell them I have the Intercessor's word David will survive."

Rachel knew she had spoken to the Intercessor at some point, but she had no idea when that would have been. The Intercessor had not been seen since the trial.

Rachel again asked the guards to move the female crew members into one cell, then promptly sent them to escort Brynna to the observation room in the infirmary. While they were on their way with Brynna, Rachel filled the women in on the situation. Each one was gravely still and quiet until Marissa broke the silence with Brynna's message. "Brynna said to let you know Arni gave his word the Captain would survive. She doesn't want you to worry."

Cheyenne teared up again, then slammed her fist on the table. "I'm so tired of being afraid and tired of crying." She looked up in time to see Arni enter the cell.

Rachel looked at the door. She was sure she had remembered the guards closing it before they left. Arni walked over to Cheyenne and knelt in front of her. The others watched him in silence. He gently called her name, "Cheyenne."

Cheyenne tried hard to blink back the tears, but they just wouldn't leave her alone. "Yes, Arni."

Arni gently placed one hand on the fist still perched on the table. "Cheyenne, the next few days are going to be very difficult, but everything will be fine. I need all of you to trust me. Your Captain will survive. I'm going to take care of him, and all of you."

Laura wasn't favorably impressed. "If allowing us to get beaten nearly to death is your way of taking care of us then count me out."

Rachel was aghast at Laura's impudence to the Intercessor. Arni turned to address Laura. "Laurel, I know you're upset. You don't understand everything that's happening right now. Everything will work out for the best. You will understand it later. I'm only here to offer you some peace of mind and comfort. What happened to David had to happen. I could have prevented it, but it would have only made things worse later. Please trust me, he's going to be fine."

Laura still wasn't impressed. "Work out for the best for whom? It had to happen? If you could have prevented it, why didn't you? It would only make things worse later for whom? For you? Are you going to save his life just in time to execute him? Why didn't you just let him die instead of making us go through this twice?"

Arni looked back at Cheyenne's fist. She had relaxed her hand with his still on top of it. He gave it a gentle squeeze then turned to Laura. "Laura, if David had died tonight then someone else would have to face this execution. Do you want your Commander or your Security Chief to take his place? He chose to die to protect you. Everything I'm doing is also for your protection. Yes, he's hurt. He will survive and because of this day, so will others. He won't die today, or two days from now. He has your backs, and I have his. I am extending mercy to him, to you and to anyone who will accept it. Someone must die for your crimes and those of all mankind. I will come to his defense, the way he has defended you. It will all make sense later."

Cheyenne looked at Rachel. "Is that true? If the Captain dies does someone else have to take his place?" Rachel nodded without speaking. She wasn't concerned about that particular part of the Intercessor's words. She was more concerned he was still talking about taking David's place.

Laura was like a bull dog. She wasn't ready to let her questions drop. "Does the Captain's pain and suffering make things easier for you? Is that why you didn't stop it? Is he messing up your plans?"

Arni could see the hurt and pain behind her questions. "Laurel, I allowed your Captain to go through this tonight for the good of the crew, not exclusively for the Captain's good, or for mine. It will affect events in the future which will mean life or death among your crew."

Laura looked at him with venom. "I don't believe you."

Arni was now standing directly in front of her. He held out his hand to her. "Do you want to see it for yourself?" She gave him a wary look. She reached out and took his hand gingerly. Arni looked up and spoke into the air. "Father, show her what would have happened if her Captain had not gone through this pain tonight." He grabbed her hand firmly.

The women saw Laura stare off into space and heard her gasp. She gripped Arni's hand firmly then she abruptly pulled her hand away from Arni's. "NO!" Laura was sitting on the bed next to Marissa. When she pulled away from Arni, Laura and Arni both looked at Marissa.

Marissa suddenly got very nervous. "What?!?"

Aulani leaned forward. "Laura, are you okay? What did you see?"

Laura looked at Arni. "It was just one of his mind tricks. It was nothing." Her words lacked a certain amount of conviction.

Arni stepped away from Laura because he knew she was now quite rattled by his presence. Looking at her purposefully he explained, "Laurel, what you saw is coming, but the ending will now be different because of David's pain. This time no one will be harmed."

Laura glanced again at Marissa which was really making Marissa nervous now. Laura sat there trying to ignore what she had just seen. It had been as real as if it had just happened. She was not the type to cry, but now she felt herself give in to tears. Marissa and Aulani moved to comfort her.

Lexi looked at the scene around her. "You said you came here to give us some comfort. Laura doesn't look very comfortable. You've somehow managed to break the spirits of the strongest people I know. I would very much like to know how you did that and why."

Something between a laugh and a scoff escaped Arni's mouth. "Soon Laura will take great comfort in what she saw. Your strength is limited by your humanity and considering what's coming, it won't take you very far. My Father can give you strength beyond understanding, but only if you ask for it. You won't ask for his help if you don't realize you need it. So yes, part of my agenda is to break your spirits. I know that sounds harsh, but I will rebuild them into something greater. The Commonwealth is about to come against you in a mighty way. You can't protect yourselves from the Dreans. How are you going to take on the whole Commonwealth? I think I've said enough for now." Arni glanced at Rachel and nodded. "Thank you, Rachel, for all you have done for them." He turned and stepped through the doorway of the cell.

Laura bolted after him. "Arni! I have one question."

Arni stopped in the hall and without looking at her answered her yet unspoken question. "No, Marissa doesn't know yet. I would appreciate it if you would keep the details of what you saw to yourself for now. It was meant only for your eyes." Arni then turned to face her. "My Father didn't show you this to frighten you. He wanted you to understand the stakes and that he has things well in hand. As I said before, because of the beating your Captain took tonight, people's priorities have changed and now what you saw won't end the same way. My Father is the ultimate tactical officer. He wants you to take comfort in what you saw, not be afraid."

Laura's eyes squinted as she studied him. "Who are you? What are you?"

Arni gave her half a smile. "My Father will reveal that information to you when the time is right. For now, I am the last surviving man from Galat III and the son of a healer." He turned and walked on down the hall. Laura shivered once then returned to the cell.

The others were talking in soft tones which stopped when she entered the room. Lexi spoke first. "Are you okay?"

Surprisingly, Laura felt calmer than she had in the last few days. "Yeah. I'm good." She sat down and tried to figure out how to view her vision as "comforting."

Cheyenne leaned forward. "Laura, what did you ask him?"

Laura made a conscious effort not to look at Marissa. She forced her eyes to focus on Cheyenne's face. "I just asked him about the vision he showed me and who he really was."

Aulani was just as curious. "What did he say?"

Laura's brow furrowed. "He said the vision wasn't meant to frighten me, but to comfort me. I'm still working on that one. He also said he was the sole survivor of Galat III and the son of a healer. He said his father would have to tell us the rest."

Marissa could stand the suspense no longer. "What did you see in your vision? I know it had something to do with me."

Laura got a little nervous considering Arni's request to keep the details to herself. She answered carefully. "I don't know exactly what caused this, but I saw a firefight on the ship. As a result, the Captain, Jake, Jason and Marissa were all shot and killed."

The women looked at each other. Aulani finally asked. "Who was shooting at them?"

Laura swallowed hard. "They were shooting at each other." By this time her voice was barely audible. The women were all too unnerved to ask her any more questions for which Laura was quite grateful.

Lexi added one last sarcastic comment. "Yeah, our crew killing each other. That's very comforting."

Rachel had enough of their lack of respect for the Intercessor. "You people really have no idea who you're dealing with do you? He has the power to give life and to take it away. Whether you choose to serve him or not, I suggest you remember the power he holds in his hands! He didn't have to ask for mercy for your crew and I know you wouldn't have gotten it if he hadn't asked for it personally. I suggest you at least grant him the respect he deserves!"

The women again got quiet. Lexi didn't really feel any differently, but she knew how to smooth ruffled feathers. "I'm sorry if we've offended you and the Intercessor. You're right, we don't really know what we're dealing with. What I do know is, we've been on a major emotional roller coaster over the last few days. We've been arrested, charged, and convicted for crimes we were virtually oblivious to. Laura gets comforted with a nightmare. Our Captain is about to be executed and was nearly killed on his way to his execution. It's the middle of the night and we've had very little sleep. So, forgive us for not being at our best!"

Rachel's anger slowly abated when she realized Lexi's point was equally as valid. "I'm sorry. I shouldn't have snapped at you. You're right, it's late and none of us have slept well in days. The Intercessor really does know what's for the best. Please try and trust him. Anything he's told you is true." Rachel intended to help give the women some comfort, but Arni's words only served to haunt her.

Aulani tried to lighten things up a little. "Laura? Why did he keep calling you Laurel?"

Laura was glad for the change in subject. "Because that's my proper name. My dad was really the only one who ever called me Laurel though. My mom called me Laurie. My dad said I was his crowning glory like a crown of laurel leaves. My dad wasn't very successful in life. He died a couple years ago. He had more marriages, jobs, and children than most people. I lost track of all his former wives and I don't even know all my half-siblings. Don't get me wrong: I love my dad. He had a good heart, just not a lot of common sense."

Aulani continued. "How did he die?"

Most men didn't die at such an early age. Laura knew she was revealing a deep dark part of her soul. "He owed some less than reputable characters money. He couldn't pay it back, and they beat him to death."

Her revelation weighed the conversation down again.

Rachel decided it was time to go check on the Captain and see what progress Captain Parker was making. She stood up to leave. She told the women her plans and assured them everyone would be safe. The guards returned just in time to put the women back in their respective cells.

Marissa grabbed Laura's hand just before they escorted her out. "Laura, there was more than what you said, wasn't there?"

A guilty look crossed Laura's face. Laura nodded slowly. "You're very perceptive. Arni asked me to keep the rest to myself for now. It wasn't really a bad thing though. You know, I'm already starting to take comfort in this vision."

Marissa gave her a weak smile. "You didn't look comfortable when it happened."

Seeing the guard's impatience, Marissa released Laura's arm. Laura smiled back at her. "I'm taking comfort in knowing most of it won't happen."

Laura moved back to her cell leaving Marissa alone. She looked around the cell. She didn't feel alone. She half expected to see Arni somewhere close by. A voice inside her whispered. "I'll always be close by. You don't have to ask for my help. You can just talk to me. I'm a great listener." She looked around again and then lay down. Marissa felt like she should be wide awake and worried, but she wasn't. The Captain was going to be fine. She drifted off quickly and soundly for the first time in days.

Lexi and Aulani talked for a long time. Laura and Cheyenne said little to each other. Cheyenne drifted off to sleep, while Laura continued to contemplate everything she had experienced.

The Moderator and her husband were sitting quietly in the observation room watching the two doctors work when Brynna was escorted in. The Moderator's husband got up and moved a chair up beside them for Brynna. Brynna politely thanked him. She wondered if he realized who she was. Brynna had quickly gotten used to being public enemy number one or perhaps number two.

The Moderator introduced them to each other. "Commander Alexander, this is my husband Edward. He teaches history at a local university."

Brynna responded hesitantly. "I see. It's nice to meet you, sir."

Being a history teacher, he would be quite familiar with who she was. Edward nodded politely, "Thank you, ma'am." He didn't reply in kind, which would have been more than Brynna would have expected. Brynna turned her attention to her own husband. She saw Saundra Tarmon studying her.

"Commander, you seem quite calm considering the circumstances." Brynna forced her eyes away from the surgery. "Moderator Tarmon..."

Moderator Tarmon interrupted Brynna. "Commander, just for tonight, call me Saundra. This is the most unusual situation I've ever been in, so let's keep it simple. You are light years away from your friends and family and in the middle of a crisis. I'm guessing you could use a friend about now."

Brynna smiled. "Thank you, Saundra. In answer to your question, as long as the Intercessor can be trusted, then David is going to pull through."

Saundra nodded thoughtfully. "I'm not sure I would be this relaxed if it were Edward, even with the Intercessor's assurances."

Brynna continued to watch the surgery but responded without looking her companions in the eye. "We've seen the Intercessor's power and we know what he's capable of. We haven't seen enough to know how and when he uses that power, or even why."

Saundra nodded even though Brynna couldn't see her. "So, at what point do you start to trust him?"

Brynna took her eyes off David and focused on Saundra. "Ask me again in five days." Saundra and Edward both stared at

Brynna. Edward was uncomfortable enough to fetch the three of them some coffee. Brynna looked down at her cup and briefly considered one of the mysteries of the universe. It seemed every world had a coffee-like beverage.

An hour later, the doctors finished the major part of the surgery. They closed David up and brought out an instrument used for mending bones. The prison only had one small unit, so it was going to have to move from one broken bone to another. It would prove to be a long and tedious process. Jason finally looked up and saw Brynna in the observation room. Keeping in mind he was still a prisoner, he asked if he could step into the observation room for a moment to let David's wife know what was happening. The two guards in the room let him through to her.

As soon as Jason entered the room, Brynna and the others stood up. Jason grabbed a chair for himself. He had Brynna retake her seat. He placed his chair facing her. He had been standing still for the last couple hours and was ready to rest a minute. Brynna appeared calm, but attentive. It seemed peculiar to him. He thought perhaps the situation hadn't been fully explained to her. "Brynna, David was gravely injured. He almost didn't make it." Brynna didn't even blink as she continued to listen. He went on to explain the nature of David's injuries, the repairs they made and the several hours of remaining bone grafting, and tissue regeneration to clean up the bruises, cuts, and abrasions. "Brynna, so long as this wasn't too much strain on his heart, he should make a full recovery." Jason watched her carefully to be sure she wasn't in shock.

Brynna took her eyes off Jason and looked back at David. "May I go in and see him now?"

Jason stood up and to let her go past him. "Yes, of course you can." Brynna gingerly stepped around him and moved quietly into the next room. The three watched her walk slowly and quietly to David's side. There were no tears in her eyes. Jason looked back at the Moderator and her guest. "Moderator Tarmon, has she been carrying on any conversation since she's been in here?"

"Yes, doctor, she wasn't overly talkative, but she was very, um, pointed in her comments. Why? What are you worried about?"

The doctor shook his head. "I don't know. I would have expected more of a reaction from her. I know she's an officer and a very strong woman, but this should have had her rattled. It had me rattled."

The Moderator's husband who'd said little this whole time finally spoke. "She's an admirable woman. She's learning and adapting quickly to her circumstances. I wanted to hate her, but it's just not happening."

Jason didn't know how to respond to his comment. "I'm going back in to check on my patient."

Brynna pulled a chair up to David's bedside. As she looked at him, she couldn't help, but see all the bloody equipment and towels that hadn't been cleaned up after the surgery. She saw the dried blood on David's face and hands. He looked like one solid bruise. His eye was nearly swollen shut and his nose was broken and bloody. She reached over gently and laid one hand on his shoulder and the other on the top of his head. Now the tears began to flow. She whispered quietly to him. "David, I'm so sorry you had to go through this. I love you. Please hurry back to me."

Jason walked up behind Brynna and put his hand on her shoulder. Brynna looked up at him. "Jason, can I clean him up? I need to do something."

Jason patted her shoulder. "I know you do. I'm afraid you can't clean him up just yet. Dr. Evans needs to collect evidence left by David's attackers. You can help me get him cleaned up after that."

Dr. Evans had stepped out to freshen up and get himself something to drink. He came back in, along with one of the medics, to start looking for any signs of DNA that didn't belong to David. The medical scanners made quick work of the search for evidence. Since they had just done the surgery, the scanner could simply scan for any DNA that wasn't David's. In a few short minutes, Dr. Evans had samples of blood and other tissues from all six of David's attackers. Once he collected the samples, he gave Brynna permission to clean David up. He instructed the medics to help her with anything she needed.

Dr. Evans paused to speak to Jason before he headed to turn in his evidence. "Dr. Adams, it was a pleasure working with you. You are an excellent surgeon."

Jason gave him a tired smile. "Thank you, sir. I appreciate you allowing me the opportunity to work with you."

The two shook hands. "I wasn't sure what to think when I walked in and found you operating in my infirmary, but you certainly know what you're doing. That patient would have died if you had waited for me to arrive. Thank you for saving him. How is it you happened to be here in the middle of the night?"

Jason rubbed his face with one of his hands. He knew this doctor wasn't going to like his answer. "I've, uh, been a prisoner in the cell across the hall from him for the last few days. I'm their personal physician." Jason pointed at David and Brynna.

Dr. Evans blinked. "I see." He took two steps towards the door and stopped. "Actually, I don't see, but you're still a phenomenal surgeon, and I'm guessing you wouldn't be out of your cell if it wasn't approved by somebody important." He turned and headed out the door with his evidence.

In the observation room, he ran into Captain Parker who filled him in on the situation. When Dr. Evans found out exactly who David was, his temperament changed radically. "Why didn't you let that low life just die? Why save his no-good life if we're just going to execute him in a couple days?"

Hearing his disparaging comments, Moderator Tarmon stepped into the conversation. "If he had died then his sentence would have fallen on that young woman in there."

Dr. Evans looked in at Brynna who was gently and lovingly washing her husband's face. His heart softened slightly. "From what I understand about this case, the whole group are guilty of reprehensible crimes. How did they even qualify for the mercy clause?"

"Because I asked for it." The group turned to see Arni Liontari standing in the doorway.

Dr. Evans had never been in the presence of the Intercessor. "I'm sorry. I – I meant no offense, Lord Intercessor."

Arni moved on into the room and looked through the glass at David. There was a quiet sadness on his face as he looked at David. The Moderator watched him closely. "Are you here to heal him, Lord Liontari?"

Arni shook his head. "No, not this time."

Dr. Evans got a puzzled look on his face. "This time? Have you healed him before?"

Arni nodded. "A couple of times."

Dr. Evans sensed he wasn't going to get many answers, so he changed topics. "So, why did I walk in and find a prisoner operating in my infirmary?"

Captain Parker decided it was time to assert himself since his tour of duty in the prison was about to end. "Dr. Evans, I shouldn't have to explain to you those prisoners are extremely high profile. You saw the man's injuries. Could your medics have kept him alive until you arrived?"

The man's pride superseded his judgment. "Of course they could have."

One of the medics entered the room just in time to hear the question and the answer. He was the one who had made the call to enlist Jason's help. He had doubted David would make it, but he wasn't certain. Jason's medical scans only served to reinforce that belief. He was concerned if the doctor pushed it, he would end up caught in the middle of a controversial debate. "Uh, sir, I seriously doubt that. The other doctor had to work on the prisoner before we could even move him. You didn't see his condition before Dr. Adams started working on him. You saw him after he was somewhat stabilized."

Anger began to build in Dr. Evans. This was his turf, and he didn't like a lowly prisoner encroaching on it. Arni turned from the window. "Be careful, Dr. Evans. Everyone's guilty of something. Don't let pride be your crime. These people are guilty of blindly serving the Commonwealth. They never physically laid a hand on anyone on Galat. They even saved some lives there."

Dr. Evans' anger was momentarily disarmed. "So why were they found guilty?"

"Because they didn't believe me when I told them what would happen. They reported the people to the Commonwealth, which got them killed." Arni looked around at their reactions.

The Moderator was saddened by the entire situation. "Perhaps, I was too hasty in bringing charges against them. I'm not sure anyone on this planet could have given them a fair trial."

Edward finally spoke up to defend his wife from her own guilty conscience. "Saundra, they're guilty of spying on Galat, on us, and anywhere else they've gone. If they hadn't gone to Galat and reported the presence of the Intercessor, the people of Galat would still be alive. They may not bear all the blame, but they bear a great deal of it."

Saundra looked at Arni gravely and asked, "Is it too late to undo this?"

Arni grimaced slightly. "Let me take the Captain's place." Saundra's eyes grew wide. "Intercessor, their guilt is questionable, you are undeniably innocent."

Arni stepped forward. "But, I'm the only one who can and will return from death. I am still a man. I can still feel the sting of pain and death, but I can escape it."

"Intercessor, you are also the only one who is guilty of nothing, and we would not want to incur the wrath of your father."

Arni gave her one more thing to think about. "You gave me the title of Intercessor, yet you don't allow me to intercede." He walked in to visit with Brynna and Jason without saying another word.

Jason glanced up when Arni walked in. "You've got a lot of nerve showing up here now. Where were you when the Captain was getting beaten to a pulp? You wait until we're done with his surgery to heal him? He's supposed to be important to your plans, but you let this happen to him?"

Brynna stood up and touched Jason's shoulder gently. He turned and saw she intended to address Arni herself. He stepped aside for her. "Arni, why are you here now?"

"I told the women of your crew this had to happen. It gravely affects your future and the lives of several of your crew. I would not have allowed him to die, just as I promised you. I didn't come to heal him either. He has to handle this one himself. I just wanted to check on you and offer you whatever reassurance you need."

Brynna looked over at David, then back at Arni. "I don't understand.

Why would you agree to take his place? Why is he so important?"

"You misunderstand. I do have a plan for him, but I also have one for you, and you, Jason. It's not his life, but my death that's so important."

Jason shook his head. "Apparently, he's suicidal."

Arni didn't flinch but responded to Jason rather matter-of-factually. "I don't want to die. You need me to die. You've seen what my Father is capable of. He has given me this task to die once and then he will give life back to me and give everyone who chooses to serve him a new life with him."

Brynna was exhausted mentally and physically. "I don't have a clue what you're talking about. This is just too much for me to process right now."

The instrument repairing David's bones made a soft beeping sound. Jason moved to re-position it, leaving Brynna somewhat alone with Arni. Brynna, embarrassed by her tears, turned and took a couple of steps away from Arni. She was a commander. Commanders were supposed to be in control. She was feeling incredibly out of control.

Arni moved up behind her. "Brynna, I know you're tired in body and soul. I just want you to know that I don't want to be your enemy. Every human life is precious to me. I don't take any life or any death lightly. I love every human being more than you can possibly understand. It's not easy for me to see needless suffering. My Father is just trying to put things right. Mankind wasn't meant to live like this."

Brynna turned to see tears streaming down his face. The look on his face told her his tears were genuine. Arni continued. "I love each and every member of your crew enough to take this punishment for them. I don't want to die, but I don't want you to die even more. Not you, not David, I wish to spare you all."

"That makes no sense. You've only just met us a couple months ago.

How can you say you love us?"

"Brynna, I have known you since before you were born. Nothing is hidden from me. You may not have known I was there, but I've always been near you. Do you remember playing ball in your yard when you were nine? You chased the ball into the street and ran into the path of an oncoming vehicle?"

Brynna blinked. "Yes. That vehicle was coming really fast. I don't know how he missed hitting me, but he did. How did you know about that? My brother is the only one who saw it, and he was six."

"I stopped that car from hitting you. It was green with gold trim. I was also there when your parents told you they weren't renewing their marriage contract. You took your sleeping bag and pillows and put them in the bottom of your closet and slept in there for weeks. You cried for hours that first night. I wrapped my arms around you and held you while you cried."

Brynna now looked stricken. No one knew about that. "I remember crying and wishing someone would just hold me tightly. I put my head down and closed my eyes and it felt like someone was really holding me. I was scared to move or open my eyes because I thought whoever was holding me would leave. Tell me the truth. Was that really you?"

"Yes, Brynna it was. That's one of those things you shouldn't have had to face. My Father didn't intend for anyone to have to deal with that kind of pain. I also helped bring your mom and dad back together a couple years later like you asked me to."

"Like I asked you to?"

"Yes, you were crying, and you specifically asked for somebody to bring your mom and dad back together. I heard your cries, and I worked as hard and fast as I could. I told David I would never control any of you. I didn't control your parents either. I had to set the scene for them to choose to get back together. I couldn't force them to do it. My Father gave everyone the right to choose their own path, and I won't take it away from anyone."

Brynna's mind was in turmoil. It was jumping back and forth from the present to the past without a good place to land. Memories and emotions flooded her mind and she began to sob openly. She folded her arms across her chest and grabbed them as though she could protect herself from the flood of emotions. Arni slowly stepped towards her. He gently put his arms around her and gave her the hug she desperately needed. She laid her head on his shoulder and sobbed openly again. She was right. These were the arms she remembered holding her as a child crying in the closet.

Jason looked up from tending to David and although Brynna did not appear to be in danger, he didn't like the position she was in. He quickly finished his task and moved to interrupt the two. It was up to him to protect his commander while she was so obviously vulnerable.

As he started towards her, Dr. Evans re-entered the room and asked him for an update on David's condition. Jason gave him a full report. He tried again to move on, but the prison doctor had more questions. Now that he knew who Jason really was, he wanted to be sure this prisoner actually knew what he was doing. Dr. Adams began to feel patronized by the pedantic nature of Dr. Evans' questions. "Dr. Evans, a few minutes ago you were complementing me on my abilities. I take it my politics have offended you and suddenly caused you to doubt my abilities."

Dr. Evans was startled by the harsh comment, although he shouldn't have been. "What? What are you suggesting, Dr. Adams?"

"I'm suggesting you found out exactly who I am, and because I'm a member of the Commonwealth, I'm apparently no longer a capable surgeon. I'll have you know I am a very experienced physician and surgeon. I have worked in the best and worst conditions possible. This man has been my patient for months, and his life is more important than my own. How dare you suggest I would give him less than acceptable care? I told your medics the thing that would give me the most trouble would be knowing the specifics of using unfamiliar equipment. Your people were very helpful in that area. I am a doctor. My politics don't affect how I care for patients. Now, either I did a good job, or I didn't. So, which is it?"

Dr. Evans was suddenly embarrassed by his actions. "I'm sorry, Dr. Adams. It appears my politics do affect my actions as a physician. I apologize for offending you. You did do an excellent job. I was just taken aback when I discovered you were a prisoner. I really didn't know anything about your training or background. Forgive my impertinence." Dr. Evans noticed Jason was distracted by Arni and Brynna. Dr. Evans reacted with awe and reverence to what he was witnessing. Jason seemed intent on interrupting it. Dr. Evans couldn't understand Jason's reaction. He did the only logical thing he could. He pulled Jason back and softly asked him about it. "Dr. Adams, I am confused by the attention you seem to be giving to the Intercessor and your Commander. You seem upset by their interaction."

Jason looked harshly at the doctor. Was he being petty again? The man's face showed genuine confusion. "My commander is extremely vulnerable right now. Her husband and Captain nearly died. The Captain is still marked for death in two days. That man is the Commonwealth's sworn enemy. He's embracing the leader we are going to look to after our Captain's execution. Her defenses are down!"

Dr. Evans looked even more confused. "Why?" He really wasn't sure what questions to ask. The whole conversation was confusing and upsetting.

Jason looked back at the man. "Why, what?" What kind of a question was "Why?"

Dr. Evans thought a minute about how to clarify his questions. "Why is he the enemy of the Commonwealth? Why does he upset you? He is the most revered person on this world and others. He is the one who introduced us to the ways of his Father. His ways are greater than our ways. He wants only the best for us. I think every person on this world would give anything to get that kind of attention from the Intercessor."

Jason looked at Dr. Evans like he had lost his mind. "He's the one who declared the Commonwealth to be his enemy. He's demanded we serve him and forsake the Commonwealth. The Commonwealth has worked with thousands of worlds to bring peace to this Galaxy. It was only when he started showing up that the peace was threatened. We had three hundred years of peace until he came along."

"The Intercessor has killed no one. Your people wiped out an entire planetary population. Yeah, I can see why you don't trust the Intercessor." Dr. Evans replied sourly. He walked on over to David and began another assessment.

Jason stood there blinking and thinking about the doctor's cutting remarks. He made a peculiar amount of sense. Jason walked over to the couple as Brynna got her crying under control. Arni released her from his hug. Brynna thanked him for his compassion. Before Jason could say anything, Arni took the doctor's elbow. "Take her to him. He's waking up." Startled, Jason looked over at the Captain who was moving weakly in the bed. The Doc saw him take a deep breath and cough. Jason forgot all about Arni and escorted Brynna to the Captain's side.

Dr. Evans raised the head of the Captain's bed slightly. Brynna offered him a sip of water. His lips were so swollen, he had trouble drinking it without dribbling it down his chin. Dr. Evans began asking David questions to assess his cognitive abilities. "What's your name?"

David coughed again. In a raspy voice he answered, "David. What's your name?"

Brynna smiled weakly. David saw her and tried to smile, but his busted lip refused to cooperate.

Dr. Evans took it as a good sign but continued to ask questions. "David, do you know where you are? Do you know what happened to you?"

David looked around for a moment. "Med... bay?" He paused to catch his breath. "Six lowlifes... beat the crap out of me?"

Dr. Evans nodded. "Okay, good. That's good." David moaned. "Didn't feel good to me."

The doctor blinked for a minute. "Umm, sorry. That was a poor choice of words on my part. I'm just glad you don't have any brain damage."

David moaned again. "Not so sure… about that." Dr. Evans didn't know what David was trying to say, so he asked him to explain. David's speech was broken and slurred. "Took on… six guys... alone. Must have… brain damage."

Dr. Evans patted David's shoulder. "No, I assure you, your brain is working fine."

David twisted slightly in his bed trying to get more comfortable. "No, brain damage – before the attack." Dr. Evans finally realized David was cracking jokes, which was even more encouraging. Brynna rolled her eyes at him. Jason smiled and looked very relieved.

David saw Brynna watching him intently. He could see the mixed emotions on her face, even though his vision was distorted by the bruising and swelling to his left eye. He slowly lifted his right hand to touch her face. His arm was weak and unsteady. Brynna reached down to steady him. Jason scooted a chair up behind her. Brynna sat down, so David didn't have to reach so far to touch her. She gently held his hand against her cheek. She handled his hand gingerly. The skin on his knuckles was broken and raw from the blows he had landed on his attackers.

Dr. Evans gave the couple a semi-private moment, then stepped back up to move the bone grafter to the one bone he hated doing the most. It would take the least amount of time because of its size, but its small size meant precision aim and positioning. The doctor had to manually adjust the position of David's nose, keep him from moving during the grafting, and keep the grafter from moving. Dr. Evans took advantage of Jason's presence and enlisted his help. David started to object, but Dr. Evans gave him a sedative before he knew it was coming.

Brynna hadn't seen it coming either. All she saw was David becoming unconscious again. "What happened? Is he alright?"

Dr. Evans paused to look at her worried face and realized he should have prepared her. "I'm sorry. Yes, he's fine. I just sedated him, so I could do the bone graft on his nose. It seemed like he was starting to fight his treatment, and the nose is so precarious. If he moves during the repair, his nose could heal crooked."

Brynna smiled then laughed softly. Jason and Dr. Evans both gave her confused looks. "Did we miss something?" Jason queried.

"After what he did to me on Medoris, he deserved that."

Jason nodded and smiled as he remembered her anger at David for drugging her on Medoris. Dr. Evans was still in the dark. As the two continued to work on David, Jason told him the story.

Brynna was injured on Medoris and David had ordered her to be sedated, so she wouldn't stop him from taking on a local inhabitant in a battle to the death. The Captain knew he would be in a second duel to the death when he faced Brynna again.

Dr. Evans grinned slightly. He still wasn't comfortable with these three people, but the story was amusing. He looked over at Brynna. "I guess he got a return on his investment. I'm sorry it wasn't your idea though. That would have made it even better, I suppose." The two were done with his nose in just a couple minutes. It was just in time. The sedative had been short acting, and David stirred again. David's nose was the last bone to be grafted. Dr. Evans reached for another instrument to regenerate soft tissues such as muscle, tendons, ligaments, and skin. He started working on David's face first, but David kept trying to push him away. Dr. Evans told Jason to sedate David again. David pushed Jason away. "Don't... Don't... Stop. I... don't . . ."

Brynna stepped forward and pushed Jason out of the way herself.

She asked the two men to give her a second. "David, what's going on? Why are you pushing them away? They're just trying to help you." David mumbled something unintelligible. Brynna looked helplessly around the room. She knew David wanted to say something and it was important to him, but she couldn't make it out.

Arni had been standing quietly on the other side of the room. He walked over to David's bedside. David gave him a look that told Arni not to touch him in no uncertain terms. Despite the pained look on Arni's face, he clasped his own hands behind his back, then told Brynna what David wanted. "David doesn't want to be healed. He believes that if the bruises are gone, those who harmed him before will have reason to do so again. He does not want to be healed, by me specifically."

Arni addressed David directly. "I will honor your request not to heal you, but I can assure you, no one will try again to harm you. There's no reason to keep your bruises."

Brynna looked at David. "Is what he says true?"

David coughed and swallowed. "Yes," he replied in the same raspy tone. "Just make sure I can walk to – to my own execution." The haze from the sedative was starting to clear, and the repairs done to his lungs were taking effect slowly, but surely.

Brynna scowled. "Doctors? Is he mentally capable of making that sort of decision for himself? Should he be sedated again until you finish?"

David grabbed Brynna's arm with surprising firmness. "Brynna, I did this, and I'll take whatever they dish out. Don't sedate me." His voice was more steady than it had been.

Brynna winced. She knew it would disturb him greatly if she defied him over this. She looked up at the two doctors. "Honor his wishes, please." Brynna sat back down beside him and spent the next hour talking softly to him.

The guards came and escorted Jason back to his cell. Captain Parker made rounds to each of the crew's cells and assured them nothing like this would happen again. He updated them on the Captain's condition. Brynna was allowed to stay with David. That afternoon David and Brynna were moved to the joint cell they were told about. They were not supposed to spend the extra night together, but considering the circumstances, no one could find a reason not to allow it. It was also the only reason Dr. Evans agreed to release him from the Infirmary.

David was stiff, sore, and weak. He walked slowly to his new cell and sat down on the bed as soon as he entered. He immediately took a nap. Dr. Evans called to check on David a couple hours after moving out of the med bay. The doctor was opposed to letting David leave the Med Bay while he still needed healing. Brynna told him how much the walk to the cell had worn David out. When Dr. Evans checked in on him again late that afternoon, he decided, despite David's previous objections he needed more of a physical boost. The doctor gave him injections to reduce swelling and pain as well as an energy boost. As soon as David felt a little better he forced himself to move around and do a severely moderated exercise regimen. His bones were intact, but he still bore the bruises and swelling from his beating. His exercise regimen leaned more towards stretching instead of body building. He wanted to be sure he could walk confidently to his own execution. He wasn't sure why it was important to him. He just knew it was.

DEATH'S END

The next two days were a blur. David and Brynna had some hard discussions about the disposition of his body and the cover story to explain how he died. The story had to be sufficient to protect this world from the Commonwealth coming to investigate or seeking retribution. David told Brynna to bury him in space, so no one could investigate his death forensically. He instructed her to launch him into the sun prior to leaving the solar system. David contacted Rachel and asked her to give a copy of the last will and testament and burial instructions, recorded the previous night, to Brynna. He cautioned Brynna to alter the file log entries to backdate his last wishes. He was afraid it would arouse too many suspicions if it looked like he made out a new will days before his own death.

The story they decided to tell was that certain political factions on the planet, who remembered the Commonwealth, strongly objected to their presence. A group of rebels from one of these factions tried to assassinate the crew which resulted in David's death. Brynna silently decided she would spin it to make David as the one who saved them from the assassination plot. She knew if she said anything to him about it, he would object. He wanted to keep it as low key as possible. Brynna wanted him to receive the heroes honors he deserved. By agreeing to this plea agreement, he was saving the lives of his crew and everyone living on Drea III. If that didn't deserve a posthumous hero's recognition, then what did?

Brynna had more questions for David. These weren't easy questions to ask. She swallowed hard then asked. "Where do we go when we leave here? Do we continue the mission or head back to CIF headquarters?"

David thought about it for a few minutes. His plan, before they were arrested, was to return to Medoris and reprogram the data modules they left behind. He no longer wanted them to notify the Commonwealth of any contact with Arni, at least until he could be sure of what was going on between the Supreme Executor and Admiral Garcia. He still held onto his loyalty to the Commonwealth but knew sometimes individuals within any organization could be suspect. He wasn't ready to say the entire Commonwealth should be abandoned over the poor choices of one or two individuals. He also wasn't sure how to abandon an organization controlling the entire Galaxy. He paced back and forth in the confined space weighing her options then decided all he could do was advise her. It was ultimately her decision. "Brynna, this is a decision you'll have to make for yourself. You'll have to leave this planet, dispose of my body, and make the appropriate log entries. You and the crew will need to make sure your stories are mostly in agreement. Small discrepancies won't get anyone's attention, but large ones will. You'll need to notify my uncle and CIF of my death and file the reports. I had planned to go by Medoris and reprogram the data modules to stop them from alerting the CIF if Arni shows up there. You could go there then get back on a course coming from Drea before contacting CIF. If they know you went back to Medoris, they're going to want to know why. Perhaps you can find a legitimate reason to go back there."

David continued. "I don't know if they'll insist that you return or not. They may ask you if you're able to continue the mission alone. It's possible they could pull you off the mission, but each couple will have to decide for themselves whether they want to go on."

Brynna had a thought. "Maybe that could be our reason for returning to Medoris. I could take the crew there purely to regroup after a mission gone wrong. It's now considered Commonwealth territory. I'm not sure I want to take a three-week trip back with an overly stressed crew. What do I do about the investigation?"

David shook his head. "I would leave it alone for now. If the opportunity presents itself to ask some discreet questions fine, but we – uh you... the crew may find itself under a lot of scrutiny. I don't suggest you rock the boat any harder. If you get backed into a corner, tell them I turned and you had to execute me. Explain that you just didn't want my family to be embarrassed or disappointed in me. Just make sure they don't find out Arni has a presence here. Don't get yourself in any deeper."

Brynna began to tremble. "You want me to tell your uncle and your family that I..." She couldn't finish the sentence. Tears began to stream down her face again. David realized maybe he was asking too much of her. He sat down beside her. Putting his arm around her, he took her hand. "I'm sorry Brynna. Ask Jake to take the responsibility for it if you need to. He might even get a medal. It won't be a stretch for him. He's already threatened to shoot me. I would rather go out as dying in the line of duty, instead of as a traitor, but if it protects you and the crew, well, do what you have to. Maybe you're right about taking some time off on Medoris." The two sat there for a long time in silence just holding each other.

After a time, they laid down and fell asleep in each other's arms. Their sleep over the two days was erratic. They would sleep some and talk some. Between the emotional stress and David's weakened physical condition, his stamina wasn't up to par. Brynna found it easy to sleep when David did. The few times she wasn't able to sleep she contacted the crew and gave them updates.

Amid the difficult conversations, taking care of business, and David's needed rest breaks, the couple managed to have a few quiet intimate moments. Neither one was quite sure about how appropriate it was. Brynna was worried about David's unhealed injuries. David was worried it would make saying good-bye harder on Brynna. Ultimately, they let their feelings guide them more than their reason.

Captain Parker stopped by their cell to inform the two Brynna would be returned to her cell the next morning at 9:00 a.m. He didn't want the two of them getting caught off guard. He was also kind enough to ask if the couple needed anything. Brynna politely told the Captain they didn't need anything. David's situation was starting to affect his mood. He wryly responded to the Captain's question, "I could really use a full pardon."

Captain Parker winced. "I truly wish I could get one for you. I really do." The prison captain had dealt with criminals his entire career and this ship's crew just didn't fit the profile. He remembered David's comment about being a "prisoner of war." He had never dealt with wartime prisoners before. Maybe that was what made the situation feel so different.

David and Brynna's last night together ended all too quickly. David slept fairly well, but his pain medications were probably the sole reason he got any sleep at all. He woke up early in the morning feeling stiff, but good for the first time since his attack. He lay there in bed and watched Brynna sleep, trying to fill his mind with one last pleasant memory. He studied every curve of her face intently. He tried hard not to disturb her, but his love for her proved to be too much for him to resist. He reached over and gently caressed her face. Brynna stirred and let out a happy sigh. She opened her eyes and smiled at the sight of her handsome husband. The memory of where they were and what they were about to face had not yet touched her mind. The brief moment of innocence was a beautiful sight to behold. David saw it and recognized immediately when it did touch her. A sadness seeped into her eyes. She continued to smile, but the intensity paled by comparison. She was always happy to wake up and see his smiling face. She sadly realized if Arni didn't do as he promised, this would be the last time she would wake up and see his smiling face. David apologized for waking her then pulled her close to him. He wrapped his arms around her and held her for as long as he could. This was how the two had gone to sleep the night before and probably the only reason Brynna got any sleep. Somehow, she had quickly learned to feel safe in his arms which made sleep easy.

All too soon, their wake-up call sounded. The two slowly got up and began to shower and dress. They sat down at the table by the food processor and attempted to eat a light breakfast. Captain Parker had cautioned David about eating a heavy breakfast. He didn't really need to warn them because neither David or Brynna felt much like eating. They pushed themselves to eat a little because they knew their bodies would need it later. David needed it enough to get him to his execution, but no further.

A few minutes before nine, the couple began to say their final good byes.

"David, this just seems so surreal. I keep thinking somehow, we'll find a way out of this. I don't want to lose you. I hoped we would extend our marriage contract and start a family together. You are the most wonderful man I've ever met. You're so good, kind, and caring. You're one of the most intelligent people I know. I can't believe anyone could just erase your existence like this, as though you mean nothing. David, please, if Arni offers again to take your place, let him. He has amazing power, maybe he can bring himself back to life." Tears began to stream down her face again. David wrapped his arms around her as she began to sob.

"Brynna… Brynna… shhh…. Brynna, I wish I could let him take my place, but you know I can't. My orders are very specific about this. If I did let him take my place, it would definitely be treason. I have some serious doubts where the Commonwealth is concerned right now, but I'm not quite ready to take that step. You may have to do that in the near future, but only after you know all the facts. Brynna, I need you to be a strong commander. Make sure I don't die for nothing. Get the crew safely out of here, protect this world and others from senseless annihilation, find out who's responsible for Galat III, and make them pay for it."

Brynna was forcing herself to listen ever so carefully to every word coming out of David's mouth. She never wanted to forget his words. She quickly forgot her tears and felt an anger well up within her. Oh yes, someone was definitely going to pay for this travesty of justice. The irony of David's last sentence hit hard. Brynna pulled back from David, her face still wet with tears, but the fire of anger in her eyes. She gave him a look that suggested he had lost his mind. He was very driven in his discourse to her, but now he was hesitant. "What's wrong? What did I say that you objected to?"

Brynna blinked then answered. "You want me to protect the crew, avenge your death, investigate the Supreme Executor and the Admiral's board, and protect the galaxy from senseless violent deaths from an explorer class ship?!"

David took a deep breath before responding. As her words took their toll on him; he felt the wind leave his sails faster than it had filled them. "Okay, so maybe I'm asking a little much. I just don't want you to lay down and die with me. I want you to live a full and wonderful life. Find someone else to love and to love you. You deserve to be happy."

The guards reached the door and opened the privacy screen. They glanced at the clock. It was exactly 9:00 a.m.

Brynna knew David needed to know she would survive. "I will do my best to do everything you've asked, but no man can replace you, David. I love you." They exchanged one last passionate kiss and embrace as the guards tried to 'not' watch, without sacrificing being as observant as their job required.

As they completed their kiss, David replied to Brynna's promise. "That's my girl. You are the strongest, most beautiful woman I've ever known. It's been an honor to have you as my first and only wife and an honor serving with you as an officer on my ship. I turn the Evangeline and its crew over to you, Commander Alexander. I wish I could give you the field promotion as well, but that would really arouse suspicions."

Brynna stepped back and saluted. "I accept command, sir!"

David returned her salute and as the guards began to pull her away, he called after her. "I love you!" He watched as the guards escorted her away.

The Captain noticed, since his attack, the number of guards had greatly increased. He was somewhat relieved by their presence, even though it had been guards who attacked him before. He also noticed they were changed out frequently. When Captain Parker stopped by the evening before, he told David all six men had been apprehended. The men were now facing a military tribunal and the charges included attempted murder. Jake identified each one of the men and the DNA samples confirmed the identifications. Although the video surveillance had been disabled, the men were identified as entering the facility and no one could give them an alibi for the time of the attack. One of the men had been the one who slapped Cheyenne the evening they were arrested. Captain Parker told David he had the right to record a statement to be given at sentencing if he wished. David told the Captain he would give it some thought, but he didn't want to take any time away from Brynna. Now it seemed he had a couple hours to kill before they killed him.

David sat down by the computer to contemplate what message he would send to the ruffians who nearly killed him. As he considered his words, David was suddenly aware of someone in the room with him. Without looking up, he said, "Hello, Arni."

Arni moved over and sat down opposite the Captain. "That's good. I'm glad you can recognize my presence. You'll need that ability soon enough."

David looked up at Arni and raised one eyebrow. "Since I'm scheduled to be dead in less than three hours, would you mind telling me how such a skill is going to come in handy?"

Arni shook his head. "No, not yet."

David leaned back and folded his arms over his chest. "Oh, by all means take your time. I've got all the time in the world. Oh wait, I almost forgot. I do have an appointment at noon. I hope that won't inconvenience you at all, but I plan on being dead for the better part of the day."

Arni's facial expression didn't change. "This day will unfold the way my father intends."

David threw up his hands. "So, what did you come here to tell me? Or ask of me? Not that I have much to give at this point. I gave my ship and crew to Brynna and I'm giving my life to the Dreans. I guess I can give you the last two and a half hours of my time."

Again, Arni's face didn't change its serious look. "I'll take whatever you're willing to give, but you have far more than this lifetime to offer. Your body can die, that much is true. The thing which makes you all that you are, is immortal. It cannot die. Do you remember standing in the fire circle on Medoris looking for the shuttle?"

David nodded, and Arni continued. "You were quietly wishing you had a god to pray to. You told the Akamu you have never seen any gods. Today you will stand in my father's presence and you will know what it is to be in the presence of power beyond your comprehension. He will show you all you need to know about your immortality and what's at stake. He will tell you what it is he wants from you, but the decision is still up to you as to what you do with the information."

David sat there staring at Arni. The thought that Arni had some sort of mental disease crossed his mind, but he seemed so stable David had trouble accepting that explanation. There was also the question of why the Supreme Executor didn't want Arni dead. Perhaps this was an elaborate deception. If he were insane, why would it matter? Several other questions formed in his mind. Why would Arni send him to see Pateras? Why wouldn't Arni just tell him whatever he needed to know?

Before he could voice his questions, Arni began to answer them. "When you stood in that fire ring wishing for a god to pray to, my father was rekindling a deep desire within you, and all of mankind. No man wants to die and certainly not alone. My father was there with you, but you haven't learned to know his presence. You're getting closer. I'm here with you now, because you still don't want to die alone. I'm sending you to my father, because he's the only one you'll believe. Right now, you believe I am either insane or a liar. With the power I have at my disposal, you had better hope I am neither of those things."

As David considered Arni's last statement, his heart began to pound. Any being, capable of bringing the dead to life and reading minds, would be a formidable force to contend with, but if such a being were also dishonest or insane? David shuddered. Arni was certainly right on that point.

Arni had one more point to make. "David your decision to die for your crew is truly admirable. It is a level of loving and caring beyond any other. Wouldn't you agree?"

David nodded. "I suppose. I think I would prefer to spend another fifty or sixty years demonstrating my love by being there to care for my wife and crew with my life rather than my death."

"Of course you would. I want you to have that as well. My question is this; would you not consider giving one's life for another the greatest sacrifice of all? The greatest gesture of love?"

David shrugged. "I suppose. I'm proud of my crew. They're a good crew, but I'm not sure love is the right word for it."

Arni leaned forward and propped his arms on the table in front of him. "Let's take Brynna out of the equation. Brynna is released free and clear. She's safely back on the Evangeline. Would you still give up your life to save the rest of your crew?"

David pictured the faces of his crew. It took him a minute to align his thoughts with Brynna out of the equation. He began to nod, "Yes, I would still do this."

Arni nodded. "Let's take it a step further. What if the entire crew was released except one? What if it were say, Jake? Would you give your life to save Jake's?"

David scowled. What exactly was Arni getting at? David had to think a second longer. Jake had been a thorn in his side from day one, but he was also a trusted and valued member of his crew. He also had to consider what was best for the entire crew. He knew at some point he might need to send Jake or any other crewmen on a suicide mission, but this was different. Arni interrupted David's thoughts to make the decision clearer. "Let's say the plea agreement is still under discussion. The judge and the prosecutor have agreed to release the entire crew, except one person has to die and they don't care who. Is it your security chief who's responsible for protecting you and the rest of the crew, or is it you? Who do you choose?"

"I would still do this. I'm responsible for my entire crew. I can't expect my crew to give their lives for me if I'm not willing to do the same. If the entire ship were in trouble and I was in the middle of command decisions on the bridge, I would send another to die if needed to save the rest of the crew, but that's not this situation."

Arni shook his head. "Actually, that is this situation, only my father is in command and he's sending me to die to save the other lives at stake. Would you die for a total stranger?"

David scowled again. "Accept a death penalty for a stranger? Let me think… uh, NO!"

Arni leaned back in his chair and rubbed his chin thoughtfully. "A madman starts killing people randomly in the streets. Would you put yourself between him and a total stranger?"

David nodded. "Okay sure, I might do that, but I'm not going to take on crimes I didn't commit to save the life of someone who's guilty."

Arni smiled. They were making progress. Arni could have told him straight up what his point was, but David needed to arrive at his own conclusion. "Okay, now, suppose you knew beyond a doubt, Galat was going to be destroyed and you ordered the crew to file false reports, but Brynna deliberately filed the correct reports. Galat's population is destroyed and Drea demands her life as payment. Do you let her die?"

The thought of Brynna's death was not pleasant to David at all and he was losing patience with Arni's cat and mouse game. He bolted out of his chair and began to pace restlessly. He really had to think about this one. In Arni's new scenario, David had "falsified records" and committed treason while Brynna had followed the regulations, but it resulted in the death of an entire civilization. Arni waited quietly while David considered his options. David finally turned back towards Arni. "Ultimately, I am responsible for any member of my crew and their actions so yes, I would take her place. Where are we going with this anyway?"

"I want to know at what point do you let others pay for their own crimes and how far do you go to save their lives?"

David placed his fists on his hips. "I don't know."

"One more time. You and the entire crew are released. Brynna and Jake report you as being corrupted by me and she defies your orders to keep my name out of the reports. You catch her just as she's about to send the reports to CIF Headquarters. She's committed mutiny. What do you do with her and Jake?"

David was getting vexed. "I suppose it depends on why they did it and whether I thought they could be trusted anymore or not."

"So, you need to know what's in their hearts? You want to know if they are misguided or guilty of treachery?"

"Yeah, I guess so. There's a lot to consider."

Arni pushed still further. "A lot to consider for just two of the people who are accountable to you, but what if you were responsible for all of mankind?"

David's eye brows seemed to be irreversibly knit together at this point. "All of mankind? Are you referring to the Supreme Executor? Are you blaming all of this on him?"

Arni shook his head again. He leaned forward again. "What if you knew the hearts of all men both good and evil? What if you knew the penalty for their crimes was a death so horrible and so eternal you would do anything you could to try and prevent it. Would you do it?"

"You're waxing a bit philosophical, aren't you?" David spoke before he realized Arni's facial expression still had not changed. He was quite serious.

Arni knew he had stretched the situation beyond what David could realistically imagine, but he intended to push him that far, like a balloon that needed to be stretched before it could be inflated. Now it was time to relax the stretching of the balloon and try again to inflate it. "Let me bring the scale down a little. You're being executed for what happened on Galat. What if this world was also condemned to be destroyed by the Commonwealth and the only thing that could stop it, is your death? Would you die to save this world? Would you die to save the billions of lives on this world, Moderator Tarmon, Rachel Johan, Captain Parker, Colonel Bernt to name a few? You know there are criminals here. You've met at least six of them. Would you die to stop the destruction of Drea?"

David felt a weight descend on him. "I – I don't know. Maybe."

Arni stood up and moved towards the door to David's cell. He stopped and turned to face David. "Here's the one thing you need to know. That horrible painful death is the coming destruction mentioned in the Ancient Texts. Every single human being will face it. No one will escape unless they choose to stand with me. But before I can protect anyone from it, I have to face it myself. I must lay my life down to offer protection to others. That's why I have to die and why Luciano doesn't want me to die. He knows how much it hurts us when our people die without hope. I want you to live, that's the reason I have to die."

David shook his head. "You know the United World Council won't go for that even if I did."

"David, that piece of you and of all men I told you was immortal, it still feels pain. Remember that when you make the sentencing statement for those six men. There's still a chance for them, if you give it to them."

David looked at the computer and realized as soon as he did Arni had left him. He looked back around his cell to confirm what he already knew. Yes, he was alone again. David moved to the computer and recorded his statement.

"I would like to say this to the men who nearly beat me to death. I forgive you. I know you were angry at the deaths occurring on Galat III. What I suppose you didn't know was if I had known for a fact what was going to happen to them, I never would have filed those reports. I didn't know your Intercessor spoke the truth. I had just met him. It would seem you don't trust strangers any more than I did. The knowledge I had at the time was that the Commonwealth had declared war on the House of Liontari, so as any good soldier, I reported the location of the enemy. Knowing what I do now, I would not make the same mistake again. The deaths on Galat hit me and my crew hard as well. We ask for your forgiveness for the mistakes we made."

"To the body who will decide the fate of these men I would like to say this. Your Intercessor is a wise man. He asked me to consider my words to this court carefully. He suggests there is something within these six men worth saving, so I ask this court to be lenient with them. No situation like this has ever happened before and it presented them with a temptation so great, how could they resist? Their desire was to help the Intercessor by taking revenge on me in his behalf. It was a mistake. I think we would all agree on that, but again I ask you to take these things under consideration in deciding their punishment. They did not kill me, although by the time you hear this I will be dead, but it was not by their hands. There's been far too much blood shed. Please don't shed any more on my behalf. Their deaths won't help me, and it won't do them any favors either. Thank you for your consideration."

David thought he could feel Arni smiling. He shook his head. It had to be his imagination. David recorded time delayed messages to each of his crew members then puttered around the cell straightening the only things possible in the room. He made the bed, disposed of the dirty laundry and dishes then laid back down on his bed to wait.

David's execution was scheduled for noon. Half an hour before his scheduled execution time, four guards showed up at his cell along with Captain Parker. Captain Parker stood at the door to David's cell. "Are we going to have a problem with this?"

David was still lying on his bed staring at the ceiling. He sat up slowly and looked at the four guards. He shook his head. "No. I won't resist."

Captain Parker nodded to his men. One of the men opened the door. Two men entered, flanked the doorway and drew the disciplinary rods David had encountered his first day in jail. One of the guards ordered David to stand up, face the back wall, get down on his knees and place his hands on his head. Captain Alexander complied. He moved slowly, in part to keep from spooking the guards and secondly, because he was still stiff and slow. David got into place and waited for the guards to reach him. The second two men approached. One of them watched him carefully while the other pulled his hands behind his back and attached the binders to his wrists. Now secured, the prisoner was escorted down the hall by the five men. None of them said anything more than necessary. The weight David felt before seemed to return. He hadn't really taken the time to mourn his own death. He had kept his mind on business and on trying to take care of Brynna and the crew. He felt like every beat of his heart was loud enough to be heard by everyone around him.

Captain Alexander was taken to a small auditorium where he was placed between two columns. Two of the guards drew their rods again to insure their prisoner's cooperation. The other two removed his binders and placed one arm on top of each column. Each wrist was secured in place with a fixed set of binders.

His method of execution was by a radiation energy pulse capable of burning him from the inside out. The Dreans had determined this was the pulse used on Galat III based on the residual energy signature. This pulse would kill humans and some animals without destroying the physical structures or plant life. A ring of energy rods was positioned above his head and pointed directly at him. They were dark and lifeless now, but they would light up with an invisible radioactive fire soon enough.

David looked around at his surroundings. The room was lit using sky lights and lots of small windows in the walls near the ceiling. The sun was high enough in the sky to be in his eyes. David moved his head around to get a better view of the room. Directly in front of him was what appeared to be a control panel. Behind and above the control panel were observation rooms angled around his platform. Two doors in the rear of the center room opened. His crew was ushered in and their binders removed. The crew caught sight of David and moved to the front of their observation area. Brynna gently placed her hand on the glass, trying to be as close to him as she could get.

Movement in one of the other rooms caught David's attention. He saw Moderator Tarmon, Arbiter Navid and several other dignitaries taking seats. He also saw Colonel Bernt standing in the rear of the room. Was it his imagination or were they having trouble making eye contact with him? He took a small amount of comfort in thinking they regretted executing him.

As the time for the execution approached everyone was asked to take their seats. Rachel Johan entered the room with the crew. She encouraged them to take their seats.

A door opened to David's left. Arni entered and walked towards him. It felt as though everything was moving in slow motion. He could hear his heart beating slowly and loudly in his ears. As Arni came near him, David saw Brynna jump up and touch the glass again. He wondered why she reacted so strongly to Arni's presence. She knew his presence would change nothing. David looked back at Arni as he stopped directly in front of him. David attempted some weak humor. "Trying to make sure you got a front row seat?"

Arni ignored his question. "You will survive this. You have my word. You may not see me, but I will always be with you. Don't be afraid, no matter what you see."

Captain Parker suggested the Intercessor take his seat. Arni moved away to a discreet distance.

Captain Parker went back to the control panel to begin the ceremonial part of the execution. He began by reading off the crimes David and the crew had been convicted of. He read the terms of the Mercy Agreement, which admonished the crew to honor the sacrifice of their Captain by preserving the lives of others threatened by the Commonwealth. Captain Parker asked the crew. "Do you accept your Captain's death in your places and this agreement?" David had ordered them to comply when he met with them to give them their final orders. The crew grudgingly accepted the agreement. David could see looks of anger and fear on the crew's faces.

Captain Parker continued his discourse. "As per the conditions of the plea agreement, the prisoner known as Captain David Liam Alexander will suffer the death intended for himself and his eleven other crew members. His face will be covered as an act of mercy. The method of execution prescribed is meant to fit his crimes. The people of Galat were killed with a weapon of an unknown energy signature. The courts found a radioactive energy pulse with a similar signature. While the most humane death would be instantaneous, the Captain has volunteered to take on the punishment of his entire crew. His death will be prolonged purposefully. He will be hit with twelve metered pulses. The last of which will be fatal."

Captain Parker paused to let everyone catch their breath and for his words to sink in. He looked at the room where the dignitaries were seated. Moderator Tarmon looked at her companions to see if anyone wanted to say anything. Chancellor Torrell volunteered a curt, "Get on with it." Moderator Tarmon returned her gaze to Captain Parker. She nodded to him to continue. The Captain looked at the Intercessor who had not yet left the room. "Intercessor, would you like to speak? You are by far the most wounded party."

The Intercessor walked to the control panel and faced the assembly. "My father gives you much more today than you understand. He is both just and merciful. Moderator Tarmon, I charge you with the task of seeing the one death that happens here today pays the full price for all crimes. Do not let others try to deter you from what I have asked. Today I will lay everything down for all of mankind and the war with Luciano Hale is settled. David, your crimes against me and my father are forgiven." The Intercessor walked away from the control panel.

One of the guards leaned over and whispered to Captain Parker. "I'm not sure I understood a thing he just said."

Captain Parker shrugged and whispered. "Me either."

Captain Parker moved back in front of the microphone to finish this difficult task. "Crew of the Evangeline, remember the sacrifice your Captain makes here today. His pain was meant to be your pain. His death should have been yours. Never forget the agreement you made on his behalf. Mercy has been granted to you; give the same mercy to others. May Lord Liontari have mercy on his soul and on yours."

Captain Parker asked David. "Do you have any last words?" David glanced over at Captain Parker and nodded.

Captain Parker told him to proceed. "Crew of the Evangeline, it has been an honor serving with you. There's no finer crew in the Commonwealth. I stayed to try and protect this world from the same fate as Galat III and it has cost us dearly. Don't let me die for nothing. Follow my last orders. Keep to the agreement, no matter what."

His eyes moved from the crew to Brynna. As he focused on her beautiful face that was covered with sorrow, he spoke passionately. "Brynna, I love you."

He looked around further to find Arni. "Arni..." Arni stepped forward again. "Arni, I'm sorry. I didn't know what they were going to do. I've been a part of something that turned out to be very wrong. Please, can you ever forgive me?" Even though Arni had already conveyed his forgiveness, David had to express his own regrets and again ask for forgiveness. It was more because he couldn't forgive himself.

Arni placed his hand on David's shoulder. "I forgive you."

David looked at Brynna's face. He wanted more than anything to stay alive and be with her. He too had hoped they would extend their marriage contract and one day have children together. He looked back at Arni. Arni tightened his grip on David's shoulder. "You will see her again, sooner than you think. My father would like to speak to you first." David's heart continued to pound faster and louder in his ears. He suddenly felt very heavy as though the weight of the world were on his shoulders. He didn't feel like he was about to pass out. It was unlike anything he had ever felt before. "Your father is here?" David suddenly wondered if this were a ploy to protect Pateras El Liontari's location.

Arni smiled knowing David's thoughts. "No, you're going to where he is." David watched Arni turn and walk away.

Arni walked over to Brynna, smiled and touched the glass where her hand was resting. She felt a sense of calm wash over her. She sat down in her seat again. Marissa sat down beside her and held her hand. Lexi sat on the other side and grasped her other hand. Brynna felt her hands grow cold. She gripped the hands of the other two women firmly.

A guard walked over to David and discreetly placed a mouth guard between his teeth. He softly told David to bite down on it before the first jolt, to ease his discomfort a little, as well as focus any desire he might have to scream. It was meant to help him protect his image as a man of strength. Next a hood was placed over his head.

David began to breathe faster. He couldn't see more than lights or shadows because of the hood over his head. The air inside it quickly grew stale. The Captain bit down on the bite guard in his mouth. He was really hoping to die with a certain amount of dignity. He took several slow deep breaths. He heard a motor start up and begin to hum. Although he could see little, he did see the rods aimed at him begin to light up.

Captain Parker continued his speech. "I will read the names of each of the men and women granted mercy as each pulse is applied, so you will never forget your Captain's sacrifice beginning with the lowest rank to highest."

David heard Captain Parker call out "Chief Petty Officer Jacob Holden." Remembering his conversation with Arni about whether he would give his life for Jake, David thought it ironic Jake was the first name called. David heard a crackle and felt a hot jolt run through his body, then nothing.

Jake sat on the other side of Marissa and held her other hand. He was angry. Angry with himself for not insisting they leave this planet, for not fighting back, for not defending the Captain in their cell, angry at the Captain for not letting him take his place, and angry the crew had to watch this.

Brynna was trying hard to be a commander and not a wife because the crew would take their cues from her from this point on. When the first jolt went through David's body, she saw him jerk and twitch as all his muscles tightened then released. She heard him groan. Where was Arni? Arni said he would save David. She tried to think. What were Arni's exact words? He said not one of the crew would die on this planet. Did David count as one of the crew? She had thought that was what he meant. He also said he would take David's punishment. Was Arni wrong? Was she wrong to get her hopes up? Was she wrong to trust Arni?

Captain Parker called out the second name, "Ensign Cheyenne Dominick"

Brynna and the crew watched helplessly as David was hit with jolt after jolt. With every jolt Brynna caught herself squeezing the hands of Marissa and Lexi. Cheyenne was sitting next to Lazaro. Lazaro had his arm wrapped around her while she cried quietly on his shoulder. When Captain Parker called her name out she buried her face in Lazaro's chest and sobbed openly. Lazaro did his best to comfort her but stared angrily at the proceedings.

"Ensign Aulani Ryder"

Thane sat with his arm around Aulani. He was torn between sorrow and anger. He squeezed Aulani's hand. Aulani returned his firm grip. She never made a sound, but tears ran silently down her face. When her name was called she gripped Thane's hand even more tightly. She wanted desperately to close her eyes. She forced herself to watch to honor the Captain's sacrifice even though he couldn't see her watching.

"Lieutenant Junior Grade Marissa Holden."

Marissa's heart was breaking despite knowing that somehow, everything would be okay. When her name was called, she instinctively gripped Jake and Brynna's hands as though her own life depended on it. Quiet slow tears slipped down her face. A thousand thoughts vied for a place in her mind. Was Arni trustworthy? Did she dare think he would get her Captain out of this? Would he resurrect the Captain the way he had brought her back to life? Was this really the end for the Captain? The questions continued to flood her mind making the whole thing surreal.

"Lieutenant Junior Grade Laurel Adams"

Jason and Laura sat there grasping each other's hands with stricken looks on their faces. Since Jason was a doctor and Laura a trained medic, the two were more accustomed to having a professional disconnect. This was harder than anything they had ever encountered. Laura jumped when the jolt meant for her caused the Captain's weakened body to convulse and his knees to buckle. It was several seconds before she realized she had stopped breathing.

"Lt. Thane Ryder"

Thane's jaw was set firmly in place as he gritted his teeth and held Aulani. A muscle in his jaw began to twitch as his name was called. Aulani offered what little comfort she could to him. He couldn't help but grip her hand more tightly as they heard the moans of pain from the dying man. Thane watched him get pulled against his binders by the painful, invisible pulses causing his body to convulse and writhe.

"Lt. Alexia Flint"

Lexi stared in horror as she tried to keep her emotions in check for Brynna's sake. She had both of her hands holding one of Brynna's hands. Brynna squeezed tighter with each jolt. When Lexi's name was called, she couldn't help but squeeze back.

"Lt. Commander Jason Adams"

By this time, Jason wanted to jump up and take the Captain's place. The sight of it sickened him. He had worked feverishly to save this man's life just two days ago, and now he was in part responsible for his pain and death. A doctor's job was to save lives, not take them.

"Lt. Commander Lazaro Dominick"

David and Lazaro had developed a bond in the Sorley village on Medoris. Lazaro sat there trying to comfort Cheyenne, but inside he was torn between being grateful, and feeling lost and angry. He held Cheyenne closer and blinked back tears of his own.

"Lt. Commander Braxton Flint"

Braxton was sitting next to Lexi. Braxton had one arm around her shoulders and gripped the arm of his chair with the other. He was having trouble believing this was actually happening. He had a tremendous amount of respect and admiration for the Captain. The man seemed invincible. He had rescued Lexi from her kidnappers, survived the fire ring – twice, and survived a tornado. He kept the crew safe. Braxton realized the Captain was still doing it. He still had trouble accepting that David was about to be dead.

"Commander Brynna Alexander"

Brynna could not stop the tears from flowing down her face. She remained silent and composed, despite her tears and feelings. As the number of jolts got closer to twelve, the crew could tell they were taking their toll on the Captain. The binders kept him from collapsing to the floor, but his body sagged weakly. He had been unable to stand after the third pulse. After the eleventh jolt, there was a pause as if to give everyone a chance to prepare themselves.

Captain Parker read the last name on the crew manifest. "Captain David Liam Alexander."

The last jolt hit prompting a more forceful cry of pain. Something wasn't right about the sound. Brynna had never seen her husband in a situation even remotely close to this one, but something wasn't right. As soon as the last jolt passed through his body and was gone. She jumped to her feet. She couldn't help but cry out, "David!" The tears that had already been silently streaming down her face stopped.

Marissa's heart was breaking for Brynna, and she could stand it no longer. She jumped up and hugged Brynna. Brynna couldn't take her eyes off the limp body in front of her. How could this be considered an act of mercy? How could an advanced society be so cruel?

One of the prison guards walked around and scanned for any signs of life. Seeing none he looked over at Captain Parker, "It's done. He's gone." As soon as the words came out of his mouth the room went dark and a tremor shook the entire building. Everyone looked up at the sky lights, but it appeared to be pitch black outside. The internal lights operated on a light sensor and came on seconds later. The Moderator looked around stunned at what just happened. Instead of demanding intelligence reports, she sat there gripping the arms of her chair looking at the collapsed body in front of her. The room around her was full of turmoil. Some clamored to get out of the building for fear another quake would cause it to collapse. Some activated communication units to find out what happened. Captain Parker was no longer concerned with David. He was more concerned with whether his other prisoners were still properly confined.

Arni's words still ran through Brynna's mind. She stood there looking at the limp body in front of her, remembering the last cry of pain she heard. It didn't sound like David. She looked up at the sky lights. It was still several hours until sunset, but it was like the darkest night she had ever seen only there were no stars. She gently extricated herself from Marissa's hug. She turned to Rachel who was confused by the sudden turn of events. "Rachel, I need to see his face!"

Rachel, still stunned, had trouble making sense of Brynna's words. "What? What do you need?"

Brynna swallowed hard. She knew this wasn't going to make sense to anybody and she knew it would sound like she had lost her mind. "I need to see his face. Something isn't right. I need to know if that really is David."

Rachel glanced at the others. Lexi volunteered an explanation. "Sometimes a person has to have some validation for their grief. She's wrestling with the grief stage known as denial. Please let her see him."

Rachel nodded and left the booth still feeling stunned.

Brynna looked at Lexi. Her mind was clear and sharp. "Where's Arni?" The crew looked around to see if they could see him. No one remembered seeing where he went when he left the execution chamber.

Rachel went directly to the Moderator who had trouble hearing for all the commotion. She finally called out to everyone. "Silence!" Rachel explained again what Brynna wanted. The Moderator followed Rachel back to the room where the crew was being held.

Moderator Tarmon addressed Brynna and the crew. "You have my deepest sympathies for your loss. Commander, I understand you wanted some time with your husband's body? I'm afraid we cannot allow you to touch the body until the third day when we release him to you. It's to insure no deception has occurred, no drugs imitating death were used, that sort of thing. I know it sounds insane, but it is meant to prevent even the appearance of impropriety. I hope you understand."

Brynna persisted. "I don't need to touch him. I just need to see him, to know for sure he's the one who's dead."

The Moderator thought Brynna was grasping at straws. "Who else would it be? You saw him there before the execution."

Brynna was trying very hard to keep herself under control but was fast reaching a point of desperation. "You know it wasn't David. You know exactly who that was."

The Moderator looked at Brynna. For a second, she thought Brynna had lost her mind until she remembered the Intercessor's words just prior to the execution. Her face went white. Rachel was afraid the woman was about to pass out. "Wait here!" The Moderator ordered as she brusquely left the room.

Rachel wasn't sure whether to go or stay. She looked at Brynna. "What are you thinking? Who do you think is out there?"

Brynna felt herself shiver. Rachel was significantly shorter than Brynna. Brynna looked down to make eye contact. "It's Arni, your Intercessor." This time, it was Rachel's turn to look pale as she recalled the Intercessor's words in recent days.

The Moderator went directly to Captain Parker. She instructed him to get the body onto a gurney immediately and to bring him over in front of the observation room where Brynna and the crew were waiting. Captain Parker frowned. "Moderator Tarmon, I need to make sure the prison facilities are still secure after that quake. I will get to..."

The woman was not interested. "No, Captain! The prison can wait. This woman needs to see her husband's face and so do I. Do this now!"

The Captain, seeing how rattled she was and seeing Brynna's anxiety from across the room, quickly complied. As Captain Alexander had earned his respect in the short time he had known him, Captain Parker ordered his men to treat the body with the utmost respect. They gently removed the binders, lifted the body onto the gurney, and covered it with a sheet. Captain Parker had only known David briefly, but he had learned David was a man of integrity. He thought, under different circumstances, they might have been friends. The men rolled the gurney over near the window. The crew gathered close to the window.

Captain Parker stood between the body and the crew. He didn't want the crew to see him remove the mouth guard in case it was bloody from the Captain accidentally biting himself. He pulled the sheet back and started gently removing the hood. He pulled the mouth guard out intending to wrap it in the hood. As soon as the hood was clear of the head, he and the Moderator both gasped. Brynna had been right. There in front of them lay the body of Arni Sotaeras Liontari, their most important religious leader. Captain Parker backed away. Terrified, he fell to his knees. As he moved away, Brynna and the others could now see it wasn't their beloved Captain. A wave of shock and relief passed through the room. Arni had somehow switched places with David as promised. So where was Captain Alexander?

David heard nothing, felt nothing. Why did he feel nothing? He couldn't see anything. There were supposed to be twelve jolts not one. He felt heavy at first then he experienced a falling sensation. Had something gone wrong? He was falling faster and faster. He wondered if he were dead or just unconscious. A light became visible in the distance. Maybe he wasn't dead. It grew larger and brighter until he was surrounded by a light so brilliant it seemed to pass straight through his body. He halfway expected to look down at his hands and see the outline of his bones through the skin. He couldn't see his bones, but his skin did seem to have a peculiar glow. He tried to get his eyes to focus on what was around him. The light was too bright. Was this death?

A voice spoke to him. He seemed to hear it both with his ears and in his mind simultaneously. "No, you aren't dead."

There was smoke blowing all around him. He couldn't see anyone to go with the voice he heard. David tried to take a couple steps, but he couldn't make out much because the smoke was so thick. He finally asked. "Who's there? Who are you?"

The voice spoke again. "You know who I am, David. I am Pateras El Liontari."

The smoke swirled away from him. David began to make out a set of stairs and the vague image of someone sitting on a throne. The young captain strained to see a face, but as he came nearer, two large men with swords stood in front of him. They drew their swords and held him at bay. David raised his hands in surrender and backed away a couple steps.

"Okay fellas, take it easy." The two men didn't relax. "Why can't I come any closer? I just wanted to see your face and look you in the eye."

Pateras spoke again. "My power is too great for your human body to handle even looking at. No man can see me and live. I would like to keep you alive."

David backed further away feeling frustrated. "Why? Why do you want me alive?"

The mysterious voice of Pateras explained. "First, I created you. You are my child. I created all of mankind, and I don't want harm to come to any of you. There are more humans than you can count, and I created them all, each one unique. Even those you call identical twins have differences. The second reason is I need someone who will go up against the Supreme Executor. I want you to be my voice and a warrior in my army. I want you to bring me into the Commonwealth."

David shook his head. "I think I need more reason than that to commit treason. I've already faced one death penalty today."

"I could give you many reasons, but you would not trust any of them because they came from me. I am still a stranger to you. You haven't learned to trust me yet. You do believe I am less of a threat than you were initially led to believe. What I will do though is, I will tell you where to look to find the answers for yourself. Would that seem reasonable to you?"

"Why do you ask me questions you already know the answers to?" David queried.

Pateras returned his query with interest. "Why do you have doubts about me when you already know what I am capable of? You know who and what I am. You know I have done nothing but help you. I have protected you and your crew. I am not the one who wants to destroy you. Luciano Hale would like nothing more than to hurt me the only way he can. He cannot harm me directly as much as he would like to. The only thing he can do is destroy what I have created. I took great joy in creating mankind. You were created with such beauty and innocence and now there is blood on your hands. I will show you the full extent of what the Dark Lord has done to you."

David looked down at his hands. The whiteness that had been there before was now gone and the same blood he had seen in his dream now covered his hands, arms and was splattered on his shirt and pants. In a flash, he saw the actual death of every man, woman and child on Galat.

He also saw every selfish moment in his life, every lie he ever told, the toy he had stolen from another child in school, the fight he picked with another boy when they both liked the same girl. The night after his graduation from the CIF academy and the girl he had been with. He could never remember her name, until now. The list of bad moments in his life was longer than he realized.

David's mind flashed back to his early days in the CIF. He had been sent on a police action to a new Commonwealth World still in its period of unrest. Some dissidents were cornered on a rooftop. He had his laser rifle trained on them as they fought against the troops closing in on them. David received orders to take them out to prevent further loss of life. He fired taking the life of the first one. A second man, seeing the direction David had fired from, returned fire. David promptly fired again and killed the second. He moved his aim to the third who was in the process of dropping his weapon. He took no chances and dropped the third man despite his apparent surrender. He had shoved the incident into the back recesses of his mind and tried to justify his actions. His superiors had no qualms regarding his actions and had given him a commendation. Deep down he knew his actions were wrong.

When the magnitude of all the wrongs he had committed began to descend on him, it weighed so heavily on him, it brought him to his knees. The power and brightness of Pateras surrounded him. The smoke swirled around him. He could feel the light pass straight through his body. It now burned within him. His chest began to feel tight and heavy. David felt a conflict between the darkness within him and the light from Pateras. He wanted to run away or hide but couldn't move. The heaviness pushed him further down onto his hands and knees. Every fiber of his being felt like it was on fire. His lungs refused to draw air in and he no longer felt like he could breathe. "Please… stop! I can't take… anymore." The weight began to lift, and the smoke cleared. David sat back on his heels and took a deep breath. "I don't – understand. What just happened to me?"

Pateras' voice now sounded very sad. "You saw the evil within you as it touched the good I created. You felt the weight of your own guilt for all the wrongs you have done at one time. The guilt and shame are easy to ignore when you see only one event at a time. Now imagine that ugliness multiplied by every human who ever existed. I never wanted any of you to live with that."

David took another deep breath. "What do you want from me?"

"Allow me to show you." A wall of the smoke separated, and David looked around. He caught his breath and felt like he was about to fall. He appeared to be in space and heading for a planet. A man appeared at his side and grabbed his arm to steady him. David looked at the man beside him. "Who are you?"

The man, who stood a full head taller than David, introduced himself. "Your Lt. Lexi Flint knew me as Gabe. My appearance is not as she saw me then, but I am still the same person."

David's eyes narrowed. He doubted the man's word. "I thought Arni was the one who appeared as Gabe."

The man remained undaunted. "My Lord was the one who sent me to protect her. I told her everything my Lord asked me to tell her. I was there as his representative."

David accepted the explanation and moved on. "Where are we going?" As they raced through the stars, David saw one planet growing larger in the distance. "Is that planet where we are going?"

Gabe nodded, but said nothing. David was still trying to make sense of his surroundings. Space was cold and had no air, but David wasn't cold, and he wasn't suffocating. The two descended onto the planet's surface. As they came down, David expected his ears to start popping due to the changes in altitude, but again, nothing happened like he expected. Gabe escorted David through a beautiful garden. The grass was the softest he had ever walked on. He reached down and touched it. It was soft enough to lay down and sleep on. The garden was filled with fruit trees, vegetables and a wide variety of flowers.

David asked Gabe again. "Where are we?"

Gabe spread his arms wide. "This is a world created for your people to live on. David looked around at the scenery. Everywhere he looked, everything was beautiful and peaceful. The sun was just coming up over the horizon. A rustling from behind him caught his attention. He turned in time to see a large furry beast, belonging to the cat family bounding towards them. David prepared to bolt for the nearest tree. Gabe put a reassuring hand on his shoulder. When the animal reached Gabe, it stopped and laid down at Gabe's feet. Gabe smiled and reached down to pet the large beast. The beast began to purr like a kitten. David looked up at Gabe who nodded. Captain Alexander cautiously reached down and gave the animal a few strokes as well. He was amused such a large animal could be so playful.

Gabe saw the tension on David's face drain away. "Just in case you run into this animal on another world, it is a dangerous animal. The animals on this world are all herbivores, but their counterparts on other worlds are carnivores. Don't take this liberty elsewhere."

David glanced down at the animal suspiciously. He stopped stroking the cat and stood up. "So why are we here?"

Gabe pointed to two buildings on the horizon. "Those buildings each contain springs of water. One contains the Eternal Waters, the other contains the Waters of Understanding. The Waters of Understanding are forbidden to drink from. The people placed here were told never to drink or even touch those waters. They were told to teach their children this one law must be obeyed. Luciano came here and began enticing and tricking those who live here to drink of the forbidden waters. Luciano is not human. He is a being like myself, but he became proud and thought he could overthrow the rule of Pateras."

David was already getting lost in Gabe's explanation. "Wait. Wait. I don't understand. What's wrong with the water? Why is understanding a bad thing?"

"It is forbidden. Drinking of this water brings death. It corrupts you and every generation following. This world and its inhabitants were made from the sheer joy and love of Pateras. Pateras could not allow you to see him because you are a child of one who drank from the Waters of Understanding. Drinking of the Waters of Understanding allows your genetic code to degrade causing it to burn itself out. Humans were not made to die. Those who remain here have not touched the waters and may commune with Pateras freely, forever. They do not carry the stain of wrongdoing within them. Pateras doesn't want anyone to serve him out of fear or because they are forced to. He only wants to be served out of love. Without the option of choice what kind of service would it be. You would be nothing more than machines. Pateras does not want the love of a machine. He placed the one fountain with the one command to never touch it. If you love and trust Pateras you would obey the one command gladly. You were told he would take control of you. He wants you to serve him, but he wants you to choose it for yourselves and to choose to love him. He will never force this on you. Luciano lied to you. Your choices, and their consequences, are yours and yours alone.

"The understanding is to understand the difference between love, goodness and obedience versus hate, evil and disobedience. Once you have chosen to cross into disobedience, the concepts of fear, hatred, evil and others are also learned and passed onto future generations. The people here are innocent. They do not understand what evil is unless they touch the waters of understanding."

David looked at the two buildings then looked back at Gabe. "So why is it called the Fountain of Understanding? Why not call it something less appealing? How about the Fountain of Evil or Death?"

Gabe smiled briefly at David's naivety. "Because they have never seen death or experienced evil. It would be like explaining ice to someone who only knows tropics."

David scowled at his own ignorance. Various people began to approach the building housing the Fountain of Eternal Waters. To his surprise, no one was wearing any clothing. David tried looking away, but there were people now coming from all directions. He decided the safest place to look was at the ground. "Gabe, why are they ignoring us, and um... why aren't they wearing anything?"

Gabe looked at David who was trying to make eye contact but was nervous about looking up. "We are hidden from them. They cannot hear us or see us. They have no need of clothing here. The weather is perfect, and as I told you before, they are innocent, completely innocent."

David noticed the people make obvious attempts to avoid the second building. He attempted to distract himself from their nudity by continuing their previous conversation. "What happens to those that drink from the Fountain of Understanding?"

David saw deep pain on Gabe's face. "They are condemned to die. They are relocated to another home where they must work hard for their food, they will grow old and die. What comes after death is even worse, and since human souls never die. The suffering will never, ever end."

A boy, who appeared to be in his early teens, was playing with other young people throwing a piece of fruit around. One of the throws went wild and the piece of fruit bounced just inside the door to the building housing the Fountain of Understanding. The boy walked cautiously to the doorway. He slowly stepped inside to attempt to retrieve his projectile. His friends yelled at him to let it go. When the boy didn't, his friends took off and ran away. The boy stepped in and picked up the fruit. David heard a voice speak to the boy. The boy stepped back and started to run, but the voice was very calm and reassuring. He moved further inside the building.

"Can we go in there and see what's going on?" Gabe gave him a concerned nod. The two went inside and saw an attractive woman talking to the boy. She smiled pleasantly at him.

David continued asking questions. "Who is that?"

This time Gabe's face was angry. His reply was laced with venom. "When Luciano was banished for his treachery, he took one third of my people with him. He's one of the banished. He can change his appearance, just as I can. He seeks to corrupt the boy. I cannot interfere."

David was beginning to understand what was at stake. "Can I interfere?" He asked quickly for fear time was fast escaping.

Gabe answered simply. "Pateras keeps us invisible to the evil ones and the inhabitants of this world. Neither of us can touch or speak to either the boy or the evil one."

David hesitated, the answer wasn't "no". He looked around quickly as he saw the woman sit down by the water and begin to drink from it herself. She was showing the boy how harmless the water apparently was. The boy had dropped the piece of fruit. David picked it up and threw it hard at the woman. It caused her to slip and splash in the edge of the water. She pulled herself out of the water angrily and looked around for whoever had thrown it at her. The boy was now sufficiently spooked and ran away.

The woman before him now transformed into a large creature, fifteen to twenty feet tall. The creature had four wings and four faces. Its body was covered with eyes. David heard rumors of tricksters who would have others believing in alien life forms. In all his travels, he had never seen anything remotely resembling an alien, until now. At the very least, he was unnerved. Gabe sensed his discomfort and placed a hand on his shoulder, to steady him. The creature looked around carefully, yelled out something he couldn't understand, then vanished. "What did she – he – it say?"

Gabe shook his head. "It's not important. We need to return to Pateras. You have seen what he wanted you to see."

The two began to rise through the roof of the building, through the clouds and back through space. They once again entered the courts of Gabe's master. David peered into the thickest part of the smoke and called out cautiously. "Lord Liontari?"

Pateras' deep rich voice answered. "Yes, my child?"

David glanced at Gabe, who gave the Captain a reassuring nod. "I got the feeling there's more to this so-called story?"

Pateras' voice came back slow and sad. "Yes. I had to do something to protect my creation. I had to do the only thing possible, no matter how hard it was to do. I sent my beloved child, my son, to pay the price for all of mankind. He is born of me and born of humanity. He is the only way and the only one who could provide a guiltless death to pay for all the crimes against me. He is the only one who could provide a way to bring mankind back to me. I didn't want to put him through that. He could have refused, and I wouldn't have blamed him, but he couldn't bear to see your people suffer any more than I could."

Realization set in. "You told me I'm not dead. It's because you sent Arni to take my place. It's my fault the people on Galat are dead and now it's my fault your son is dead?"

David dropped to his knees again. He wasn't sure how to feel right now. That sick feeling in the pit of his stomach returned along with a wide variety of other emotions. Mostly what he felt was shock and sorrow. He shouted up at the cloud shrouding Pateras. "Why? Wasn't there enough blood on my hands? Why didn't you just let me die?" David wasn't the type to cry easily, but tears began to fall slowly down his face.

"I love you. I don't want you to die, nor anyone else. This was the only way to protect you. I sent my son to be your defender and the defender of all of mankind."

Gabe knelt beside David. He put a hand on David's shoulder. "David, do you remember the pain you felt when Pateras showed you the magnitude of your crimes against him?"

David felt more tightness in his chest. He gave a slight nod, and Gabe continued his explanation. "If you had died, you would have been subjected to that pain for all of eternity, that pain and much more. Pateras didn't want that to happen to you. He's giving you another chance. The other reason is, Arni will not stay dead. Pateras will give him life again." "What about all those people on Galat? Will he bring them back again as well?"

Gabe shook his head, but his countenance wasn't sad. "No, they are quite happy where they are. To send them back now would be cruel. They have desired nothing more than to be with Pateras. To take them from his presence would bring them incredible sadness. It also would make them an even greater target for Luciano. He destroyed them once, and his determination would increase many times over."

David shook his head and looked down at his hands again. "I don't understand. Why did Arni have to die if you can – I mean – if you're just going to bring him back to life how does that serve a purpose?"

Pateras took up the explanation. "The cost of disobedience is eternal death and pain. Death alone is not a pleasant experience neither is the pain associated with death. All humans, save those on the one planet I have hidden, must pay the price of death and the eternal torture that comes after. I don't want that for anyone, but the evil within all of you cannot exist in my presence. Think of it like the matter and antimatter that helps propel your ship. What happens when the two are introduced to each other?"

David's eyebrows raised. "If it isn't controlled, a giant explosion could occur. It's why we have to maintain a containment field to keep them separate."

"I am the one that has no beginning and no end. I have contained myself to protect you and all of mankind until a way could be made to rescue you. I offered up my son to pay the price for all of mankind. Mankind may still die a physical death, but in giving Arni life again, I am also offering man a new life of joy without end. I only ask one thing of man. He must accept my gift of my son's life and serve me. He must claim the forgiveness I have already given."

"When? How long until... I don't know how to ask this. How long will Arni be dead?"

Although David couldn't see Pateras' face, he could feel the joy in his voice. "My son will return to begin the war against Luciano the morning at the end of the execution waiting period, on the third day."

David looked up to the swirling smoke again. "What does serving you involve? What do you want from me?"

Pateras answered him. "I will never force you to do anything you do not want to do. I do know what is best for you. If I ask you to do something, you need to trust me. I may not ask the same things of any two people. I just want your love, trust, and obedience. I can offer so much more than what you already have. Even if Luciano offers you good things, it's only good for this lifetime and it will cause eternal suffering in the next life time. What I want from you is, to introduce me to the rest of the galaxy."

"Uh, that's a pretty big order. I'm not sure I'm capable of doing that.

No, I know I can't do that." David argued.

"I'm not asking you to do this alone. If I give you a job, don't you think I have the power to equip you to handle the job? My power has no limits." Pateras pointedly replied.

David was getting close to turning, but his analytical mind continued to question. "How do I know what you're saying is true? Where's the proof about Executor Hale? I saw the creature by the Fountain of Understanding, but that isn't proof Luciano Hale is one of those things. How am I supposed to know for certain who's telling the truth?"

"First, I will give you the gift of discernment. I gave you a portion of this gift when I created you, but now I will greatly increase it, so you can see others for what they truly are. Prepare yourself for it though. The others will not see what you see. Those you see will not know you see them as they truly are. If you speak of it, the others will not understand. If you tell Luciano what you see, he will try to destroy you."

"Second, I will tell you where to find the answers you seek. There is a small world along your route controlled by the Commonwealth. It is a penal colony where my followers are sent. They are drugged, brainwashed, tortured, and killed. The only thing they have done is to follow me. The other thing you are to do is to access the Ancient Texts. Get Cheyenne to translate them for you. They will tell you more of the history of my people. Once you have the information I have pointed you to, it's up to you what you do next. It is time for you to go, but I would like to tell you one other thing before you leave."

The great power in front him and the darkness within him made it seem appropriate for David to assume a subservient position. Although he had not chosen to serve Pateras, David was beginning to understand how great and powerful Pateras was. He slowly looked up towards where a face should be above the throne in front of him. "Yes sir?" His military training still governed his behavior despite the incredible new experience. "Thank you for protecting the boy from the evil one. I appreciate it very much. I hope you will use your new knowledge wisely."

"You're welcome? I hope I didn't break any rules."

"You did not break any rules. I will speak with you again whenever you wish. It's time for you to go."

David stood up. "What is the name of the world I need to look for?" For a few seconds, everything went dark. The light from Pateras had been so bright the normal ambiance of an ordinary room seemed dark. David's eyes focused in a few seconds and he saw Gabe standing next to him. They were back in the cell where David and Brynna had spent the last two days. Gabe started to walk away from him. "Gabe! Wait! I have more questions. What's the name of the world I need to look for? And how do I explain what happened to me and to Arni?"

Gabe walked outside the cell door and turned to face David. "Stay here and say nothing. Answer questions as they are put to you, but volunteer nothing. I will close the cell and leave you here for them to find. No one will harm you. In three days when Arni returns, you will be freed. Go to Mara. You will find the penal colony there. If you have more questions, speak them to Pateras. He will hear them and answer them in his own time."

Gabe touched David's shoulder. David felt a warmth and energy flow through his body. He gave a Gabe a questioning look. Gabe didn't wait for David's question. "Your gift of discernment."

Gabe closed the cell and left David alone. David sat down on the edge of the bed to think about what just happened and to wait for someone to find him. He wasn't sure how eager he was for someone to find him considering how these people felt about him before Arni died. The whole incident seemed so surreal. It suddenly occurred to David perhaps Arni wasn't dead yet. Maybe there was still time to stop it. He moved quickly to the computer panel and tried to contact Captain Parker, Moderator Tarmon, and lastly Rachel Johan. None of his calls went through. He left messages for all three then resorted to yelling down the corridor for any guards who might hear him. There wasn't supposed to be anyone in this cell block, so no one was there to hear him.

In a few minutes, he sat down again to wait. Inwardly he felt conflicted. The Supreme Executor ordered him to protect the life of Arni. As a normal compassionate human being, he didn't want to cost another man his life. He especially didn't want one who appeared to be as good and kind as Arni, to die in his place. On the surface, he understood why Pateras wanted Arni to die, but he couldn't justify the unfairness of it. Only the guilty deserved punishment, not the innocent. When he thought about his own guilt, the memory of what Pateras revealed to him made him sick to his stomach. No, this had not been a dream. David knew he was the one who deserved to die, not Arni.

Moderator Tarmon recovered from the shock of discovering the Intercessor's body enough to order the immediate lock down of the building. The building housed the courtrooms, jail, and execution chamber, along with other related facilities all in one. It proved to be more secure than moving prisoners from one facility to another. If a prisoner were sentenced to a term of incarceration then they would be moved to another facility, but only after the courts were done with the individual. The offices of the members of the UWC were also located within the building. By locking the entire building down, she could ensure no prisoners escaped if the quake damaged the building or security functions. She also locked down all outgoing communications. The Intercessor's face was covered, and he was immediately evacuated to the infirmary. Moderator Tarmon ordered the crew moved back to their cells and secured with the same heavy guard complement they had been given over the last few days.

As was customary for executions, Dr. Evans was already present when the Intercessor's body was brought in. Assuming he was merely there to pronounce death, he got up slowly to do a thorough scan of the body. Moderator Tarmon was only a few steps from the body. She was determined not to let it out of her sight. Upon seeing the doctor's lack of concern, she started barking orders. "Doctor, you have to revive this man at all costs!"

The doctor stopped in confusion and stared at the woman. Moderator Tarmon knew the only way to impress the importance was to show him. She grabbed the sheet from the Intercessor's face and jerked it down hastily. The doctor now stood still from shock instead of confusion. Moderator Tarmon was about to lose all control. "Doctor! Move! Now!" Her desperate tone shook him from his stupor and he turned his equipment on as fast as he could. He began supplying oxygen and respiratory support then cardiac stimulation in every form known. The scanners continued to give him the same hopeless readout. The doctor worked feverishly for the next thirty minutes for any indication at all, but not a single blip showed up. One of the medics worked frantically alongside the doctor. The doctor finally reached a point where he didn't want to stop trying to save the man in front of him, but he knew it was useless to continue. He finally stopped moving and looked up at the Moderator. He slowly shook his head and softly said the one thing she didn't want to hear. "I'm sorry, Moderator Tarmon. He was already gone.

There was nothing I could do."

The Moderator's face went white as a sheet. Her knees started to buckle. The guards who transported the Intercessor to the infirmary grabbed her and helped her to a chair. The Doctor quickly gave her something to steady her. As she gathered her wits, the doctor made entries into the medical log indicating time of death and started a scan to determine cause of death.

Moderator Tarmon sat quietly in her chair, staring at the sheet covering the Intercessor's body. Although she wasn't the planetary ruler, the planet's leaders did look to her for guidance. What was she going to tell the rest of the world? The Intercessor's plea to honor the "one death" as paying the full price had been recorded. Yes, that was the ticket. The Intercessor's words were her way out. Per the Intercessor's words and his sacrifice, the debt for the deaths on Galat was now paid and it was his dying wish the crew would be released. So where was Captain Alexander?

Saundra looked up in time to see Captain Parker and Rachel Johan walk in. Their faces were drawn and gaunt. Rachel, seeing the covered body of the Intercessor, teared up immediately. Captain Parker was blinking back tears of his own. His job required he be in control of his emotions, but this shook the very core of his being. His mind was conflicted more than anyone else. He had already promised the Moderator his resignation, but misplacing a prisoner on death row and executing the wrong one? This was a mistake that could never be fixed. The fact that it was the Intercessor only magnified it. He knew it was only a matter of time before someone started trying to lay blame on him.

Rachel hesitated, to pull herself together, then formally presented herself to the Moderator. She stood directly in front of the woman and bowed her head. "Forgive me, Moderator Tarmon, this is all my fault. I knew the Intercessor planned to do this and I should have alerted you immediately."

Captain Parker approached the Moderator with the Counselor. When he heard her confession, Captain Parker gave her a startled look. "What? This isn't your fault! This is my fault. I take full responsibility ma'am." Saundra forced her eyes to focus on the two. She looked at Captain Parker. "And just how do you suppose this is your fault, Captain?"

"I executed an innocent man. I am responsible for whatever happens on my watch."

The woman nodded. "I see... Captain Parker, I would be careful about accepting responsibility for things you clearly didn't do. We all saw Captain Alexander secured to the columns, we heard his last words and saw your man cover his face with the hood. He never left our sight. Only the Intercessor himself could have done this. We just need to make sure everyone knows it and accepts it."

Suddenly the Moderator had new energy. "Captain, I need you to conduct a search of the entire facility. We need to find Captain Alexander and he had better be alive and well. Also, I saw Colonel Bernt at the execution. Clear him to leave and send him to their star ship to see if perchance the Captain is there. Make sure there is a full complement of guards on the Intercessor's body at all times. I don't want there to be any appearance of impropriety. I'm going to the conference rooms to work. Rachel, I could use your help. I want to see all footage of the Intercessor for the last few days. I need to put out a statement to the press, but it has to be accompanied with the Intercessor's last requests or we'll have rioting in the streets."

Captain Parker ordered escorts for the two women and the extra guards for the Intercessor. He also ordered the window in the observation room covered. He went to his office and organized the search for David. Moderator Tarmon looked out the window. She could see lights from other buildings and on the streets and vehicles, but the sky was darker than she had ever seen it. She and Rachel set to work collecting whatever recent audiovisual records of the Intercessor they could. Saundra programmed the computer to do a facial recognition search for the Intercessor then divided the records up between the herself and Rachel to review. The two were looking for any mentions of the Intercessor's plans.

The address given at Captain Alexander's execution gave them a good solid start.

Captain Parker was in the habit of checking his messages frequently and with a high-profile day like today, he was even more diligent. After he dispatched teams to search the entire building, he returned to his office. He gave his list of messages a quick perusal until he spotted the one from David. Captain Parker listened to the message then recalled one team of four guards and headed for David's cell.

Captain Parker found David sitting dejectedly on the edge of his bed. He was leaning forward resting his forearms on his knees and staring at the floor. As soon as David saw the men at the door he jumped up quickly and moved to the door. "Am I too late to stop the Intercessor?"

Captain Parker was not in a congenial mood. "Shut up! Turn around, get on your knees and put your hands on your head."

David slowly complied with Captain Parker's order. He backed away from the door. While placing his hands on his head, he cautiously turned around and knelt as ordered. "Captain Parker, this wasn't my idea. I didn't have a choice. You have my word as an officer, I didn't have anything to do with this."

Captain Parker ignored him. Deep down he knew David couldn't have done this, but it was easier to be angry at David than the Intercessor. Two of the guards placed binders on David then jerked him up. They spun him around until he faced Captain Parker. "Captain Parker, I'm sorry about the Intercessor. He didn't ask for my cooperation and..."

Captain Parker grabbed David and slammed him against the nearest wall. He looked at his men briefly. "Clear the room!" Three of the men cleared the room without question.

The fourth man was higher ranking and stopped near the door. "Sir, you did say we were ordered to bring him in alive and well. Do you know what you're doing?"

Captain Parker kept his eyes glued on David. "Lieutenant, don't question me. Just get out." The Lieutenant reluctantly stepped out of the cell. Captain Parker told the voice activated door to close. He heard the door seal then ordered the privacy screen to activate. The front panels of the cell went white shutting out the witnesses. Captain Parker got right up in David's face. "I strongly suggest you say as little as possible. I know you could not have escaped and put the Intercessor in your place. Only the Intercessor himself could have done this. I know you didn't do it, but you need to realize not everyone else is going to recognize those facts. Most people on this planet wanted you dead before this day started, and the only thing stopping them from taking matters into their own hands is the fact you were scheduled to be executed today. For the moment, that's off the agenda. The only thing keeping you alive at this point is Moderator Tarmon and me. The Intercessor should never have died. He's done nothing wrong, unlike you. I would like nothing more than to wrap my hands around your throat and squeeze the life out of you myself. The Intercessor has done more in the three years he's been coming here than your Commonwealth could ever do. You and your entire Commonwealth aren't half the man he was." After his tirade, Captain Parker relaxed his grip on David and backed away. "You do exactly as I tell you if you want to stay alive, understood?"

David's response was short, sweet, and to the point. "I understand." He waited for Captain Parker to relax before he said more. Captain Parker's breathing seemed to be more at ease, so David ventured to speak to him. "Captain Parker, I didn't want to die, but I didn't want him to die in my place. Pateras said it needed to happen for the good of all mankind. He showed me just how much I deserved it. I should have been the one to die. I'm sorry for the grief I seem to have caused. Do whatever you need to with me."

Captain Parker scowled at him. "Your fate isn't up to me. I have my orders. I need to get you safely to the Moderator. I'm afraid you aren't going to like what I need to do to keep you safe."

David glanced at the cell door. He knew Captain Parker had to put the ultimate fear into his men, so they wouldn't try to take matters into their own hands. He nodded. "Do what you have to."

Captain Parker stopped and studied David's face. "Wait a minute, Pateras said what? Pateras talked to you? What happened to your bruises? Your face was covered in bruises including two black eyes. There's no sign of bruising on you."

David ran his tongue over the spots on his lips that had been split.

His lips felt normal. David shrugged, "The Intercessor?"

Captain Parker thought back to the moment when he had lifted the hood off the Intercessor's body. He remembered seeing the split lip but hadn't thought about it until now. Since he was expecting to see David's face, he expected to see the split lip. Captain Parker suddenly changed his mind about how to handle David's safety. "He literally took your punishment. He took your pain, your cuts and bruises, your death, everything. I can't touch you, not even to protect you."

"I can't say I'm heartbroken over that," David replied wryly.

"If you are by some means responsible for the Intercessor's death, I warn you. You won't live to see a proper execution and I will make your last minutes as painful as I possibly can."

David could tell by the look on the guard's face, he was deadly serious. "Captain, I didn't do this." David didn't offer any oaths or beg Captain Parker to believe him. He knew the man would either believe him, or he wouldn't, and his words would make little difference. Sometimes less is more.

Captain Parker studied David's eyes and saw pain in them. It was clear David was trying to mask the pain he felt. It was still visible to the trained eye. If David had been trying to get away with something, there would have been no sign of pain. Captain Parker backed away from David. "I believe you. What happened to you out there?"

"Arni said he was sending me to his father. I went somewhere and spoke to Pateras and a being named Gabe."

Captain Parker stared at David for a moment. He finally gave David some final instructions. "I need to get you to the Moderator. I'm going to tell everyone you are under Pateras' protection. Don't talk where others can overhear you. Speak only when necessary. You need to be as mysterious as possible, so everyone is afraid to hurt you. Tell your story only to people who need to hear it. Got it?"

David nodded. "Yeah, I got it." It was the same message Gabe had given him.

Captain Parker moved further away from David and turned the privacy screen off and opened the door. The men expected to see David writhing or unconscious on the floor with Captain Parker standing over him. They were quite surprised to see the men on opposite sides of the cell and David was uninjured. Captain Parker gave the scene a moment to sink in then he stepped outside the cell and closed the door behind him. His lieutenant was still wearing a concerned look on his face. "Captain Parker, is everything alright?"

Captain Parker looked through the glass at David. "He has the protection of Pateras."

The guards exchanged curious glances. "I don't understand. How do you know, sir?"

Captain Parker waved his hand towards David. "That man had bruises all over his face two hours ago, and his lips were split in three places. The Intercessor had those exact injuries on his face when we found him. Captain Alexander didn't just get his bruises healed. Those bruises were moved to the Intercessor's face in the exact locations and the exact stage of healing that his face had been in. I saw those bruises myself. Gentlemen, we need to make certain no one touches him. They could incur the wrath of Pateras himself."

Now all the guards were staring wide-eyed at David. David was feeling rather conspicuous. He looked away from the men. The men recovered from their Captain's startling revelation, stepped into the cell and gently removed their prisoner. Word spread quickly among the guards. Most accepted the information and resolved to handle David with the utmost care. A few postured and blustered, proclaiming it was all a sham and they weren't afraid. Captain Parker did add one other suggestive message. He casually mentioned he hoped no one touched the Captain for fear Pateras' retribution could fall on them all. He didn't mean to take advantage of Pateras' reputation of being a harsh judge, but he knew it would help protect Captain Alexander.

When Captain Parker delivered David to the Moderator, the women stopped working to interrogate him. The Moderator sat there for a moment staring at the Captain. How does one politely ask, "Why aren't you dead?" She finally decided on the best way to word her question. "Captain Alexander, would you mind explaining what just happened to you?"

David looked at the darkness outside the window. "How long was I gone? What time is it?"

Moderator Tarmon slammed her fist down on the table. "What do you mean, 'What time is it?' It's been one hour since your supposed execution and here you sit. I need some answers mister, or I will walk you back down there and execute you again myself."

David looked outside again. "I'm sorry, Moderator Tarmon. I'm not sure if I can explain what happened. I thought I was having one major hallucination. I was placed in the chamber and secured. The sun was in my eyes. I remember getting hit with a jolt then I had what felt like a really crazy... dream?"

"Tell me about your dream, Captain."

David hesitated then ventured. "First, could I let my wife know I'm still alive?"

Moderator Tarmon didn't blink. She continued giving him a cold stare. "Not until I decide to leave you alive. There's no reason to cause her such grief twice."

Rachel interrupted briefly. "Captain, she's seen the Intercessor's body."

Moderator Tarmon knew Rachel had to do what was best for her clients, but she wished Rachel had waited just a little longer to tell the Captain. She gave Rachel an annoyed look then turned her gaze back to David.

David nodded. "Yes ma'am. I'm not sure if you'll believe anything I tell you, but here goes. I think Arni took my place. He told me he was sending me to see his father. I saw, well, I'm still trying to figure out what I saw. I talked to a wall of smoke and some really big guys with swords. A voice identified himself as Pateras El Liontari. He told me no man can see him and live. He sent me to some unknown planet with a garden with two fountains of water. One was forbidden. It was called the Fountain of Understanding. He told me Luciano Hale was once one of his most trusted officials but rebelled along with one third of his followers. There were people living there who were totally – uh – innocent."

David stopped talking when he saw the two women exchange a look he couldn't interpret. "What is it?"

"Captain, have you been reading the Ancient Texts?" Rachel ventured.

David shook his head. "I tried looking them up, but you don't have them translated into Intergalactic Standard. We never downloaded any of your current language files once we determined your people were fluent in Intergalactic Standard. I saw there was some sort of controversy in your news files about translating them. I wasn't able to glean much from my research. Why?"

Moderator Tarmon exchanged another look with Rachel. "So, you have no idea what's in the Ancient Texts?"

"No ma'am, Pateras told me to search out a copy of the texts and get them translated, so I could read them. I don't suppose you could help us with that, could you? He seemed to think it was really important."

"You seem rather sure you're going to walk out of here, Captain." Saundra glared at him.

"I'm beginning to think I'm only along for the ride. This is my life, and I don't seem to be in control of it anymore. I have superior beings on both sides of me trying to tell me what to do. I get the feeling neither you, nor I, are making the decision whether I live or die. Pateras has some plans for me and they don't include dying. He's sending me to another world to show me something Luciano Hale is responsible for. I need answers and Pateras El Liontari is the only one being straight with me right now. Once I get the answers I need, I'm taking control of my life back."

Moderator Tarmon continued to stare at him. David knew she needed to hear one more thing. "He told me one more thing that should help you to know I'm telling you the truth."

Moderator Tarmon folded her arms across her chest in a defiant posture. "I'm listening."

David swallowed hard. If this was a massive hallucination, it would definitely mean the end of his life. At least it would buy him a couple more days. "Pateras said Arni would be returned to life on the third day to lead all the worlds against Luciano Hale."

The woman still stared at him coldly. "Are you willing to bet your life on that?"

"That's all I have left, and I shouldn't even have that. I'm already living on borrowed time. Since I should have been dead an hour ago, what's a couple more days."

Moderator Tarmon leaned forward and placed her elbows on the table in front of her. She clasped her hands together. Her eyes narrowed, and her tone was cold and harsh. "Here's the deal, Captain. If the Intercessor hasn't risen by noon on the third day, you will be secured in the execution chamber between the pillars and I'll hit you with a charge guaranteed to destroy you once and for all. Then I will hit you with twelve more charges just for show. Do you understand me?"

"Is my crew's deal still intact? Are they still going to be protected?"

Moderator Tarmon slammed her hand down on the table again. "You are not in any position to bargain, Captain."

"I'm not trying to bargain, Moderator. My crew had no part in what happened. I just wanted to know if you intend to honor the last wishes of the Intercessor. I'm just as concerned for the welfare of my people as you are for your people. I didn't ask your Intercessor to take my place. That was his choice. Pateras said he sent his son to pay the price for all crimes committed against him. He said it's up to each individual whether they accept his sacrifice or not. So, no, I'm not bargaining. What you do next is entirely up to you. If you execute me and it isn't what Pateras wanted, he's a powerful being. He can bring me back to life if that's what he wants. I'm just concerned about my people."

David looked out the window again. David felt his inner being settle into a gentle peace. He was no longer concerned for his own life. Rachel and the Moderator sensed something was different about him as well, but they couldn't quite figure out what it was. David looked back at the Moderator again with a puzzled look. "I do have one more question. If it's only been an hour since my execution, why is it dark outside? Is there some kind of shielding on the windows or is it actually dark because I'm not seeing the sun, moons, or stars."

The two women stared at him. They exchanged astonished looks. Moderator Tarmon's patience was at an end. She couldn't even discuss it with him. Rachel had a little more patience. "Captain, Pateras El Liontari is the creator; the maker of all there is. He has no beginning and no end. No one is his equal. He has, but one son, who just died. If we understand his teachings and add what you have said to it. The Intercessor just died taking on the punishment of every man, woman and child in the entire galaxy. Did you really think creation wouldn't notice and react when its creator suffered such a horrific pain?"

David looked outside again, then back at the women. "It, uh, makes sense when you put it that way." David looked outside one more time. As he surveyed the skies and the depth of the darkness, reality set in. A light as bright as the one that emanated from Pateras went on in David's mind. The only words he could say spoke volumes. "Oh... my... God." David stood and walked over to the window. He stared out it looking towards the dark empty sky. The two women could see the wheels turning in his head. He turned to look at the women again. "He's not just A superior being, he's THE superior being. Isn't he?"

Rachel nodded, but held her tongue. She didn't want to interfere with his train of thought.

David continued. "We were taught this was all there is. There were no supreme beings and no life after death. We were lied to. Why?"

Moderator Tarmon had regained her calm. "Captain, your Commonwealth tried to get us to put aside our beliefs in Pateras. That's why they destroyed our space exploration program. It wasn't just that we were a divided world. There was a minority who refused to let go of their beliefs. The minority were hunted down, tortured, brainwashed, imprisoned, or killed. Those who were sympathetic to that minority began to take up their fight and hide them. There was an unbelievable upsurge of those who sought to serve Pateras. It threw our world into turmoil. The Commonwealth decided we were a lost cause. They destroyed our space program, left those satellites in place, told us what we needed to do to join the Commonwealth, then left. They captured several of the underground leaders, took them off-world to try and convince them to change their minds about following Pateras. My father's name was Donald Leal. He was a strong follower of Pateras. The Commonwealth took him when I was a small child. I don't remember much about him. I just know what my mother told me about him. I suppose you were lied to because it doesn't fit your Commonwealth's idea of what the ideal society should look like. It might also be because your Supreme Executor has declared war on Pateras."

As everything David learned started to fall into place, he felt tears roll slowly down his cheeks again. He began to mentally kick himself. How could he have been so stupid? No normal human, not even a con artist, could do the things they had seen Arni do. David stood there and wondered what he was supposed to do next because the one man who could answer his questions was now dead. David looked up again. "You gave him the title 'Intercessor' didn't you?"

Moderator Tarmon nodded. "Yes, it was one of many titles he was entitled to have, but we felt like it was the most appropriate."

"How does he intercede?"

"He is an intermediary within our government to settle disputes, and he intercedes on our behalf with Pateras El Liontari, who is our judge. I suppose he has now made the ultimate intercession."

David meekly replied. "I suppose he has. What happens now?" Moderator Tarmon pressed a control on the table. "Captain Parker,

when you have a moment, I need to see you along with an escort."

A voice came through the speaker. "Yes Moderator, be there momentarily."

Moderator Tarmon looked at David sternly. "I'm going to keep you and your people safe as promised. I will also execute you as promised if the Intercessor doesn't rise from the dead at the appointed time. If I have to execute you again, then your people will have to wait here three more days if they want to take your body with them. As Rachel said your people already know the Intercessor was the one killed and not you. I will leave it up to you if you want to communicate with them or not. If it were me, I wouldn't put them through this again. They don't have to watch your second execution. I can tell them you simply vanished. Give it some thought, Captain. Your people shouldn't have to deal with this twice. If I end up executing you again, I can tell them about it after the fact."

David nodded. "I will give it some thought."

Captain Parker and four guards entered while David and the Moderator were talking. Once their conversation was complete, the woman turned to Captain Parker. "Captain Parker, I need to be sure the Captain and his crew are kept safe for the next three days. The Captain's execution has been rescheduled for noon, day after tomorrow. I am canceling all other legal proceedings scheduled in this building for the next week. Get any unnecessary prisoners shipped out of here. This building is closed except for dealing with this one situation. There will be no United World Council meetings or any meetings unless I call them myself. Understood?"

Captain Parker nodded. "Yes ma'am."

Saundra waved at the Captain. "Get him back to the cell where you found him. Keep him under heavy guard, and you can restore his communication privileges. If he so chooses, his wife may be permitted to rejoin him in his cell."

Captain Parker looked perplexed. "Moderator Tarmon, I'm afraid I don't understand. Why be so generous with his privileges while putting him back on the execution schedule? Is he responsible for the Intercessor's death, or not?"

The Moderator stood up and turned around to face the Captain of the Guard. "Captain Parker, given the unusual circumstances, I will overlook your insubordination and answer your question – this time. His guilt has not been determined, yet. It will be decided for certain, day after tomorrow. If the Captain has told me the truth, he'll go free that morning. If he hasn't spoken the truth, he'll die for his lies and deception. Does that satisfy you, Captain Parker?"

"Yes ma'am. I apologize for my insubordination ma'am. It won't happen again."

Moderator Tarmon's tone became frosty. "It had better not, Captain."

Captain Parker moved over to escort David out. David nodded politely to the two women as he headed for the door. Moderator Tarmon turned around briskly to ask one more quick question of David. "Captain Alexander, what happened to your bruises?"

He shrugged his shoulders, as well as he could with his hands still bound behind him. "Arni?"

The Moderator silently shook her head then turned her attention back to the video screen in front of her.

Back in his Spartan cell again, David sat down wondering what to do next. Moderator Tarmon was right, he didn't want to put the crew through the torture of watching him die again, but he wanted to talk to Brynna badly. He finally decided to let them know he was alive and well. He decided not to tell them about his next execution, at least not yet. He took his first step towards trusting Pateras. "Pateras, I really hope you were telling me the truth." It felt strange to him to talk to someone he couldn't see, but he was certain Pateras heard him. He punched the control to speak to Brynna. A couple hours later, arrangements were made to escort her to his cell.

Moderator Tarmon didn't want to wait too long to have her press conference. She knew the entire planet was near the point of panic. David had the computer monitoring the news channels for the Moderator's address while he went through his workout regimen. As soon as it came on he stopped his workout to listen. He watched as the Moderator stepped up to a podium. The woman had always seemed so calm and cool, but now she looked very nervous and unsettled. She wet her lips one more time before she began to speak. "Ladies and gentlemen of Drea III. I know you are all concerned by the darkness of the skies and the rumors have already begun to circulate. I wish to replay a message given to us by the Lord Intercessor Arni Liontari. She pressed a button and the words of the Intercessor from David's execution replayed.

"My Father gives you much more today than you understand. He is both just and merciful. Moderator Tarmon, I charge you with the task of seeing the one death happening here today pays the full price for all crimes. Do not let others try to deter you from what I have asked. Today, I will lay everything down for all of mankind and the war with Luciano Hale is settled. David, your crimes against me and my Father are forgiven."

Saundra felt like she was hearing the words for the first time now that they were in perspective. Her heart beat faster as she struggled to maintain her composure. As the audiovisual record concluded, she gave the words time to sink in before she continued. She took several sips of water and a deep breath. "Ladies and gentlemen of Drea III. It is my sad duty to report... the Intercessor has given his life to pay for the crimes of another." She paused again. "If we are to understand his last words, he has paid for the crimes all of mankind have committed against his father, Pateras Liontari. The Intercessor was pronounced dead at 12:42 p.m. The Intercessor took the place of a prisoner without official notification or due process approval. The situation is being investigated fully to be certain there was no impropriety.

"I am declaring a period of mourning starting immediately. I am requesting all non-essential offices and businesses be closed for the next three days. If it is found the prisoner, who was spared by the Intercessor, was in any way responsible for the Intercessor's death, he will be executed promptly.

"The Intercessor's body will lie in state in the covered courtyard of the World Council Justice Center Building for three days as soon as his autopsy is complete later today. Visitation will be allowed by all."

"I know you are all concerned about the darkness. I wish I had answers for you, but I don't. The information I have access to indicates the darkness shouldn't last more than the three days of mourning. I suggest everyone spend time praying to Lord Pateras El Liontari. I know you may have questions, but I have no answers for you. Get your answers from Pateras."

Moderator Tarmon walked away from the podium. In her hurry, she failed to turn the audiovisual feed off. She headed quickly back to her office which was just down the hall. Rachel had been with her, along with their security detail. Two of the security guards followed the Moderator back to her office. Rachel approached the podium and discreetly turned the feed off. She walked silently back towards Moderator Tarmon's office.

Rachel reached the outer office and found the Moderator's guards posted outside the door to her inner office. They quickly informed Rachel the Moderator didn't want to be disturbed right now. Rachel sat down at the desk belonging to the Moderator's assistant. She thought about everything that had happened. She wasn't sure what to do next. Was there anything left unfinished? She had been distracted from her position of defense counselor. There was nothing she could think of. She supposed she could go home, but something kept nagging at her. She wasn't done yet. A light came on in her head. Yes, there was something she needed to do. She worked at the computer for a few minutes then told the Moderator's guards she would be back shortly. Taking her own guards, she headed for the detention center.

David sat there staring at the computer screen for a few minutes after the press release. He had seen all of it firsthand, but it still hit hard. He thought for a minute. He hadn't seen everything. He hadn't seen Arni's body. He looked up to see Rachel and her guards walk up to his cell. He stood up as she entered the cell. "Counselor, to what do I owe the honor of your visit?"

Rachel stood there nervously. She wasn't sure if she was doing anything wrong or not, but she would rather not find out the hard way. "May I sit down, Captain?"

The Captain waved her over to the bench that served as a sofa. David switched the view on his computer screen to a view of the exterior of the building. It helped ward off claustrophobia. David frequently put up similar things on the viewers on the ship. He was really starting to miss his ship.

"What can I do for you, Counselor?"

Rachel glanced at the guards to see if they were paying attention to her. They were. "You are my client, Captain. It's my duty to check on you."

David sat down in one of the chairs at his dinner table keeping a significant distance between himself and Rachel. He sensed something was up and didn't want to get accused of anything. "I'm fine, Counselor."

"Captain, could we put up the privacy screen?"

Most meetings between attorney and client happened in the conference rooms, not in the cells. Rachel was a visitor and had no access to the screens. David wasn't comfortable with that. "I'd rather not. What's on your mind, Counselor? I'm already a convicted murderer. I really don't have anything else to hide."

"You told the Moderator you hadn't seen the Ancient Texts and Pateras wanted you to seek them out and read them." Rachel casually stuck her hands in her pockets.

Her movements weren't as casual as she thought. David noticed immediately. His eyes followed her movements. He forced his eyes not to tarry on her hands. He didn't know what she was up to but getting his own attorney in trouble didn't seem prudent. "Yes, that's true. If I understand the situation, some of the Dreans want the text translated, but the older population still remembers the Commonwealth. The older population want to keep their native languages alive and they were afraid if the texts were translated, their languages would die."

Rachel nodded. "I think you have a good grasp on the situation." Rachel took her hands out of her pockets. She crossed her legs and turned her back more towards the front of the cell. The guards no longer had a good view of her right hand which was closed in a fist.

David was still watching her movements curiously. He continued to keep the conversation going as casually as he could. "Is it a criminal offense to translate the texts?"

Rachel winced. "That's a tricky question. The publishers have an injunction against it, but there are no laws against an individual translating them for their own personal use. I'm not sure how the law would view it if one were to just hand over language files and the texts at one time knowing that's how they would be used. If it were done off world, I'm certain there wouldn't be a problem, but to do it here and now? I just don't know." Rachel slipped her right hand into the crevice between the back and seat cushions.

David could tell she had pushed something in between them, but he couldn't see what it was. The urge to look at the guards to see if they had noticed washed over him. He fought the urge and kept his gaze neutral. "I'm sure Pateras will find a way to get the files to us if we were meant to have them."

Rachel smiled and nodded. "I'm sure he will. I wanted to let you know I don't know what the next few days will hold, but I am still at your disposal. It was the Intercessor's will that I do all I can for you. Is there anything else you need?"

"Now that you mention it. I need to talk to my crew. Can you arrange a meet in the conference room? I wasn't going to tell them about the possibility of getting executed again. I'm reasonably certain Pateras will revive Arni on time. I don't want to worry them unnecessarily."

Rachel shook her head at him. "You like to live dangerously. How are you going to explain this to them?"

David grinned. "I'll just claim ignorance if I have to. I'm pretty ignorant where Pateras is concerned. There's one more thing." David stood up and moved around restlessly. "I – I need to see him."

Rachel's mood changed to match David's. She stood up and moved closer to the cell door. "I don't know if I can arrange that, but I'll see what I can do. Is there anything else?"

David shook his head. "No, Brynna's going to be brought back in here shortly. That's the only other thing I needed." David sat back down in his chair. "Rachel, thank you for everything."

Rachel turned around to answer him and gasped. David looked up at her. She was looking at the computer screen. David turned to see what had gotten her attention. The sun was again shining. Both breathed a sigh of relief. They both knew what would happen to the planet if the sun were permanently gone. They both believed everything would be fine now.

Rachel knocked on the glass to get the guards to release her. She hurried out to talk to the Moderator.

248

DEATH'S END

PAID IN FULL

The Moderator still wasn't taking calls, so Rachel arranged with Captain Parker for David to go to the observation room in the infirmary to see the Intercessor's body. The Captain was kept in binders and under heavy guard. The Intercessor's body was moved over near the window, and the sheet covering his face was gently laid back. Arni didn't quite look the same as he had on Galat. On Galat, the men wore beards, but here Arni was clean shaven. His face bore the cuts and bruises David had worn hours ago. David stood there staring at him. For a moment, he shut out everything around him and mentally spoke to Arni.

"Arni, I'm sorry you had to go through this. I don't understand who or what you are, but I really hope Pateras is right. I hope you will return soon. I think I'm ready to listen to you now. I'm sorry it took so many deaths to bring me to this point. I really hope you can forgive me for not listening to you sooner."

As David's mental speech concluded, he began to pay more attention to his surroundings. The first thing he became aware of was the silent tears escaping his eyes and running down his face. The second thing was a conversation behind him. Two of the men who had escorted him in were whispering in a clearly disapproving tone. He decided it was time to leave. He knew most of the guards would be angry and blame him for Arni's death. Dwelling too closely could get dangerous. David nodded his thanks to Dr. Evans and turned to Rachel. "Rachel, thank you. Please give Captain Parker and Dr. Evans my thanks as well."

Rachel, seeing the tears on his face, reached into one of her pockets and pulled out a tissue. She wiped the tears from his face, and then gave a stern look of disapproval to the two guards at the back of the room.

Captain Parker entered quietly and was standing at the back of the room glaring at everyone. He sent two of the guards into the hallway with David but stopped the two who had been expressing their distaste. "Gentlemen, I am not a scholar of the Ancient Texts, and I don't pretend to understand the desires of Pateras. I do know he knows our thoughts and hears our whispers. I also know he has a special plan for Captain Alexander. This man must be under his protection. Why else would he allow his son to die in the Captain's place? Be very careful not to let anything happen to him." As Captain Parker spoke, he kept his tone low and looked around as though he suspected someone of eavesdropping. His plan worked. The two men became sufficiently spooked and adjusted their attitudes.

Captain Parker escorted David and his guards back to his cell where Brynna was waiting. David thanked Captain Parker for allowing him to see the Intercessor. As Captain Parker left David's cell, he heard the guards talking again in hushed tones. He couldn't make out everything they said, but he caught one significant phrase. "He actually had tears in his eyes." Captain Parker breathed a sigh of relief.

Moderator Tarmon's computer flashed a silent notice every time she received a call. She needed time to grieve and try to make sense of the day's events, but the constant notices kept pulling her back to reality. After a long time of staring out her window and pacing, she finally reached a moment of calm. Just as her stress level began to dissolve, the sunlight returned. She stepped out onto the balcony and basked in its warm rays again. A few minutes of breathing in the warm air and feeling the sun on her skin restored her to her professional self. She moved back inside and reviewed the list of calls she had missed. She listened to the various messages left for her and began to deal with each one.

Rachel had left a message telling Moderator Tarmon about the Captain's requests to meet with his crew and to see the Intercessor. The Moderator pressed a button to return her call. She told Rachel the Captain should remain in his cell for his own protection, and she was not approving either of his requests.

"Moderator Tarmon, I need to apologize. You were unavailable, and I took the liberty of arranging for the Captain to see the Intercessor already. He has been returned to his cell and is unharmed. He viewed the Intercessor from the observation room and was not granted any closer access to him. Captain Parker oversaw it. There was a total of ten guards present plus Dr. Evans."

Moderator Tarmon frowned. "Well, what's done is done. I just wanted to be sure we avoided any appearance of impropriety, as well as protect Captain Alexander. I think you handled it quite well, but I would rather have not left any questions in anyone's minds about the Captain's involvement."

Rachel didn't care much for the Moderator's answer. "I'm sorry you didn't approve ma'am, but I think it was quite appropriate. The Intercessor took the Captain's place. I think the Captain deserved to see the face of the man who saved his life. I also think it cemented the Captain's position that it wasn't his desire for the Intercessor to die for him. The guards even changed their attitudes after seeing the Captain mourn the Intercessor's loss."

The Moderator declined to let David out of his cell again for any reason. She wanted to see him protected from any further retribution. She wanted to be certain if she needed to execute him later, he was alive when the time came. She did agree to allow Brynna to meet with the crew on his behalf. Rachel conveyed the information to David and Brynna. The meeting with the crew was set up for the next morning.

The Intercessor's body was dressed in his most formal attire, which was still simple and subdued. He was placed in a clear, airtight coffin in the garden-like patio outside the building. Colonel Bernt provided troops to protect the coffin and the building. Lines began to form well before the area was opened for visitors. Dignitaries began planning trips to be there for the funeral. Moderator Tarmon set the date of his funeral for one week from the day he died. She decided not to put too much time and effort into it before three days had passed. If she woke up on the fourth day and the Intercessor was still dead, she would worry about it then. She wanted to spend this time finding answers, so no one would doubt her. She arranged for around the clock audiovisual to cover the procession. The woman worked tirelessly. There were pesky details like parking, shuttles from remote locations, and restroom facilities among other things. She had just issued a request for businesses to close for a period of mourning, and now she needed people to work. The irony of it was frustrating.

The Intercessor died on Friday just after noon. His body was placed on display around 6:30 pm that evening. Captain Parker and Moderator Tarmon arranged for the security personnel to go through the viewing before it was opened to the public. The procession of people started moving through immediately. Their reactions ranged from silent shock to loud cries of despair. People came all throughout the night bringing tokens of their love for the Intercessor and laying them around his casket. The tokens became so numerous the security guards had to periodically come through and move them around the perimeter of the area. They felt bad about having to remove them. When the numbers reached a point of saturation, they would close off the area to the visiting mourners, move the flowers, pictures, symbols, and other items, and then reopen the area. The area remained flooded with guests all day Saturday and into the night.

David decided it was time to trust his crew and hold nothing back. He briefed Brynna on the Moderator's decision including the threat to execute him if Pateras didn't bring Arni back to life. Brynna looked like she was about to cry again. David assured her everything would be fine. Brynna wasn't convinced. "David, I've just gotten you back only to find out I may lose you again? What makes you so sure?"

"Because everything Arni told us has happened exactly like he told us. I'm going to be fine."

"But Arni's dead. How does that prove things are going to be fine?"

David looked slightly at a loss. He wasn't sure how to explain it. He was "at peace." He told her about his "dream" and everything that happened to him. "Brynna, I believe Pateras is capable of all the things he said. I don't believe I was hallucinating and I don't believe I was lied to. I don't know for certain all he said about Executor Hale is right, but I intend to find out. Pateras is very powerful, and he knows I intend to get some answers. He wants me to get those answers, so he's going to do what he can to help me. That includes keeping me alive and well."

David did hold back on one piece of information. David wasn't comfortable telling her about Pateras' revelation of his crimes. It was something so extremely personal and painful, he couldn't share it, not yet. He did tell her about the Ancient Texts and how Rachel had discreetly provided him with the tools to translate them. He told her where they were hidden and asked her to get them to Cheyenne, but to be cautious with them until they were back on the ship.

Brynna met with the crew and Rachel that morning. She passed the data crystal to Cheyenne and warned her the guards might take issue with it. She told her what was on the crystal and what the Captain wanted done with it. Cheyenne concealed it in her uniform.

Late that evening after numerous meetings, Moderator Tarmon was well beyond weary. Chancellor Noe, Chancellor Torrell, Arbiter Navid, and Prosecuting Attorney Gunter Finley had all been nipping at her like small dogs. They each had differing opinions about what should happen with Captain Alexander. They hadn't wanted to agree to the plea agreement, and since the Intercessor was now dead, they wanted it revoked. Moderator Tarmon finally reached her breaking point. Full of anger she stood up from her desk with such force she knocked her chair over. "Enough!! How dare you?! These were the last wishes of our beloved Intercessor. May I remind you his father still lives? I will not dishonor his memory. His father sees all and knows all. Perhaps you do not believe what the Intercessor has taught us about his father. Perhaps you never believed in Pateras at all! There is reason to believe Pateras will raise the Intercessor from the dead, and I intend to wait for that to happen. If it doesn't, then I will punish Captain Alexander myself, at noon on Sunday! Are we clear on that?"

Everyone's faces went from looks of shock and indignation to looks of concern as the Moderator's face went from pale to blood red, and then back to white in a matter of seconds. She gasped trying to catch her breath and weaved dangerously before passing out. Rachel was standing closest to her and caught her.

Arbiter Navid jumped to help Rachel. The two quickly moved her over to the sofa. Captain Parker was also in the meeting and called Dr. Evans to the Moderator's office.

Dr. Evans arrived with a medic and a stretcher. He wisely sent everyone out of the room except for Rachel and Captain Parker. He knew the Moderator had been leaning heavily on the two of them and felt their presence would be beneficial. Rachel called the Moderator's husband, Edward. She didn't have a diagnosis to give him yet, but she wanted him to get on his way as quickly as possible. Edward had fixed a simple dinner for his workaholic wife and was already in route. Captain Parker sent guards down to meet him on the street. One guard took his vehicle and parked it, while another escorted him quickly into the building. By the time Edward reached the building, the Moderator had been moved to the infirmary. Dr. Evans determined the Moderator was suffering from stress and exhaustion. He gave her a sedative and advised against moving her just now. He assured Edward his wife would be fine. She needed rest and the meal he brought would be helpful when she woke up. Edward thought she would rest better if she were at home in her own bed. Dr. Evans agreed, however he believed the trip home would disturb her too much right now. Her heart was clearly too closely intertwined with the things happening here at work. He was afraid she would react badly if she were forcibly removed from the premises. They both agreed the Moderator would need to be awake, alert, and agree to leave on her own for her to rest properly. They also both sensed she would somehow know and fight the sedative if she were moved. Their final diagnosis was an acute case of stubbornness.

Chancellor Torrell and Counselor Finley were the two most dissatisfied with the situation. As soon as Moderator Tarmon became incapacitated, the two started looking for an opportunity to reverse her decisions. They began to discuss their "concerns" with the others. Chancellor Torrell was next in line after Moderator Tarmon in the United World Council. He promptly declared himself to be in charge until the Moderator could resume her duties. The group met late into the night reviewing all the "evidence" that might point to the Intercessor's resurrection or his last wishes. They weren't looking for confirmation, but a loophole. They weren't the only ones up late.

The ship's crew had a little trouble going to sleep themselves. Tomorrow would determine the Captain's fate. It was quite late when the last one lay down. Cheyenne lay down and tossed and turned for more than an hour. She finally decided Laura was sound asleep, so she got up and went to the computer. She kept the sound and display brightness turned down. She pulled out the data crystal and started to work on translating the Ancient Texts. Before she realized it, two hours had passed. She looked at the time and saw it was after 2:00 am. She was finally starting to get drowsy but wanted to get to the end of the section she was working on. She continued to work despite feeling like it was time to stop.

Two guards made their usual rounds, and even though the women had their privacy screen up, they could see light from the computer display flashing through the opaque glass. The guards deactivated the privacy screen to see what was going on in the cell. Cheyenne hadn't heard them approaching and her back was to the door. They watched her intently to see what she was doing. When the guards realized she was translating the Sacred Texts, they rushed into the cell. Not being well- versed in the law, they assumed all translations of the Ancient Texts into Intergalactic Standard were illegal. Cheyenne tried to close the program down and hide the data crystal, but the guards were ready for her. The two cuffed her and pulled her from the cell. Cheyenne knew she only had seconds to let Laura know what was happening. "Laura, Laura! Wake up! Laura, call the Captain! Laura, I'm in trouble. I screwed up. Laura!" Laura woke up slowly. By the time she was coherent, she was alone in her cell. Marissa heard the commotion and got her privacy screen down in time to see the guards dragging Cheyenne down the hall.

Marissa quickly went to the comm panel and tried to call the Captain and Commander, but after-hours communications were shut down. She knew she was allowed access to her legal counsel at any time, so she attempted to reach Rachel Johan, but didn't get an answer. She quickly left a message and tried Moderator Tarmon. Again, there was still no response.

The guards locked Cheyenne in a holding cell still bound. It only took a few minutes for word to reach Chancellor Torrell.

When he heard what she had been caught with, he was ecstatic. He woke the others, and an hour later they assembled in his office. Arbiter Navid had barely gotten to sleep when the Chancellor summoned him back to the UWC building. He was tired and annoyed. Prosecutor Finley was equally as annoyed and more vocal. "Chancellor, I don't understand why you brought us back in here for this. The woman hasn't broken any laws. It's not illegal to translate the Ancient Texts into Intergalactic Standard, just to distribute them."

Chancellor Torrell was still elated. "Captain Alexander told the Moderator, he hadn't read the Ancient Texts. He said he didn't have the native language files. This data crystal has both the Ancient Texts and the language files. He lied."

Chancellor Noe had a cooler head and wasn't out for blood. "The Captain hasn't had contact with his crew since before the execution. How are you going to prove he had the access?"

Chancellor Torrell countered. "His crewmen could have passed the information to him via our own communications network or when they met with their legal counsel."

Chancellor Noe shook her head. "I think I need a little more proof." Chancellor Torrell reluctantly gave in to her demand. He sent the crystal to be analyzed for fingerprints, DNA and usage logs. He also had Cheyenne brought to his office. Chancellor Noe put in a call for the woman's legal counselor. He was unable to reach her.

Cheyenne was brought in and sat in a chair in the middle of the room. Chancellor Torrell circled around her like a shark. He started out will some less aggressive questions. "What is your name and rank, young woman?"

Cheyenne knew enough to be careful with this man and his questions. "Cheyenne Dominick. My rank is Ensign."

Chancellor Torrell continued treading lightly. "What are your responsibilities on your ship?"

Cheyenne began to get nervous. She could see where this was headed. "Where is my legal counsel? I need to speak with her."

The Chancellor spoke slyly to her. "Surely your duties are not secret, are they? Are your duties something we should be suspicious of?"

Cheyenne still hesitated. "Under the articles of war, I am allowed to have my commanding officer present when questioned."

Chancellor Torrell was taken aback by her comment. He looked around at the others in the room. "So, this one thinks we are at war." He gave a hearty, but sarcastic laugh. "Answer my question, or I'll have you in the execution chamber."

Chancellor Noe and Arbiter Navid started to object, but a stern look from Torrell shut them down. Cheyenne was scared, but stubborn and well-versed in human behavior. She knew he was trying to bully her. "Do whatever you think you can get away with. I'm not saying another word until I have either my lawyer or my Captain present."

Chancellor Torrell was losing patience with her. He slammed his fist on his desk and let out a couple expletives. He started to backhand her, but Arbiter Navid blocked his hand. "What could it hurt to bring her Captain up here. Perhaps he will implicate himself." Chancellor Torrell relented and sent for the Captain and the Commander. He thought it might be helpful to have the Captain's wife nearby.

It took nearly twenty minutes to get the Captain and Commander brought into the office. The Captain took one look at Cheyenne and knew what had happened. Cheyenne could clearly see he was disappointed in her carelessness.

Chancellor Torrell recounted the situation to the Captain. David's first question was expected. "Where is our attorney? I would also like to know where Moderator Tarmon is."

Chancellor Torrell's temper flared again. "Your attorney is apparently unreachable. We have made a good faith effort in attempting to reach her. Moderator Tarmon is currently on medical leave. I am in charge until she is able to return, and I want some answers."

David wasn't in a hurry to back down. "And I want an attorney."

Chancellor Torrell looked like he was about to blow his top. His eyes landed on Arbiter Navid and the red color in his face slowly faded. "Fine, Arbiter Navid will serve as your attorney until Counselor Johan can be reached."

The look on Arbiter Navid's face was priceless. He looked like he had swallowed a small live fish. David grinned. "You are joking, right? You want the man who sentenced me to death to be my defense attorney."

Chancellor Torrell charged forward. "Captain, that's the only choice you have. Take it or leave it, but before you choose, know this. If you choose not to answer my questions, I will revoke your plea agreement and execute your entire crew before breakfast."

David studied the man's face. He could see the Chancellor was quite serious. "Where is Moderator Tarmon?"

Chancellor Torrell gave David this last answer before he started pushing again. "You have pushed Moderator Tarmon to her breaking point. She is in the infirmary under sedation. She can't help you, Captain."

The Chancellor turned back to Cheyenne. "Now, Ensign Dominick, what are your duties aboard your ship?"

Cheyenne looked to the Captain for guidance. David looked at Arbiter Navid who simply shrugged. David nodded for Cheyenne to answer. Cheyenne looked back at the Chancellor and nervously answered his question. "My primary responsibilities are linguistics, communications, and computer programming."

Chancellor Torrell smiled. He began to question her about what she was doing with the data crystal. His next line of questioning she refused to answer. "Where did you get the data crystal? Who gave it to you, and how long have you had it?"

When she refused to answer despite the Captain's approval, Chancellor Torrell looked to the Captain again. "Instruct her to answer, Captain. I'm losing patience."

David nodded then knelt on one knee in front of her. "Ensign, answer his questions honestly and completely. Don't leave anything out."

Cheyenne's eyes teared up. "Captain, I can't. This was my fault, not yours." Cheyenne looked down and away from him.

David put himself back in her line of sight. "Ensign, it may not look like it right now, but everything's going to be fine. I promise. I need you to tell them exactly what happened. Please, Cheyenne."

Cheyenne nodded. She looked at Chancellor Torrell. "Commander Alexander gave it to me this morning."

Chancellor continued his relentless questions. "What was on the data crystal, and what were your orders? What were you supposed to do with it?"

It was clear from the quiver in her voice she was unnerved by the questions. "The Commander ordered me to translate the Ancient Texts. The crystal contained the language files necessary to start the translation and a copy of the Ancient Texts." Cheyenne looked like she had more to say. Her eyes were darting back and forth between Chancellor Torrell, Captain Alexander, and Commander Alexander.

Before Chancellor Torrell could jump on what was obviously an omission of information, David beat him to it. "Cheyenne, don't omit anything."

Cheyenne blinked back tears again. "Yes sir. The Commander said the Captain needed them translated when he got back to the ship, and I should be careful with the crystal until we were back aboard the ship. She said the guards might not like finding the files. I couldn't sleep because I was worried about the Captain. The privacy screen was up. I turned the audiovisual outputs down, so I wouldn't wake Laura. I didn't think the guards would – would see it." Cheyenne could fight her tears no longer. With her hands still bound behind her there was little she could do about them but let them flow down her face unimpeded.

David glanced at Chancellor Noe, then at Cheyenne. His eyes told her what he wanted, but she was not one of the dominant personalities in the room. He decided to give her a little help. "Chancellor Torrell, unless you are afraid the Ensign intends to harm you in some way, would you please unbind her and allow her a small amount of dignity?"

Chancellor Noe jumped on the opportunity. "Damarion, show a little compassion. You're pushing her awfully hard. Who's she going to hurt when you have her Captain and Commander locked up?"

Two of the guards looked at each other. They had been the ones escorting Laura into the conference room the day one of their companions slapped Cheyenne. They had seen what she was capable of while her hands were bound. They weren't convinced removing her binders was a wise move. Chancellor Torrell grudgingly ordered the guards to remove her binders. The two guards watched her closely while releasing her hands. Cheyenne wasn't feeling threatened physically, so she had no reason to attack or fight back. Chancellor Noe provided Cheyenne with a cloth to wipe her face with. She regained her composure and began to use the cloth as a stress reliever, twisting it tightly in her hands.

Chancellor Torrell began again. "Ensign Dominick, what sort of skills does it take to do your job on the ship?"

Cheyenne was caught off guard by the question. "I'm not sure what you're asking. I have a degree in linguistics, and I am fluent in six languages. I also have degrees in Computer Science and sociology."

Chancellor Torrell leaned back in his chair in a relaxed manner and folded his arms across his chest. "I don't doubt you're an expert in your field, but if you were somehow unavailable to do your job, who among your crew could take your place? What if you got sick or resigned? How many people aboard your ship would be capable of translating the Ancient Texts?"

Cheyenne's heart began to beat faster again. Now she knew where he was headed with this line of questions. "Given the language files were already on the crystal, anyone on board could do it."

Chancellor Torrell wasted no time. "So, your Captain could have used those files to understand the Ancient Texts?"

"Yes sir."

"Does he also have the capability to create a file of completed translations then delete it from the data crystal? Could he have passed that file to you in an attempt to cover the fact he had already translated the information he needed? Is it possible he wanted you to get caught with that file to try to prove he didn't know the Ancient Texts?" Chancellor Torrell was now on his feet leaning over his desk firing questions at Cheyenne. His voice was getting higher and louder as he fired question after question at her. "Is your Captain capable of such a deception? Does he have the skills? Has he ever shown himself capable of deception aboard the ship? Has he? Answer my questions!"

Cheyenne was crying again. If this had been a normal day in the line of duty, she wouldn't have been so easy to upset. Yes, she was more emotional than most of the crew by nature. She was still a Commonwealth Soldier. The things they had been dealing with on this voyage were beyond anything her training had prepared her for. She was not trained to deal with Superior Beings who had the power over life and death, could appear and disappear at will, and read one's mind. This was too much.

David stepped quickly between Cheyenne and Chancellor Torrell. "That's enough! What is it you want Chancellor?"

Chancellor Torrell moved around from behind his desk. He got right up in David's face. He spoke softly, so he wouldn't be heard over Cheyenne's sobs. "Personally, I'd like to see you and your crew dead, permanently. I'd also like to get my hands on your ship to restart our space program now that you have shut down those satellites."

David didn't back down. "I hate to disappoint you Chancellor, but if you attempt to enter my ship without proper authorization it will activate the self-destruct sequence and an automated distress call to the Commonwealth. As far as those satellites, they're programmed to reset themselves when shut down. We'll have to resend the shutdown codes before we leave. The one satellite may be too damaged to reset, but that leaves a very narrow window for your people to escape orbit. We agreed to give you the codes to the satellites once my ship and crew are in space. I still stand by that agreement. So, I ask you again. What do you want?" The Chancellor's breath was hot on David's face as his tone grew louder. "I want you to admit you are responsible for the Intercessor's death and used that data crystal to gain knowledge of the Ancient Texts to hide your actions against the Intercessor."

David matched his tone to the Chancellor's. "That didn't happen. If I confessed to it, I would be lying. I don't think your truth-seeking justice system would approve. Yes, I had the data crystal. Yes, I intended to translate the Ancient Texts, but I only had possession of it after the death of the Intercessor. As far as being responsible for the Intercessor's death, I am just as responsible as you are."

The Chancellor broke away from David and turned to the rest of the room. "There, you heard it! He confessed to having the crystal. He was using it to translate the Ancient Texts and he admits to being responsible for the Intercessor's death."

Arbiter Navid shook his head. "I'm sorry, Chancellor. That's not going to stand up in any court anywhere. According to what he said, we should execute both of you."

The chancellor was startled at the suggestion. He stood there quietly for a moment, thinking. His face went from blood red back to its normal hue. When he began to speak again, he was calm and confident. "Everyone, except the Captain, wait in the outer office. I think the Captain and I can come to an understanding. As a matter of fact, guard, unbind him. We can talk like civilized beings. Take the binders off his wife as well."

The guard did as he was instructed. The others filed out of the room quietly. David gave Cheyenne's shoulder a reassuring squeeze and Brynna a quick hug. As he hugged her, he made eye contact with Chancellor Noe and softly said. "The Chancellor plans to threaten me off the record. He may harm you or Cheyenne if I try to call his bluff. If there's no record of this meeting, I may have to plead guilty to things I haven't done to protect you." David made sure Chancellor Noe heard him as she walked past the two.

The group walked out into the reception area and Chancellor Noe excused herself from the others. She stated she needed to go to her office for a moment. She raced to her office and tried to turn on the surveillance in Chancellor Torrell's office. The Chancellor had shut it down.

Everyone in the building was currently required to have an escort. Security guards had access to things officials might not. She looked up at the security guard. "Sergeant, I need you to override the audiovisual monitoring in Chancellor Torrell's office. He's alone with a convicted murderer in his office and the prisoner isn't even bound. I need to keep an eye on him to see he isn't harmed in any way."

The security officer hesitated. Chancellor Noe had a valid point, so he did as she requested. The man insisted on staying to oversee the situation. Chancellor Noe quickly began recording and sent a duplicate recording to her personal files.

Chancellor Torrell invited the Captain to sit down in the chair vacated by Cheyenne. "Captain, you asked me what I wanted. I want to be the one responsible for bringing the

Intercessor's murderer to justice. It will go a long way towards furthering my political career."

David yawned. It was the middle of the night and he was missing his sleep. His main goal at this point was to stall until Arni was brought back from the dead. He wondered exactly what time it was supposed to happen. His yawn seemed to really annoy Chancellor Torrell, which was part of David's strategy. "So, you expect me to fall on my sword, just so you can win your next election? You can't win on your own merits? Never mind, don't answer that question. I already know the answer."

Chancellor Torrell could feel his blood pressure rising. He knew the Captain was just trying to make him angry. Despite his efforts to resist, it was working. "You seem overly confident, Captain, but I hold all the cards right now. You see, I can set aside your plea agreement in the Moderator's absence. I can have you and your entire crew executed. As a personal favorite, I think I will have you executed last and let you watch every one of your crewmen die, one at a time starting with your pretty wife."

David sobered his attitude. "You've never cared the slightest for the Intercessor. You've only pretended to care just for your own personal gains. You know he can see right through you."

Chancellor Torrell grinned. "Maybe he could when he was alive, but not anymore."

David grinned. "Wanna bet?"

"Captain, I'm tired of this game. You're going to confess to being responsible for the Intercessor's death, and I'm going to execute you for it."

David folded his arms across his chest. "Please tell me why I would do that."

Chancellor Torrell leaned forward and propped his arms on his desk. "I told you, I can revoke your plea agreement."

David was nonplussed. He slid down in his chair and crossed his legs at the ankle presenting an even more relaxed posture. "And I told your people, if my people aren't allowed to leave, the Commonwealth will come here looking for us. For that matter, they may already be looking for us. We have been out of touch for a week already."

Chancellor Torrell was angry but keeping his temper under control. "Fine, I will release you and your people. You are free to leave this morning once you are processed out of the system."

David was suspicious. He sensed a "but." "What's the catch?" "Oh, your little Ensign and your wife will have to stay and face charges of conspiracy, failing to comply with an injunction, and attempting to undermine the religious and political structures of the United World Council." Chancellor Torrell grinned. If they had been playing chess, Chancellor Torrell would have called "check."

David shook his head. "That's not going to fly, and you know it."

Chancellor Torrell continued to grin. "It may not, but you will be required to leave this planet before tomorrow morning and abide the terms of your plea agreement giving us control of those satellites. Your wife and Ensign will be stuck here until this ugly legal mess can be straightened out. I figure it will be straightened out right after we get control of those satellites. In the meantime, there could be any number of rumors circulated around about who's actually responsible for the Intercessor's death. Both of those lovely ladies could end up as unfortunate targets of someone seeking revenge."

David remained in his relaxed position. "Is that the best you've got? Hypothetically speaking, if I left here without my crewmen, my ship could have a malfunction in its firing mechanisms and accidentally take out the top half of this building. It was damaged when we landed. We could have missed something when we made our repairs."

"All right, Captain, you win. I'm declaring your plea agreement null and void unless you confess to your crimes against us. We will destroy your ship ourselves. When the Commonwealth comes, we will show them the damaged satellites and tell them we helped you with your repairs and you left the planet a few days ago. We'll take our chances with the Commonwealth. The Intercessor is no longer here for them to find. I think we'll be fine."

David sat up in his chair. "You would risk your entire world's safety just to destroy me and elevate your own social standing."

Chancellor Torrell stood up and walked around his desk. He leaned back against the edge of the desk and crossed his own legs at the ankles then folded his arms across his chest. "Captain, I really don't have anything personal against you. I just found the perfect opportunity to discredit Moderator Tarmon and move into her position, permanently. Now I suggest you agree to this or I'll send those two women out to be executed right now."

David was still trying to find ways to stall. "What happens when everyone finds out I did nothing wrong? Won't this come back and bite you? There is evidence in my favor."

Chancellor Torrell paced in front of his desk for a moment. He wondered what evidence, but he knew David would never reveal that information. "I think I can handle any evidence you try to throw at me from beyond the grave. Do we have a deal, Captain or do I start executing your crew?"

David sat there contemplating his options. He maintained his cocky attitude although the feeling behind it was not there. "When do plan on executing me? Moderator Tarmon had an appointment already set up for me at noon. Do you plan to keep the same time?"

"No, I want this over with as soon as possible. I'm sending you off to be executed as soon as you issue your confession."

David still had the assurances from Arni and Pateras everything would be fine. The thing most concerning to him was they would not control individuals, which he assumed included the Chancellor. David got up and walked over to the window. He stood there with his hands clasped behind his back looking out the window at the darkness. If he tried to call the Chancellor's bluff, it could cost one or more of his crew their lives. He wasn't willing to risk anyone's life, but his own. He did want to do what he could to protect Rachel and Moderator Tarmon. "You're not giving me much of a choice. How do I know you'll keep your word once I'm gone?"

Chancellor Torrell stopped grinning. "You don't. All you know is what will happen if you don't cooperate."

There it was, the place to call his bluff. "Find my lawyer. I'll do what you want, but I need to talk to Rachel first."

"Captain, you'll do what I want right now or I'll start the executions now. Do you understand what I am capable of?" Chancellor Torrell's icy stare gave David a chill.

"Do you understand what I'm capable of?" David returned his icy stare. "You are alone in the room with a convicted killer. I have extensive combat training. I need to talk to my lawyer to be sure you can't hurt my people. You give me that, or I'll be on you before you can make a sound." David felt a twinge of remorse. He had now lied twice to the Chancellor. The memory of Pateras revealing his own soul to him still weighed heavily on him. David knew those satellites wouldn't reactivate on their own. It was true David was young and well trained in combat, but it was highly unlikely he could attack as quickly and quietly as he claimed. He also wasn't a coldblooded killer. He could kill to defend himself, but he wasn't capable of attacking and killing an unarmed man.

Chancellor Torrell hesitated and stared at David. He realized he had backed David into a corner and he might just be desperate enough to carry out his threat. "Fine. I'll have her located. If she isn't found in the next hour though, you'll have to send her a recorded message."

David assumed a more defeated posture. With his back to the window, he made one last request. "Can I have a few minutes alone with Cheyenne and my wife?"

The Chancellor started to say no, but realized he was already rushing this through and his supporters might rebel if they realized exactly what he was doing. "I'll send them in now, then I'll send them back to their cells."

Brynna and Cheyenne walked into the office and the door shut behind them. David held up his hand to tell them to wait. "Chancellor Noe, if you are watching and recording this, and I hope you are, don't get caught. Chancellor Torrell is willing to murder me to become the next Moderator. Make sure you have a strong backing before you try to take this man down or he'll take you down. I'd really appreciate it if you could let Moderator Tarmon know what this man is up to and capable of. Don't let him find out what you're doing."

David turned his attention to the women. "Please tell me she wasn't out there with you."

Brynna shook her head. "No, she excused herself right away. David, what's going on?"

David reached out and gently rubbed Brynna's arm. He wasn't anxious to tell her what was about to happen. He decided they would take it better sitting down. He escorted the two women over to the couch and sat down with them. "Cheyenne, Brynna, I'm sorry. I had to agree to his terms. I'm going to confess to causing the Intercessor's death. He's going to execute me as soon as he has what he wants. I . . ."

"Captain, no! This is all my fault! You told me to be careful. I screwed up. I'm so sorry. How can I fix this?"

David grabbed Cheyenne's hand. "Cheyenne, he was going to do this one way or another. This just gave him an easy way in. This isn't your fault. He wouldn't have known the significance of the data crystal if he hadn't been searching for a way to trap us."

Brynna knew she had to hold herself together for Cheyenne's benefit. "David, what are you going to do?"

David didn't want to give her any more information than he had to in case Chancellor Torrell was now watching. "Chancellor Torrell is allowing me to talk to Rachel to help insure the safety of the crew. I just need you two to be strong for me. Arni said I wasn't going to die. I can only hope he meant despite two executions and not just one."

Brynna swallowed hard. "I hate to mention this, but perhaps Arni couldn't see past his own death."

David gave her a disgruntled look. "I hate for you to mention that too. He told you no one would die here. I'm just going to hold onto that thought." David took Brynna's hands in his own. "When this is over, I'm going to owe you one serious vacation."

The two stood up and hugged tightly, then David gave Brynna a passionate kiss. Cheyenne moved to the window and stared into the darkness to give the couple a moment of privacy.

David turned around to Cheyenne while still holding Brynna's hand. "Cheyenne, do me a favor." Cheyenne turned to look at him. "Don't give him the satisfaction of seeing you cry again."

Cheyenne snapped to attention and saluted the Captain. "Yes, Captain."

Chancellor Torrell re-entered the room along with the others. He ordered the guards to escort the women to the observation room of the execution chamber. David turned around abruptly to face Chancellor Torrell. "What? You said you were sending them back to their cells!" Chancellor Torrell smiled again. "I decided to have a little insurance in case you decided to act up. I can send them back once you're secured between the posts if that is your wish. Now please tell everyone what you decided to tell me."

David sat down in the chair in the middle of the room again. He glanced outside looking for the sunrise. It was still pitch black. "I take full responsibility for the death of the Intercessor. I will make a full confession once I have spoken to Rachel Johan."

Arbiter Navid was quick to question his change of heart. "Were you coerced in any way to do this?"

The Captain looked at Chancellor Torrell. "No, not at all." His gaze stayed locked on the Chancellor until the Chancellor grew uneasy and looked away.

The group discussed a few trivial details of the arrangement and vented more about the plea agreement. They had no personal dislikes of the crew. They simply felt like the Commonwealth had attacked them again and didn't want them to "get away with it."

David wanted to make eye contact with Chancellor Noe to see if she had gotten his messages. He knew it would be dangerous for her if he did. He moved over to the window and continued to stare out it while the others continued their pointless banter. Chancellor Noe got up to leave the room. Damarion Torrell was concerned about her lack of enthusiasm. "Chancellor Noe, is everything alright?"

"I'm just worried about Saundra. Since we're still waiting on Counselor Johan, I thought I would take a minute and check in with Dr. Evans before the execution. I promise I won't disturb the Moderator. I know she desperately needs her rest." She stepped over more closely to Chancellor Torrell and spoke softly. "I appreciate what you are doing Damarion, but you know this stuff isn't my style." She gave him a disarming smile and walked on out. His eyes followed her suspiciously for a moment then decided he was just being paranoid. Her guard followed her out.

After the two were well away from the Chancellor's the guard broke protocol. "Chancellor Noe, may I ask a question?"

The Chancellor turned to look at him and the cameras scattered throughout the halls. She scowled at him. "Sergeant, if you are to be trusted as my guard and protector then I suggest you only ask questions that won't endanger that trust."

The Sergeant looked over his shoulder to see what had her attention. His eyes landed on the audiovisual recorders. He turned back towards her. "I'm sorry ma'am. I apologize for the breech in protocol. It won't happen again."

The Chancellor smiled at him. "I appreciate your wise choices, young man."

The guard had watched the entire conversation between Chancellor Torrell and the Captain when they were alone in the Chancellor's office. He had said little about it, but Irena knew he was shocked. She had given him one brief warning not to mention what he had seen to anyone. She also took the liberty of sending copies of the recorded files to Colonel Bernt, Captain Parker, Moderator Tarmon, and the Premier of Raanan, Damarion's direct superior.

While watching the interchange, she also stole a quick look at the forensic report on the data crystal. The evidence showed the crystal was new and had never had anything on it prior to the two files it now contained. Aside from the guards who confiscated the crystal, the only DNA and fingerprint evidence found was of Cheyenne, Brynna and Rachel Johan. The Captain's DNA was conspicuously missing. When she sent out the files, she included the forensic evidence and created her own data crystal with the same information.

The two continued to the infirmary. As they walked in the door to the observation room, Irena discovered why no one had been able to reach Rachel. She was asleep in a chair with her head on Captain Parker's shoulder. Captain Parker looked up apologetically. "Forgive me for not standing Chancellor Noe. The Counselor is exhausted."

Chancellor Noe gave him a weak smile. "I'm sorry Captain, but I'm going to have to wake her." Chancellor Noe touched Rachel's shoulder and shook her gently. The Captain gently slid his shoulder from under her head. Between the Chancellor's gentle prods and the Captain's movements, Rachel began to move and open her eyes. The Captain pulled a chair over for the Chancellor. She nodded her thanks and sat down in front of Rachel. Irena asked the Captain to get Rachel a glass of water, so they could talk alone for a moment. The Chancellor was still afraid she was being watched, so she chose her words and movements carefully. "Rachel, are you awake enough to talk, dear?"

Rachel nodded. "Yes Chancellor, I'm awake."

The Chancellor took Rachel's hands in her own and held them tightly. "Rachel, I need you to listen to me. Listen carefully dear, I know you're still sleepy, so this may not make a lot of sense." Every time she said the word "listen," she squeezed Rachel's hands tighter. Irena could see Rachel wiping the cobwebs from her mind as she sat up straighter in her chair.

Rachel gave a simple, "I'm listening" as she waited for Irena to go on with whatever was on her mind.

Captain Parker stepped back in with the glass of water. Sensing his presence was an interruption, he set it down quickly and quietly on the table next to Rachel. He started to move away from the women, but Irena decided he should stay. She asked him to sit down and informed him she had orders for him after she finished talking to Rachel.

The Chancellor carefully began to explain to Rachel why she was there. "Rachel, I know you have worked hard to protect the Captain and his crew. I am impressed by all the hard work you've done despite your true feelings about them."

Rachel gave the Chancellor a puzzled look and started asking questions. "Chancellor, what's this about? Has something happened?"

The Chancellor squeezed Rachel's hands even harder causing her to wince. "Just listen Rachel, we don't have a lot of time. Listen carefully. We can talk about this more later, but for now I need to you to understand me. Chancellor Torrell found evidence Captain Alexander lied about his knowledge of the Ancient Texts. The Chancellor believes the Captain is responsible for the Intercessor's death. One of the Captain's crew members was found with a data crystal containing translation files and the Ancient Texts."

Rachel, knowing she was responsible for those files started to offer an explanation to the Chancellor. "But Chancellor, he didn't -"

Irena squeezed her hands tightly again. "I know he probably didn't tell you about it. He's a deceptive officer of the Commonwealth. Chancellor Torrell has been working on accessing the numerous audiovisual records to gather as much information as possible to support his case. He and several others believe Moderator Tarmon has not handled this situation as well as she should have. Captain Alexander has agreed to give a public confession, but he wants to see you to ensure the safety of his crew first. Chancellor Torrell has only given us one hour to find you. Your job is to convince the Captain, by whatever means necessary, his crew will be protected, so he will make his confession. Chancellor Torrell will then have him executed before the Moderator wakes up and is forced to deal with him again. The Chancellor doesn't want to burden the Moderator any further with this. Go quickly to your office and freshen up. You probably have several messages for you from the Captain and his crew and a couple from Chancellor Torrell. After you've had a chance to freshen up, go to Chancellor Torrell's office to give the Captain whatever reassurances he needs to finish this once and for all."

Rachel sat there trying to make sense of the whole thing. She heard the words coming out of the Chancellor's mouth, but somehow, they were all wrong. Rachel managed to respond although it was not much of a response. "Okay, if you say so." Chancellor Noe smiled and gave her hands a more gentle squeeze then carefully extricated her hands from Rachel's.

Captain Parker was looking very perplexed. He knew there was more going on than what he could see. He looked at Chancellor Noe waiting quietly for her orders, despite the numerous questions popping up in his mind. "Captain, you need to prepare for Captain Alexander's execution. After he confesses his crimes, he will be executed within the hour. The other thing you should be aware of is there are some who may disagree with the way Chancellor Torrell is handling this. Anyone who opposes him could be in danger –uh - be dangerous. So, you'll need to arrange protection for Rachel, people you know you can trust. Since she is representing our sworn enemies, her loyalties could be under scrutiny. That's where your security override will come in handy. Do you understand?"

Captain Parker shook his head. "No ma'am, but I know my job and that's all I need to understand. Get the auditorium ready for another execution and protect Rachel. That's all I need to know. It will be done."

Chancellor Noe smiled. "That's a good soldier." The couple headed off towards Rachel's office. Irena hoped everything connected for the couple, but not for Chancellor Torrell.

Irena stepped on into the infirmary and found Dr. Evans sipping on a cup of coffee while he was typing a report. Edward was sitting at his wife's bedside, sleeping with his head down on the edge of Saundra's bed. Irena asked softly if they could talk. Dr. Evans nodded and followed Chancellor Noe back into the observation room after glancing back at his patient. "How is Saundra doing, Doctor?"

Dr. Evans hadn't had such a busy schedule since his days working in a local hospital. He took this job because he wanted a slower paced schedule. His plan hadn't been overly successful of late. "She's doing fine. A couple days of rest and relaxation and she'll be good as new."

"Do you have any idea how long she'll sleep?"

Dr. Evans folded his arms and leaned against the wall. "I can't really say for sure. I gave her a sedative which should keep her asleep for another two to three hours. As worn out as she is, she could sleep longer. Of course, she could fight her way back up sooner if she's got too many things on her mind."

"Well try your best to see she sleeps as long she can. Chancellor Torrell is trying to clean some things up for her. If she wakes up too soon, it could seriously raise her stress level." Chancellor Noe reached up and wrapped her hand around the doctor's arm as she spoke. She squeezed his arm gently. "She and the Chancellor don't always agree on methods and I'd hate for her to wake up and have to tangle with him again. He's only trying to do what's best. I'm sure Chancellor Torrell will be watching her progress personally. I'm also sure there will be plenty of things she'll want updates on after she wakes up." She gave his arm a tight squeeze. "Please let us know when she's awake." She gently pulled her hand back without squeezing again. Dr. Evans gave her an odd look as she turned to walk away.

Chancellor Noe rejoined the others. She reported finding Rachel and she would be coming to the Chancellor's office as soon as she freshened up. Chancellor Torrell began to question Irena. "So where did you find her?" Irena told the suspicious man exactly what she had done minus a few discreet details. He appeared to be placated by her answers. He had been watching her on the surveillance feeds and she told him everything as he had seen it. Irena had heard Captain Alexander's warning and was heeding it.

Minutes later Rachel arrived. She appeared to be extremely stoic and perhaps a tad cranky. She walked in and asked what was so urgent it couldn't have waited a couple more hours. Chancellor Torrell gave her a brief rundown of the situation, or at least his own version, then asked everyone to again leave the room, so the Captain could speak to his lawyer as requested. He also warned the Captain not to give Rachel too much information.

In the outer office, Damarion had one more question for Irena. "I saw that you looked at the forensic report on the data crystal."

She gave him a harsh look. "Of course I did, but there's nothing you can use to help your case. If the others see it, they may not be as supportive of your position. I suggest you get the Captain's confession as quickly as possible then get him executed before anyone else gets ahold of it."

Seeing the two talking in hushed tones, Arbiter Navid approached the couple. "Is there a problem?"

Chancellor Noe volunteered to answer the Arbiter's question. "It would appear Counselor Johan and Captain Parker may be developing a relationship." She spoke softly because Captain Parker was standing on the other side of the room talking to his guards. Her performance was quite convincing as the Arbiter looked casually over his shoulder then grinned. It only took a moment for him to spread the gossip to Counselor Finley.

Chancellor Torrell nodded his approval to Chancellor Noe. He walked slowly past her to the receptionist's desk and whispered. "Impressive, I think I underestimated you."

David and Rachel waited for everyone to leave the office before they began to speak. Rachel spoke first. "Captain, what's going on? You confessed to being responsible for the Intercessor's death? How is that possible?"

David was staying near the window watching the silhouettes of clouds drift across the moons in the night sky. He needed to choose his words wisely. "Rachel, I know you could care less about what happens to us. You made that quite clear the day we met. You seemed like you were genuinely trying to defend us as a favor to the Intercessor. I guess now that he's dead, you feel like you don't owe him anything more."

"Captain, I don't-"

David quickly interrupted her. "Please just let me finish. I will admit, I was suspicious about why you brought me that data crystal and now I know. You wanted to entrap me. Were you working with Chancellor Torrell or was this a convenient set of circumstances?"

Rachel stood there with her mouth open, unable to speak.

"Never mind, don't bother answering that." David looked around the room to the various cameras and spoke loudly. "I know you are watching and listening Chancellor. Did you put her up to framing me?"

Rachel looked at the cameras. Had the Captain lost his mind? No, he hadn't. She realized it was his way of warning her to be careful what she said. She decided it was time to play along. "Captain, have you lost your mind? You're seeing conspiracies where none exist. Yes, I planted the data crystal in your cell, but not under Chancellor Torrell's orders. I just saw the opportunity to discredit you with Moderator Tarmon. I know she promised to execute you for lying, I wanted to make sure she could catch you in a lie. You couldn't have tricked or manipulated the Intercessor to die in your place, but those stories you told us afterwards? Come on, you had to have read them in the Ancient Texts. Did you expect me to believe you hadn't? I just had to make sure Moderator Tarmon could see through your lies. She's a good woman and you were taking advantage of that. Now Captain, you obviously don't need legal advice, why am I here?"

David recognizing the change in Rachel's tone and demeanor, he knew he had gotten through to her. The woman was quite convincing. David almost felt insulted by her tirade. "I need two favors from you. I know you only took our case as a favor to the Intercessor, but please, in his name and in his memory, do these two things for me. First, I recorded my final wishes on the computer in my cell. Please get those transferred to a data crystal and to my wife. Second, please see that my plea agreement is honored, and my crew gets off this planet safely. Don't let Chancellor Torrell anywhere near my people. He is an evil man with his own agenda. He's willing to murder me to further his own political goals, so he's probably willing to do the same to anyone else he perceives as a threat."

Rachel eyed him cautiously. She felt like he hadn't cemented his cause for demanding to see her. "So, you woke me up tell me something you could have said in a recorded message?"

David weighed her response carefully. "No, I needed to look you in the eye to see if you intended to keep your agreement with the Intercessor to give us your best effort. Will you honor my last requests? Will you protect my people? For him?"

Rachel shifted uneasily. Her answer was easy, but it didn't need to come too easily. "Fine, but only in his memory. Is there anything else you need?"

David moved to look out the window. He turned and gave her a serious look that didn't match the words coming out of his mouth. "I need to see the sun rise." It sounded like an emotional plea for more time to live life, but the look on his face was saying something entirely different. Rachel didn't respond to his last request. She wasn't sure how to respond. She gave him a curt nod then walked out of the room.

She headed straight for Chancellor Torrell. "Chancellor Torrell, I think Captain Alexander's brushes with death have affected his mind.

He's seeing conspiracies where none exists." She leaned in and softly whispered. "I have to confess. I did plant that data crystal in his cell, but he deserved it."

Chancellor Torrell smiled sadistically. "I won't tell, if you won't."

Rachel laughed nervously. "I'm not going to say anything. I'd lose my ability to practice law. I was just hoping you wouldn't be upset with me. Once the Captain is dead, he can't testify against me. You will need to plant his DNA on the data crystal though."

Chancellor Torrell nodded and watched the woman hurry out of the room. The smile faded from his face. Only one person could have told her about that forensics report. He had been watching Chancellor Noe carefully, but apparently not carefully enough. He would have to deal with the two women, and quickly. Maybe he could kill two birds with one stone. Before walking back into his office, Chancellor Torrell sat down at the receptionist's desk and issued a couple more orders.

David stood by the window awaiting the Chancellor's return trying to think quickly for more ways to stall. He stood there looking out the window. It was still quite dark outside. He finally spoke. "Pateras, I really hope you stand by your word because I don't think I can get out of this by myself."

Chancellor Torrell returned to his desk and gave David a very simple statement to read as his confession. David was hoping he could use his own words to confess. His intention was to make his confession last as long as possible. That was no longer a viable option.

David read through the confession and stopped when he got to a certain point in it. The confession implicated Chancellor Noe and Rachel Johan. He looked up to see the Chancellor smirk. "You thought you had me fooled, didn't you, Captain? As soon as we begin your execution, the two women will be placed under arrest. With your testimony, it will be easy to get a conviction."

David was now angry. He slammed the data tablet containing "his confession" on the desk. "This wasn't part of our agreement. I'm not taking out your enemies for you." David was still trying to bluff.

Chancellor Torrell wasn't buying it. "Captain, your legal counselor slipped up. She let me know she had seen the forensic report. She had no way of knowing the thing even existed unless someone told her about it. The only ones who knew what that report said were Chancellor Noe, the forensic technician, and myself. I've been watching Chancellor Noe, I never saw her tell Rachel about it. Apparently, Chancellor Noe has been passing information I haven't seen. It makes one wonder, what other information she's been passing. I need people around me I can trust. You will read this confession as it is, and you'll do it now, or shall I start the executions without you?"

David glanced out the window again. There was no sign of light and the two moons had dipped below the horizon which made it even darker. David suddenly felt defeated and helpless. A familiar voice whispered in his mind. "Trust me, I've got this."

David picked up the tablet and read it again. He set it down in front of him and nodded to the Chancellor when he was ready to begin.

"My name is David Liam Alexander. I am Captain of the Commonwealth Interstellar Force Star ship known as the Evangeline. I was granted mercy by the Courts of Drea III and by the Lord Intercessor for my part in causing the deaths of the inhabitants of Galat III. In so doing, I confess I am guilty of causing the death of the Intercessor Arni Liontari. My crew was incarcerated and had no knowledge of my actions."

David reached the point in his confession where he was to implicate the Chancellor and Rachel, but he couldn't force himself to do it. He had no trouble confessing his own guilt, but he couldn't lie, not about this. Chancellor Torrell motioned for David to continue.

"I manipulated those around me through hypnosis and medications to participate in the effort to free me and put the Intercessor in my place. I obtained medications from my stay in the infirmary. I incited the men who attacked me, so I could get into the infirmary. Those who helped me didn't know what they were doing and are innocent of all wrong doing. I created and acted on this plan alone. I accept this punishment for my crimes."

David stopped speaking and glared at the Chancellor. "You want to take those women down? You'll have to do it on your own. I'm not going to help you."

The Chancellor sat there and drummed his fingers on his desk deciding what to do. He pushed a button on his desk and two guards entered. "Very well, Captain, have it your way. I'll do it my way. Guards, bind him and take him to the execution auditorium."

David reacted instinctively to defend himself. Before the first punch was ever served, the Chancellor put a stop to it. "Captain, may I remind you, your wife and ensign are already in the auditorium?"

David relaxed his stance. He turned around slowly, lowered himself to his knees, and placed his hands on his head. The guards moved in and locked the binders around his wrists quickly. They pulled him to his feet and started to escort him out. David twisted out of their grip for a second to address the Chancellor again. "Chancellor, things aren't always what they seem to be. I used to think the Commonwealth was the most powerful force in the galaxy. It's not. I've found something considerably more powerful since I've been here on Drea III, something inescapable."

The Chancellor grinned. "Captain, flattery will get you nowhere."

David grinned in return. "You misunderstand, Chancellor. You are the one who won't be able to escape. Arni's coming for you."

The Chancellor broke into an all-out laugh. "Get him out of here."

The two guards ushered him down the hall. They talked to each other as though David weren't even there. "I don't get it. The first time we took this guy to be executed, he didn't even try to resist. Why fight back this time?"

The second guard shrugged. "Beats me. I don't try to understand, I just do my job."

David gave the two men a perturbed look. "You could ask the guy.

He might have a good reason."

The first guard was more interested in understanding than the second one. He looked at his partner. "You know if it weren't against regulations to talk to prisoners on their way to execution, I might ask him why."

His partner gave him an annoyed look but didn't respond. David looked at the two men again. "I suppose I'll just have to talk to myself. I wouldn't want to get anyone in trouble. I suppose there are several reasons why a man might or might not resist going to his own execution. Personally, the first time I was guilty, and I accepted it. This time I'm not."

The second guard who was determined to abide by the regulations grabbed his disciplinary rod and pointed it at the Captain. "I'm going to ask nicely this time. Shut up. Next time I won't be so nice."

David nodded and waited for the man to put the rod away then added one more hasty comment as they stepped into the elevator. "I think I'd

also want to know why the Chancellor is moving so fast while the Moderator is out of commission."

The man grabbed his rod again and jabbed it into David's side. David convulsed, fell to the floor and began twitching. "I warned you to keep your mouth shut."

The first man gave his partner an annoyed look. "Great. Good job, man. Now we're gonna have to drag him the rest of the way." The two just left him on the floor until the elevator reached the appropriate floor. David tried hard to shake the cobwebs from his mind. He wasn't trying to buy himself time. His intent was to plant doubts. He was hoping to avoid the discipline. He decided to take advantage of the situation and allow them to drag him instead of trying to walk.

The two griped and snapped at each other the rest of the way to the execution chamber. They dropped David on the ground by the two columns in the center of the room and started to prepare the binders for him. The shock from the rod had worn off enough for David to have most of his muscle control back. While the guards were distracted, David rolled to his feet and walked over to the glass where Brynna and Cheyenne were being held. He mouthed the words I love you to her and winked at her. Her hands were free, so she reached up and touched the glass as close to him as possible. A movement behind her caught his attention. The door at the back of the room was opened. The rest of David's crew was being ushered in. David started to get angry, but decided it wasn't worth it. They would either see him die like they expected, or they would see the power of Pateras.

The guards got the binders ready and looked back at the empty spot where they had left David. For a second a wave of panic ran through them until they saw David standing calmly a few yards in front of them. The trigger-happy guard reached for his wand a second time until his partner gave him a jab to the ribs. "You don't learn too quickly, do you?"

The two drug David backwards to the columns. Before they removed his binders, the second guard asked him a pointed question. "Are you going to resist this time?"

David looked at the man and answered bluntly. "No, the Chancellor is holding my wife hostage. He promised to execute her and one of my ensigns if I don't behave." The guard gave him a confused look then promptly released David's binders. His partner looked at him like he had lost his mind. He grabbed one of David's wrists and swiftly attached him to the top of the column. The guard behind him gently pulled David's other arm to the second column. The guard gave the two pedestals an odd look. They were too far apart. David's arms wouldn't reach. When he discovered the problem, he sent his partner to the control panel to adjust the width of the two columns. The safety engaged forcing them to remove David from the platform before the pillars would move.

Chancellor Torrell and his entourage arrived and looked annoyed to see David was still not strung between the pillars. David was torn between resting in the belief Pateras had everything under control and fighting for his life. He finally decided there wasn't any way to escape without putting his crew in danger. If he was going to go out, he might as well have some fun. He looked at the guard who was holding his arm. "Should I go hold my arms out to see if he has the measurement right or not?" The guard started to smile then realized what David was saying. He looked at his prisoner as though he had lost his mind.

David looked at the windows and sky lights for any sign of daylight. There was nothing. He turned towards the guard again. "What time is it?" The guard gave him the same strange look as before, then asked, "Have you got some place you need to be?"

David shrugged. "It would be nice to know what time it is when I die. I do have another appointment to be executed by Moderator Tarmon at noon if Pateras doesn't bring the Intercessor back to life. I wouldn't want to miss that appointment. C'mon, really, what time is it?"

The guard jerked David around to face him. "You're insane. You know that, right? My buddy over there wouldn't have been as patient with you as I am. He would have hit you with the disciplinary rod a couple times by now. Here's what I can do though." The guard landed one swift hard punch into David's solar plexus. David doubled over and tried to catch his breath.

The crew milled around the observation room near the glass. Brynna gave them a brief explanation of what was happening. As she gave them the explanation, she watched Cheyenne for a reaction. Cheyenne managed to disconnect her emotions. She sat there next to Lazaro tightly holding his hand. Jake was on Brynna quickly. "Isn't there anything we can do to stop him?"

Brynna shook her head. "David has taken steps to stop Chancellor Torrell, but I don't know how successful he's been."

Thane saw David talking to the guard then saw the guard react violently. "What's he doing?"

Jake gave his assessment. "It looks like he's trying to antagonize the guards.

Brynna scowled. "He's trying to buy time."

Now it was Jake's turn to scowl. "Buy time for what?"

Brynna stared at David as he struggled to stand upright again. "Time for Pateras to raise Arni from the dead."

Jake sat down and said nothing. One by one, the crew took their seats. Brynna refused to sit down yet.

David finally caught his breath and pulled himself up to his full height. He faced the guard who had punched him and stopped being cocky. "I'm not insane. Chancellor Torrell is attempting to usurp Moderator Tarmon and he's executing me to do it. He's going to arrest Chancellor Noe and Rachel Johan. He may even try to execute my entire crew."

The guard shook his head incredulously at David. "You just don't learn, do you?" The guard closed his fist and attempted to land another punch to David's abdomen.

David was ready for him and caught the man's wrist. David and the guard struggled discreetly for power. David finally told the guard. "You're going to have to pick sides very soon. I hope you'll choose the right one. I'm going to let go now. I'll understand if you need to try again, and I won't stop you. I just needed to make my point."

The guard relaxed his arm and turned away from David. Then he turned back to David. "If what you said is true, then I'll back the Moderator, but in the meantime -" The man reared back and landed his punch unimpeded.

David groaned and doubled over again. In a minute, he caught his breath and asked the guard, "Can you tell me what time it is now?"

The guard gave him a look of annoyance and walked him up the platform to the columns. He secured the Captain between the pillars. David said nothing else to the man.

Chancellor Torrell got everyone settled in the VIP observation room, and then he headed out to the main chamber. A large number of guards began to fill the room. Chancellor Torrell started giving directions to each group as they entered. He sent them to cover all the exits. He sent several heavily armed men to the back of the room where the crew was seated. David and Brynna exchanged knowing looks. Several were also sent to cover the VIP room, but those were in a more relaxed stance. David made eye contact with Rachel and Chancellor Noe. He nodded towards Chancellor Torrell then mouthed the words "He – knows." The two women looked around at all the guards and knew David was right. They were fairly certain they had no way out. They stood up to try and slip out, but Chancellor Torrell moved to the podium. "Ladies, please return to your seats. We are ready to finish this."

Chancellor Torrell had summoned a few of his loyal supporters who were now in the observation room with Arbiter Navid, Prosecutor Finley, and the two women. Rachel and Irena returned to their seats. Captain Parker had been in and out, staying obviously busy.

Chancellor Torrell began his speech about the Captain's lies and how the Moderator had been deceived as well. He bragged about getting the evidence and a confession from the Captain. He played David's confession for the others to watch then began to comment on it. "Unfortunately, the Captain continues to lie even during his confession. In return for his confession, I agreed to spare the lives of Ensign Dominick and Commander Alexander who were both conspirators in this. Since the Captain lied in his confession, I declare that agreement null and void. His entire crew will be executed, and we will be rid of these Commonwealth troublemakers once and for all. Gentlemen stand ready."

The guards in the observation room readied their weapons. The weapons they carried were not like the Tri-EMP's. These weapons fired deadly invasive projectiles. The crew was on the edges of their seats ready to react, but afraid to move before the time was right. David jerked at his binders and yelled out at the Chancellor. "Chancellor Torrell, we had an agreement! You can't just shoot them where they sit!"

Chancellor Torrell looked like he was high on Adrenalin. He wore the largest sadistic grin on his face and strutted around like he owned the world. For the moment, he did. Chancellor Noe stood up to challenge the man. Before she could speak, he played the clip of Rachel admitting to planting the data crystal and then her comment about the Captain's DNA not being found on the crystal. He addressed the clip as proof, Rachel and Chancellor Noe were working with the Captain to subvert the ailing Moderator. "Rachel Johan confessed to giving the crystal to the Captain under the guise of planting it. In actuality, it left him a way to claim innocence because he never physically touched the crystal. He also pointed out the only ones who knew about the forensics report was Chancellor Noe and himself. "Guards, place the two women under arrest please."

Two guards in the VIP room moved to arrest the women when another voice called out from behind Chancellor Torrell. "Belay that order!"

The startled guards stopped in their tracks. The voice had come from Moderator Tarmon. Behind her stood Dr. Evans. Chancellor Torrell quickly tried to cover his actions. "Moderator Tarmon, there is a conspiracy involving the Captain and those two women."

Moderator Tarmon was nearly as angry as he had seen her just before she collapsed. "Oh, there's a conspiracy all right, but it started with you. Gentlemen put away your weapons and stand down!"

Chancellor Torrell waved for the guards to stay put. "No, hold your ground, gentlemen. The Moderator is not well, she doesn't know what's happened. She's being taken advantage of."

Dr. Evans spoke up. "Moderator Tarmon is merely suffering from exhaustion and is of sound mind."

Moderator Tarmon knew she needed to push hard and fast before Chancellor Torrell had a firm foothold. "Guards arrest Chancellor Torrell. The rest of you stand down or face a court martial."

No one moved until Captain Parker nodded to them. As soon as he nodded, the group in the observation room with the crew holstered their weapons and abruptly left the room. The ones in the VIP room had been handpicked by the Chancellor and weren't as quick to respond. They did move to the back of the room. They were waiting around to see if the Chancellor would again get the upper hand. Captain Parker had chosen the guards assigned to execute the crew, so despite their foreboding appearance, they would not have fired under any circumstances. Two guards moved to arrest the Chancellor. He backed away from them, then turned to run, only to find himself behind the executioners control panel. The guard who was manning it had been running one last diagnostic and wasn't concentrating on the scene unfolding around him. Chancellor Torrell grabbed the technician's weapon and knocked the man to the floor.

The guard who had punched David twice in the stomach, edged closer to the pillars David was bound to. He attempted to reach up and release David's restraints. He wasn't fast enough. Chancellor Torrell fired his weapon at one of the pillars to warn the man to stay back.

Captain Parker started edging closer to Chancellor Torrell. Since the chamber was designed for various methods of execution, the control panel was shielded. The guard who had been manning the control panel tried to take back his post. The Chancellor anticipated his move. He fired his weapon causing the man to collapse on the floor.

Chancellor Torrell decided he had only one chance. He moved to the edge of the shield then pointed his weapon at the Moderator. As the weapon discharged, Captain Parker threw himself onto the Moderator, taking them both to the ground. The weapon pierced the Captain's back and left him unconscious on the floor. Knowing the weapon was potentially deadly, Rachel gasped and jumped to her feet.

David looked over his shoulder at the guard who had tried to release him. "Get the Moderator and her husband to safety." The man nodded. He raced to the Moderator's side. He helped her to her feet then pulled the couple away from harm. He attempted to pull Dr. Evans as well, but the doctor refused to go. He chose instead to see what he could do for Captain Parker. Rachel bolted for the door. The guards refused to let her leave the safety of the room. Although they sided with Chancellor Torrell, they now saw the wisdom in rethinking their choice.

Chancellor Torrell was growing angrier and more desperate by the moment. When his attempt to kill the Moderator failed, he decided he had only one more option. It wouldn't help him escape his fate, but he would be a lot happier. He reached down and powered up the energy charge that would irradiate the Captain. The Captain heard the machine powering. He immediately looked around to see if anyone else was close enough to stop the man or to release him. There was no one. He saw a light through the windows. He rejoiced for a second thinking it was the sunrise. His heart sank as it disappeared then flashed again. Rain began to hit the sky lights. It was storming outside.

Chancellor Torrell took one more moment to gloat. "Captain Alexander, I was going to have your crew shot in front of your eyes seconds before I had you executed, so you could watch them die. Since that didn't work out, I'm just going to have to be happy with executing you alone. This time it's programmed to kill you with one blast." He raised his free hand dramatically over the firing mechanism. He held it there momentarily to prolong the Captain's suspense. When he was satisfied he had gotten all he could from the Captain's distress, he brought his hand down hard and fast towards the control panel. Just as his hand descended the lights went out. The building shook and vibrated. Except for a brilliant flash of lightning seen through windows and the eerie glow from the control panel, there was no light. Brynna, along with several of the crew, held her breath. She couldn't bear to see this happen again. David strained against his bonds. It seemed like an eternity, although it was mere seconds. Nothing happened.

They could hear nothing, except the hum of the generator, which had its own separate power supply and a voice cry out. "Noooo!"

David had clenched his jaw to prepare for the expected jolt. The lights came back on, and David breathed a sigh of relief.

The Chancellor was standing there with a desperate and stricken look on his face. Arni stood at the Chancellor's side holding the man's arm just above a button on the control panel. Arni powered the machine down.

Once he recovered from the shock, Chancellor Torrell began to beg and plead for mercy. Two guards ventured close enough to take the Chancellor into custody. The guards were in awe of Arni's presence. They had been in awe of his presence every time they had seen him before he died. They were well beyond awe at this point.

David called out to Brynna who breathed a sigh of relief to see David smiling at her. She jumped up to touch the glass again. She looked behind the control panel to catch Arni's eye. She mouthed the words "Thank You," to him. Arni smiled and nodded. Brynna and Cheyenne were both so relieved they grabbed each other into a tight hug. This time Brynna was the one who cried.

The guards who arrested Chancellor Torrell escorted him past the Moderator. When he saw the Moderator, he begged and pleaded with her to ask the Intercessor for mercy. She looked at the guards. "What's he talking about?"

One of the guards stopped long enough to answer. "The Intercessor stopped the Chancellor from executing the prisoner."

Saundra looked past him towards the execution chamber. "The Intercessor?"

The guard nodded. "Yes ma'am. It was unbelievable. The power went out and when it came back on he was there. He was suddenly just standing there, keeping the Chancellor's hand from hitting the button to execute the prisoner."

The Moderator ran straight back into the chamber with her husband close behind. They found the two injured men sitting up and talking. The Intercessor had healed them both. Moderator Tarmon headed straight for the Intercessor and knelt in front of him. Rachel had managed to get past the guards and was at Captain Parker's side.

Upon seeing Moderator Tarmon kneel before the Intercessor, all the Dreans in the auditorium followed her example and knelt before him as well. The crew stood there watching the scene unfold with curiosity.

The guard who pulled the Moderator to safety, returned to release David from the pillars. The task was much easier when a madman wasn't shooting at them. As the guard released the second binder he looked at David and said, "6:57."

David massaged his wrists and gave the guard a puzzled look. "What?"

The guard grinned. "You wanted to know the time. It's 6:57." David shook his head and laughed.

THE AFTERMATH

The ship returned to Medoris after leaving Drea. The crew was in dire need of shore leave in friendly territory after their ordeal on Drea. David zipped his jacket all the way up. It was getting chilly now that the sun was setting. He was starting to see his breath. They hadn't been gone from Medoris IV very long, but the harsh climate of this world made the summers short and the winters long and hard. David wasted no time in walking down to the creek after arriving. He needed to be alone for a little while. Before he stepped foot off the ship he told Brynna everyone was on leave, but subject to recall if necessary. The computers were set to automatically notify him if anyone approached the ship or if any communications came in from the Commonwealth.

The entire crew had been testy during their journey back to Medoris. They tried to get along, but the tension was so great, it was hard to control. David thought back over the events of the last four days. Moderator Tarmon had the crew released from custody within an hour of Arni's resurrection. She quickly shuttled them back to their ship before holding a press conference touting the return of the Intercessor. The Intercessor also addressed the press conference with shrouded prophecies making little to no sense to David. He was still struggling with Arni's death and resurrection. What he couldn't understand was why it meant so much. If Arni could cross over between life and death the same way David walked through a door, why did he feel so indebted to Arni? He hoped the matter would be settled in his mind soon. He didn't like this feeling. Speaking of feelings- "Hello, Arni."

"Hello, David. I told you I would see you on Medoris."

Arni had pulled David aside just prior to their departure and promised they would get a chance to talk again on Medoris. David thanked Arni again for saving his life and the life of his crew. He was torn between wanting to learn more about Arni and wishing he could just forget the whole thing.

David and Arni talked for the next couple hours. David tried to understand the significance of the events on Drea and what Arni was expecting from him. "Arni, I know your father is the most powerful being in the universe, but do you understand what the two of you are asking of me?"

"Yes, we are asking you to give up everything. We are asking you to turn your back on your friends, your family, everything you have ever been taught to be the truth and follow what will look like nothing, but a primitive ghostly superstition. Does that about cover it?"

David sighed. "Yeah, that pretty much covers it. Pateras wants me to bring him into the Commonwealth, but my Commonwealth mission takes me directly away from the Commonwealth. How am I supposed to do that?"

"Don't worry, we'll take care of that part. My goals are to do whatever is needed to show you the truth about the Commonwealth, secure your trust, and the trust of your crew."

David nodded thoughtfully. "For whatever it's worth, I truly am sorry for – for all those things Pateras showed me, especially the deaths on Galat. You show me proof the Commonwealth has become the monster they claimed you were and you'll have my allegiance. In truth, I've already committed treason. I had Ensign Dominick alter the programming on the data modules. They will no longer notify the Commonwealth of your presence here. They will only contact the Evangeline. I haven't chosen to follow you yet, but I won't set up another planet for destruction. Depending on what I learn next, that could change. I can't speak for my crew though. They are under orders to destroy me if I ally with you. You'll have to convince them for yourself." Arni leaned casually up against the same tree several of the crew had previously found comfort leaning against. "I'm already working on it. I plan to spend time with your crew one on one."

The two continued to talk long past sunset until David was having trouble staying warm. He didn't complain about the cold, but Arni could see him shiver periodically and watched him tuck his hands under his arms trying to keep them warm. Arni was the one who suggested they head back to the ship. As they reached the base of the steps, David had one last question he desperately needed an answer for. His other questions could wait. "Arni, I am grateful you saved my life and my crew's lives, really I am, but..."

"You're thinking it wasn't a big deal for me since I can die and return to life at will. Do you remember what my father revealed to you about yourself?"

"Yes." David shivered again, but not from the cold this time. "When I died, I felt the physical pain of each jolt sent through my

body. I also felt what Pateras showed you and it was multiplied by the number of humans across all of eternity. It wasn't as quick and easy as you think. I died an infinite number of painful deaths at one time. Consider that, while you warm up inside. I'll be around." Arni turned to walk away. David watched him walk away into the night then headed inside quickly.

David went to the dining hall for a cup of coffee. Brynna and Cheyenne were already sitting there, drinking coffee and talking. David's hands were cold enough he was having trouble making his fingers bend. Initially, he dropped his coffee cup before he poured any coffee into it.

Brynna got up and moved to the dispenser. "Captain, you look cold. How about a little help?" She took the cup he had just picked up from the floor and put it in the bin for dirty dishes. She grabbed another and filled it up with coffee. She placed it gently in his hands and wrapped her hands around the outside of his warming them up faster.

David smiled. "Thanks, Commander."

Brynna smiled back at him. "You may want to take a nice hot bath or shower before coming to bed. I have a hunch your wife wouldn't appreciate those cold hands."

David's smile changed to an impish grin. "You think so?"

Brynna winked at him and planted a gentle kiss on his cheek. "I know so."

Cheyenne grinned, but averted her eyes. It was almost like watching one's parents being playful. She began to feel like three was a crowd when Brynna released David's hands and sat back down near her. She didn't know if it was acceptable to ask but needed to change the subject. "Captain, what's our plan from here?"

David took a few sips of his coffee before answering. "For the next few days, I intend on giving shore leave to the crew. We do have some things to accomplish while we're here. I want you to start that translation, but I want you to have some time off too. Lexi needs to interview the entire crew. We've just been through some traumatic events. I want to make sure everyone's dealing with it appropriately. Personally, I'd like to get in a few games of Zone."

Thane and Jason walked in the door about that time. "Zone? Did somebody mention Zone? I'm in."

The Captain smiled. It was good to hear the enthusiasm in Thane's voice. Jason seconded Thane's opinion. "Yes, gentlemen, that's part of my agenda while we are here on Medoris. I also want to check in briefly with the Kimbra, Akamu, and Sorley, but nothing heavy duty. We'll have a staff meeting in the morning and make everything official."

Jason, being the more pragmatic one, asked, "What time is the staff meeting?"

"Let's just have it with breakfast in the morning, say around 8:30 a.m.?"

"8:30?" Thane whined. "I thought if we were getting shore leave I could sleep in."

David rolled his eyes. "We do have some business to tend to, so make it 9:00. Is that better?" David gave Thane a look that said, you better not object.

Thane grinned. "Much better, sir. Thank you, sir."

Despite Thane's protests to rising so early, he was one of the first to enter the dining room and seemed as awake and as alert as ever. He was in rare form this morning, pestering anyone he could. His first victim was Marissa, who was not a morning person and gave him an elbow in the gut for his troubles. Jake was at her side when she elbowed Thane. He gave her a puzzled look, and then encouraged Thane to annoy someone else.

Marissa wasn't typically so easily ruffled. Jake pulled her over to a table away from the others and quietly asked her if she was alright. She stared at him for a moment before answering. "I didn't sleep well. I'm still exhausted. I have a headache and a crick in my neck." She paused a moment then whispered, "and I'm cranky. I hate being cranky!" Jake blinked. He wasn't quite sure how to handle her bluntness. He finally reached up and gently massaged her neck. His thumb hit the knot in her neck and she winced. He stopped massaging for a moment until she relaxed then he started on the spot again only more slowly and cautiously. He saw her face start to relax, which made them both feel better.

A few minutes later the entire crew was assembled. David finished his breakfast first and started the briefing while everyone else continued to eat.

"Everyone, listen up while you eat. For the most part of our stay here, you're on shore leave. There are a few work items that need to happen. Lt. Flint, I need psych evals done on every crew member. Wait at least one day before starting those. I want everyone to have a little time to unwind. You can do them as formally or informally as you would like, but I need to know how everyone's holding up."

"Ensign Dominick, I understand you've already started working on that translation?"

Cheyenne set her fork down to respond. "It's pretty much done, sir. I put the files into the computer and let the computer do the work. The only thing left is to check words having multiple meanings. I need to go through the words the computer flagged and make sure it chose the correct definitions. You could feasibly read it now."

"Fine, then forward a preliminary copy to me and to the Commander. Ensign Ryder, see what you can do to help her out with that, but it doesn't have to be completed right away because the primary goal for now is shore leave."

"We can expect visits from the neighbors. The Commander and I want to speak to the leaders of all three populations. We want to warn them about the possible consequences of allying with Arni. I don't want any more blood on my hands. If they choose to ally with him after our warning, then it's on them, not on me. If the Commander and I are away from the ship and one of our neighbors comes for a visit, just let them know we'd like to check in with them. I'm not leaving anyone on active duty only passive duty. I'll take volunteers first and commandeer as needed."

David knew he sounded cold, but he also knew Jake was watching and listening closely. He needed Jake's trust. Jake had seen Arni save David's life twice. The chief knew David's moral character would cause him to feel ingratiated to Arni. He did feel indebted to Arni, even more so since their talk the previous night. David needed Jake to drop his guard and not worry about the Captain's loyalty.

"I told you to work on preliminary reports in route to Medoris. Here's what I want. In deference to our agreement, there is to be no mention of Arni. Mention the Intercessor as vaguely as possible, and don't mention his death and coming back to life. We reached a plea agreement giving them control of the satellites in return for our freedom. Chancellor Torrell is a radical within their own government who tried to seize power. I am recommending to the Commonwealth, due to their history, we not contact this world for another twenty-five to fifty years. Any questions?"

Lt. Flint scowled. "How are you going to explain the psych evaluations? I mean, I know you want them because we watched you die once and nearly saw it a second time. If we didn't see you die, then will the Commonwealth understand why you ordered them?"

"You never saw me executed. You saw the Intercessor intervene and protect me from two attempts on my life. I was removed from the execution chamber and returned to my cell by the Intercessor. You saw me nearly executed. The Commander's life, Ensign Dominick's life and each of you were threatened. We were all sentenced to death, but we bribed our way out of it with the Satellite codes. Is being locked up for over a week, sentenced to death, and nearly watching your Captain die sufficient reason to ask for psych evals?"

Lexi's brow was still furrowed. "I suppose it is, but I really don't like lying to our superiors, sir."

David nodded. "Noted, Lieutenant. I don't care for it either, but until I can find out for certain who's responsible for the death of Galat III, I'm not going to give them the chance to take lives needlessly. If it really is the Supreme Executor, then I'll take any heat for this. None of you will go down for it. Is everyone clear on that point?"

Scattered affirmations came from the crew. Some came with more enthusiasm than others. The looks on their faces were very somber. It was time to get their shore leave going. "Take today off then finish your reports tomorrow and get them to me some time tomorrow. Lt. Commander Adams and Lt. Ryder, I have one more job for you. This is a mission of vital importance. Chief Holden, I'm going to need your assistance."

Jake leaned forward with a serious look on his face. "Yes sir, what do you want me to do?"

David walked over and put a hand on Jake's shoulder then turned to look at Jason and Thane. "I need you to help me school those two in playing Zone."

Jake's somber look changed. He grinned eagerly. "It would be a pleasure, sir."

Thane wasn't about to let that comment go. "Oh no, I'm sure we'll be the ones schooling you two and it will be our pleasure." With that comment, their business was concluded, and their shore leave had commenced.

Days later, the crew seemed to be in much better spirits. Everyone was relaxed and having a good time. Some of them seemed to be having too much fun. David had to start chasing their reports down. He finally had everyone's reports except Lexi's. He wasn't overly surprised by that since she also had evaluations to do on everyone. He caught up to her as she was sitting outside on the ground in the sun working on her data pad. "Lt. Flint, mind if I join you for a moment?"

Lexi looked around herself at the ground. "Of course not, sir. Pull up a patch of ground and have a seat."

David plopped down in front of her. "I just wanted to see how you were coming on your report on Drea."

Lexi set her tablet down and sighed. "I'm just finishing it up now. I'm sorry it's taking so long to get it done. I've been trying to get all the psych evaluations done, but Marissa and Jake are avoiding me."

David nodded. "I see. Has Jason done your eval?"

Lexi nodded. "Yes sir, the crew are showing signs of stress and confusion, but they can be counted on to do their jobs. I do get a sense there are several crew members who have things they aren't ready to talk about yet, including you."

David smiled. He thought back to his evaluation. He knew she picked up on his deliberate omissions. "There were some things I just don't know how to put into words yet. You let me know if you think they are affecting my ability to command. Don't pressure the others to talk until they are ready. If the others experienced anything like I have, they... just don't know how."

Lexi smiled and nodded. "Understood, sir."

David stood back up. "I'll speak to Jake and Marissa. I want you to finish up and get some R and R. We can't stay here much longer. Winter is about to hit this place."

Lexi frowned. "That's a shame. I haven't seen snow in a long time."

David grinned. "I bet the crew would enjoy a good snow ball fight. I'll see what I can arrange."

A big smile spread across Lexi's face. "Really?"

David smiled even bigger. "Hey, I'm the Captain and my ship's psychologist just told me it would be good for crew morale. How can I not? Let's just keep this between the two of us though." David walked away leaving a smiling crew member behind.

The Captain found Jake sparring with a defenseless punching bag in the gym. From what he could see, the punching bag was no match for Jake's fury. The Chief was so focused he never heard the Captain approach. "Chief... Chief... Chief Holden... Jake!"

The Captain finally tapped Jake on the shoulder. The startled security chief spun around with his left fist flying. David was ready for him, but not as ready as he would have liked. He leaned back quickly to dodge Jake's fist. Losing his balance, he fell backwards onto the floor. When Jake realized his mistake, his eyes widened. He wiped the sweat off his brow and offered the Captain his gloved hand. "CAPTAIN, I'M SORRY! I DIDN'T HEAR YOU COME IN! LET ME HELP YOU UP!"

David grabbed Jake's wrist and allowed him to pull him up. "Jake, what was that all about?"

Jake gave him a puzzled look. "WHAT?"

David returned Jake's puzzled look. He was apparently having trouble hearing, so the Captain raised his voice and tried again. "JAKE, WHY ARE YOU YELLING AT ME?"

The Captain saw realization on Jake's face. The chief walked over to the bench where he had laid his personal items. He pulled off his gloves and pressed a button on his communications bracelet. "Sorry, Captain, I had music playing. I guess I had it a little loud. You startled me, I didn't mean to swing at you, sir." Jake grabbed his towel and wiped his face again.

David wasn't going to drop the incident so quickly. "Jake, are you having some trust issues? If you're concerned about somebody sneaking up on you perhaps you should face the door while punching."

Jake sat down on the bench and wiped his face again, but this time he was trying to clear his mind rather than his face. "I'm really sorry, sir. I guess I just had too much on my mind. I suppose I should go talk to Lexi, but…"

David grabbed a nearby chair. He sat down straddling the chair backwards. He folded his arms and rested them on the back of the chair. "But what, Chief?"

Jake looked down at the floor and shook his head. "I don't know. It's Marissa. We're supposed to be relaxing and having some fun, but she's wound up tighter than ever. She won't even talk to me."

David's brow furrowed. "Both of you need to sit down with Lexi and get your evaluations done. Maybe Lexi can shed some light on the situation. Go ahead and make your appointment with Lexi, and I'll talk to Marissa."

Jake nodded glumly. "I just wish I knew what was wrong with her." David shrugged. "You just never know with women. I mean sometimes we do something wrong, but have no idea what we did, and sometimes it's just a woman thing."

Jake sat upright. "You really think it might just be a woman thing? You know, it might be a woman thing. That could explain – uh – a lot of things."

The Captain had no intention of interfering in the relationships of his crew, but he was glad Jake's spirits were lifting. The Captain stood up to go on about his business. "Get with Lexi – today. I'll talk to Marissa about her appointment."

David went in search of Marissa. A computer search showed she was not currently on board the ship. The computer notified David there were riders approaching from the south. It appeared they were about to get a visit from the Sorley. David made a mental note to catch up with Marissa later in the day. He sent a quick message to Brynna and headed outside to greet their guests. He grabbed some chairs on his way.

Lexi was still outside working on her reports when she saw the Captain carrying several chairs. She immediately looked around the horizon for visitors. She spotted the horsemen riding in from the South and knew who they were. She hastily got up and helped him set up the chairs. The riders turned out to be Kasen, the Sorley leader, Tharen,

Kasen's son, and Jager, Tharen's best friend, along with a small warrior escort. Brynna joined the group before they had a chance to get settled. Kasen inquired as to why they had returned to their world so soon. David wanted to jump in and explain but waited to hear Brynna's explanation.

"Kasen, it is good to see you and your people again. We have come back here for two reasons. First, we wanted to warn you. Someone in the Commonwealth destroyed another world that were followers of Pateras." Kasen's face clouded with hostility. "Have you come to threaten us?"

Brynna quickly addressed his concerns. "No, Kasen, we lost people we were quite fond of when the world known as Galat was destroyed. We know you have never followed Arni or Pateras. We just wanted to warn you if others come here, their objectives may be less noble than our own. We do not want to lose any more friends. We have begun to doubt the motives of some of our leaders. The one you have seen, known as Arni, has saved all our lives, several times. We have never seen him do anything dishonorable. This is your world. We still consider you our allies, but if the Commonwealth sends others here, be careful what you say to them if you choose to follow the Liontari household."

Kasen nodded. "What is the other reason you have come?"

Brynna had to think a minute to explain shore leave to him. "Our people needed some time to rest and relax. The last world we visited was hard on us and we needed to return to friendly territory to get some rest."

Kasen smiled. "We are glad you see us as friends. If this other world you visited was harder than we were on you, then we are highly honored to count you as friends. You are strong people; this world is harsh, and I was hard on you. If you considered us better to you than this other world, you must have been in a truly difficult situation."

Brynna smiled. "You are indeed a strong people living on a harsh world. We are honored to count you as friends. Tharen, I'm glad to see you have healed well. I trust you have no lingering side effects from your injury?"

Tharen smiled enthusiastically and nodded. "I am as strong as before, and I have taken a wife since you were here last. She would not have agreed to marry a weak man."

David laughed. "That was a very short courtship, shorter than ours." His translator beeped at him and flashed on the word courtship. The men only got part of David's message and gave him puzzled looks. David frowned. "Dating relationship?" Again, his translator rejected his words. Apparently, the concept was foreign to the Sorley. They had no words for it.

David finally explained their own concept of dating to them. "Our people choose someone they may want to marry and spend time together for several months. If they find they enjoy each other's companionship enough they will commit to be married. Then they go through a period of being engaged or betrothed which usually lasts a few more months until they marry. We have marriage contracts which last an agreed period of time and can be extended if desired."

Kasen frowned. "Your people make things too hard. Find someone you cannot live without and marry them. Then you live with them until you die. It's not hard."

Jager deferred to his superiors, but since the conversation had digressed, he asked a question that had been bothering him. "There is something I don't understand. Are you still loyal to the Commonwealth, or do you serve the ones you warned us about?"

Kasen and Tharen were surprised by his question but didn't stop him from asking. They waited quietly for Brynna's answer. Brynna glanced at David who gave her no help at all. She glanced at him again and got nothing, not a blink or a nod, just a cold stare. She finally took a deep breath and answered the best she could. "We are disturbed by some recent events. We don't know if these events were caused by criminals within the Commonwealth or if the Commonwealth itself has become corrupt. The enemies we came to warn you about have tried to tell us our leaders are responsible for great evils. Until we know who's responsible, we will continue to do the job we were ordered to do. The job we are doing is to help people and gather information. We intend to still reach out to help people. We're just being more careful about what we do with the information we gather. We don't serve the ones we warned you about, but we're no longer convinced they are the kind of enemies we thought they were."

Jager nodded thoughtfully. "I see." He didn't really understand.

Kasen and Tharen were just as unclear about the situation, but how much could they expect to understand from a people who couldn't even handle a simple marriage? These people had great power, but Kasen felt like their power had robbed them of the good things in life. It did give him a sense of hope they had chosen this world to find time to rest on. Maybe there was hope for the Sky People after all.

The Sorley, seeing their presence wasn't needed, visited with the crew-members that were available, then headed back to their encampment to the south. They were going to be moving off to their next encampment location in two more days and had lots of work to do.

Jason, Laura, Marissa, Cheyenne, and Lazaro had gone into the Kimbra cities to shop in the markets. Thane and Aulani were hiking in the woods to the north. The only other crew-members that were around to visit with were Lexi, Braxton, and Jake. Kasen asked Brynna to give his regards to the others, then he rode off swiftly to the South.

That evening as the crew gathered into the dining room, David suggested a trip to visit the Akamu. The entire crew wanted to spend a little time visiting with Manton and Vesta. Despite their rocky start, they had grown fond of the Akamu couple. Since everyone wanted to go, the Captain suggested they go in two shifts, so the ship wasn't left unoccupied. He split the crew into two groups. He and Brynna would take Jake, Marissa, Jason and Laura in the morning, then switch out after lunch. He didn't want to overwhelm the Akamu with the entire crew and didn't want to miss the Kimbra if they came for a visit.

Brynna cornered David that evening and asked him why he left her to answer Jager's question. David decided to be blunt with her. "I've put my life on the line by trusting Arni and questioning the Commonwealth. My allegiance is under question in my own mind. I can only imagine how this looks to you and the rest of the crew. I needed to have some idea what you're thinking."

Brynna gave him a pointed look. "Were you testing my loyalty? Are you testing my loyalty right now?"

David wanted to walk over to soothe her ruffled feathers. He knew that was exactly the wrong thing to do. He sat down and continued his blunt approach. "Brynna, I love you, and I can only hope you love me as much as I love you. I am seriously having doubts about the Supreme Executor and what the Commonwealth's actual goals are. I would much rather have you abandon me here than throw me out into space. So yes, I am testing your loyalty. If you think I need to be relieved of command, do it now because I am going to pursue this to the end. I'm not declaring allegiance to Pateras. I am having issues with the Commonwealth, which may lead me to change my alliance."

Brynna wasn't sure she was ready for that much bluntness. Her shocked stare told him he might have moved too quickly. The two had been getting ready for bed. All activity now ceased. Brynna sat down on the foot of the bed near David's chair. It was a full minute before she could respond. "We're into some dangerous trust issues, aren't we?"

David had been leaning forward resting his forearms on his lap and rubbing the palms of his hands together. He finally stopped staring at the floor and looked up into her loving face. Yes, it was a look of love he saw, not a disarming flirtation meant to deceive. "David, I realize you could be setting a trap for me by saying that, but I don't want there to ever be deception between us. I – I'm having the same doubts. I told Arni on Drea if he spared your life, he would earn my trust. I have no intention of relieving you of command when I'm in no better situation than you are." She started speaking slowly, then rushed to get the words out before she lost her nerve. By saying so, the Captain had the authority to leave her behind on Medoris or execute her in space. If he was attempting to trap her, it was working. She held her breath hoping she hadn't misjudged her own husband.

David continued to search her face for any signs of deceit. The longer he waited the more fear he saw on her face. He finally reached up took her hand. "Just when I think I can't love you any more than I already do... I will make this agreement with you. No matter what I decide, I'll be honest with you. If you think I'm no longer fit to command, I'll willingly walk away."

The fear slipped gently from Brynna's face. She squeezed his hand firmly. "I will be completely honest with you as well, no matter the consequences. I promise to walk away, as well. I'll have your back, always."

David cocked his head to one side. "Does it feel like we just got married again?"

Brynna laughed. "It did, strangely enough."

David stood up and pulled her closer to him. "If we just got married again, does that mean we get another honeymoon?"

Brynna laughed and pushed him away. "Get ready for bed." David grinned. "Yes, ma'am."

Morning seemed to come all too soon. Maybe it just seemed that way since the days were getting shorter and it was still dark outside. The crew was taking full advantage of their shore leave and only the crew members headed to the caves were up early. The crew took the shuttle to the cave entrance. David and Brynna met alone with Tarin to give him the same warning they had given the Sorley. This time Brynna added the explanation Jager had asked for. Tarin seemed no more pleased than Kasen had been. He appreciated their candor and their friendship though. Tarin arranged for a tour of the caverns showing them the improvements they had made. David asked for a guide to take them further up the side of the mountain, so they could get a view of the area. Tarin sent Manton and Vesta to guide them. Jason wouldn't allow Vesta to go until he had done a scan to determine her physical condition. She was quite physically fit despite her bouts with morning sickness. The medications Jason had left with her were helping.

The group went through the inner caverns until they were halfway up the mountain then moved outdoors. Manton and Vesta led them to a cliff stretching a quarter of the way around the mountain. It wasn't the top of the mountain, but it was close enough to give them a breathtaking view. The crew took a long and relaxing look at their surroundings.

It was time to head back down the mountain all too quickly. David told Brynna to occupy Jake, so he could have a moment with Marissa. Manton and Vesta led the group back towards the upper caverns. David stopped Marissa from joining the rest. "Lt. Holden, is everything alright?"

Marissa gave David a look that could only be described as a cross between guilt and fear. "Yes sir."

An alarm bell went off in David's head. She didn't ask why he asked. She stopped with the short answer. "Lieutenant, you aren't a very good liar."

Now the look on her face intensified. "Excuse me, sir?"

David started moving at a slow pace the same general direction as the others had gone. He gently encouraged the Lieutenant to walk with him. "You've been avoiding your psych eval. Is there a reason for that? No, that wasn't the right question. What's the reason for it?"

"I – uh, I just haven't felt very well lately. I'll get with Lexi first thing tomorrow, sir. I'm sorry for the delay, sir."

"Why don't you let Jason check you out this afternoon? Maybe he can get you back up to speed."

"No sir! I mean, that won't be necessary sir. I'm feeling better."

David stopped walking when Marissa balked so strongly. "You aren't acting better Lieutenant. I'll make it an order if I have to."

Her voice now rang with panic. "Please, Captain, I'm fine. I don't need to be checked out by the doc."

"Marissa, we've all been through a lot. You and I more than the others. If there's something going on, I need to know about it. Lexi knows there are things we aren't ready to talk about yet. She's not going to pressure you, but why are you resisting seeing both her and the doctor?" Marissa continued to stand there looking terrified. She knew she needed to answer him, but even she didn't like the answer.

"Captain, please don't let the doctor examine me, please." Marissa was on the verge of tears.

David was starting to like the blunt approach. "Give me a reason why I shouldn't, and I'll reconsider."

He started walking again, but Marissa had a response ready. "Even if it's something you would have to report?"

The Captain stopped in his tracks. He turned around and looked at her. "Marissa, we're all in precarious positions right now. If there's something I need to know, I suggest you tell me now."

Tears began to roll down her face. Her hand shook as she wiped them away. "I – I . . ." She took a deep breath then tried again to say one of the most difficult things in her life. "I'm pregnant."

One's initial response was to say "Congratulations," but the tears in her eyes didn't seem to call for such a response. David chose to ask a question that wasn't much better. "How is that possible?"

Marissa stared at him with a look that said, "Don't be stupid." When he realized how silly his question sounded on the surface, he rephrased it. "You were temporarily sterilized, so you shouldn't have been able to get pregnant. If the doc didn't examine you, how do you know for sure?" Marissa gave him another look not much different than the first. "Captain, I am a trained field medic. I know how to use a medical scanner on myself. I checked myself out when the doc was off the ship then purged the records."

The Captain pushed her to keep moving before someone came back to check on them. "Does Jake know? No, never mind, he doesn't know. What are you going to do?"

"How did you know I hadn't told Jake?"

The Captain had always been perceptive, but by this point his "gift" of discernment seemed to be working. He thought for a minute. "Arni healed you – completely. He healed you which made you able to get pregnant. You didn't know to take precautions. That was not the most helpful thing he could have done. I knew you hadn't told Jake when I found him trying to work out his frustrations on a punching bag yesterday. So, what are you going to do?"

Her tears started flowing again. "Captain, I don't know. I love being on this mission with Jake, but the regs are clear on this. I either have to leave the mission or end the pregnancy. Captain, there's something else. I wasn't supposed to be able to ever have children. They did the temporary procedure on me just as an additional precaution. I never expected to have children. I don't know how to deal with this."

"By regulations, you only have three days to decide."

"I don't want to be responsible for the death of another innocent. After the things Pateras showed me, I just can't. I don't like either option, Captain. I don't know if Jake will want to leave the mission and I don't want to leave without him. Jake and I have never talked about having children. What should I do? What are your orders, sir?"

David stopped in his tracks. "I can't give you orders on this, Lieutenant. This decision is yours and Jake's. I will tell you this. I still need you to get your psych evaluation done. Get with Lexi tomorrow. You don't have to share this with her unless you want to. You don't need to see the doc, so long as you monitor your own condition discreetly. I will keep this between us and the Commander for now."

"The Commander won't report it?"

"The Commander and I have an understanding. She won't report it, for now. Marissa, none of us are sure about this mission anymore, so I'm not in a hurry for your decision. You've got a couple months before anyone notices."

Marissa wiped away her tears again. "Thank you, Captain. Arni said I should trust you with this. He was right."

David was caught off guard. "Arni? When did you talk to Arni?"

Marissa took a deep breath. "He talked to me the day I found out. It was the day after we landed."

David just stood there a moment. "Captain, are you upset with me?"

The Captain had been staring at the ground. He looked up at her and smiled. "No, Marissa, not at all. We've all been thrown into circumstances we are severely unprepared for. You're doing the best you can, just keep me apprised of any contact with Arni and of your condition. I will probably need to adjust your duty schedule, discreetly."

"Captain, what about Jake? If I tell him, he'll force a decision. You know he's a stickler for following the regs to the letter. I'm not sure I can tell him just yet."

David started moving slowly down the mountain again with Marissa still in tow. "You're right about that. He deserves to know, but that's your call. I will do what I can to protect you and the baby for now. I do suggest you smooth things out with Jake. He knows something's wrong, but he thinks it's a woman thing, if you know what I mean. He'll expect you to get back to normal soon."

Marissa rolled her eyes at the Captain's aversion to discussing female biological processes. She understood what he meant but wasn't sure how to do what he asked. "Captain, how do I do that?"

David stopped again and gently grasped her elbow. "Focus on the positives for one. You're going to have a baby, Lieutenant. Congratulations, mama. Your husband is going to be a daddy. You don't have to make any decisions right now. There's no pressure from the regs. You also have three people to confide in."

"Three?"

"Yes, three. Brynna, Arni, and me. You do need to give me a little time to tell Brynna though."

Marissa nodded and teared up again. "Thank you, Captain." She grabbed the Captain and hugged him.

The Captain was caught off guard again. Thankfully, his communicator beeped at him. "This is the Captain."

A voice came through. "This is Chief Holden. Is everything okay, Captain? We're ready to head back into the caverns, but we still don't see you two, yet."

"Sorry Chief, I'm still working out some of the kinks from that beating I took. We'll pick up the pace."

They came around a bend and caught sight of the others. Minutes later the entire group headed through the caverns. Brynna matched David's pace for a few minutes and watched him. He began to notice her attention on him and asked her what was up.

She eyed him suspiciously. "You're keeping pace quite well, so what was that line you fed Jake about."

"Lt. Holden has been delaying her psych eval. Jake just got his done yesterday. I was trying to find out what was going on. I need to fill you in on the details later. Jake won't be suspicious of my flimsy excuse because he knows I was going to talk to her about her evaluation. He'll take it for what it is."

"You're seem pretty sure of yourself."

"On this I am. I'm not so sure about a lot of other things."

The group made their way through the caverns and said their farewells. David told Tarin, the others would be back to visit in a couple hours. The crew got back to the ship and changed places with the ones they left behind. David and Brynna went to their quarters to finish their conversation. The two sat down on their sofa. Brynna pulled her shoes off and stretched out across the couch facing David. She promptly plopped her feet in his lap. David angled himself towards her as well.

"So, why's Marissa scared of her psych evaluation?"

David sighed. He absentmindedly massaged Brynna's feet while he talked. "She has a secret and was afraid Lexi would find out if she went for her evaluation."

"What could be that traumatic? Does it have something to do with Arni?"

David continued rubbing Brynna's feet. "Not directly. I told her I would talk to you about it, but no one else. I promised her we would keep her secret."

"Has she changed her loyalties?" Brynna asked the question so casually David stopped rubbing her feet.

"I didn't ask, but I don't think so."

Brynna's curiosity was eating her up at this point. "So, what is it?" "When Arni brought Marissa back to life, he healed her… completely."

Brynna's look showed no indication of understanding where he was headed. "Yes, I know."

"Her body is healed of all scars, and man-made imperfections." David saw her start to connect the dots. He finished connecting the last dots for her. "Marissa's pregnant."

Brynna sat straight up pulling her feet out of David's lap. "What?

What's she going to do?"

David scooted closer to Brynna. "Nothing, for now."

Brynna's shock level increased. "David, the regulations are very clear on this matter. She has to end the pregnancy or leave the crew. What's the problem?"

"Brynna, you know what the problems are. The Commonwealth has been lying to us, sending us on missions of a questionable nature. What happens if she leaves this mission? She's going to come under a great deal of scrutiny. They're going to want to know why she didn't just end the pregnancy like any good soldier would. What if Jake doesn't leave with her? He's got that right."

Brynna moved from shock to confusion. "So, why doesn't she just end the pregnancy?"

David's comfort level was dropping quickly. He didn't like discussing these female topics. "She's seen too many innocents die already. She didn't say what Pateras showed her, but she said it affected her decision not to end the pregnancy. I am supporting her decision for now. She'll tell Jake when she's ready, but for now, you and I are the only others who know. Are you going to be okay with this?"

Brynna sat there processing the information. Mentally there were red warning flags going up, but as she thought more about the situation she realized David made the right call. "Yes, I think so."

David went on to tell her about Marissa's state of mind and what he had attempted to do to encourage her. He also told her about his plans to adjust her duty assignments. He didn't want her on anymore security details. The conversation slowly worked its way around to a more personal nature. The couple began to discuss their own future and thoughts about having children themselves. It was a pleasant topic but was overshadowed by their uncertain future.

Later that afternoon, David and Jake took on Jason and Laura in a game of zone. Jake seemed to be in better spirits. After the game, Jake pulled the Captain aside. "Captain, what did you say to Marissa?"

David immediately claimed ignorance. "What are you talking about Jake?"

Jake wiped the sweat off his face. "Aw, come on Captain, I know you talked to her about her psych evaluation. I know she hasn't done it yet, but she's in a much better mood. So, what did you say to her?"

David looked thoughtful. He knew he needed to give Jake something, but he had to be careful what. "I don't know the specifics, but she was upset about something Pateras showed her. I told her we've all seen things we're having trouble talking about. I guess I just took some of the pressure of the psych eval off her. There are some things I saw, that I don't even know how to put into words."

Jake smiled. "Well, whatever you said, it helped. It's like I got my wife back."

David looked thoughtful again. "Well, it might have been what I told you, or it might have been the other thing I told her."

Jake stopped smiling. "What other thing?"

David looked at Jake and grinned. "I told her to lighten up on you, because you were driving the rest of us nuts."

Jake laughed. "Yeah, that must've been it." David was glad Jake's mood had improved.

The next day David and Brynna visited the Kimbra and gave the same warning as the other two societies. They did a little shopping in the market themselves. Brynna found a necklace she liked. David wasn't much into shopping, but he enjoyed watching Brynna shop.

The visit with Cashel, Jabre, and Auryon concluded their business on Medoris, so David scheduled a staff meeting for the following morning. At the staff meeting, they laid out their plans for their next few stops. David assigned Marissa to plan their trip to a planet called Mara, then on to Tudoren II. He reminded the crew he still had an investigation to conduct into the deaths on Galat III. The plans for the day were to prepare for launch the next morning.

Lexi turned in her evaluations. Her basic conclusions were listed in a summary report. The entire crew was functioning adequately in their assigned roles, although all were unsettled by recent events. Their moods and abilities had improved after their shore leave. No further actions or follow up were required at this time. The only exceptions were the Captain and Navigator, who were showing more signs of stress than the rest of the crew.

David and Brynna took the reports from Drea and edited them. They made sure there were no references to Arni, only the Intercessor, and no mention of his death. David had promised the crew he would protect them from any fallout from Drea. His report indicated rebels within the government tried to execute them, and the government was still unstable.

He made sure the Commonwealth knew the population remembered their last encounter and advised against contacting them for another twenty- five to fifty years.

The next morning the crew got ready for launch. Diagnostics were complete, navigation was laid in, and the ship took off from Medoris and headed for Mara, after a brief stop further north for a snowball fight. During takeoff and landings, a full bridge crew was present. David, Brynna, Thane, Marissa, Aulani, and Jake were on the bridge. Braxton and Lazaro were in engineering. They set course once they reached orbit. David always kept the observation panels open while leaving a solar system. It was a personal indulgence on his part. He never grew tired of watching the planets go by. The rest of the crew seemed to enjoy it as well. As soon as they cleared the solar system, he ordered the panels closed. Engineering charged the tachyon net. The net reached capacity and David ordered the tachyon drive engaged. Everyone always breathed easier once it was fully engaged.

The crew didn't disperse so quickly this time. The weight of everything concerning Galat and Drea was about to be churned up again when they reached Mara. Everyone was anxious to talk about it. David sent the reports in, requested a communication back from his uncle, Admiral Deacons, then joined in the casual conversation.

Thane turned away from his station to ask, "Captain, what do you expect to find on Mara?"

David had been deep in thought wondering the exact same thing. He was leaning to one side resting his chin on his fist. When Thane interrupted his train of thought, he sat up straight in his chair and forced his eyes to focus on Thane. "I don't really know,

Lieutenant. Hopefully there will be some kind of proof about who's telling the truth."

As the two continued to talk, the other crew-members on the bridge began to pay attention. Aulani asked a question that was probably better left alone. "Who do you think is telling the truth?"

Marissa turned around to hear his answer, and her eyes landed on Jake. His face showed no emotion whatsoever. It was a face that always worried her. Marissa jumped in before the Captain had a chance to respond. "There's a little truth in all sides of a dispute. Neither side is bound to report things exactly as they are."

The Captain nodded in agreement. "That's typically true."

Aulani, being a communications expert caught the "but" he failed to verbalize. "You think Arni is telling the truth. You aren't sure the Commonwealth is trustworthy anymore."

The Captain swiveled his chair to face the Ensign. "And you're putting a LOT of words in my mouth." David had also seen the look on Marissa's face as she tried to sidetrack the conversation.

The stern look on David's face caused Aulani to quickly back off. "I'm sorry, sir. I meant no disrespect."

Jake started to get up from his station and spilled his coffee on his uniform. "Ahh, man! I don't believe I just did that. Excuse me, Captain, I need to go change and get a fresh cup of coffee. Anybody else want some when I come back?"

Thane grinned. "No, thanks. I'm not sure I trust you to carry it."

Jake glared at Thane. "Alright, smart aleck, you can get your own coffee." He moved towards Aulani and in his sweetest voice asked. "Ensign Ryder, may I get you a cup of coffee? Perhaps you would also like some cream or sugar? I would be glad to get it for you if you like." He took her hand and kissed it gently. Aulani gave the chief a bewildered stare.

Thane came out of his chair like he was on fire. "Hey, that's my wife! Kiss your own wife and keep your hands off mine!"

Jake let go of Aulani's hand and gave Thane a perfunctory salute then turned back to Aulani. "I apologize my dear. I do hope I haven't offended you."

David and Brynna were caught slightly off guard by Jake's antics. They soon realized he was merely trying to push Thane's buttons and began to snicker quietly.

Jake took two long quick steps and knelt in front of Marissa. He gently took her hand in his. "I apologize my darling wife. I hope I haven't offended you, either. Perhaps, it will make amends if you would allow Lt. Ryder to kiss your hand in return?"

Marissa tried to keep a straight face, but by this time she was having trouble. The corners of her mouth were twitching. She was torn between balking or playing along. "Um – I – uh." Luckily, she didn't have to respond. David and Brynna were now laughing hysterically at the looks on Thane's face.

"I'm not going to kiss Marissa!" Normally Thane would have been the one clowning around and Jake would have been the serious wounded party. Thane looked around the bridge and realized what happened. He glared back at Jake and mumbled, "Brat!" Sitting back down at his station, he turned his back on the crew.

Jake marched off the bridge with as much pomp and circumstance as he could muster in a coffee-soaked uniform. The crew continued to laugh and joke about Jake's antics for a few minutes. They gave Thane a moment to collect himself before they included him in the fun. Marissa confirmed Jake was indeed capable of such antics, but usually only with family.

The conversation settled down and Marissa moved over to talk to David. "I'm sorry, Captain for interrupting earlier, but I didn't want you to say anything Jake might use against you."

David nodded. "I appreciate that, Lieutenant."

Marissa started to walk away then turned to ask one more question. "Captain, you can't keep dodging him. What are you going to do about him?"

David looked at the anxiety on her face. "Nothing. There's no reason to do anything. Maybe Arni can reach him, because I seriously doubt I can say anything to change his mind."

"I can ask the next time I see him, but he won't force himself on Jake. You know he won't."

"Captain, what if Arni's telling the truth? What are you going to do?

Will you change sides?"

The bridge went silent. Everyone had been listening quietly and continuing their work at their duty stations. Now, no one moved or spoke. David looked around at the anxious faces around him. He gave the only answer he could. "I don't know for certain who's telling the truth, but if Arni's being totally straight with me, I can't remain loyal to the Commonwealth. Let's just say for now, I don't know."

PART SIX

PRISONERS WHO AREN'T

DOWNWARD SPIRAL

Treason? Were the Captain and crew really considering it? Jake shut off his computer. He saved the recorded surveillance to a file and labeled it, "weapons inventory." He reasoned the recording was a weapon of sorts and hopefully no one would find it. He also attached a voice print password identification code to secure the file. As security chief, it was Jake's job to keep the crew safe, but now his job was changing. The recording proved the Captain was willing to betray his commission and commit treason. The most disturbing part was Jake's own wife, Marissa, didn't seem to have a problem with it.

Jake considered everything they had been through the last few months. Would they force him to report them for treason?

Originally, the crew's orders were to have no interaction with the allies of Pateras Liontari. It was considered far too dangerous. The Commonwealth told the crew Pateras controlled his followers telepathically. Once an individual was conscripted by Pateras, no amount of threats, punishment, re-education, or even bribery had been effective in returning the individual's loyalties to the Commonwealth. Several of Pateras' followers had been executed to prevent the spread of the infestation.

The very first world the Evangeline visited was a peaceful planet known as Galat III. It turned out to be the home planet of Arni Liontari and his mother. Their instructions were straightforward. Get out before you are taken over by the enemy. Captain Alexander evacuated his crew as quickly as possible and reported the find to the Commonwealth Interstellar Force (CIF) headquarters.

Medoris IV, the ship's next stop, was harsher than Galat in both climate and societal temperament. The crew nearly suffered numerous casualties, and in fact suffered one definite death. Arni followed the crew to Medoris and saved the lives of Captain Alexander and Lt. Marissa Holden, Jake's wife. Marissa was killed in a storm but revived later by Arni. Both she and the Captain were healed from all their injuries in ways none of them expected.

Jake was grateful his wife's life had been saved, or at least restored. Was she considering treason because Arni restored her? Was it because of the deaths on Galat? Or perhaps it was because Arni saved all of them on Drea.

In the crew's run-ins with Arni, he volunteered several pieces of important information. Some things were in direct conflict with the previous Commonwealth intelligence. Arni could manipulate energy and mass. He was capable of healing injuries or illness all the way down to a cellular level. He could travel instantaneously anywhere in the galaxy he wanted, and was capable of restoring life to the dead, including himself. Arni claimed he would never control anyone's mind, despite the Commonwealth's claims. The crew's instructions were expanded to allow them to spend time with Arni to collect as much intelligence as possible. The head of the Commonwealth, Supreme Executor Luciano Hale, took notice of the crews' resistance to Arni. He granted David special permission to talk to Arni at length.

Jake wondered if this greater latitude had been the cause of the Captain's now precarious state of allegiance.

With the help of the Captain and the ship's psychologist, Jake was learning to keep his emotions in check. It was going to take every ounce of his control to stop the Captain and crew from committing treason. Jake made it his personal mission to set things right.

The Captain set course for Mara. The handsome, young, energetic Captain was not the same since leaving Drea. He seemed distracted, moody, and perhaps a little depressed. He had good moments and bad. It was obvious something happened to him on Drea. He said very little about what happened during the time he was missing from his own execution. The crew knew the Captain met Pateras El Liontari. They also knew Pateras was sending the crew to Mara to find some much needed answers.

Lt. Thane Ryder, the ship's pilot was on duty on the bridge with Cheyenne. Cheyenne's husband, Lazaro was at his station in engineering.

There wasn't much to do on the voyage portion of their trips, and boredom had a way of setting in. Thane leaned back in his chair and rocked back and forth staring at the ceiling. He finally twisted around to face Cheyenne. "Hey, Cheyenne, do you know what the Captain's been up to? I haven't seen much of him since we started this trip. He hasn't played Zone with us since we launched from Medoris."

Cheyenne looked up from her station. "I don't know. I haven't seen much of him either, not since I gave him a copy of the Ancient Texts."

"I saw the copy you gave him. That was a hefty file. It's going to take him a long time to get through it."

Cheyenne nodded. "Have you read any of it?"

Thane shook his head. "No, I thought I would wait to see what the Captain said about it. If he thinks it's worth it, then I'll read it. I'm more into reading technical manuals, not history books or novels or whatever that thing is."

Cheyenne started to respond until her station began to beep at her. She gave Thane a quick, "Wait a sec." She pressed a button on her station. "This is Ensign Dominick of the Evangeline. Go ahead."

Thane watched her listen to the voice coming through her ear piece. He saw her posture change subconsciously, even though the speaker wasn't seeing her. It was definitely someone important. "Yes sir, stand by." Cheyenne pressed a couple more buttons hailing the Captain. "Captain, I have Admiral Deacons for you. Shall I connect it to your office?" Cheyenne waited for the Captain's response.

The Captain was studying the Ancient Texts in his office and didn't hear Cheyenne's call. "Captain, are you there? I have Admiral Deacons for you."

David's eyes jumped off the screen and he looked around the room to see who was talking to him. He slowly realized the voice had come across the communications network. It took another second for the memory of what he heard to replay in his mind and be processed. Finally, he reached over and pressed a button to respond. "Sorry, Ensign, put him through."

Seconds later the Admiral's face appeared. "Admiral, a pleasure to hear from you, sir."

The Admiral had a distressed look on his face. "David, I just read your reports. I suppose I'm calling more as your uncle rather than your superior. Son, you are getting into some rather bad habits. These reports nearly scared the life out of me. Are you alright?"

David was still slightly distracted by the texts he had been reading. His focus was not on the Admiral's question. There was a noticeable lull between the question and his answer, but it was only noticed by David. "The crew and I are fine, sir. Lt. Flint said we are exhibiting the signs of stress, but we're all still capable of fulfilling our duties. We took some shore leave back on Medoris, so we're almost back to normal." David stared at the Admiral waiting for his response.

The pause between David's answer and the Admiral's reply was significantly longer than David's previous pause. When he finally spoke, the distress in his eyes was evident in his voice. "Son, I want the truth, not the textbook answer. Per your reports, you were tried and convicted of war crimes. That's got to have a profound impact on you and your crew. You said you were nearly executed."

David knew he needed to be very careful how he answered. He didn't want to give the Admiral any reason to suspect his reports were anything, but totally accurate. "Yes sir, it did take a toll on me and the crew. It took an unbelievable amount of diplomacy and a fair amount of bluffing on my part to get us out of that one. My crew suffered quite a bit, emotionally speaking. They suffered a whole lot more than I did in that respect."

"So, why did you choose to go back to Medoris for shore leave and not one of the Commonwealth Colonies. Medoris nearly killed you too." David stretched and leaned back in his chair a bit. "I had several reasons. I wanted to go someplace quiet for one. Second, I wanted to go someplace friendly and familiar. I thought..."

"Friendly and familiar! You have a strange definition of friendly.

David, are you sure you have your head on straight?"

"Admiral… Uncle Rob, I know we had a rough time on Medoris, but we've been accepted as friends and allies by three major societies on the planet. My crew was pretty shook up by what happened on Galat. They just needed to see their hard work on Medoris wasn't for nothing."

The Admiral studied David for a moment. "Galat was a colony established by Pateras. You know why they had to be stopped."

David was trying to keep careful tabs on whether it was his uncle addressing him or the Admiral. He sensed it was more the Admiral this time. "Admiral, no one is questioning that. The crew just spent several weeks getting to know the people, improving their way of life, and to have it all gone suddenly made them feel like they were wasting their time. They put a lot of hard work into that world only to have it destroyed. Between that and getting arrested, tried and convicted, they needed to know Medoris was okay."

"By the way, how did you find out about Galat?"

"We picked up a trader passing through the system. We hailed them to find out why they were in a non-space faring system. They were cutting corners by passing through the system. They had apparently seen the devastation on Galat and asked if we knew anything about it. I think they were afraid we would report them for violating the travel regulations and wanted to offer us a distraction. I let them go on with a warning to stay out of the Drean star system."

The Admiral studied David again for a moment. "What is your current destination?"

"We're heading for Tudoren II." David tried very hard to keep from giving himself away. Tudoren II was past the penal colony on Mara. From their current position and trajectory, either place could be identified as their destination. The Captain knew someone in the Commonwealth was responsible for the deaths on Galat. Whether it was the action of a radical or if it was truly sanctioned by the Supreme Executor of the Commonwealth, he didn't know for certain. Captain Alexander was treading on dangerous ground. If he accused one or more of the Admirals and didn't have proof, his career would be over before it even started. If he accused the Supreme Executor, his life would be over. The Supreme Executor could simply issue an order to have him executed as a traitor.

Admiral Deacons hesitated again after hearing David's answer. "Captain, can I sidetrack your mission just a little?"

David gave the Admiral a puzzled look. "Yes, sir. What do you need?"

"Do you think you have enough pull to get back onto Drea if need be?"

"If the reason were important enough, they might let us through.

Moderator Tarmon owes us a favor."

The Admiral scowled at David. "I'm not sure I see what you're seeing, but I'll take your word for it. I need you to go to the penal colony on Mara and pick up three prisoners who are to be released. I don't have any other ships in the vicinity. They need to be returned to Drea. The prisoners have been determined to no longer be a threat to the Commonwealth. We're cleaning house on Mara. We anticipate with this new mission to need the space to house followers of the Liontari very soon. If you think you can get in, then pick up the three prisoners and take them home."

David sat there considering the Admiral's words. "Who are the prisoners?"

The Admiral glanced at a data pad before answering. "There's a husband and wife, Noah and Aleah Simons, and another man named Donald Leal."

David recognized the name of the last prisoner. He again tried hard not to let his uncle know. It wasn't that he didn't trust his uncle, but he didn't want to put his uncle in danger. David remembered the Admiral's warning from a previous communication that even the secure channels may be monitored. David quickly moved the conversation forward. "May I ask what these prisoners were incarcerated for?"

The Admiral answered without checking his tablet. "They were political prisoners. They weren't guilty of anything violent if that's what has you concerned."

David nodded. "Since I only have one full time security officer and a skeleton crew, it did cross my mind. I suppose if they worry me, I can either keep them in stasis or confined to quarters. I'm pretty sure I can get them home though."

The Admiral appeared to relax a little. "It will probably take you an extra day to get to Mara, and a day to get back to Drea, so you'll only be two days behind schedule as long as there are no hold ups on Drea or Mara. How long do you expect to be on Tudoren?"

David scowled. He wasn't prepared for that portion of his mission, so he didn't have a solid answer. "I don't have the information in front of me, but my understanding is there are four separate inhabited continents. I imagine we'll be there at least a month if we spend only one week on each continent. We could easily be there for up to four months."

The Admiral seemed to relax a little more and managed a slight smile. "Good, good, I'm glad you're moving ahead despite your recent setbacks."

David smiled back at the Admiral with an equal amount of enthusiasm. "Was there anything else you were concerned about, sir?"

The Admiral took a deep breath and shook his head. "Please tell your crew how pleased I am with the way they've handled themselves under such difficult circumstances. No other crew has been through the things you have, and I am not sure the others are holding up nearly as well. I'm proud of you, David. I really underestimated you, son."

"Yes sir, thank you, sir. I will be sure to let the crew know what you said."

"My love to you and Brynna. Oh… yeah… one more thing."

David looked puzzled and annoyed. He wanted to get back to studying the Ancient Texts. "Yes, Admiral?"

The Admiral's face got more serious. "David, contact your mother. She's driving me insane asking about you, and this stuff is not something I can tell her about. I wouldn't want to tell her about it even if I could. So, while you have some down time, contact her. That's an order, Captain!"

Now David was even more annoyed, but he knew the Admiral wasn't joking. "Yes sir, I'll do it as soon we're done, sir."

As soon as his communication with the Admiral was complete, the Captain hailed Cheyenne and asked her to connect him with his home on Raesii. Cheyenne put the communication through to him. shortly. David spent the next thirty minutes apologizing to his mother, assuring her he was fine, and promising to call more often. His mother, in rapid-fire sequence, told him about his new nephew, how his sister was managing being a new mother, his grandmother's health issues, his younger half-brother's skills and achievements in school, and several other mindless details he really didn't want to know right now. David tried to tell his mother about the more enjoyable parts of his job, but he sensed his mother knew he was hiding things from her. As their communication was coming to an end, David's stepfather stepped into view. David didn't dislike the man, but even after knowing him for the last sixteen years, it still felt wrong to see him and not David's father with his mother. David's father and mother had not renewed their marriage agreement when David was in his early teens. The man greeted David warmly, and David returned the sentiment. "Steven, how are you? Are you taking good care of my mom while I'm gone?"

"I'm trying to, but she's a hard woman to take care of, especially when she's worried about her children. Did you tell him about your dream, Jess?"

As soon as Steven mentioned dreams, the smiles left both their faces. David had gotten accustomed to having nightmares since meeting Arni, but he never imagined they would touch his mother. "What dreams, mom?"

Jessica shook her head. "Oh, it's nothing. I just had one of those types of dreams that makes you worry until you talk to the person you dreamed about and know they're okay."

Steven shook his head. "She's had the same dream several times.

She dreamed you were attacked by a wild dog."

David stared at his mother for a moment. His mind flashed back to the dream he had when the crew left Galat III. David had dreamed a pack of wild dogs attacked and killed the people on Galat then one of the dogs turned and attacked David. The dream continued to haunt him. His second visit to Galat using the Drean wormhole technology where an actual wild dog attacked him, did nothing to relieve his dreams or anxiety. He knew he needed to reassure her. He wasn't sure he could do that without lying to his own mother. He also didn't want to put his family in danger by telling his mother what he already knew her dream meant. "Mom, I think your dream just represents your anxiety over what you know is a dangerous assignment for me. I'm fine and I promise to be careful around wild dogs. Look, see no bites." David stood up, backed away from the screen and turned around, so his mother could see him from head to toe.

His mother scowled at him. "Don't try and snow me young man. I know the doctors can heal wounds, so you would never know they were there."

David smiled. "I'm not trying to snow you, mom. I was just trying to make a little joke to lighten your mood. The doctor has only treated me one time, and it wasn't related to wild dogs."

His mother scowled at him. "What did he treat you for?"

David shook his head. "I got into a fight with some dissidents. I'm fine. It was nothing."

His mother began to rant again. David nodded respectfully. While he was listening to her, Brynna slipped into his office quietly. David hadn't heard her come in. His mother's lecture finally pushed David to his breaking point. "Mom, I said I'm fine!" He slammed his fist on the desk.

Jessica looked stunned, then hurt. Steven looked at his wife then back at David. "David, there's no reason to talk to your mother like that. It sounds like you aren't as fine as you say."

Brynna was still standing silently behind him. She was also shocked by his outburst. She slipped quietly into a chair to allow him to finish talking to his mother.

David shook his head back and forth. "I'm sorry. I didn't mean to yell at you. Yes, I'm a little stressed and frustrated. I've got the Doc constantly trying to be sure I'm alright. The ship's psychologist is doing the same thing. Brynna, well… she seems to be able to see right through me and knows when I'm alright and when I'm not. Every time I file a new report, Uncle Rob's calling to make sure I'm okay as well as other officials in the chain of command. Did you know Uncle Rob opposed my entry into the command track?"

Jessica nodded. "Yes, he told us right after you applied. He didn't expect you to succeed, but he was so proud when you did."

"So, why is he so worried about me? This is a tough job, and I knew it when I started. I don't have any regrets. From my perspective, I think I'm doing a good job."

Jessica smiled. "You are doing a good job. Your Uncle doesn't give me a lot of specifics because your mission is classified, but he brags on you all the time. He thinks of you like a son since he never had any children of his own. I believe he worries about you the same way he would his own child, but David that's not enough to get you this upset." "Mom, I just don't want you to worry. When I said Jason had only treated me one time, well, I nearly died that one time. I was beaten, almost to death, by six men. It took Jason and a second doctor to keep me alive. I was able to protect the life of one of my other officers. I left some marks on the guys who attacked me, and I don't have any emotional scars from the incident. I'm not having any bad dreams about it, no panic attacks. I even made an appropriate sentencing recommendation for the men who did it. The men were caught and charged with attempted murder. I requested leniency for them. It's like everybody expects me to fail. I'm not failing, and that seems to bother everyone. I suppose I'm not accomplishing everything I should, like calling my mother often enough,

but I'm not failing."

The looks on Jessica's face went from concern and worry to shock and terror while he spoke. As he continued to speak, she forced herself to relax. As soon as he mentioned not calling her often enough her face changed again to a look of annoyance. "Well, son, I hate to disappoint you, but I'm a mother. I'm going to worry. I would worry less if you would call more often. Just don't feel like you should hide things to protect me. I married your father while he was in the infantry. I know how to handle worry. I would rather know what you've gone through than let my imagination fill in the blanks. That doesn't include the stuff that's classified. I know you can't talk about that."

David promised to call more often and spent another few minutes chatting with his mother and stepfather then excused himself to get back to work. He pressed the button to close the communication. He turned to see Brynna scowling at him. He wasn't sure how long she had been there, nor how much trouble he was in. He knew there wasn't much of a chance of avoiding another annoying conversation. The look on her face told him she saw enough of the conversation with his mother to have concerns of her own. They sat there in silence for a minute looking at each other. Brynna waited on David to explain himself, and David waited on Brynna to ask whatever questions she had. David wasn't willing to volunteer anything, so Brynna finally spoke first. "Would you like to explain that outburst to me?"

David wanted to say, "No," but knew that would only open the door to larger problems. "I was just busy trying to read and understand these Ancient Texts. They're not easy to understand. Some things are very straightforward, but others aren't. The Admiral interrupted me, and then ordered me to call my mother. I was just annoyed on several levels."

Brynna continued to stare intently at him. She finally decided to let the matter drop with one strong suggestion. "David, you need to take a break from the Ancient Texts. You need to get some exercise and have some fun. You're getting cranky, and the crew's noticing. What did the Admiral have to say?"

David leaned forward on his desk and gave Brynna a puzzled look. "You aren't going to believe this, but he wants us to go to Mara, pick up three prisoners, and return them to Drea."

Brynna's jaw dropped. "Are you serious? I wondered how we were going to explain our presence on Mara. What are the chances something like that could happen?"

David shook his head. "I don't know. I'm certainly glad it did."

Brynna cocked her head sideways. "Do you suppose Pateras or Arni had something to do with it?"

"I suppose it's possible. He wants us to go there, so it stands to reason he would do whatever he could to get us there."

"Do you suppose we'll have any trouble getting back into Drean space?"

David's brow wrinkled. "I hope not, but I intend to be extremely cautious." He sat there for a moment then hailed Cheyenne. "Ensign, I need you to contact Moderator Tarmon on

Drea and tell her I need to talk to her as soon as possible. Let me know as soon as she responds."

Cheyenne acknowledged the order then, since it was nearing the end of his duty shift she asked. "Captain, do you want me to notify the Commander if she calls back after you've gone off duty?"

David's attitude hadn't improved. "No Ensign, I said let me know, and that's what I want you to do. Is there a problem I should know about?" He snapped at the young Ensign.

Cheyenne was taken aback by the Captain's tone and message. "Uh– No sir, no problems on this end, sir. I just wanted to clarify your orders, sir."

As soon as she acknowledged him, the communication was cut from the Captain's end. The communication audio was turned on, and Thane had heard the entire conversation. He turned around to face her. He gave her an incredulous look. "No problems on this end? Are you looking to get put on report for insubordination?" He shook his head at her subtle smart remark to the Captain.

She scowled back at Thane, "I didn't say anything that wasn't accurate. Besides, he deserved it."

Thane shook his head and laughed. "Maybe so, but you should leave it to someone of higher rank to give it to him. Don't be too surprised if that comes back to bite you."

The Captain was annoyed at his order being questioned and cut his communication off with Cheyenne before he said too much. He looked back up to see Brynna's glare. "What now?"

"The Ensign asked you for a simple clarification. She wasn't challenging your authority. She knew you were about to go off duty, and from what I could tell she was being thoughtful and considerate. Why did you just snap her head off?"

David glared back at her. "I didn't snap her head off! Why are you questioning me, Commander?"

Brynna ignored his attempt to move the discussion from husband and wife to Captain and Commander. "Yes, David, you did, and she was right. The problem wasn't on her end, but yours. I suggest you get your head screwed on before we have to make this official." Brynna stood up to leave the office.

David stood up when she did and continued to glare at her. "Is that a threat?"

Brynna stood by the door giving him a cold and sober look that made the room feel noticeably cooler. "No, Captain, it's a crime to threaten a superior officer."

Brynna made a hasty exit from the office. She heard the Captain yell behind her. "COMMANDER!" She continued on her way.

Brynna headed to the dining hall to grab a cup of coffee then to the bridge. She nodded curtly to Cheyenne and Thane as she entered the bridge. She sat down at her station and reviewed the duty logs and ship logs. Thane and Cheyenne quickly noticed her mood and kept their conversation to a minimum. Moments later David hastily entered the bridge. He gave the two bridge officers a similar curt nod and moved immediately to Brynna's side. He whispered softly. "Can I see you privately for a moment?"

Brynna looked up at him still angry. "Who's asking, the Captain or my husband?"

David leaned over her and tried to soften his tone and demeanor. "Whoever it needs to be."

Brynna knew if she refused, he would make it an order, so she got up from her station, picked up her coffee cup, and followed him back to his office. The two sat down at the table opposite each other. David stared down at the floor for a minute before speaking. "Do you mind telling me what all of that was about?"

Brynna sighed. "What was all of what about, David? I thought I was pretty clear earlier. What is it you don't understand?"

"I guess I just don't understand what you're so upset about. Why did you storm out of here? Why did you feel the need to threaten me?"

"David, I told you when I walked in here you needed to take a break. You just yelled at your mother, and you snapped at Cheyenne for asking for a simple clarification. You aren't acting like yourself. You accused me of threatening you."

David scowled at her. "You threatened to take official action against me. I haven't done anything except get a little cranky. You don't have any grounds to take action against me."

Brynna continued to glare at him. "I didn't say I had grounds to bring any official action against you – yet. I don't want to take action against you. I want you to get your head screwed on straight. I was trying to warn you that your behavior is becoming erratic."

The urge to stand up and loudly protest surged through the young Captain. He knew that would only serve to prove her point. David fought the urge. He looked at Brynna's face. Behind her anger, he thought he could see pain in her eyes. He remembered standing before Pateras and all the wrongs he had ever committed flashed before his eyes. The experience had been crushing. He was left feeling empty and disgusted by his own life. He remembered having trouble being able to stand or even breathe. The thought that this might be added to his list of wrongs struck a chord within him. The pain, anguish, and sorrow came rushing back.

David knew he needed to try and make this right. He leaned forward and reached across the table for Brynna's hands. Her hands were resting on the table, and she made no move towards him. David reached a little further and took her hands in his own. She looked away but didn't pull her hands away. There it was. The sadness in her eyes now outweighed the anger. David called her name gently, "Brynna."

She forced herself to look him in the eye. She was done talking at this point. It was definitely his turn. David didn't disappoint her. "I'm sorry. You were right about everything. I'm not sleeping well, I'm tired and I'm cranky. I'll see what I can do to get some rest and relaxation. I promise to apologize to Cheyenne."

Brynna searched his face. The anger faded, but the sorrow didn't. She knew he was dealing with the symptoms, not the actual problem. She wasn't entirely sure what the problem was, but it had something to do with Arni. Finally, her mind formulated an appropriate response. "I'll accept your apology, but you need to deal with whatever's really bothering you. I wish you would talk to me about whatever it is."

David pulled away from her. He stood up and turned his back to her. He finally looked over his shoulder. "I'm not sure I can tell anyone about it."

Brynna moved over behind him. She laid her hand on his back.

"David, at least tell me what it is."

David turned around to face her again. "Pateras showed me…" David sighed. He didn't want to talk about this, but knew he needed to. "He showed me every wrong I've ever done including every man, woman, and child who died on Galat. I saw them all in seconds. The images and the feelings flooded my mind so fast. I felt them all like they were happening right then. The weight of the guilt was – was unbearable. It permeated every fiber of my being. I couldn't stand up under it. I – I couldn't even breathe."

Brynna saw a horrible pain, and tears welling up in his eyes. She never thought it possible to see him broken to the point of crying. She started to placate him with the "everybody makes mistakes" speech but decided against it. "Why would Pateras show that to you? What does he expect to accomplish by showing you every bad choice you've made?"

"I've asked myself that same question over and over. I just don't know the answer. Maybe he wants me to know how much I owe him. I can never repay that kind of debt, no matter how hard I try. There were over six million people killed on Galat because of me. How do I pay that kind of debt?"

"David, I can't speak for Pateras, but you saved over three billion lives on Drea by not reporting his presence on Drea. That should count for something. You're human. You've made mistakes, but you're a good man."

David huffed and looked away from her. "You just threatened this good man with punitive action."

Brynna's face fell. "I'm sorry, David. It was just to warn you that you're not behaving right. You haven't been yourself for days. You are a good man. Talk to Arni. Ask him why Pateras showed it to you and what to do about it."

David shook his head. "I don't want to talk to him until after I've been to Mara."

Brynna nodded. "I understand. Do me a favor, and don't be so hard on yourself. Don't be too hard on the crew either."

"I'll try. I'll start by going a few rounds with the punching bag in the gym unless you want to do some hand to hand combat sparring."

Brynna shook her head. "With the mood you're in? I don't think so. I think the punching bag is the safest opponent for you right now. I don't want to take a chance you're still angry with me."

The anger had dissipated between the two, but a heaviness remained in the room. David promised to get some rest. He went to the gym and worked out, then to the dining hall. Lazaro, Thane, and Cheyenne were now off duty as well and getting something to eat. David grabbed a sandwich and stopped at the table where the three were eating quietly. He was certain they were talking less now than they had been before he entered the room. "Cheyenne, I need to apologize to you. I was rather short with you earlier, and I'm sorry. You were right, the problem wasn't on your end. I'll try to take better care of my end."

Cheyenne glanced quickly at Thane and swallowed hard. "Yes sir. I'm sorry I smarted off to you, sir."

David gave her a curt laugh. "No, you're not. You meant it, and I deserved it. I'm sorry I pushed you to it." David excused himself and went back to his quarters to eat. It was his intention to get some sleep, but he just wasn't tired yet. He pulled the Ancient Texts up and began to study them again. He had two days until they reached Mara. He wanted to know as much as he could before they got there.

Once the three crew members were alone again, they discussed the incident in more detail. Thane sat back in his chair and shook his head. "Wow, I thought you were dead meat."

Lazaro looked confused. "Dead meat? What did I miss? Did the Captain say you smarted off to him?"

Thane laughed. "Did she ever?" Thane proceeded to tell Lazaro what his wife had done.

After hearing the tale, Lazaro gave his wife a stunned look. "Chey, why would you do that? You know what kind of mood he's been in lately."

Cheyenne assumed a more sanctimonious posture. "You heard the Captain. He said I meant it, and he deserved it. It would be insubordinate to argue with him."

Lazaro buried his face in his hands. He finally raised his head up to look at her again. "Woman, you are going to make me an old man before my time."

Thane laughed heartily at the couple.

MARAN SECRETS

The Evangeline entered orbit around Mara. David hailed the penal colony. "Maran Penal Colony, this is Captain Alexander of the CIF star ship, the Evangeline. We're here to pick up three prisoners for transport to Drea."

A voice came back through the speaker. "This is Commander Chase Landon. I've been expecting you, Captain. Do you have a shuttle, or will you need to bring your entire ship down?"

"We do have a shuttle, Commander. Give us instructions, and we will get those prisoners off your hands."

"Of course, Captain. As much as we would love to have visitors, it's a security risk to have a long-range ship on the planet. Please only bring a minimal compliment, and I am feeding you the approach and landing coordinates now. You may bring personal sidearms only. They will need to be checked in with the security officer when you land. I strongly advise against stowing any extra weapons on board your shuttle. What time can I expect your arrival?"

"We should be there in about an hour, Commander."

"Make sure you dress warmly. The landing bay is shielded, but not warm. Once you get inside the complex, you can stow your gear and be comfortable. Will you be coming down yourself, Captain, or will you be sending a detail?"

"I haven't decided on the escort detail, but as of now, I am planning on coming. My security chief may try and talk me out of it, but I plan on being there."

The Commander smiled and nodded. "I completely understand, Captain. Knowing what I do about Captains and security chiefs, I look forward to meeting the two of you shortly. Watch those cross winds when you come in. They can be tricky."

The Captain acknowledged the Commander and closed the communication. He turned to see Jake scowling at him. Before Jake could object, David addressed the security issues. "I want to set up a security protocol, so if something goes wrong, we can deal with it. Ensign Ryder, tell Lt. Commander Flint to report to the Dining Hall, and have Dr. Adams and Lt. Adams report to the bridge. Commander, Chief, Lt. Ryder, and Lt. Holden report to the Dining Hall. Ensign, you and Lt. Commander Dominick link in."

Aulani got busy notifying the personnel the Captain named to their assigned positions. The bridge crew exited the bridge and headed to the lower decks. The Captain stayed on the bridge until the doc and his wife came to take over the helm and navigation stations. As soon as the couple settled into their stations, David headed down to meet with the crew members waiting on him.

David entered the Dining Hall with a data pad in hand. He glanced down at it as he moved to the emptiest side of the room. Jake had grabbed two cups of coffee and handed one to his wife as he took his seat beside her. Marissa wrapped her hands around the cup to soak in its warmth. She wasn't cold, but the warmth seemed to relax her. The others were still taking their seats. David encouraged them to move faster to their places, so they could get started.

"Settle in people. We've got work to do. Here's the plan. Lt. Ryder, you're piloting the shuttle down to the surface. Get the landing instructions and coordinates from Ensign Ryder. Chief Holden, you and Lt. Commander Flint are going down as our security detail. Commander, you'll be in command until we return. Lt. Holden, you are in charge of security. I will give you the phrase, 'I've got an encrypted message for you', if everything is fine. If we're in trouble I will either not give you the phrase or I will tell you no encryption is necessary. Repeat that back to me."

The Captain was rattling things off quickly, and it took Lt. Holden by surprise when he demanded a quick response. She hesitated for a second then answered him. "If you're fine you will tell me you have an encrypted message, but if the crew's been compromised you'll either leave the message out or you'll tell me no encryption necessary."

David paused weighing whether to say something about her hesitation. He decided it would be a waste of time, and time was a priority in his mind right now. "If I don't give you the safe phrase then what I want you to do is to allow us to land as though nothing is wrong. Re- pressurize the shuttle bay then once the shuttle doors are open start bleeding the air back out of the bay and increase the gravity to incapacitate everyone in the shuttle bay instantly. Once everyone is incapacitated, restore the controls to normal as quickly as possible and move in to take custody of anyone causing trouble. This will require precise timing between you and engineering. Lt. Commander Dominick, did you get all of that?"

Lazaro was tied in through the computer from engineering. "Yes, Captain, I got it." David continued to be sure he did understand. "Make sure you only affect the gravity of the shuttle bay and not the whole ship. Lt. Holden, don't go in until he tells you the gravity and air have been restored to normal. I don't want you – or anyone else – getting hurt. You'll have to use Ensign Dominick, Lt. Flint, and the Commander as your security team. I want weapons handed out to all crew members until we have safely left orbit."

David had chosen his words carefully when addressing Lt. Holden. Marissa gave the Captain an understanding nod. She continued to play with her coffee cup without drinking any of it. The computer files on pregnancy advised against drinking caffeine while pregnant. A small amount wasn't dangerous, but she didn't want to take in any more than necessary. She finally decided she had better at least look like she was drinking it before someone, especially Jake, questioned her about it. She raised the cup to her lips and barely moistened them with the liquid. She was grateful the Captain and Commander had agreed to keep her secret. The Captain continued to give instructions. "Commander, Lt.

Holden, you are under no circumstances to cave in to any hostage negotiations. If you have to bleed every drop of air out of that shuttle bay or watch every one of us die, then do it. Do not hand this ship over to a bunch of criminals. Are we clear on that?" David looked around making eye contact with every member of the crew to be sure they understood. Everyone returned solemn nods. David rounded out his explanation to settle the crew back down. "I'm not expecting trouble, but I would be a fool not to prepare for it. Our guests are in their seventies and eighties. I will assess the threat level, but if at all possible, they will be treated as guests not prisoners."

Jake had his chair leaned back against the wall and balanced on two legs. When the Captain indicated his intentions, the security chief nearly came out of his chair. "Captain, you can't be serious! You're going to allow convicted criminals free reign on this ship?"

The Captain was still suffering from overwork and a lack of sleep. It was his own doings, but the results were the same. "Mr. Holden, do you think I am incapable of doing a simple risk assessment or that my brain is addled? I don't intend on giving them free reign of my ship, Chief. The bridge and engineering will be strictly off limits to them. Internal sensors will be programmed to track movements and the Doc will place internal sensors in them to make tracking them easier. You challenge my orders like that again, and I'll put you on report for insubordination so fast, it'll make your head spin. Is that CLEAR, Mr. Holden?"

The crew sat there stunned. The Captain was red faced with anger. They had never seen him angry before. They had seen him under stress, annoyed, frustrated, purposefully stern, and even cranky, but never full blown angry. Jake was accustomed to feeling the brunt of the Captain's frustration, but not anger. Once Jake got over the shock of the Captain's tirade, he swallowed hard and answered the Captain. "Yes sir, I understand. I apologize for my outburst, sir. It won't happen again." For once Jake looked like his feelings were hurt. In reality, he was caught between shock and concern for the Captain's state of mind. Brynna stared at David, just as shocked as the rest of the crew. She and David had more than their share of squabbles recently, but nothing like this.

During his angry rant, David had gotten right down in Jake's face. Jake's instinct was to push the man out of his personal space, but he controlled his urge. Once he apologized, the Captain backed away from him. As soon as the Captain turned his back to walk back to the place he was addressing the crew from, Jake gave Brynna a look that spoke volumes.

As David turned back around he caught the expression on Brynna's face. He gave her a quick look that told her to keep her mouth shut, which she complied with, for now. He quickly gave them a run down on the prisoners they would be transporting. The husband and wife, Noah and Aleah Simons, and the single man named Donald Leal. "I talked to Moderator Tarmon as soon as I found out the names of the prisoners. Donald Leal is Moderator Tarmon's father. He was a leader among the followers of Pateras and fought the Commonwealth's attempts to eliminate the worship of deities."

Jake wanted to at least make the appearance of getting back in the Captain's good graces. "I'm sorry, Captain. I don't understand. Is Pateras considered a deity? I thought he was simply a superior life form. Which is he?"

David searched Jake's face to understand his intentions. Seeing no contempt, the Captain answered his question. "I'm not sure it matters. He is definitely a superior life form and he has the ability to squash people like bugs. Does that qualify him as a god? Maybe, but ultimately, he is what he is. Does it matter what label you put on him?"

Jake nodded thoughtfully. "I suppose you're right. Is Mr. Leal dangerous?"

David shrugged. "I doubt it, but that's why I said I would do a risk assessment. I will talk to Commander Landon and the prisoners before I make that determination. Mr. Leal's the one who's in his eighties. He's eighty-two to be exact."

Thane decided to take some of the heat off Jake. When the mission had started several months ago, Jake and Thane were often at odds. Over the past few months they had come to trust and respect each other. They still had a healthy rivalry, but they also had each other's backs. "What about the other two prisoners, Captain?"

"I gave Moderator Tarmon their names and they didn't ring any bells with her to begin with. She researched the names and contacted me again. Aleah Simons is the older sister of Hugh Kelly."

Jake couldn't help himself this time. "Hugh Kelly? The old man who slugged you? The engineer who helped repair the ship on Drea?"

David was annoyed at the reminder. He had allowed the older man to slug him to help him vent his frustrations. Later that evening, he had put up with Jake's incessant cajoling over the incident until Brynna and Lazaro discovered the truth. Hugh blamed the Commonwealth for the death of his sister and her husband. David thought it was best to let the old man take his anger out on him in order to protect the ship and the crew. "Yes, that Hugh Kelly."

Jake's intention was not to poke fun at the Captain. He truly was confused. "He said his sister was dead, not missing. I don't understand." The Captain shook his head. "Moderator Tarmon didn't either. I assured her I would look into it. She also provided me with a list of others they thought were dead." The crew members who were present had more questions, but David quickly put a stop to the asking. He had no answers for them. He gave those heading to the planet an admonition about wearing cold weather gear, then gave them ten minutes to get loaded up. Brynna followed David back to their quarters to talk to him while he gathered his cold weather gear. As soon as the two were alone, David told her point blank. "I don't have time to talk about Jake right now."

Brynna ignored his comment and followed through on her intentions. "I hadn't planned on discussing your reaction to him right now. I did want to ask you privately about assigning Marissa to the security detail. I thought you were going to back off on her security duties."

David stopped what he was doing and stared at her for a moment. "I can't take her completely off security details without arousing suspicions. I don't think this is going to put her in any danger. If you think it's a problem, change the assignments after I leave."

Brynna shook her head. "I'll be there to back her up. I was just confused by your choices. As far as Jake is concerned, we can discuss that later. I can wait."

David rolled his eyes then grabbed his gear and headed out the door. Brynna stared after him. Something was definitely wrong with him, but she was not sure what or how to fix it. She made a mental note to talk to Lexi at her earliest opportunity.

Jake picked up his cold weather gear and issued weapons to the landing party. Marissa issued weapons to the crew members staying behind. Minutes later the shuttle took off and headed for the planet's surface. Since the Evangeline was such a small ship, they didn't have space to store a wide variety of survival options. The distance between their landing site and the climate-controlled section of the prison was only a few hundred feet. A good heavy coat with hood and scarf would have been sufficient, but the crew's only cold weather gear was almost sufficient to stand the cold of space. The crew had one-piece hooded jumpsuits with an optional face mask that could filter and warm the air as needed. The jumpsuits included overshoes, so they could step into or out of them easily. The crew put their suits on before the shuttle launched, and Thane left the heat turned off.

Thane followed the landing instructions carefully. The group landed without incident. The four exited the shuttle. The landing pads were inside large bunkers, which shielded ships from the elements, but not the cold. The group walked across the floor of the bunker to an elevator. There were no guards present in the bunker or anywhere near the elevator. The crew stepped into the elevator. Once the doors closed, the elevator descended without any verbal instructions or the pressing of any controls. Jake looked like a nervous cat. The Captain watched him mentally counting the number of seconds it took for the elevator to reach the bottom. Surprisingly, it didn't take long for them to reach the bottom. The prison was forty stories down and used geothermal heat to keep the complex warm.

As the elevator headed down, the warmth increased to the point they were unfastening their jump suits even before getting off the elevator. The elevator came to a stop, and the doors opened to reveal a high security area. They found themselves in an area set up as a military level kill zone. There were weapons turrets pointed at them from all sides. David looked down at his chest and saw several conspicuous laser sites trained on him. He looked at the rest of his crew and saw the same thing on each of the others. David recognized Commander Landon's voice come across a speaker. "Sorry for the cold reception gentlemen, but it's standard operating procedure. Take your cold weather gear and your weapons and place them in the secure containers to your left, then come one at a time through the scanner portal. Place your hands on the scanning pads in the portal. As soon as your identities are confirmed you may pass through the portal. If you attempt to leave the portal before your identity is confirmed, you will be shot. Again, I apologize for the reception. It's automated and out of my control."

The crew glanced at the Captain, who gave them a curt nod before moving to a wall of drawers with hand print locks. The Captain opened a drawer, took his cold suit off. Folding it neatly, he placed it in the drawer, with his sidearm positioned carefully on top of the cold suit. He slid the drawer shut and programmed the sensor lock to open only to him. The crew followed his example. David headed for the portal as instructed. He looked down at his jacket. The lasers still followed him every step of the way. Before he could step into the portal, Jake called out to him. "Captain, do you mind if I -" Before he could finish his sentence the Captain backed away and waved Jake through. Jake's identity checked out and he walked on through. The Captain went through next, followed by Braxton and Thane. They headed down a narrow corridor to a door.

The crew stepped through the door and were greeted more cordially by Commander Landon. The Commander stretched out his hand to the Captain. "It's a pleasure to meet you, Captain."

David politely shook the man's hand and forced himself to smile. He had his mind on business, not pleasantries. For a split second, he thought perhaps he should have sent Brynna on this mission because he was too emotionally involved in this one. He shook the thought out of his mind and turned to introduce his crew. "This is my security chief, Jake Holden, my pilot, Lt. Thane Ryder, and this part is going to sound strange, but this is my architectural and structural engineer, Lt. Commander Braxton Flint."

Commander Landon shook hands with each of the men, then turned his attention back to the Captain. "You're right, that does sound strange. Am I allowed to know why you have an architectural engineer?"

David smiled a little more genuinely this time. He knew he needed to establish a rapport with this man if he intended to get his cooperation. The information David was looking for wasn't going to be found in any official record. "Our mission is mostly diplomatic and involves offering aid to those who are technologically behind. My crew is small, but diverse. They are highly-trained and specialized."

Commander Landon nodded. He didn't fully understand, but he also recognized he wasn't going to get detailed information. "How long can you gentlemen stay? We don't get many visitors here, and we would love to have somebody new to talk to. I have five officers and eighteen petty officers stationed here. I've heard all their tall tales. I'd love to hear some new stories. Can you stay through dinner? We get regular shipments of fresh food in here, and we have a hydroponics garden. My people aren't gourmet chefs, but it's bound to be a little better than the prepackaged stuff you've been eating."

Commander Landon's invitation and description got Thane and Braxton's attention. Despite the broad nature of his description, their mouths were already watering. They looked anxiously at the Captain, hoping he would accept the invitation. A little part of them felt guilty for getting to enjoy a good meal while their crew mates were stuck on the ship. The Captain saw the two men looking like anxious children and despite his mood, found it amusing. "Well Commander, I think I would be inciting my men to mutiny if I didn't accept your offer. So yes, we'll stay. I do need to let my ship know there will be a delay in our return. We will need to leave right after dinner though. Admiral Deacons promised this would only take two days out of our schedule. I prefer to stay on schedule if I can."

Thane and Braxton grinned when David accepted the invitation.

Jake didn't. He said nothing, but everyone knew his thoughts.

Commander Landon took the group on a tour of the facility. The facility was capable of holding five hundred prisoners, but now held less than fifty. After their tour, the group ended up in the staff lounge. David pulled the Commander aside and asked if they could talk privately. The Commander nodded and took the Captain to his office. The two sat down and began their discussion. "What is it you would like to talk about, Captain?"

David reached into his pocket and pulled out a data crystal. "I was wondering if you could tell me if you knew about the status of the people on this list. We've been trying to improve relations with Drea, and things are somewhat improved, but I thought if I could give them a few answers, it would help."

The Commander plugged the crystal into his computer. He scowled. "Captain, these names are classified. Where did you get these?"

David eyed the Commander carefully. "I checked with the Drean authorities to be certain we would be allowed to land and return these prisoners to them unhindered. They checked out the names of the prisoners before agreeing to it. Two of the prisoners you are sending with me were reported by Drean authorities as dead. The third was presumed dead but known to be a prisoner. They agreed to allow us back on the planet with the prisoners, but kindly requested any information on the names on that list. I told them I would see what I could do."

The Commander returned the Captain's intense gaze. Neither was sure the other could be trusted. The Commander finally asked, "Do you know the Commonwealth's history with Drea?"

David inhaled. "I know the Drean side of things better than I wanted to. We got caught in a highly political tug of war on Drea and nearly executed because of the ill will remaining there."

Commander Landon shook his head. "The names on this list will only make things worse, not better."

David squinted at the Commander. "These people were here, and now they aren't. There are well over five hundred names on this list, and this facility can hold five hundred. I'm sure I can safely assume some of those people actually died on Drea, but the rest were brought here, weren't they?"

The Commander grew uncomfortable under the Captain's gaze and hastily got up from his desk. He began to pace back and forth in the office. He finally came to a stop with his back to David. "I was told to trust you. Can I trust you?" He turned around to see David's face.

David hesitated. "Trust me to do what? Who told you to trust me? Admiral Deacons?"

The Commander blinked. David took that as a yes to his last question, but the Commander still seemed hesitant. "The Admiral did, but someone else did too. Who?"

A familiar voice spoke softly in David's ear. "I did."

The voice was so real David looked around expecting to see the man who spoke to him, but no one was there. He looked at the Commander. "You know Arni Liontari?"

The Commander grew wide-eyed. "Are you a follower of Pateras?" Now it was David's turn to pace. He weighed his answer carefully. He turned to face the Commander.

He gave the man a blunt answer. "No. My mission is to seek out his followers and report them to the Commonwealth."

The look on the Commander's face went from anxious to fearful, and finally settled on sick. He realized he had probably tipped his hand to a man bent on destroying followers of Pateras. He moved slowly over to his desk and sat down again. His hands placed firmly on top of his desk.

David grimaced. "You're a follower of Pateras."

The man seemed too scared to answer. He leaned forward in his chair and looked at David for some sign of mercy or compassion. "Please, don't report me. I'm close to retiring, and this outpost is secluded. I can't hurt anyone out here."

David finally relaxed his cold stare for a moment. If his next words were going to get him executed, then so be it. He had escaped being executed more than once. He was already living on borrowed time. "I am not a follower of Pateras, but Pateras sent me here to find out something. He didn't really tell me what I was looking for, other than the truth about the Commonwealth."

The color in the Commander's face began to return. "Captain…"

David held up his hand to stop the man. "Commander, while we are having this discussion, call me David. This is more personal than business."

The man nodded. "You can call me Chase. It's been a long time since anyone called me by my first name. I suppose it's only fitting. If it were Captain Alexander asking for this information, I would have to refuse to give it to you. Since it is David asking at the instruction of Pateras, I will give you the information you asked for."

David looked puzzled. "Why does that make a difference?"

Chase leaned forward on his desk. "My orders say this information is classified by the Supreme Executor himself, and even though you outrank me, you still can't order me to give you the information. Pateras outranks Luciano Hale. Pateras has ordered me to give you this information." Chase turned to face his computer. He pressed some controls and approximately five hundred files downloaded onto David's data crystal. He gingerly handed the crystal back to David. "You realize that information could get me prosecuted or killed, right?"

David nodded. "The fact that I am asking for it puts me and three billion other people on Drea at risk. Can you tell me basically what's on here?"

Chase nodded. "Eighty percent of those people died here. They were either executed or tortured to death. Ten percent of those people now work for the Commonwealth. The remaining people were never here."

David sat back down with the crystal in his hand. He stared at it intently as though he could read the data with the naked eye. He looked back up at Chase. He was torn between being nauseated and feeling overwhelming guilt and pain similar to what he felt when he entered the presence of Pateras. "Why were they here, and why were they executed?" Chase was feeling the same nausea and disgust David was feeling. "They were followers of Pateras. Some were political leaders, and some were technological geniuses. A few were simply hostages intended to affect the behavior of other prisoners. There were spouses and children here for a period of time. I've reviewed the records of this prison at length. It's not pretty. As soon as the prison was full, the administrator at the time was ordered to execute certain prisoners immediately in a public display to make a point."

"What about the prisoners still housed here? Who are they?"

Chase shook his head. "Except for the three you're picking up; the rest are bona fide criminals going through reprogramming. They are from a half-dozen worlds in this sector. We will be shipping them out in a couple months for relocation. I reclassified the three you're taking as no longer a threat. I was afraid they were going to get classified as enemies of the state and scheduled for execution just to get them off the books. I've been trying to find a way to get them home for over a year. They are elderly and don't need to be around real criminals. They can't defend themselves anymore. I've done everything I can to protect them."

"Do they serve Pateras?"

Chase's face now seemed to almost glow. "They've never wavered, not once. They are the reason I chose to follow Pateras. They've been prisoners here for nearly fifty years and refused to renounce him."

His face fell, and the glow disappeared. "I'm sorry to say, I did my share of trying to turn them through torture, but they couldn't be turned. They were willing to die if necessary. There were four of them back then. One day I couldn't stand it any longer and lined the four of them up. I threatened to execute them right then and there if they didn't recant. They were all strangely at peace. They weren't relieved to see the end of their torture and imprisonment, but excited to meet Pateras. They started singing. I was so angry. I – I shot one of them. I had the guards throw her body out into the snow." Tears began to flow down the man's face as he recounted the events.

David gave the man a chance to collect himself. "How long ago was that?"

Chase sniffed and wiped away more tears. "I was assigned here fifteen years ago. That incident happened eleven years ago."

From the man's emotional reaction, David expected to hear a much more recent timetable. David grew uncomfortable again. He got up and paced, stopping to look at the scant decorations adorning Chase's office. He finally turned around to continue the conversation. "So, what convinced you to change sides?"

Fresh tears began to stream down the Commander's face. "When my three remaining prisoners saw their comrade fall in front of them they began to sing and jabber even louder. They seemed like they were rejoicing. I ordered my men to beat the three of them and return them to their cells. I took two guards outside with me to retrieve the woman outside."

"Retrieve her body? Why?"

Chase looked up at the Captain, his face now soaked with tears. "I only stunned her. I hadn't killed her. I thought maybe she would still be alive, and I could use her as a bargaining chip. I was going to offer to send her to the infirmary and save her life if they would recant. She suffered a heart attack from the cold. Before she died, she wrote one simple sentence in the snow."

David was enthralled with Chase's story. "What was it?" Chase wiped away more tears. "I forgive you."

The two men went silent. David flashed back to the moment when he stood on Drea about to face his own execution. He had asked Arni to forgive him for his part in the deaths on Galat. Arni had genuinely forgiven him for the deaths of over six million people. He somehow didn't feel forgiven.

Chase took up his tale again. "I brought her body inside and tried to revive her, but she was gone. She died with a smile on her face. I had the other three brought to the infirmary and treated their injuries from the beating. When I was alone with them, I asked why they wouldn't recant. I asked them what was so special about Pateras. They explained their decisions to me, and they forgave me for killing their companion. I chose to serve Pateras that night. I can't serve a Commonwealth who claims to be civil and peaceful, and then asks me to treat people so cruelly. These people weren't violent, ever. I've given them responsibilities in the prison I wouldn't trust others with and left them unsupervised. With the rumors I've been hearing, I decided a year ago I needed to get them out of here. The day will come very soon when I will be ordered to execute them outright. I can't do that. You must get them home quickly.

"In order to stop them from sending me any changes in orders, I might have a problem with my communications network. My communications network will probably be out of commission for a day or two. I hope yours doesn't have any problems. I hope it's not a computer virus. I suppose I could've passed it to you when we talked."

David returned to his chair. "Did you pass a virus to my ship, or do I need one?"

Chase shook his head. "No, I didn't give you one, but I have one if you need it." He reached into his desk and started to hand David a data crystal.

David waved him off. "I will contact you when we return to the ship. Send it in the transmission just in case anyone tries to track it. It will look like an accidental infection."

The Commander had a private bathroom in his office. He stepped into it and washed the tears from his face then came back and asked the Captain a pointed question. "You obviously know who Pateras is, so why haven't you chosen to follow him?"

The Captain shifted uneasily in his seat. "I've got a million times more blood on my hands than you do. Pateras is pure goodness. He needs people better than me."

Commander Landon's sorrow was now gone, and he seemed somewhat excited. "But, that's just it. The Ancient Texts say that when the son of Pateras dies for crimes not his own, the debt for all crimes will be paid. If we choose to give ourselves over to Pateras, he will apply the payment of his son Arni to our debt."

David fought back tears of his own now. "You don't understand. I am partially responsible for over six million deaths on Galat III and for the death of Arni Liontari. How can I serve Pateras now? He has to hold me in such contempt. I don't know why he didn't strike me dead a long time ago."

Chase stared at him for the moment. "Arni died? When?"

A voice from the other side of the room startled the two men. "I died a little over two weeks ago." At the sight of Arni Liontari, Chase moved out from behind the desk, knelt on one knee before him and bowed his head. David did quite the opposite. He stood up as though he were glad to see the man then turned away from him. Arni walked over to Chase and greeted him. He encouraged Chase to return to his seat.

Arni moved over to David. "David, you know I have offered you my forgiveness for Galat. My Father does not hold you responsible for my death. My Father sent me to this existence for the sole purpose of dying. It was not a pleasant experience, but I would have done it even if you were the only human being alive."

David shook his head. "I didn't ask you to do that for me."

Arni grabbed David's arms and shook him to emphasize his point. "I know you didn't. My Father asked me to do it for you and for everyone else. He would have asked me to do it if you were the only one whose life it would save. My Father and I are responsible for my death, not you." David twisted out of Arni's grip.

Chase shook his head at Arni. "He doesn't understand."

Arni nodded in agreement. "He's close though." Arni turned back towards David. "David, why did you make the agreement to die in your crew's place on Drea?"

David gave Arni an annoyed glance. "You know why. It was the only thing I could do to save their lives. I'm responsible for those people. It's my job to keep them safe."

Arni looked at David soberly. "And I'm responsible for you. You care about your crew the same way you care about your family. My Father created all of humanity. You are his family and you're headed down a dark road to a very bad ending. Of course, he's going to do everything in his power to protect you. All he wants is for you to accept his help. David, you're drowning in a stormy sea, and all you have to do is reach out your hand and I will pull you into the safety of the boat."

The analogy seemed rather trite to David. He didn't understand how Arni could pay for the crimes of everyone else with one execution. Arni knew David's thoughts and shook his head at him. "David, you seem to think there isn't enough forgiveness in the universe for your crimes. You're wrong. You're not the worst man who's ever lived. I hold those who nearly beat you to death as more guilty than you. They are no less redeemable, but their crimes are by far more vicious and violent. You killed the population of Galat out of ignorance. They attempted to kill you purposefully."

The Captain's weariness weakened his defenses against the turmoil going on inside himself. As he remembered the events of that night, anger welled up inside him. He balled up his fist and punched the wall nearest him.

Jake had noticed the Captain leaving the lounge and followed him. He was waiting in the reception area outside Commander Landon's office. When he heard the Captain's fist hit the wall, Jake charged into the room. He had no weapons, so he didn't know how he intended to handle whatever just happened. He looked around the room. He saw the Captain standing by himself near the door gripping his arm. The Commander and Arni were standing several feet away from the Captain. The Commander looked stunned and Arni had the same frequent sad eyes Jake had seen many times before. Jake looked back at the Captain. "Are you okay, sir?"

The Captain grimaced. "Yes, Mr. Holden, I'm fine. I appreciate your diligence, but the only one intent on harming me, seems to be me. I got angry and slammed my fist into the wall. Forgive the outburst, please."

Jake gave a questioning nod. He wanted more information but knew better than to ask for it. He glanced over at Arni. "What's he doing here?" David didn't want to give Jake any reason to report the Commander, but he didn't want to lie to him either. "I would have to assume he's following me again."

Jake looked warily at the other two men then nodded towards the Captain's fist. "Did he make you do that?"

David shook his head. "Not really. I did this all on my own."

Jake frowned as he looked at the Captain's hand. "Did you break something?"

David tried to open his fist and grimaced again. "Ow, maybe. It's swelling up pretty fast, and I can't seem to open it all the way."

Jake looked at the Commander and at Arni. "Commander, could you have your facility medic come in here and treat the Captain?" Jake didn't want to cause the Captain any more discomfort by having the rest of the crew know what he had done. The Commander nodded and moved back over to his desk.

Before he could open the channel to the infirmary, Arni blocked his hand. "David, I can heal your hand. You know that I can."

David shook his head slowly. "I don't deserve any favors from you, Arni. I deserve a lot more pain than this. I'll get my doc to look at it when we get back."

Jake gave his Captain a bewildered look. He looked back and forth between his Captain and Arni. "Sir, I don't understand. You haven't done anything wrong. What is it you think you're guilty of?"

David looked down at his swelling hand. "Quite a lot, Jake. Arni and Pateras are the source of all good things in the universe. I've managed to play a significant role in destroying some of those good things. I don't have the right to ask for his help."

Arni took a couple cautious steps towards David. David heard Arni speak in an icy tone he had only heard once or twice before. "My Father gave you that right, and only he can take it away. Stretch out your hand again." His tone was so cold David was afraid to disobey. He stretched out his hand. It hurt and popped a couple times, then got warm. The pressure from the swelling began to dissipate. David looked up to speak to Arni again, but the man was now gone.

Jake and the Commander looked around for Arni as well. Jake shook his head. "Well, he's gone again."

The Commander looked back at Jake and the Captain. "Does he do that often?"

David gave the man a curt reply. "Pretty much whenever he wants to."

Jake looked back at the Commander. "I take it you've never seen him before." The Captain was still looking at his hand. When he heard Jake's question, he looked up quickly.

The Commander wasn't sure how to interpret the Captain's reaction, but he answered honestly. "No, I've never seen him before. I have heard quite a lot about him though. My prisoners have said plenty about him. Their stories seemed rather incredulous at the time."

The Captain was ready to usher Jake back out of the office before he asked too many questions. "Jake, I appreciate your diligence, but I'm fine. I promise not to hit anything else, so you can return to the lounge." Jake recognized his invitation to leave. He nodded and turned towards the door. "Yes sir." He stopped just short and turned towards the Captain. "Captain, I don't normally agree with Arni, but you're not an evil man. You're a better man than I am. That may not be saying much, but I've always admired you as a leader and a good man. I've got a long way to go to be half the man you are."

The Captain was surprised by Jake's admission. "Thanks, Jake. I appreciate your candor." Jake left the room and headed back to the lounge.

As soon as he was gone, David breathed a sigh of relief. He looked back at Commander Landon. "You've never seen Arni before?"

The Commander shook his head. "No, but somehow I knew who he was as soon as he appeared. His voice was familiar. What was that look about when Jake asked about Arni?"

"Our mission orders included instructions on what to do if any of the crew chose to follow Pateras. Jake has been a little trigger happy. He's quick to try and defend the crew against Pateras. I'm glad you answered the way you did."

"I spoke the truth. So, your man can't be trusted. What about the others?"

David looked pensive. "As far as I know, none of my crew serve Pateras, but they all have doubts. Jake has doubts, but he isn't about to give in to them. He's going to follow the regs to the very end. I doubt any of them would betray you, except Jake. I wouldn't put it past him at all." The Captain had laced his explanation with so much ambiguity the Commander decided it was better to be safe than sorry. "Perhaps we should rejoin the others, now that you have the information you came for."

David reached into his pocket and fingered the data crystal. He was anxious to look over the information. Unfortunately, this wasn't the time or place. "Yes, we probably should, Commander. I do have one question. Don't give me details because I don't need to know. I don't want to know. Have others on your staff changed alliances? Will you be alone here when we take these three?"

The Commander realized the Captain was trying to avoid putting other lives at risk. The Commander answered simply. "I won't be alone." The two moved back to the lounge where they found Jake pretending to be involved in a conversation as he intently watched the door for the Captain's return.

The crew enjoyed a delicious meal with the prison staff and lots of enjoyable conversation. The crew told about their adventures on Galat, Medoris, and Drea, at least the non-classified portions. A great deal of the conversations dealt with the Captain getting a fist to his face. The Captain took the ribbing in stride. He did return the favor by telling the story of Jake dancing around the bridge in a coffee stained uniform kissing Thane's wife's hand. Thane sat there looking annoyed a second time over the incident. The group ended up laughing hysterically over Jake's antics. The group also enjoyed the Captain and Braxton's tale of the artificial gravity failure. Braxton described Lazaro's acrobatics in trying to reach the controls in only ten percent gravity.

The Captain felt at leisure to add his own twist on the story. He told the men sitting around the table how the entire bridge crew had heard the scene play out over the audio speakers. David laughed heartily for a change and continued to tell his side of the story. "So here I am, trying to be the proper stern Captain, and the bridge crew is cracking up. Thane is doing his own set of acrobatics trying to capture hot bubbles of coffee back into his coffee cup. I'm sitting there trying not to laugh myself. I finally couldn't hold it in any longer, so I ask Braxton and Lazaro through the open channel if there was a problem. They didn't know the channel was still open and for a second, you could've heard a pin drop, if a pin could drop at such a low gravity. I ordered them to get my gravity back up, and Lazaro to report to my office as soon as things were squared away. I went to my office and looked at the record of what happened and cracked up. It was so funny. I laid my head down on my desk. I was laughing so hard my sides were about to split. My Commander comes into my office. She sees me shaking with my head down. She thought something was seriously wrong. I lifted my head up and she sees these tears streaming down my face. So, for a second she really thinks something is wrong. You should've seen the look on her face when I took a deep breath and laughed so hard I thought I was going to fall in the floor."

Thane slapped his own face and shook his head. "Captain, I thought you were really ticked off at them and us for laughing. You were just as amused as we were?"

The Captain laughed and nodded. "It really was a bad breech in protocol, so I couldn't let you know I was amused. I had to be the bad guy."

Braxton sat there looking like a nervous cat. He shook his head. "From what Lazaro said, I thought we were on the verge of being court martialed. I never knew you were laughing at us."

David gave Braxton an evil grin. "You won't know it next time either."

As dinner wound down, Commander Landon had his three prisoners brought into a holding cell to be handed over to the Captain. The Captain asked for a moment alone with the three who were sitting there with binders on. Jake objected. The Captain asked Thane and Commander Landon to keep an eye on things from the observation room next door. He positioned Jake and Braxton immediately outside the door. Jake reluctantly agreed.

The Captain stepped into the room to talk to the three. His questions were short and blunt, but he was looking to shock them into answering honestly. "Do you intend to try and take over my ship when I get you aboard, or are you going to behave as proper guests?"

The three gave each other startled looks. Noah Simons was the first to speak. "Sir, we're a little too old for that sort of behavior. We don't intend to resist or fight. Our manners may not be quite so practiced, but we'll do our best to avoid rudeness."

The Captain searched each of their faces carefully. "Do you still serve Pateras?"

The three suddenly became fearful their days of torture might begin once again. The eldest of the three, Donald Leal answered for the three of them. "We do, and nothing you do to us will change that."

The Captain nodded. "Then swear to me, in his name, you will behave yourselves while in my care and do everything you are ordered to do. You keep your word, and you will be guests on my ship, not prisoners."

Mr. Leal gave Captain Alexander a quizzical look. "Do you follow Pateras?"

David shook his head, "No, I don't. I do know if you follow him and swear in his name, you will keep your word."

The three looked confused, but they all swore to David as he asked. Aleah Simons seemed to be staring intently at David. David finally asked. "May I ask you a question?" The elderly woman nodded. "Why are you staring at me? Is there a problem?"

The woman lowered her head. During the last fifty years, she had learned the value of appearing subservient. "I'm sorry, sir. I meant no offense. Forgive my impertinence." The two men lowered their heads as well.

David began to realize how abused these elderly people had been, and they were genuinely afraid of him. He knelt in front of the woman. He gently lifted her chin with his hand. "You and I are not enemies. I'm not your jailer unless you do something to cause me not to trust you. I will treat you as guests. My people and I are soldiers, and we will defend ourselves if attacked, but we are also diplomats not a police force. You should respect me, not fear me. I have no intention of harming any of you." David assumed the woman was staring at him because she was afraid of some new line of torture. He tried to do what he could to reassure the three but was certain nothing he said would truly make a difference. He decided not to waste any more time. He stood back up and moved towards the door.

David wasn't in the mood for the distraction and brought the topic of conversation back on target. "I will have Commander Landon remove your binders since I have your word you will behave. Do you have any personal effects you need to take with you?"

Noah shook his head. "The day we were brought here all of our personal belongings were put into a pile and burned in front of us. We were forced to watch as our jewelry was taken and smashed with a hammer. We have nothing, but prison uniforms. We have no pictures, no mementos, nothing."

David turned and waved for the Commander to come in. The man came in with the intention of releasing the three from their binders. David spoke softly to the Commander as he passed him in the door way. "My men and I will be in the hallway, if you need a minute. Those three will need some cold weather gear." His intention was to give them a chance to say a farewell that wouldn't be appropriate for a warden and prisoner type relationship. He did expect their shared following of Pateras gave them a bond beyond what they should have had. David also had it in mind to protect the man from betrayal by the crew. The Captain pulled his people into the hallway as promised, while he stepped into the observation room alone. He watched the man release the binders from each of the prisoners then hug each of them. None of them seemed surprised by his actions, and they returned their jailer's hugs. To the paranoid Captain it added another piece of evidence supporting the fact that his prisoners could indeed be trusted to keep their word. He watched as the group said their farewells, and then moved back into the hallway.

The Commander escorted the three into the corridor. A team of two prison guards escorted the group back to the room just outside the elevator. The Commander had one last request to make. "Captain, I don't have any cold weather gear to spare. I can give them suits to wear to get them to your shuttle, but I need the suits back."

The Captain nodded. "We can do that. Let us get them on the shuttle, get it powered up, then we'll get the suits back to you."

The crew and their guests donned their cold weather gear. The group, including the two guards, rode the elevator back up to the landing bunker. The crew escorted their guests to the shuttle. Thane moved ahead of the group to get it powered up and heated. The crew boarded the shuttle. David moved to the co-pilots seat. He told the three Dreans to sit wherever they wanted but suggested moving away from the door for warmth. Jake and Braxton moved to the rear of the shuttle. They buttoned the hatch and once the temperature seemed to be close enough to comfortable, David took his gear off first. Once he got his gear off, he nodded to their guests to take their suits off. Jake and Braxton collected the three suits. They opened the hatch and quickly passed them to the guards waiting outside. Once the hatch was again secure, Jake, Braxton, and Thane took their gear off. As soon as everyone was buckled in, the shuttle took off.

The three prisoners began to talk quietly. The three had spoken Intergalactic Standard fluently, but David realized they were speaking something else. He could only assume they were using their native language from Drea. The thing he was most worried about were the looks he kept getting as the three spoke to each other. He noticed the three were watching only David, not the other crewmen. David quietly pressed some controls on the panel in front of him. He continued pressing buttons only to give up in frustration. He angrily slammed his fist on the panel.

Thane looked over at the Captain. "Is everything okay, Captain?" The Captain kept his voice low. "We never downloaded those language files from Drea. Cheyenne has the written language on the data crystal with the Ancient Texts, but not the spoken language. I want to know what they're talking about."

Thane glanced over his shoulder. "Can you record it and get Cheyenne to work on translating it later? You could also order them to only speak in I.S."

David considered his options for a moment then hastily punched another couple controls on his panel. He didn't bother letting the Lieutenant know his decision. Thane didn't ask any more questions but went back to his job. The rest of the trip was rather quiet and short.

The shuttle landed in the bay and the bay re-pressurized. David opened the shuttle hatch and walked down the three steps onto the deck. He touched his comm unit. "Ensign Ryder, we are disembarking from the shuttle. Stand by for all clear signal."

Noah Simons exited first. David helped the older man down the steps. The man turned and held up his hand to help his wife down the steps. The couple moved slowly but were surprisingly steady on their feet. Aleah smiled appreciatively at her husband. As she reached the deck, she continued to hold his hand. The couple acted like newlyweds despite their gray hair and wrinkled skin. David found their behavior intriguing. He turned to help Donald Leal down the steps as well. He led the three across the deck and touched his comm unit again. "Ensign Ryder, I have an encrypted message for you. Download the files from the shuttle please."

Donald, the oldest and probably still the most astute of the three, turned around to David. "I'm guessing that was your all clear signal?"

David didn't miss a beat. "Did you think I wouldn't have one?"

"I didn't know if you would consider three old timers such a risk or not. It certainly tells me something about you."

The group continued to talk as David escorted the group towards the infirmary. "If it tells you anything else about me, the security phrase was more for a scenario not involving you and your companions, but to guard against other prisoners trying to escape Mara."

Donald looked thoughtful. "So, you don't consider us to be much of a threat?"

David replied honestly. "I admit you are a potential security risk, but I'm taking you home Why would you risk your freedom? I also recognize that your age and physical conditions reduce your security risk. They don't eliminate it."

Noah turned and asked a more pointed question. "How far were you prepared to go to protect your ship, Captain?"

Again, David didn't hesitate. He wanted the three to know his limits or lack thereof. "As far as I needed to."

The group grew silent after David's admission that he would do whatever was necessary to protect his ship and the bulk of his crew.

David ordered Jason to do a full physical on all three of their guests. He failed to give the three former prisoners any advanced notice. As the three entered the infirmary, they assumed the worst about their circumstances. They saw the beds and instruments and feared they were about to be used in some sort of medical experiment or simply be put to sleep, permanently. Aleah whispered something desperate under her breath. David whipped around to see fear in her eyes and concern in the men's eyes. Despite his cranky mood, David had compassion on the group. He sent Jake to get Lexi. Jake hesitated to leave the Captain without back up but chose to follow his orders without question.

Jason and Laura began to move to guide their new patients to exam beds. David waved the two off and asked them to wait out in the corridor for a few minutes.

Once David was alone with his guests, he sat down on one of the beds to talk to them. "I gather you still don't trust me. Did Commander Landon tell you to trust me?"

The three were afraid to volunteer any information. Noah finally spoke up first. "He did. He said you had been touched by Pateras."

David huffed at his explanation. "I suppose that depends on your definition of touched. It's accurate enough, I guess."

Donald picked up the response to David's inquiry. "I'm sorry, Captain. Trust is a hard thing for us. We've spent the last fifty years being tricked and lied to. We are in the habit of expecting the worst from people."

David nodded then hopped off the bed. He headed to the nearest computer and activated it. "Computer, give access to all files on Drea III to Donald Leal, Noah Simons, and Aleah Simons."

He pulled up a list of files and scanned down the list. He touched two files and ordered the computer to play the video logs. The first was a video recording of Lt. Commander Lazaro Dominick meeting with the Drean Engineers in the ship's engineering dept. He explained to the three, the ship's need for repair and the Drean officials' desire to be rid of the

Commonwealth ship as quickly as possible. He told the group the Dreans sent two of their best engineers to help with the repairs. The video record showed a recording of discussion between the engineers.

Noah and Aleah were very well acquainted with the subjects they were discussing. Aleah suddenly looked puzzled. Noah seeing the look on her face looked at the Captain. "What is it that you want us to see, Captain?"

Aleah moved closer to the screen. She looked at Noah then back at the screen. "That man looks like my grandfather, but that's not possible. My father would be much older than that if he were even still alive."

David reached out and took the woman's hand to steady her for what he was about to tell her. "That's your younger brother Hugh, Hugh Kelly. He helped us repair our ship a month or so ago. He also decked me with a right cross, but that's a story for another time."

The woman wavered briefly making David glad he had held her hand. "That's Hughie? He was just a boy the last time I saw him." Her eyes welled up with tears.

David pressed the control to play the second file. It was a recording of Moderator Tarmon meeting with David and Brynna just prior to their departure from Drea. She was courteous, but glad to see them go. The conversation was extremely businesslike. It showed that they bore some hard feelings towards each other but were parting with an understanding.

Donald stared at the images. "The woman reminds me of my wife. Is she some relation to me as well?"

David nodded. "She's one of the most powerful individuals on Drea. She's admired and highly respected by all of Drea and by my crew. Her name is Saundra Leal Tarmon, Moderator of the United World Council of Drea."

"Saundra? My baby girl?"

Noah was less emotionally involved and asked, "What is the United World Council?"

David explained briefly about the governmental changes on Drea. He told the three the Dreans created the Council to try and unite the world. During the early days, the UWC was the world's attempt to make themselves ready to join the Commonwealth.

Drea now used the UWC to maintain peace between the various nations and provide their own commonality. "The Commonwealth doesn't have any relations with Drea. We were there only a couple weeks ago. Our visit was not particularly pleasant for either side. I've given you access to all our files on Drea. Feel free to review them as much as you like. You'll only be on this ship for a day. I want our doctor to check you out for your own benefit. I want you to feel safe. I am doing just as I said. I am transporting you home. That's it."

The infirmary door opened. Jake and Lexi stepped slowly through the doorway followed by Jason and Laura. Lexi waited by the door for the Captain to acknowledge her. The Captain waved her and the others forward to introduce them. "This is our ship's psychologist, Lt. Lexi Flint, the ship's doctor, Jason Adams, and his wife, Lt. Laura Adams. Laura is the ship's botanist and serves as a medic or nurse for Jason. I really would like you to let the doc check you out, but I will leave it to you to decide for yourselves. He's not going to harm you. I just want to make sure you are in the best of health when you see your families again." Either their confidence was growing, or they were ready to test the Captain's honor. Captain Alexander was ready to leave the crew to do their jobs. Noah stepped into his path. "Why didn't you consider our well-being fifty years ago, Captain?"

Aleah's eyes grew wide with fear that her husband was inviting retribution. Lexi started to step in and defend the Captain, but he waved her off. Jake stepped closer and bristled. David decided to turn off the filter in his brain that kept him from losing control. "First of all, I wasn't born until 20 years after you were taken. I couldn't get a pass to leave my daycare to come rescue you. Second, I am only here now to rescue you, and yes this is a rescue, because your – your God, Pateras..." The word was difficult for him to use. "Your God, Pateras, arranged it. I have a great respect and fear of Pateras, but I am not his servant or puppet. I owe him my life several times over. I will at least do what he wants with you, and I will do my best at it. Are we clear on this point? I don't know how he did it, but he got the Commonwealth to order me to pick you up and deliver you back to Drea. There is also something he wants me to learn from you. I don't know what it is, so I don't even know what questions to ask. If you're worried about this being part of some elaborate scheme to question you, well, maybe it is, but it's by Pateras' design. The Commonwealth has nothing to do with it." David wasn't angry, but he knew the three needed to see he wasn't just putting on a show for their benefit. The words had been difficult for him to say. He had trouble accepting the concept that there could be something such as a "god."

Noah glanced over David's shoulder at his companions. The two nodded approval to him. Noah stepped out of the Captain's path. "We will do as you ask. In the name of Pateras, you have our trust, for now."

The Captain took another couple steps towards the door, then stopped and turned back around. "I'm afraid you have one more decision to make. This is a small ship. We have one crew compartment open. Our quarters are designed for only two people. There is a sofa in the sitting area. The three of you can share the one compartment or one of you, or all three are welcome to stay in the infirmary. Lexi can show you around after you're done here. The choice is yours. You would have more privacy in the guest quarters, but it's up to you. Let me know if you want to talk later."

David turned and made a hasty exit. As he passed through the doorway, he hollered over his shoulder, "Jake, with me." Jake scowled again and took off quickly to catch up to the Captain.

Lexi's eyes followed the Captain as he left. Her eyes revealed serious concern. He was calmer than he had been earlier that day, but he was still extremely touchy. Aleah noticed the young lieutenant's concern. "He will be fine. The Spirit-Wind of Pateras has stirred his soul. As soon as he accepts it, he will change to be an even better man than he is now." Lexi looked at the woman in utter confusion. "I mean no disrespect, but I have no clue what you just said. The captain is already one the greatest men I have ever met. He's just going through a difficult time right now."

Aleah smiled knowingly. "You let me know if you want me to try and explain it to you later." The woman sat down on the bed Jason was guiding her to.

Jake caught up to the Captain in the lift. The two rode it up to the bridge. Jake stood there quietly waiting for the Captain's orders. As the two moved down the corridor, David finally spoke. "Jake, those people have been tortured and abused for nearly fifty years. If you feel the need to keep an eye on them, do it through ship's surveillance. I'd like to at least give them the feeling I trust them."

Jake squinted at the Captain. "Sir, they've been in a military prison. They have to know we will watch them pretty much anywhere."

The Captain paused to correct him. "They know the surveillance is there. They don't know if we are using it or not. They do know if you're following them around."

David and Jake stepped onto the bridge. Jake immediately went to his station to monitor the activity in the infirmary. David checked in with Brynna, then leaned over Aulani's shoulder to look at the files she had downloaded. The recording of the conversation aboard the shuttle wasn't going to be helpful without running it through the translation software. "Get this to Cheyenne right away. Also, get with Jake and get any additional conversations to her. She may need a lot more to get a baseline for the translation. I need to know what they were talking about. I got the feeling it was important."

The Ensign acknowledged her orders and set to work. The Captain, while standing over Aulani's shoulder, hailed Commander Landon. "Commander Landon, this is Captain Alexander of the Evangeline."

The panel showed an open connection on both sides, but for several seconds there was no reply. Commander Landon's voice finally came through and face appeared on the screen. "This is Commander Landon. I gather your trip back was uneventful?"

David had been carrying a data pad and chose this particular moment to set it down on Aulani's console. He set it right on top of the warning beacon that would've alerted her to the presence of a secondary file being uploaded onto her console. The Captain was expecting it but hadn't had time to warn Aulani. He didn't want to warn her in front of Jake, either. The Captain continued to talk to the prison Commander while the virus uploaded. "No problems to report. I do have one question though. Do you have any language files on Drean languages?"

"No, Captain, I'm afraid I don't. It's a standard prison rule that you speak Intergalactic Standard, or you don't speak."

David gave the Commander a frustrated look. The Commander glanced down at his own console and gave the Captain a subtle nod. David acknowledged the man's nod and continued the conversation. "We appreciated the hospitality, and it's been a pleasure meeting you and your staff. I hope you get a chance to enjoy a long happy retirement."

While the Captain was speaking, Aulani reached down to move the data pad off her display. The Captain casually put his hand firmly on top of it and held it in place earning him a puzzled look from the Ensign. The two men completed their conversation and bid each other farewell. David leaned over and quietly whispered to the Ensign. "Not everyone needs to know what's there." He glanced up. She followed his line of sight until it landed on Jake. She understood part of his concern. As David walked away from her, she reviewed the communication logs to see what was there that he didn't want to draw attention to. When she saw the file, and began to examine it, she looked up at David just before he stepped off the bridge. He caught her eye and shook his head at her. She knew a virus when she saw one. Now she wasn't sure what to do with it, so she began looking at how to repair any damage they might incur related to it. She didn't want to implement the fix until the Captain ordered her to, but she wanted to be ready the instant he said so. She scowled at it as though she could scare it into submission with a dirty look. Her other question was why would the Captain allow this? What purpose did it serve? No, he was not behaving normally.

David headed to his office without taking Command from Brynna or ordering the ship to leave orbit. Brynna scowled thinking he may have done so to deliberately keep her busy on the bridge. "Lt. Holden, get our course plotted to Drea. Lt. Ryder, take us out of orbit. As soon as you have the course plotted, prepare to initiate the tachyon drive." The two heard the tension in her voice and each silently hoped whatever was going on with the Captain would resolve soon. The two worked quickly to get their course locked in. As they passed the orbit of the last planet in the system, Brynna hailed engineering. "Lt. Commander, prepare to engage tachyon drive." She punched another control to hail the Captain. "Captain, we've left the Maran system and are preparing to engage the tachyon drive."

There was a brief pause before the Captain acknowledged the information and ordered her to carry on. As soon as the ship was up to speed, Brynna ordered Thane to take over as the watch officer. She headed straight for the Captain's office.

"Captain, may I have a word with you?"

David sighed at the sound of her voice. He looked up from his computer screen. He waved at the chairs in his office. "Yes, please come in. I need to update you on some things. I apologize for not doing that earlier. I had my mind on other things."

His words sounded hollow to the both of them. Unfortunately, Brynna had to accept his hollow platitudes, even though she didn't put much stock in his words. "Fine, you can bring me up to date, then we can discuss what I came in here for." David stared at her for a moment before moving on. His thoughts ran quickly through the scenario he saw coming in his future and how he might handle it. He didn't come to any clear conclusions.

The Captain reported the events on Mara, including his discovery that the Warden and some of his staff now followed Pateras because of the three prisoners on board. When he reached the part about the virus in the Communications system he decided Aulani needed to know about it. He reached over to his comm unit and asked her to step into his office for a moment. Aulani came in as ordered and joined Brynna at the table in the Captain's office. The Captain moved from behind his desk over to the table, only he remained standing as he addressed the two women. "Commander Landon was concerned about possible orders coming to execute our three guests in the very near future and he wasn't comfortable with it. He did everything he could to see they got out of prison safely. In order to get them safely back to Drea without receiving any new orders, he infected his communications system with a virus. His system may have accidentally infected our system as well."

Brynna was both shocked and angry. "What?! You agreed to that?

Are you out of your mind?"

David gave her a cold look. "Are you questioning my orders, Commander?"

"What orders, Captain? You haven't given me any orders to question, Sir!"

Aulani chose this moment to jump in to try and diffuse, or at least sidetrack the discussion. "The virus is already in the system and working. We should start having communication losses in about an hour from what I can tell. I have also already been working on the algorithm to counter it and I have set up some safety measures to prevent it from getting into the rest of the computer systems. I haven't implemented the algorithm yet. I was waiting on the Captain's orders. Sir, you should know that if I hadn't contained it, it could have gotten into all the computer systems including the tachyon drive." Aulani was afraid her last comment might put the discussion right back to the point it was when she tried to derail it.

When neither the Captain nor the Commander responded, she added one last comment. "Captain, I understand what the intention was, but Commander Landon's systems aren't the same as ours. He couldn't have known the dangers of such a thing." Her cleverly disguised point was that Captain Alexander should have known the dangers.

Aulani's words and her intent finally hit home. The Captain finally pulled a chair out and sat down. He was no longer glaring at Brynna. He slowly looked over at Aulani. "Do you mean this thing could have crossed over into the tachyon drive and disrupted the tachyon field?"

Aulani gave him a serious look and nodded. "Yes Sir, engineering uses the same language code as the comm system. I think I stopped it before it crossed systems."

David rested his elbows on the table and buried his face in his hands. "What have I done?"

Brynna knew he was at point where he would listen, but this wasn't the time to challenge him. "Ensign, what are the risks if we don't flush the system right now?"

Aulani shook her head slightly. "I think I have it contained, but if I missed something, it could still be a threat."

David's head popped up and looked at Aulani. "Is there something you can do to confound the comm system that would mimic the symptoms of a computer virus?"

Aulani thought for a moment. "I could run some concurrent overlapping diagnostics and give it a fail-safe code where it would continue running until I alone shut it off."

David seemed almost excited. "Great! Let's do that. I will return to the bridge shortly. You report the discovery of the virus and that you have managed to confine it, but it's going to take a while to cleanse the system. I'll order you to take care of it, then you flush the virus and run the diagnostics. How does that sound?"

"I would feel better if I could go ahead and flush the system now, sir."

David's mood swung back the other direction. "Fine, get started on it. Don't let Jake know what you're doing. As a matter of fact, go back to the bridge and get started, then call me to the bridge to report the virus." Aulani stood up to go. She glanced at the Commander prior to leaving with a look of concern. Brynna nodded towards the door. Aulani headed out quickly and back to her station.

Once they were alone David looked at Brynna. "Just don't say it. I really don't need to hear it right now."

Brynna's tone and demeanor changed drastically from her original intent. "David, I'm worried about you. The David I know wouldn't have missed something so obvious. Something is very wrong with you. You aren't sleeping. You were red-faced with anger at Jake this morning. You allowed a virus onto the ship that could have killed us all and may still do so if Aulani didn't contain it quickly enough. This isn't you, David."

David stood up and began to pace again. His agitation was obvious, but it was aimed inward not outward. "I know. I know. I KNOW!" He balled up his fists again then remembered what happened when he hit the wall in the Commander's office and forced himself to relax his hands.

Brynna looked at his fists then back to his face. She spoke to him as gently as she could without sacrificing the importance of her words. "David, I love you and respect you."

"But...?" He knew from her tone there was a "but."

She took back her sentence. "I love you and respect you, but something isn't right, and if you can't find a way to fix this within three days, I will relieve you of command. I'm telling you this off the record and as kindly and gently as I know how because I love and respect you. Something is terribly wrong, and someone is going to get hurt if you don't sort this out."

"You have no grounds for such an action. If you say anything about the virus you are putting the Commander of Mara at risk for being discovered."

"David, I don't have to put Commander Landon at risk. Aulani can simply testify that you purposefully downloaded a virus into the computer system. She doesn't have to say where it came from. I'm quite sure Jake would agree you have been irrational and behaving erratically. Lexi and the doc will probably agree as well. If things haven't improved with you in three days, I will ask you to voluntarily take yourself out of command, or I will remove you from duty myself. I will have you escorted to the med bay for a full diagnostic and a sedative to make you sleep. I'm not bluffing, and I'm not threatening you. I'm worried about you and about this crew. I will do what I must to protect everyone concerned. Do you understand?"

David tried to scowl at her. For some reason, he was more hurt than angry. "I understand." David's comm unit suddenly whistled at him and Aulani's voice came through requesting his immediate presence on the bridge. She hadn't wasted any time on her assignment. David thought this virus must have really rattled her.

David and Brynna stepped onto the bridge together. Aulani made the expected report. David began barking out orders to her. She acknowledged them hastily. Jake stopped watching the ship's guests who were still in the infirmary and watched the interaction quietly, but intently.

David turned to Thane, "Disengage tachyon drive, but allow the ship to continue its current trajectory."

David touched the comm unit to address engineering. The communication wouldn't go through. He glanced at Aulani. Noting his unasked question, she volunteered. "Internal channels have been affected, but comms on your bracelet should be unaffected because they don't have to go through internal channels."

David touched his bracelet and contacted Lazaro. He warned the engineer about the virus, ordered a diagnostic on the drive systems, and told him they would not use the tachyon drive until the system was cleared.

Brynna watched David closely through the events to be sure he wasn't missing anything. Lazaro warned the Captain it would take nearly two hours to run such a thorough diagnostic. The Captain calmly acknowledged the information and allowed the man to do his job. The ship couldn't maintain the extreme speeds created by the tachyon field, even though there was nothing in space to slow them down. The tachyons were necessary to create the conditions for increased speed. Without them, their speed would automatically drop to sub-light speeds.

As soon as the crisis was theoretically past, David headed to the gym and took more of his frustrations out on the punching bag. At this rate, they were going to need a new one before their two-year mission was up.

David tried hard to get some sleep that night. He couldn't seem to stay asleep. When he did doze off, his sleep was full of unsettling dreams. He got up two hours early, pulled on some clothes, and went to the dining hall for a cup of coffee. No one else was around because it was late in the current shift. The next shift wasn't up yet. David picked up his data pad and began to read the Ancient Texts again. He kept going back and forth between new sections he hadn't read yet and one section he had read repeatedly. The new sections were some sort of prophecies about one who would come and rescue all that were cast off the birth world. The writer seemed to have the promise from Pateras himself that everything would be made right again. The texts were full of prophecies of doom, but more full of promises. David looked back at the section he couldn't seem to get away from. It described a world of immense beauty and lush vegetation. A world where animals, no matter how large or small, were submissive to humans and never attacked. The planet contained two springs of water, one was free to all, but the other was forbidden. The writer told about his own desire to increase his knowledge. His desire was to be closer to Pateras and more like Pateras. One of the banished ones appeared to him and tricked him into drinking the water. The writer lamented about losing the joy of eternity and the sorrow of falling into the disfavor of Pateras. The writer, despite his immense loss, rejoiced over the promise given to him by Pateras that the banished evil beings would be vanquished. The promise included a prophecy that the son of Pateras would come to them through a descendant of his own.

David scowled and thought. The man who wrote this part of the texts had everything. He got greedy and lost it all, but he was still rejoicing and still serving Pateras.

"Are you having trouble understanding the Ancient Texts?"

The voice came out of nowhere. David looked up to see Donald Leal standing over him. It took him a moment to make sense of the words spoken to him. He finally looked up at the man standing over him. "How did you know I was reading the Ancient Texts?"

Donald motioned to one of the chairs. "May I sit down?" David nodded. The man sat down to answer his question. "Pateras woke me. He told me you needed help understanding the Ancient Texts."

David didn't question the man's explanation. He didn't doubt Pateras' ability to talk to people. David didn't waste any time getting to the point. "The man who wrote this had a perfect life and he let it get away from him. He regrets his decision, but he's still… still… I don't know. He's still happy?"

Donald smiled. "He has indeed lost a lot, but he hasn't lost the thing that is most important. He still has his love for the maker of all, Pateras."

"He rejected Pateras, why would Pateras want him back?" David argued.

Donald eyed David cautiously. "I assume you don't have children." David shook his head, and Donald continued. "The relationship between Pateras and us is similar to parent and child. Are you married?"

David nodded. He realized he hadn't introduced the entire crew to the man. He wouldn't have asked that question if he had known the entire crew was comprised of married couples. "My wife is my first officer. Her name is Commander Brynna Alexander."

"Is she pretty?"

David smiled at the thought of her face.

Donald continued. "I'll take that as a yes. Do you love her?"

David looked up at the man. "Yes, very much, although I haven't done much to show her lately."

"If she walked in here and told you she wanted a divorce, what would you do?"

David's face contorted in mental anguish. "I suppose I would give it to her."

Donald shook his head sadly. "I thought you loved her. You wouldn't fight to get her back?"

"I don't deserve her. You don't seem to understand. Pateras showed me exactly who I am. Even Pateras despises me."

Donald straightened in his chair. "Pateras despises no one, except the ones he banished."

"Didn't he banish us all from his perfect world?" David spit out the venom laced words.

Donald shook his head. "You don't understand. He took us off that world for our own protection. If we hadn't been removed, we may have taken a drink from the eternal fountain. If we had done that, there would be no hope for us. We would become like the banished ones. The death of the offspring of Pateras could not be applied to our crimes. We would live forever in these bodies, and when the day of retribution comes, we would receive everything we deserve for all eternity. Captain, none of us deserve to stand in the presence of Pateras. None of us deserve to have his offspring take our punishment. He created us, and we have all rejected him. You say you would let your wife go if she asked. Would she do the same to you, or would she pursue you? Pateras continues to pursue you. He wants you to choose to re-enter his favor. Don't let the death of his offspring be for nothing. When that day comes, you will understand."

David slammed his fist on the table, and his eyes began to tear up again. "That day has come and gone. Arni died, and it was in my place. I should've been the one who died. Your daughter had me on the execution block. I was ready to die for my crimes, but Arni took my place!"

Donald sat there stunned. "You've met the offspring of the Timeless One? He's dead?" The man's face became pale.

David knew he had shocked the man. He decided to put the man at ease, quickly. "I'm sorry, Mr. Leal. I forget not everyone knows Arni. Your people called him the Intercessor. They knew his name, but he was so highly revered, your daughter could barely handle calling him 'Lord Liontari.' He had to push to get her to do that. Arni is alive. He died, but Pateras restored him. Arni introduced me to Pateras. Pateras sent me to Mara to find out what the Commonwealth is capable of."

Donald was still a bit shaken. Tears of his own slipped quietly down his cheeks. "Have you found what he sent you to find?"

David slumped down in his chair. "I don't know. I guess I thought… I guess I thought whatever I found would make me automatically just change my mind and betray the Commonwealth without a second thought."

Donald reached over and tapped the data pad David had been reading. "The Ancient Texts tell us from the beginning that our choices are our own. Pateras doesn't force us to do anything except to make a choice. Who you choose to serve is up to you. I could have chosen the Commonwealth fifty years ago and gotten myself out of that prison, but I didn't. I chose to stay in prison and serve Pateras. I guess I'm a lot like the man who wrote that text you were reading. The Commonwealth would have given me great rewards if I had chosen to serve them. I could have had anything. I could have had everything, by human standards. I'm still happy with my choice. Think about that for a while." Donald got up to leave the room.

David looked up at the man. "Thank you." As the man got to the door, David decided to try something unorthodox. "Hold on a second." The man stopped and turned back around to David. David looked around the room. "Arni? Please, could you indulge me a moment and introduce yourself to Mr. Leal?"

Donald gave David an odd look. "What are you…" Arni suddenly appeared in front of the two men. He wore his traditional Drean business attire. Donald stumbled backwards. Arni reached out and steadied the man.

"Why? Why would you come here now?" Donald gasped in amazement.

Arni smiled happily. "Because it's the first time David has asked me for anything."

David thanked Arni for answering his call, then left the two talking while he went to get a shower. Instead he laid back down on the bed to relax his tired muscles for a minute and was quickly sound asleep.

The next thing he knew Brynna was waking him up to let him know he was two hours late for his duty shift. She had been the one on duty but didn't seem irate that he was late relieving her.

Realizing what he had done, David apologized emphatically. He got a quick shower and raced up to the bridge. Once there, he reviewed the ship's logs, took care of the routine matters, then began his relentless task of reviewing the Ancient Texts again.

Thane and Aulani were again on duty with him. Aulani didn't want to disturb the Captain, but she knew she needed to. "Captain?"

David swiveled his chair around to see her. "Yes, Ensign?"

"I have a message for you from Ensign Dominick. She said she doesn't have enough of the verbal Drean language to build a translation matrix. She said she might be able to record conversations while they are in their quarters, but she was uncomfortable doing that without orders."

David furrowed his brow. "Would the translation files from the Ancient Texts provide any help?"

The Ensign shook her head. "I'm sorry, sir. She tried, but without a verbal reference, it's going to take some time."

David's brow furrowed even more. He wasn't comfortable recording private conversations either. If the safety of the ship and crew were at stake, he would have no problem with it. "If I asked them outright, could she confirm the accuracy?"

After some consideration, Aulani answered. "Maybe. That's a question only she could answer."

David jumped up from his seat. He adjusted the recording mechanism on his bracelet. "I'm going to go talk to our guests and see what they can do to help." Captain Alexander found Lexi in the dining room with all three of their guests. Lexi had provided their guests with clothing from the ship's stores. She and the Captain has agreed they didn't need to return to their families in prison uniforms.

David greeted each of them casually and grabbed something light to eat. Since he was two hours late for his shift, he had skipped breakfast.

The Captain sat there eating his meal quietly. He listened to the others converse about Drea. The three guests had plenty of questions about the changes on Drea. Lexi answered their questions as best she could but didn't volunteer any information regarding the failure of their last mission. She was fairly certain their guests would not be pleased to learn the entire crew was considered convicted criminals on Drea. The dreaded questions finally came. Aleah started with a simple question. "So, has Drea finally made an alliance with the Commonwealth?"

Lexi glanced at the Captain. "No, not exactly. We've basically agreed to stay out of each other's way."

Sensing there was a lot more to it, Noah jumped in. "So how is it we rated this trip back home? Are we being used as a peace offering?"

Lexi again looked to the Captain. This time she didn't know how to answer.

David swallowed his last bite of food, took a sip of water, and slowly wiped the crumbs from his face. He wanted to slow the conversation down before it could get out of control. "I told you how this happened, at least as much as I know. Pateras wanted me to learn something and sent me to Mara. He somehow arranged for us to pick you up. We will reach Drea late tonight, so whatever I'm supposed to learn, you better teach me quickly."

The three looked at each other blankly. "Captain, perhaps you should give us a little background. We don't know what information you're looking for." Aleah volunteered.

Donald took the questions even further. "Captain, I would almost bet your answers relate to what you told me early this morning. Would you care to share with them what you told me about Saundra and the Intercessor?"

David seemed surprised Donald hadn't told the others about their earlier discussion. David nodded. "Okay. I'll tell you what you want to know, but first tell me about something. David pressed a couple buttons on his bracelet. The computer pulled up the record of the conversation aboard the shuttle. "What was this about? Everyone on Drea speaks Intergalactic Standard. We never downloaded the files for the other languages on Drea. I know it had something to do with me, but what did you say?" The group watched for a moment. David paused the recording at an emphatic point. "That! What was that?"

The three seemed a little hesitant. Aleah looked at the two men who were more hesitant, then told the Captain what he wanted to know. "I told them you reminded me of a man who was a prisoner with us at the beginning of our captivity. He was taken captive along with his wife and three children. I heard they killed his oldest daughter to secure his cooperation. He and his wife were engineers. They were working on spaceship propulsion systems."

Noah said something to Aleah in Drean and grabbed her arm. She shook him off and answered him in I.S. "It's fifty-year-old information. What good is it now? He cooperated and they took him and his family away. He's probably gotten his just reward by now." Her tone sounded very bitter. She looked back at David. "What I said, right there, was you looked so much like Elliot Paulson."

The two men looked bitterly at David. It made David uncomfortable. He switched on the recording again and caught Noah saying something that appeared equally bitter and Donald saying something less bitter, but no less sad. David stopped it again. "What about that?"

Noah looked angry. He folded his arms across his chest and refused to answer. Donald and Aleah weren't eager to answer either. Donald finally answered. "Noah was hoping Elliot got what he deserved for abandoning Pateras and Drea. I was telling him Pateras knows what he is doing. Elliot's defection was probably what protected Noah and Aleah, and what kept them alive."

David looked puzzled. "What do you mean?"

Donald sighed. "They were looking for engineers. Engineers who were working on a specific project. Noah, Aleah, Elliot, and Tyra, were working on the same project. They really only needed one of them to work on the project for the Commonwealth. They promised all the engineers and their families good lives, but they had to reject Pateras and agree to work for the Commonwealth. Tyra and Elliot had no choice. The officer in charge killed their firstborn child and was about to kill their second and third children if they didn't cooperate. Once

Elliot and Tyra agreed to work for them, they no longer needed Noah or Aleah. They didn't want to kill them just in case things didn't work out with Tyra and Elliot. They never stopped trying to get us to reject Pateras, but they were careful not to do any permanent damage to us. I don't really know why they kept me alive."

David was starting to have questions of his own. He moved over to the control panel for the computer and pulled up a copy of the prison files. He pulled up a picture of Elliot Paulson. The face of a man a little older than David appeared on the screen. The resemblance was uncanny.

Lexi looked at the picture. "Captain, he does look a lot like you."

David glanced back at Donald. The two men had been the same age when they were taken from Drea. David looked back at the computer. "Computer, age the man in this picture to show me what he would look like if he were forty-seven years older." The computer began to run the man's age forward. Before it reached its target, David yelled, "Computer, stop age progression." The age progression stopped at thirty-five making the man in the picture seventy years old.

Lexi looked at the Captain again. "Captain, did you know him?"

The Captain stood there staring at the picture. He was squinting and shaking his head. "Computer, pull a picture from my personal family album of Saul Deacons and put it alongside the current picture." The picture appeared on the screen. The two men were nearly identical.

Lexi jumped up went to the computer. "Computer examine the bone structure and facial features. Are these the same men?"

The computer responded. "There is a ninety-two percent probability the two pictures are of the same man."

Lexi looked at the Captain. "Captain, do you have any DNA profiles?"

David reviewed the prison files. "Yes. No. I have a profile for the prisoner Elliot Paulson, but I don't have Saul Deacon's profile. I wouldn't have any reason to have that."

Lexi punched a couple more buttons on the computer control panel. "Computer compare the DNA profile of Elliot Paulson and Captain Alexander. Are they blood relatives?"

The computer flickered as it did the requested analysis. The computer finally gave a response. "Results indicate that Elliot Paulson may be the maternal grandfather of Captain Alexander. Conclusive results are only possible with DNA from maternal grandmother."

David and Lexi stared at each other for a moment then both reached for the computer panel and added the DNA of Tyra Paulson into the equation. The computer paused for what felt like an eternity to add the new information into the mix. Finally, the computer responded. "Elliot and Tyra Paulson are the biological maternal grandparents of Captain David Liam Alexander."

The three former prison mates continued to watch curiously. They weren't sure what to make of what was unfolding in front of them.

David sat down stunned. Lexi finally sat down in front of him. "Captain, how are you taking this? Are you okay?"

David looked up at her. "I'm not sure how to take this. Until I figure this out, this information doesn't leave this room. Understood?" David stared at Lexi until she agreed then he looked at their three guests. "Do I have your word on this?"

Donald looked at his companions who returned blank stares. He looked back at the Captain. "You have our word, Captain."

David got up and created a data crystal for Donald. "Here's the complete files on our mission to Drea. I sent a redacted file to the Commonwealth about Drea. This file can never be allowed to reach the Commonwealth, or they will destroy Drea. If they know Drea still follows Pateras, they will wipe the entire population out. I reported the presence of the son of Pateras on a planet called Galat III. The Commonwealth destroyed everyone on the planet. We confessed to our part in this tragedy, and Moderator Tarmon had us arrested. We were tried and convicted of mass murder, among other crimes. I was sentenced to be executed for my crimes and those of my crew. What you won't find in those files is that Arni Sotaeras Liontari, the son of Pateras, is known as the Intercessor on Drea. He was the spiritual leader of Drea. He took my place at my execution. He sent me to visit his Father. Pateras showed me his side of the story and then sent me to Mara to find some hidden truth. I guess, I just found it." David shut the prison and DNA files down and locked them to open only on his password. He grabbed two cups of coffee and abruptly left the room.

Lexi fought the urge to follow him. She had a strong desire to help him make sense of this new information but knew he would need some time alone to process it first. His entire identity was now shattering in his own mind. It didn't make it any easier on her nurturing instincts.

Noah went back and picked up a lost thread of conversation. "Don, if Elliot's betrayal kept us safe, why did they start attacking us again twelve years ago? What changed?"

On a hunch, Lexi did some quick research on the computer. In a minute, she turned back around to address Noah's question. "The Captain's grandfather died suddenly in a traffic accident twelve years ago."

Aleah grabbed Noah's hand. "They were afraid Tyra would either betray them or would fall apart after Elliot's death. They were coming after us again. What stopped them?"

The three suspected Commander Landon's treason played a part in it, but they weren't going to betray him. They knew there had to be more to it than that, but what?

No one knew the answer to her question.

DREAN HISTORY

The Evangeline reached Drea late at night according to the ship's schedule and put down on the moon nearest Drea. They were out of reach of the four defense satellites orbiting the planet, but close enough for the planet to see them without their cloaking net activated.

David contacted Moderator Tarmon and told her they would make arrangements to transfer their guests to the planet after dark on the Cathal Provence's eastern coast. It would be mid-morning for the crew.

As David talked to Moderator Tarmon, she noticed he was focused on getting his business done and nothing else. She finally asked, "Captain, are you alright? You seem distracted or upset by something."

David pressed his lips together. He glanced at the bridge crew. He wanted to give her the answer she was looking for but didn't want to talk in front of his crew. He finally gave her a halfhearted and half accurate response. "It's a personal matter. I apologize if I've been rude. Perhaps the Intercessor would fill you in. This is something only he could adequately explain."

Surprisingly, Moderator Tarmon smiled broadly. "I've seen a number of those situations. I'm sure it will work out for the best and sooner than you think. It may not work out as soon as you would like, but the timing will be perfect."

David found warmth and encouragement from her smile and her words, but not as much as he needed.

The Captain had invited Donald Leal to join him on the bridge to see his daughter for the first time in nearly fifty years.

Lexi escorted the man onto the bridge while the Captain and the Moderator were concluding their business. The Captain heard them enter and turned to re- introduce the two. "Moderator Tarmon, this is Donald Leal, your father." Saundra had been anxiously awaiting the moment since David contacted her a couple days earlier. She still wasn't sure how to respond.

She stared at the old man with anxious anticipation. "Daddy?"

His face wasn't the face she remembered. He looked like the man she remembered as her great-grandfather. Both began to tear up. "Saundra? Saundra, I thought I would never see you again. You look so much like your mother."

Saundra's face was full of both joy and sorrow. She was heartbroken over the years she had lost with her father but rejoicing over his return. "Daddy, she's never given up hope. She said you would be brought back to her one day."

Donald smiled through his tears. "Your mother's still alive?"

Saundra nodded and wiped away her tears. "Yes, Daddy, she's still alive and very active. I haven't told her you were coming home yet. I wanted to wait until I saw you for myself. I didn't want to get her hopes up after all these years."

Donald continued to smile. "I can't wait to see you both in person. We have so much to talk about. Will you both be there when we land?"

"Yes, Daddy. We've all been apart for far too long. I'm not going to let another moment be lost. Noah and Aleah Simons' families will be there as well."

David interrupted at that point. "Moderator Tarmon, please make sure you have one of those satellites shut down, so we can land safely. We're sending our shuttle down with a minimal complement. I'd rather not lose anyone if we can help it."

Moderator Tarmon nodded. "Captain, just as a word of warning, if you are using my father as a way of getting those satellites shut down, you will sincerely regret it."

David snapped to attention. "In the name of Pateras, I am not using your father to perpetrate any sort of deception. My intentions are honorable."

Moderator Tarmon, knowing what David had gone through on Drea, accepted his oath and declaration. She breathed a sigh of relief. Before they closed their communication, Donald asked his daughter one more quick question. "Would it be possible to have any family of Elliot and Tyra Paulson's there as well?"

David's head whipped around to look at Donald. What was the man up to? Lexi stiffened at the mention of the name as well. Moderator Tarmon could see this meant a great deal to the Captain and to her father, but their reactions were polar opposites. She knew she needed to do as much as she could to honor the request. "I'll see who I can find, but what do I tell them? They obviously aren't coming home with you."

Donald nodded. "Tell them I have information about their missing relatives."

Saundra promised to do what she could in such a short period of time. She bid her father a warm, but short farewell and closed the comm channel.

David volunteered to escort Donald off the bridge. Lexi was concerned about the two men being alone together just now. She caught the Captain just before he stepped off the bridge. "Captain, you aren't going to do anything rash, are you?"

The Captain bristled. He whispered quietly, but sharply. "Do you really think I'm going to beat up an eighty-year-old man? If I'm giving you those kinds of doubts then perhaps you need to relieve me of my command, Lieutenant."

Lexi looked startled. She hadn't meant to suggest such a thing, but perhaps it was running around in the back of her mind after all. "I'm sorry, sir. That isn't what I meant to suggest. Forgive me. I just know you're under a lot of stress, sir. I just wanted to let you know I'm here if you need me."

The Captain gave her a brisk nod and walked out after Donald. David caught up to him at the elevator. The two rode down in silence. Donald had chosen to stay alone in the infirmary. As the two stopped at the doorway, Donald grinned sheepishly. "Captain, would you care to come in and talk for a few minutes? My home is your home. Although, my seating area is somewhat lacking." David accepted the invitation and managed a halfhearted grin.

Donald climbed slowly onto his bed and stretched out to make himself comfortable. It was late, and he was quite tired, but he knew he owed the young Captain an explanation. David did what he could to help the man onto the bed, then sat himself down on the next bed. As soon as David was settled, Donald surveyed the young Captain. He wore the visage of a man who was tired inside and out. "Captain, I know what you're worried about. As far as I am concerned, your grandfather was forced to work for the Commonwealth. He's no traitor. He did what any man is expected to do. He did what he had to, in order to protect his family. Elliot's family should know he survived and that his children and grandchildren are alive and well. I also thought you might want to meet more of your family."

"Every human being on Drea views me as a mass murderer. Do you really think they will claim any kinship to me?"

"I don't know. Whether you tell them who you are or not, is up to you. I promised you I would say nothing, and I intend to keep that promise. Because they survived, I will tell their families what happened to Elliot and Tyra. You can choose to tell them your relationship, or not."

David hadn't spent a large amount of time reviewing the prison records. He did make a copy of the files Commander Landon had given him. He wanted to keep a copy for himself and felt compelled to give Saundra Tarmon a copy. He found himself lost in thought staring at the floor. Looking back up at the old man's kind face,

David asked. "What was her name? The one they... the daughter who died? My aunt?"

Donald's face clouded as he thought back. It had been a long time ago, but he had vowed to remember the names of everyone who died at the hands of their enemies. In a moment, his thoughts came together. His eyes once again focused on David's face. "It was Abigail."

David's face went pale. "My sister's name is Abigail. My mother must've named my sister after her own sister."

Donald's eyes began to glaze over as he relaxed on his bed. David knew he should leave and let the man get some rest, but he was strangely drawn to him. He knew their time together was fast coming to an end. David hopped off the bed he was sitting on. He offered the man his hand. The old man gave David a puzzled look but took his hand. David gave him a firm hand shake. "I appreciate your candor and your help. I'll be sorry to see you leave us tomorrow. I hope Pateras grants you several more years with your family."

Donald smiled. "Thank you, young man. Pateras has great plans for you and your crew. He chose a good man when he picked you."

David winced at the man's words. He had a hard time believing him. David left the room to allow him to get a good night's sleep. He returned to his quarters and laid down on the sofa with his data pad. He decided to look over the prison files in more detail before he met with Moderator Tarmon the next morning, or night depending on how one chose to look at it. An hour later, he was sound asleep. Brynna was on duty and came in quietly just to check on him. When she saw him sleeping on the sofa she grabbed an extra blanket and laid it over him. She carefully slid the data pad out of his hand and laid it on the end table near his head. She dimmed the lights and slipped quietly back to the bridge. Since they were sitting still on the moon, their shifts were brief. Everyone would take just one two-hour shift through the night and only two people needed to be on duty at a time. She knew she would be off duty in a couple hours, so she wanted to be sure she could slip in quietly again without disturbing him.

Brynna went off duty and handed the watch over to Lazaro. She came in to find David still sleeping on the sofa. She moved into the bedroom and got ready for bed as quietly as possible. Minutes later she was sound asleep. David began to get restless on the couch. His dreams continued to rattle him. Images of the inhabitants of Galat living their happy lives were replaced with images of their decaying corpses. Wild dogs began to attack him. Considering his recent discoveries, the dogs were now attacking his uncle, mother and sister. David began to fight the dreams and thrash about on the sofa. In his dream, he and his uncle fought to protect his mother and sister from the attacking beasts. After a frenzied fight, David killed one of the dogs, and the others ran off. He turned around to see his entire family lying dead on the ground including Brynna. He fell to his knees and picked up Brynna's lifeless body. He looked up to see Arni standing over him. Arni knelt in front of him with a look of sorrow on his face. "David, let me help you. This is my fight, not yours."

David woke up with a start. He was broken out in a cold sweat. He sat up slowly and tried to clear his mind. It wasn't working very well. A wave of nausea washed over him. He bolted for the bathroom and vomited. David sat on the floor until his stomach settled down. He finally pulled himself up, got cleaned up, and headed to the gym to reacquaint himself with the punching bag. He wore the appropriate protective gear but punched the bag until his hands were bruised and his knuckles were rubbed raw and bloody.

Why couldn't he get rid of these dreams? David's strength began to fail as he continued to punch the bag. He finally walked over to a bench and sat down. He jerked the gloves off and threw them on the floor angrily. He looked down at his hands which were swollen and shaking.

He felt a familiar presence near him. He looked around and saw no one. He yelled into the air. "So, where are you now, Arni? Why don't you come torment me some more?"

Arni's voice whispered softly to him. "I'm not tormenting you. You're doing this to yourself. Call out to me when you are ready. I want to help you."

David picked the gloves up from the floor and threw them across the room. There was no one there to hit, but it made him feel a tiny bit better. David went back to his quarters, showered, and dressed for duty. He went up to the shuttle bay to make sure it was ready for departure later in the day and kept himself busy for the next couple hours doing routine activities.

Captain Alexander finally landed in the dining hall for some coffee and a pastry. He walked in to find Donald sitting there alone sipping on a cup of coffee. He managed a polite greeting despite his foul mood. Donald looked at David and shook his head. "You need to get yourself straightened out and soon. I need more sleep than this."

David gave the man a befuddled look. "I don't understand."

Donald took another sip of his coffee before offering his explanation. "I'm not used to getting up so early. I've been waiting here for you for over an hour. Pateras woke me again to tell me you needed to talk.”

David leaned back in his chair. “I see.”

Donald looked down at the Captain’s hands. “You can’t beat up an enemy you can’t see, Captain.”

“I can try.” David wryly replied.

Donald shook his head at David. “I’ve been a prisoner of the Commonwealth for fifty years, Captain. I had nothing to beat up on. How do you suppose I didn’t go insane? I was locked up for daring to defy the Commonwealth on my own home planet. I was yanked away from my family, and never got to see my only child grow up. I saw my friends beaten, tortured, and killed. I didn’t even know if I was going to live to see another day. There were times I didn’t want to live to see another day.”

David leaned forward. “How did you survive that? I’m not sure I’m surviving having my freedom.”

A distant look and a twinkle appeared in the old man’s eyes. “That’s just it. You don’t have the freedom I had. You are imprisoned by yourself and the Commonwealth. I had the one freedom no one can take away.”

David didn’t know where to begin with his questions. “I don’t understand.”

“The Commonwealth took everything away from me except my ability to choose who to serve. I chose to serve Pateras, and he never left me. You’ve chosen to serve the Commonwealth. What do you have to show for it? Who’s helping you with your pain and struggles? Your wife? Your ship’s psychologist? Your family history was even taken from you. Pateras doesn’t usually do things the way we think they should be done, but his way works out better. If I had it to do over again, I wouldn’t change anything. I’m not saying I wanted to be in a prison for fifty years. I’m saying Pateras put me there for a purpose and I would not have wanted to miss the opportunities.” The man’s face was quite serious.

David studied him carefully. It always seemed like David could relax when this man spoke to him. “You think I should betray the Commonwealth and surrender to Pateras?”

“I think the choice is yours, but I also think you would be a fool not to. The Commonwealth and Luciano Hale will fall. It’s just a matter of time. I don't know how much time, but its day is coming."

"What would I have to do? This is a Commonwealth ship. Would I have to stay behind on Drea?" David's heart was beginning to pound inside his chest. He was being drawn to the idea of surrendering to Pateras but didn't know how. He had never found Pateras' home world if he actually had one. Did Pateras have ships of his own? Did he need ships? David thought back to the one time he had been in the presence of Pateras. One of his – his assistants? His servants? Whatever the creature was, had transported himself and David through space without a ship.

Donald could feel David's mood change. He smiled. He reached across the table and patted David's arm. "That's a question for Pateras. He will accept you from wherever you are. If he wants you someplace else, he'll tell you. Can I ask you a question?"

David wasn't sure what he could tell the wise old man, but he was glad to help. "Sure, go ahead."

"I think you have all the information Pateras wanted you to have. You know who Pateras is, what he's capable of and the honor of his intentions. You know what Luciano Hale is capable of and what atrocities the Commonwealth has committed. What's stopping you from turning on them?"

David leaned back in his seat and stared at his coffee cup for a long time. He turned it around and around slowly. Finally, he stopped. He looked up at Donald and his eyes refocused on the man's face. Purpose and fullness began to permeate his gaze. "Nothing."

David got up and started to leave the room. His half-eaten pastry still sitting on the table.

Donald called out to him as he reached the door. "Captain?"

David stopped and came back towards the man. "Call me David, please."

The man smiled and nodded. "David, what were your grandparent's names?"

David seemed almost embarrassed to answer. "Saul and Kay Deacons. My uncle is Robert Deacons, and my mother is Jessica. My grandfather died under questionable circumstances twelve years ago, but my grandmother is still alive, unless something has happened recently."

"What did they do for the Commonwealth?"

"My grandfather had a position in the government as an engineer. He never really talked much about his work. My grandmother was also an engineer and worked at a research facility. She's responsible for the improvements in our propulsion systems. She perfected our tachyon drives which cut our interstellar travel times in half."

"What about your mother and your uncle?"

"My mother works for an accounting firm. My uncle is the Admiral who trained the teams for this mission. He's also the one who assigned us to pick you up from Mara."

Donald sat back in his seat and laughed robustly. David gave him a questioning look. Donald explained his outburst. "Your uncle was old enough to remember Drea. They put him in a position where they could keep an eye on him, and he got himself into a position to fight back. Your uncle probably couldn't tell you about his past, but he could send you to this part of the galaxy without raising any suspicions. He sent you to Mara, right after you went to Drea. This could only happen by the design of Pateras. You realize if your uncle's superiors find out where you've been, he could be in danger, and so could you."

David nodded thoughtfully. "I'll definitely need to watch my step. Any words of advice?"

"Talk to the son of Pateras. You seem to have an understanding with him. Always do as he tells you, even if it sounds ridiculous."

David nodded then smiled. "Go get a nap. We still have a few hours before we leave for Drea."

Donald smiled and got up slowly. "I believe I will." The two men went their separate ways.

Four hours later, David held a briefing in the dining hall with the entire crew. He informed the crew of his plans to get their three visitors home. "I'm going to take the shuttle down. Lt. Flint, I would like for you to go with me. I won't make it an order, and I won't hold it against you if you decline. The Drean mission was rough, and I wouldn't expect anyone to be happy to go back."

Braxton came out of his seat in a hurry. "Captain, you can't be serious. I thought you were sending Lt. Ryder and Chief Holden."

David gave the Lt. Commander a long hard look before answering. His inner struggle was settled, but he was still cranky from lack of sleep and improper eating habits. "That's why we have these briefings, so I can tell you what I'm thinking. Do you mind if I finish?"

Braxton looked like he had swallowed soured milk. He took his seat slowly. David turned his attention back to Lexi. "Lt. Flint, I have Moderator Tarmon's assurance we will be granted safe passage both in and out of Drean Space."

Jake knew from the Captain's recent mood he wasn't going to take kindly to any other challenges. Jake was leaned casually back in his chair. He sat upright and casually raised his hand. He worded himself carefully. "Captain, request permission to accompany you, sir."

David gave Jake a quick response. "Request denied, Chief."

Jake gave Brynna an emphatic pleading look for support. This time she took Jake's side. "Captain, I request you reconsider the chief's request. I think the entire crew would be more at ease if they knew you had a little more back up. We almost lost you here before, Captain. We don't want to risk that again."

David weighed her words carefully. "I understand, and I will consider your request. You need to consider I don't want to risk any more lives than necessary. There are three billion people on this planet and four Commonwealth satellites in orbit around it. Do you really think one extra security guard is going to help? I want Lexi with me because she has developed a rapport with our guests. Moderator Tarmon is familiar with her, and I need someone to back me up. I also don't want us to appear threatening.

"That being said, here's the rest of the plan. If we don't return within twenty-four hours, get the ship out of here, and report us as killed in action by the satellites. Under no circumstances is anyone else to come down to the planet. Don't attempt a rescue, because those satellites will fry you. I expect to spend no more than four hours, probably less, on the planet then head right back. If Arni gets involved, well things sometimes change. If I need more than twenty-four hours, I'll contact the ship and request additional time. If I don't ask for it, personally, my original order stands. Are we understood?"

Brynna acknowledged the orders. David went on with more instructions. When they left Drea, the Captain gave the Dreans the access codes, so they could use them for planetary defense. For the crew's protection, Cheyenne created a back door into the satellite programming. The Captain ordered her to be on duty and ready with the backup codes. If it came down to it, she could shut down the satellites herself. He also wanted Thane and Marissa at the helm and navigation. They had handled the ship expertly the first time they faced the satellites. The shuttle was no match for the satellites. If they activated, one hit would destroy the shuttle. David wanted the ship as close as they dared to run interference if needed. He ordered Brynna to stay in a distant orbit until the shuttle made it safely to the ground. "I'll signal you from the surface when we are preparing to return to the ship. Move back into the same high orbit until we reach you."

David dismissed the briefing and sent the crew to their stations. Lexi and Jake went to escort their guests to the shuttle. David pulled Brynna aside once everyone was on their way. "Brynna, I'm going to deny Jake's request to join the shuttle mission. I need to tell you more about why, but now isn't the time. For now, let's just say I prefer that he stay here to protect you and the crew. I told Moderator Tarmon I would only bring a co-pilot and myself. There's one other thing you need to watch out for. If the Commonwealth found out about the Intercessor, they could be using us to get past those satellites and destroy Drea. Keep a close eye on the scanners. If you have to sacrifice the shuttle to protect the planet, then do it."

Brynna gave David a stare that suggested she was very lost. "David, I think you're getting paranoid. Do you really think the Commonwealth is that desperate? That ruthless?"

David never batted an eye when he responded to her. "Considering the information I recently discovered – yes, I do. If we make it back, I'll tell you all about it. If I don't make it back, you'll be safer not knowing what I found out. To be honest, it's one of the reasons I'm taking Lexi with me. She knows what I found. It will be safer for her and the rest of the crew if this does turn out to be a Commonwealth trap. I really hope I am being paranoid." David reached up and caressed her worried face. "I really don't want this to be the last time we ever see each other."

The worried look on her face wasn't softening. "David, as soon as you get back…"

David interrupted her before she could finish. "As soon as I get back, a lot of things are going to change. We'll start with a long talk just between the two of us, and I'll explain everything to you." He pulled her closer and gave her a quick, meaningful kiss. She tried to enjoy his touch, but her worry overshadowed it. Knowing he couldn't leave his wife in charge of the ship, David abruptly changed gears to get Brynna into the correct mindset. "Any questions, Commander?"

David watched Brynna's eyes. She blinked and he saw the gears in her mind start to turn. "No, Captain." Worry still permeated her face, but it was no longer on the forefront of her mind. Brynna headed for the bridge, and David headed for the shuttle.

The ship left the moon's surface and got as close as it dared to Drea. The Captain launched the shuttle. He contacted Moderator Tarmon to be sure it was safe to approach the planet. She assured him it was and gave him final landing instructions. The shuttle traveled safely into the atmosphere. David concentrated on flying the shuttle and Lexi kept her attention focused on the scanners. She wanted to be able to let the Captain know instantly if the satellites activated or if the Drean Air Force responded to them. The shuttle descended over the ocean on the same trajectory the ship traveled on their previous visit to Drea. The shuttle leveled off and flew inland to the same military airport. As the shuttle neared the airport, the Captain received a private message from Brynna. He acknowledged her message and reported back to her that they were preparing to land safely. Lexi wondered if it was just her imagination, but the Captain now seemed irate about something. He was pushing buttons and levers more aggressively than before.

David brought the shuttle in slowly and gently despite his obvious mood change. A similar complement of military personnel awaited the shuttle's landing as before. As soon as the shuttle touched down, David shut the engine down completely then stood up to face the back of the shuttle. He folded his arms across his chest. The three passengers looked perplexed at the Captain's stance. They learned the reason momentarily. "Chief Holden! Front and center!" The security chief had been crouching on the floor in the back row of the shuttle. The chief stood up to face the music. He approached the Captain slowly. The look on the Captain's face was deadly serious. Jake reported as ordered. The Captain was clearly angry, but in a hurry. "Chief, I would ask why you disobeyed a direct order and stowed away on my shuttle, but I don't have time for your excuses right now. You have seriously endangered us with your presence on this shuttle and put the rest of the crew at risk with your absence from the ship. Take a seat and buckle yourself in. You are restricted to your seat for the duration of the time we are on the ground." Jake looked startled at the Captain's orders and objected. "Captain, since I'm here..."

The Captain's face turned red again. He spoke softer, but with no less emphasis. "Chief, take a seat now or I will put you in it myself."

The two men stood nose to nose for a moment, not blinking. Lexi sat there wide-eyed at the tension between the two men. She was scared to breathe. She finally spoke in support of the Captain's position. "Chief, you don't have all the information the Captain has. Follow your orders, Chief."

Jake cast a sideways glance at Lexi then backed away and took a seat as ordered. He slowly began to buckle himself in. As soon as he was buckled David turned to Lexi. He ordered her to get the hatch open and to start escorting their guests off the shuttle. Jake sat there looking vexed and angry simultaneously. He watched Lexi and the Captain escort the three off the shuttle. As the Captain escorted the last one to the hatch. He handed the elderly man off to Lexi then turned back around to face Jake.

Jake was looking more desperate to be of service with each passing moment. "If I leave, you aren't going to stay put, are you?"

Jake searched the Captain's face for clues to giving the right answer. "Captain, I should come with you. It's my job to protect you and Lt. Flint."

The Captain nodded. "It is your job, and I appreciate your diligence, but the Dreans are not my worry right now." The Captain turned his back and walked towards the hatch. David stopped just short of the door. "Jake, I really hope you'll forgive me for this, but I can't take chances on you disobeying my orders right now." The Captain pulled his Tri-EMP from its holster out of Jake's line of sight and set it on the lowest setting. He turned quickly, aimed at Jake's chest and fired. If Jake hadn't been restrained in the seat, he would have been out of it and on top of the Captain. He moved quickly to try and release the buckle on his straps. He was too late, by far. He managed to yell out, "Captain! No!" before he convulsed and fell unconscious. David searched him and confiscated his weapons.

Lexi chose that moment to step back into the doorway. She looked at Jake and the Captain. She was in shock and afraid to move for a moment. Her eyes finally focused on the Captain. Wide-eyed she asked, "Captain, what did you do?"

David holstered his weapon and put it out of sight under his jacket. He stowed Jake's weapons in a compartment near the door. He looked mildly repentant of his actions, but his words were less convincing. "I'm sorry, Lieutenant, I couldn't take the chance he might disobey orders again. He's only stunned. He'll be alright. He'll be mad as a hornet when he wakes up, but he'll be fine."

"Captain, you can't just – just shoot him like that. You'll be court martialed."

David needed to get off the shuttle and talk to the Dreans as soon as possible. If this turned out to be a Commonwealth trap, every minute they spent on the surface put them at an increased risk for dying there or being trapped there indefinitely. He took her elbow firmly and escorted her back outside. "Lieutenant, you're right I may be court martialed, but I don't have very many options right now. I will report to the doc for a full evaluation as soon as we get back - if we get back."

Lexi looked shocked again as they stood by the shuttle door. "If? What do you mean by if? You never said anything about a one-way mission when you asked me to come along." She started inundating the Captain with questions and demands.

David was fast getting frustrated. He spun around to face her and grabbed her arms. He gave her one brief shake to get her full attention. "Lexi, I'm going to explain some things to the Dreans, and then you'll understand my position. I'm trying to keep everyone safe, but I need you to just settle down and pay close attention. Do you understand?"

Lexi nodded. She finally managed to pull herself together. "Captain, I'm going to need you to report to me for an evaluation after the doc is done with you. Do you understand?"

David relaxed his grip on her. "Yes, I understand. In fact, after this next conversation, if you think I'm not fit to command then tell me, and I'll stay here on Drea. The decision is yours. You and Jake can go back without me." David didn't wait for her response as he saw Colonel Bernt and his entourage approach hearing distance.

David turned to face the Colonel and gave a friendly, but tenuous greeting. "Colonel Bernt, it's good to see you again, sir."

Colonel Bernt's greeting was slightly more tense. "Captain, Lieutenant."

David glanced back towards the shuttle entrance. "Colonel, I have a small problem. It's slightly embarrassing. Can we step over here to discuss it?"

Lexi stayed near the three refugees while the two men talked. She continued to a keep a wary eye on the Captain. In a moment, she saw Colonel Bernt shaking his head. The man turned and waved two of his men forward. The two approached as ordered. The Captain and Colonel stepped inside with the two escorts. A minute later the two officers emerged from the shuttle leaving the two troops inside. Colonel Bernt called two additional men forward and placed them alongside the shuttle entrance. The Colonel then escorted the group into a bus to transport them to the airport hangars and offices.

Lexi was still somewhat in shock, but she knew she wouldn't have time to ask many questions. She forced herself to move forward. "Captain, what did you say to Colonel Bernt?"

"I told him exactly what happened with Jake and that I didn't trust him to follow orders. I asked him to put a set of binders and a couple guards on Jake. If this takes too long, I wanted to be sure Jake had access to the facilities on the shuttle."

"If what takes too long sir? I don't understand why we're sticking around. We could have dropped our passengers and left. I know you just discovered your grandparents were taken from Drea, but sir, you don't have any personal ties here. What is there to discuss?"

David wanted to reassure her, but his mind was focused on the upcoming discussion. He stared out the window at the darkness and then looked back at Lexi. "It will make more sense in a few minutes."

Lexi folded her arms angrily across her chest and looked out the opposite window. She turned back to the Captain to add one last comment. "You still should've told me this might be a one-way mission. This wasn't fair, Captain. I didn't have a chance to give Braxton a proper good bye." She relaxed again. She lowered her arms to her sides and rested her hands on the seat.

David looked back at her. She looked really scared. He reached over and patted her hand. "I'm sorry. I guess I should have told you, but I really needed you to come. It was for your protection and for Braxton's." "Braxton's protection? I don't understand. Why is Braxton in danger?"

"I'm sorry, I misstated the situation. It's possible the entire crew could be in danger if we shared the information of my family's origins. It wouldn't be him specifically, but the crew in general. I was trying to separate the two of us from the rest of the crew just for their protection." Lexi's tone and mood softened. She turned back to the Captain. "That explains why you were so ticked off at Jake, but why did you shoot him?"

"To keep him from shooting me for one. Second, I need to get in, get this done, and get out quick."

The trip to the hangar only took a minute. Noah and Aleah whispered quietly to each other in excited tones. The two were teary-eyed at seeing the home planet they thought they would never see again. They held each other closely and stared out the window into the night. Donald paid close attention to the conversation David and Lexi were having. The vehicles pulled into a hangar, and the doors closed behind them. Before they stepped out of the vehicle, Donald stood up and turned towards David and Lexi. "Captain, Lt. Flint, I may not have much of a chance to talk to you later, so I'll say this now. We appreciate how kind you have been to us and for the hospitality you've shown us. Captain, I know you are starting into uncharted territory, but Pateras won't steer you wrong. You have my word on that, and his."

David reached out his hand and shook the elderly man's waiting hand. "Thank you for sacrificing your sleep for me. I hope to see you again someday."

The man smiled. "You will. I'm sure of it. Captain, is it alright if this young lady escorts me off the bus?"

David wasn't sure what the man had on his mind. He had been so wise and helpful, David gladly agreed. He wanted to hear the man's words for himself but was sure it was better this way. He nodded and moved down the aisle alone.

Lexi looked at the old man. "What's on your mind Mr. Leal? You are a very spry man. You don't need an escort."

"I just wanted to tell you that even though your Captain has been cranky lately, he's still on top of his game. He knows exactly what he's doing. Don't sell him short, and don't worry. He's about to be better than ever."

The two were only a few steps from the front of the vehicle. The old prisoner had not forgotten how to be a gentleman. He stepped aside to let Lexi step off the bus first. Lexi stepped in front of him as she pondered his words. She stopped and turned back around for a moment. "He's turned, hasn't he? He's chosen to serve Pateras, hasn't he?"

"Your Captain has chosen wisely. He can change his loyalty back again, if that is what he wants. The decision is his. He will explain his choice to you shortly. I hope you will continue to trust him."

Lexi's defenses went up instantly. She wasn't about to let this old man change her loyalties. She stepped off the bus. Her head was buzzing from the events of the last five minutes.

The group was escorted into a large conference room where various family members were waiting. Noah and Aleah's families were already gathered around them. Tears flowed freely.

Donald saw his wife sitting on the far side of the room next to his daughter and another man. He walked slowly around the tables to reach them. Saundra held her mother's hand tightly. Saundra's husband, Edward had been sitting next her. He got up and moved to the other side of Donald's wife. The woman was obviously shaking from the sight of her long-lost husband. Tears began to flow down her face as he drew closer to her. The man helped Donald's wife to stand. As Donald rounded the last corner and got close to her, his pace quickened and he called out to her. "Annalise, my love!"

The two moved quickly into each other's arms. David heard the woman crying as she spoke to him for the first time in fifty years. "Donald, I never gave up hope. I knew I would see you again. Thank you, Pateras."

As things began to settle down, Donald was introduced to Saundra's husband, Edward. The group talked quietly for a few minutes. They tried to cram fifty years' worth of information into just a few minutes. Saundra and Edward had two children waiting for them at home. Neither of them was married yet, although their son had a serious girlfriend. Saundra didn't want to overwhelm her father with a large crowd. She didn't realize that a man who had been a prisoner and tortured for fifty years was unlikely to be overwhelmed by anything.

David and Lexi stayed near the door and watched the commotion in the room. Everyone seemed to be accounted for except David's grandfather's family. Captain Alexander looked around the room to try and figure out why they were missing. As he stood there looking around, Hugh Kelly, the engineer who helped repair the ship walked up to the Captain. The Captain changed his stance to face the man. He nodded tenuously to the man. "Mr. Kelly."

Hugh's face was unreadable. "Captain, you gave me your word you would do whatever you could to make this right."

David swallowed hard. "It was wishful thinking on my part to think I could do that, sir. I apologize. Please forgive my impertinence."

Hugh nodded. "You are a man of your word and an honorable man.

I forgive you."

David held out his hand. "Does this mean you aren't here to slug me again?"

The man looked down at David's hand then grabbed the young Captain and hugged him tightly. David slowly returned the hug as he gave Lexi a perplexed look. Hugh released the Captain from his tight grip. As he backed away, David saw tears in his eyes. "I'm so sorry I hit you. Please forgive me. Why did you let me get away with that? Your man could have killed me."

David smiled. "It's never been my intention to kill anyone. I set you up to take out your frustrations on my face. You needed to do that, more than I needed my lip intact."

The man returned to his sister's side to continue welcoming her and her husband home. Lexi looked around at all the happy faces. "Isn't this the most wonderful thing you've ever seen?"

David shook his head cynically. "No, it's the saddest. These people should've never been apart." David stepped out into the hallway again.

Lexi followed him out. "Captain, you didn't cause this travesty of justice. You've helped to put it right. If we hadn't been here to lay the ground work, this moment may never have happened."

David wasn't encouraged by her platitudes. He finally relented slightly. "Don't get me wrong. I'm as thrilled as you are that we could get these people back home. That prison held five hundred prisoners. That's four hundred ninety-seven prisoners who didn't come home. There's a lot of things I'm finding lately that should never have happened."

Lexi stared at him sorrowfully. She ventured to a topic she was afraid to mention. "Mr. Leal said you turned. Is that true? Are you no longer loyal to the Commonwealth?"

David's look gave her the answer she didn't want to hear. "You'll understand why when I talk to Moderator Tarmon." David glanced through the glass surrounding the conference room. Moderator Tarmon caught his eye and motioned for him to come back into the room.

David and Lexi moved back inside and headed across the room to talk to her. "Captain, I'm sure everyone wants to go home and be with their families. Can we meet with you in the morning?"

Donald jumped in before David could answer. "No Saundra, this can't wait. He needs to get this information to you and get back to his ship as quickly as possible."

"I don't understand, what's so urgent? Does everyone need to be here?"

David shook his head. "The only ones who really need to be here are you and Lexi, although I would like to talk to the family of Elliot and Tyra Paulson."

Saundra tried to release everyone to leave, but Noah and Aleah Simons refused to leave as did Donald Leal. The Moderator became concerned. These people hadn't seen their families in so many years. Why did they want to stay? What was so important? She decided to get it over with as quickly as possible, so the reunions could continue. She asked the group to all find seats and settle in quietly. It would probably move faster if everything was done once. She had Colonel Bernt escort the only family members available from the Paulson family into the room. Tyra had a brother who hobbled in with a cane and took a seat near the door. Elliot had both a brother and a sister and their spouses come into the room.

The Moderator called the room to order. For the benefit of the Paulson family she explained what was going on to the confused family. "Approximately five hundred people were taken from Drea fifty years ago and imprisoned by the Commonwealth. Many of those taken were believed to be killed in the Commonwealth attacks. It was only three days ago we found out this was not the case. Captain Alexander brought two of the ones thought to have been killed back to Drea. They have been in prison this entire time."

As she spoke looks of anger were cast at the Captain and Lexi. Moderator Tarmon continued. She attempted to smooth things over as best she could.

"When I found out about the Simons', I asked the Captain to research all those who were lost. He brought these three back to us and has more information for us. I am grateful to the Captain for doing what he could to bring us some semblance of resolution. I know a great deal more of us need closure, and he has been kind enough to bring it to us. Captain, the floor is yours."

There were angry murmurs heard throughout the room. David reached into his pocket and pulled out two data crystals. He set them down on the table in front of him. He stood there and looked at them for a second before he began to speak. He looked up and around the room at the angry faces staring back at him. His eyes landed on Donald who smiled and nodded. David was accustomed to speaking in front of crowds, but this one resembled more of a lynch mob. Taking courage from Donald's smile he started with the only words he could.

"I know you don't want to believe this, but I am renouncing my allegiance to the Commonwealth and giving my allegiance to Pateras." His statement was greeted with sarcasm and disbelief. David continued. "The Commonwealth has taken a great deal away from everyone on this planet. It has also taken from me. I didn't know just how much until a couple days ago."

David picked up one of the data crystals and handed it to Moderator Tarmon. "This crystal contains the files of all Drean prisoners who were held on Mara. The prison on Mara can hold five hundred prisoners. Moderator Tarmon gave me a list of those who were either taken prisoner or killed during the Commonwealth attacks. I haven't compared every name on the list, but there were more than five hundred Drean prisoners on Mara. Ninety percent of them died on Mara. They were either executed, tortured to death, or died of injuries related to their torture."

The murmurs were getting louder and angrier. David handed the crystal gingerly to Moderator Tarmon. "I hope these records will provide closure to the families. Some of the names you gave me were never on Mara. Ten percent left Mara. They were given new identities and relocated on other planets. They were either forced or enticed into joining the Commonwealth."

The Paulson family had been sitting quietly in their corner trying to put the pieces together. Elliot's brother could finally take no more. "Why are we here, Captain Alexander? You obviously didn't bring our family back to us."

David glanced over at Donald again. Donald nodded at him again. David swallowed hard. "That's mostly true. I can't bring the family you lost back to you. I do have some information on your family though. Your family survived Mara."

David picked up the other data crystal and handed it to Moderator Tarmon. He asked her to load the contents onto the computer and put them up on display. As she was getting the data up, David continued to answer the question put to him. "Your family was forced to work for the Commonwealth. Elliot Paulson did die under questionable circumstances twelve years ago."

As soon as he spoke the words, Elliot's brother and sister grabbed each other in a tearful embrace. Tyra's brother watched David's face carefully waiting for the other shoe to drop. David gave the group time to catch their breath again. He looked at the older man with the cane as he spoke again. "Tyra is still alive to my knowledge, at least she was three days ago."

The siblings who had just been told about their brother's death now had a second wind and wanted a lot more answers. "What about their children? Where are they? Are they alive? Do they remember Drea? Why can't you bring Tyra home?"

David glanced at Lexi. Lexi looked like she was just as frightened as David felt. David had fought warriors in a battle to the death, but a room full of angry elders seemed much more frightening to him. He raised his hands for quiet. "The – The oldest daughter, I understand her name was Abigail, didn't survive Mara. They executed her to force Elliot and Tyra to work for the Commonwealth. The other two children are alive and well as of three days ago. The Paulson's were given new identities and relocated on another planet. Their remaining two children married. Elliot's son had no children, but his daughter has three children, two sons and a daughter. The oldest son and daughter are married, and the daughter has just given birth to a baby boy.

The man with the cane had been staring long and hard at David. He finally spoke up. "You seem to know a lot about our family. Why?"

David glanced at Lexi, then Donald. Their faces gave him encouragement. He looked over at Moderator Tarmon. "Can I access the data?" David stepped over and pulled up the prison file for Elliot Paulson. The first item in the file was the identification data, which included his name, his picture, and his DNA profile, among other details. David's grandfather had been a little older than David was now when he was taken prisoner by the Commonwealth. The picture of a man bearing a close resemblance to David materialized on the screen. Time had dulled the memory of their missing family members. Confronted with a fresh image of his likeness, the family gasped audibly as they looked back and forth between David and the image on the screen. The murmurs increased again.

David moved quickly to explain and hopefully calm the group down. "We compared the DNA code attached to this file and Tyra's file to mine. It was a match. This man is my grandfather. I knew him as Saul Deacons." David pressed another button on the computer panel. A picture of Tyra appeared beside Elliot's and below it was a picture from David's personal files of David's grandparents. The couple did appear to be an aged copy of the prison photos.

Angry murmurs began again. David heard the words "trick" and "Commonwealth trap." He glanced at Donald. He wasn't sure if he should keep talking or wait for them to assimilate the startling information.

Donald stood up slowly and motioned for silence. "I know you have no reason to believe me anymore than you do the Captain. I could have been brainwashed or tricked. I've been under the enemy's influence for fifty years. Noah, Aleah, and I have put our trust in Pateras, and we have not wavered in those fifty years no matter what they did to us. There are things that happened to us that support what the Captain is saying. I believe this is the work of Pateras, not the Commonwealth. The Commonwealth tried to destroy us, but Pateras has protected us. Let the Captain finish."

David resumed speaking. He seemed to spend as much time looking at the floor as he did making eye contact with those in the room. "If the Commonwealth is laying some sort of trap, then I am as much a victim as you are. There is a good chance it is a trap. Moderator Tarmon, I need to warn you. The reason I didn't want to wait until morning is to protect Drea. The Commonwealth knows I gave you the satellite codes. Not all of my crew are trustworthy. If my superiors found out about the Intercessor, they could be using us to get you to disable the satellites long enough for them to move in and destroy them. Commander Alexander is watching for Commonwealth vessels and she is under orders to leave us behind if necessary to protect Drea."

Moderator Tarmon scowled at David. "I wish you had said something sooner Captain. I left the one satellite inactive. I could have put it back on-line as soon as you landed if I had known there was a risk." "I'm sorry Moderator. I was operating under the assumption my wife would warn me if anyone entered this solar system, but it probably would be safer to get it back on-line now."

Saundra pressed some controls on the computer then looked up at the Captain. "I'll shut it down when you are ready to depart, if your Commander reports that everything is clear. You do need to know, I won't hesitate to put them back on line at the first sign of trouble, even if it costs you and your crew their lives."

David nodded. "I understand and fully expected that. I am sorry to say Lt. Flint and Chief Holden were not told of that possibility until it was too late. I will take full responsibility for that."

"So, why did you do that Captain? Why did you bring me here without telling me the risks?" Lexi maintained her military bearing but felt as though she deserved an explanation.

David saw a quiet fear in her eyes. "The Commonwealth has taken great pains to hide Drea from the rest of the galaxy. They took five hundred of Drea's greatest assets and either corrupted them for their own use or destroyed them. They stole my grandparents from their home, forced them to work for the Commonwealth, and forget their own identities. I'm Drean and I had never even heard of Drea until a few months ago. I have an aunt I never knew, because the Commonwealth killed her as a child to coerce my grandparents' cooperation. My mother named my sister Abigail after her dead sister. My family was forced to deny their own names and the existence of Pateras. They used my family to further their own agenda. They used me to destroy the home of Arni Liontari. I told you when I started I am no longer loyal to the Commonwealth. I hope you all will agree, I have every reason to reject them at this point. Lt. Flint, you asked why I didn't tell you about the risks before bringing you along. If the Commonwealth finds out I know who I am and where I'm from, they will destroy me and anyone else who knows. I haven't even told Brynna because I don't want to put anyone else in danger. Lexi, you were there when I found out, and I brought you to protect the crew and to protect you."

The Captain's voice had gotten angrier as he spoke then softened as he addressed Lexi's question. He finally reached out squeezed her arm. "I'm sorry if this works out badly. I really hope I'm being overly cautious"

The old man at the back of the room stood slowly and moved towards the front of the room. All eyes followed him. The room became deathly silent. The old man came to a stop in front of David. He stared into David's eyes. The first thing he saw in the Captain's eyes was an open window to his soul. He was hiding nothing. He saw David's anger and his sorrow, but he also saw resolve. David seemed to be at peace with his position. The old man asked some hard questions. "Why did you choose to serve Pateras? Did you do it to get back at the Commonwealth?"

David kept his gaze on the old man. He had thought his decision through carefully. He answered softly, but firmly. "No. Pateras does intend to take apart the Commonwealth. He's asked for my help and I have no more qualms about it. I resisted Pateras from the beginning. Despite my resistance, Pateras has been nothing, but compassionate to me and to my crew. I was willing to give my life in defense of the Commonwealth. The Supreme Executor asked me to give my life to stop the death of the Intercessor. I was prepared to do just that, but the Intercessor... Arni, took my place. Pateras showed me how much I deserved that punishment and so much more. The evil I've been a part of nearly crushed me when I saw it. He's given me a second chance. He's protected my life more times than I can count. I owe him everything. I no longer owe the Commonwealth anything."

Tears formed in the old man's eyes. He reached his hand out to David. "My name is Zachary Leeto. I am your great uncle. Welcome home, son."

David grasped his hand firmly. The man decided a hand shake wasn't sufficient. He grabbed David in a tight hug. David was surprised by the strength in the old man's grip. The surprise faded as David realized the man was now family. He slowly returned the hug. The hug reminded him of the hugs he had left behind in his civilian life. A Commonwealth Officer commanded respect and dignity. He had received very few hugs since he joined the military. He had forgotten how comfortable they could be. His mother, sister, and grandmother were among the few to cross the lines of military decorum to hug an officer. His Uncle Rob only crossed the invisible boundary twice. Once was after David graduated from officer's school. The two had been at a family celebration and wearing civilian attire. The second time was after David and Brynna's wedding.

Zachary released David from the hug and stepped back. David barely had time to recover before he was grabbed and hugged by Elliot's brother and sister, Joel and Amanda. Their spouses also grabbed David and welcomed him into their family. They each had a million questions to ask him. David answered them as quickly as he could. He had a little more business to complete. David asked the group to give him a few minutes to finish up before he continued to answer their questions. His new-found family stepped aside for him. They returned to their seats until he was ready to spend more time with them.

The Captain sat down with Moderator Tarmon to talk less publicly. "Moderator, I don't have any answers for you about the other ten percent of the people who now work for the Commonwealth. I've kept a copy of these records for myself. I'll have to be discreet in making inquiries. If I start chasing down these names, it's bound to get the wrong people's attention. This is also assuming I make it out of this star system alive."

Moderator Tarmon gave David a puzzled look. "Do you really think the Commonwealth is waiting for you to fly out of here just to destroy us?"

"Not exactly." David glanced at Lexi. "My crew is under orders from the Commonwealth to use extreme measures to safeguard the crew from the influence of Pateras Liontari. Lt. Flint is well within her mandates to either leave me behind or have me executed when we get into space. I've already publicly announced my treason. I told her I won't fight her if she chooses to leave me behind."

Lexi stood there listening to the whole conversation. Apprehension weighed heavily on her. David reached slowly for his weapon and handed it to her, butt first. She gingerly took the weapon from him and tucked it into a pocket. She then folded her arms across her chest and slipped her shaking hands under her arms. She wanted very badly to leave the room, but she knew she needed to continue her evaluation of the Captain. She didn't remember deciding the fate of her Captain being on her job description.

David looked back at Moderator Tarmon to continue their discussion. "If I can get back into space, I'll try to find answers for the remaining families on that list. If I can't, I have another idea about getting the information, but we can talk about that later if necessary. I really want to put as much space between us and you as soon as possible. The longer we stay here the more danger we put your planet in. I refuse to be responsible for the death of another civilization. Moderator, I strongly suggest you work on additional planetary defense weapons and early warning systems. The Commonwealth may leave your planet alone as long as you don't take on an offensive posture. The fact that they may have Dreans working on sensitive projects may be enough for them to keep this planet as a quiet hostage. The problem I do see is those people are getting advanced in years and may no longer be in positions of importance. I suppose their children may be. My Uncle Rob has to remember, and my mother may have some memories as well. My mother isn't in a position of influence like my Uncle Rob. My uncle is Admiral Robert Deacons of the Commonwealth Interstellar Force. He was assigned the duty of training and developing the twelve teams who are on this mission with us. He was the one who sent me to bring the three remaining prisoners home. I would say he remembers, but he knows he's being watched. I know he wasn't happy about what happened to Galat." David spent another few minutes updating Moderator Tarmon, and then he spent another hour and a half with his new family members. He showed them pictures from the data disk of all of his family. There were more tears and more hugs. The group begged David to get messages to his grandmother and her two children. He promised them he would do his best. He warned them it would put all concerned in danger if they were caught. The group was saddened, but they understood.

David caught Moderator Tarmon with one more question. The two talked together privately for a couple minutes. Lexi saw the two shake hands and go their separate ways.

After saying their farewells to their three passengers and new family, Colonel Bernt escorted the two officers back to their ship. David and Lexi said very little on the brief ride out to the ship. As the vehicle pulled to a stop, David looked up at Colonel Bernt. "Colonel, can you give me and the Lieutenant a minute?"

The Colonel gave David a curt nod and stepped off the bus. He had been present for the entire meeting and now knew David's heritage and predicament. The two sat there quietly. Lexi couldn't look David in the eye and continued to stare at the floor. David finally took the burden off her. "Lt. Flint, I have committed numerous acts of treason against an oppressive authority gone wrong. You are a Commonwealth officer. I surrender myself to your authority. Will you allow me to return to duty to right some universal wrongs, or are you going to leave me here as an appropriate disciplinary action?"

Lexi looked up with tears in her eyes. "Captain, don't do this to me." David got up and paced in the narrow aisle. "Who should I have done this to? My wife? Jake? Who's going to be fair and objective besides you? Am I being controlled by an alien intelligence?"

Lexi looked back up at him. Tears streaming down her face. "Captain, I don't know what to do."

David shook his head. He didn't want to force her hand in either direction. She needed to make this decision for herself. David came back to his seat. He sat on the edge and faced her. "Lexi, if you let me back on that ship, I'm going to use all the resources at my disposal to find those missing people. I'm going to fight Supreme Executor Hale to stop the slaughter of any more innocent people. I'm going to continue our mission as a ruse to hide my ulterior motives. I am going to call on Arni Liontari and Pateras Liontari freely. If you can live with that, then hand my weapon back to me, and we will head back to the ship. If you can't live with that or if you will feel the need to report me to our superiors, then get off this bus and climb aboard the shuttle. You don't have to even look back. You won't even have to explain to Brynna. I'll contact her myself from here. Is that easy enough for you?"

Lexi looked sideways at the young Captain. She had known and trusted the Captain for several months now. She had been training half her life to be in her current position. If she allowed him to come back, she would be throwing her entire career away. It wasn't something she could do easily.

David got up again and moved halfway down the length of the bus and turned his back to her. He knew she needed to make her decision without him breathing down her neck. She watched him walk away from her.

Lexi thought back to their time on Medoris. He had saved her life when a couple of locals kidnapped her. While she lay tied up in the dark caverns, she knew he would rescue her, and he had. While she dangled over the edge of cliff above a lava pool, he was one of the ones who pulled her and Vesta to safety. Lexi looked again at the Captain's back. She reached into her pocket and pulled his weapon out. Her choice was not complicated. She could hand him the weapon and walk back onto the shuttle with him or walk away and leave him. She gripped the weapon in her hand. She looked up at the Captain's back again. "Captain?"

David turned to face her. His face remained neutral. He looked at the weapon in her hand. It was gripped, so she could simply point and fire, but she didn't have it aimed at him. David wondered if she were holding it habitually or intentionally. "Yes, Lieutenant?"

"If I allow you to return, what will you expect from me and the rest of the crew?"

David took a deep breath. "I would prefer you not tell Jake what I've done. I would expect you to do the same job you've been trained to do. I may edit your reports to the Commonwealth, and I would also ask you not report me or my family to the Commonwealth."

Lexi still looked worried. "Captain, you're asking me to take a chance on losing everything I've worked for."

"Put yourself in my shoes for a minute. What if your ancestors were taken from Drea or some other planet and coerced into working for the Commonwealth? All twelve teams are the Commonwealth's best and brightest. What if your family didn't have a choice? My family didn't just by chance move to Raesii. We were living on Juranta. My Uncle Rob came and told us I received a scholarship to a military training school on Raesii. I know my parents kept part of those conversations to themselves.

My mom and my uncle had a big argument that night. My mom cried a lot after that, and when my parents' marriage contract came up for renewal, they went their separate ways. My mom didn't want me to be so far away, so she picked up and moved to Raesii. I got the feeling she was afraid for me to be out of her sight. It makes more sense now than it did then. What if your family was manipulated as well?"

"Captain, that's not fair. You're reading things into this you don't know are there."

You're right. I don't know what's there, but I sure want to find out.

I'll have a much harder time doing that from here on Drea."

"You aren't asking me to give my loyalty to Pateras?" Lexi chewed on her lower lip as the Captain formulated his response to her question. She wasn't sure what his answer would be or what she wanted it to be.

"I'm not asking you to change your loyalty. I'm just asking you to allow me to make my own choice, and don't report me for it. Let me even go this far. If the authorities catch me and start questioning you, then by all means report me. I don't want to put the crew at risk. I'll even confess to pressuring or forcing your cooperation. I just want the chance to put things right again."

Lexi looked down at the weapon in her hand. David's eyes followed hers. If she let him back on board no matter what he said, she was committing treason. She placed her finger inside the trigger guard. David straightened his body and stiffened up. He was really hoping she would walk away rather than shoot him. Lexi turned the weapon towards him then released her grip on the handle. The weapon was top heavy and immediately flipped upside down with her finger still inside the trigger guard. She held the weapon out to him. He looked down at it, and then looked back up at her. He reached out and took the weapon gently from her hand. Her eyes met his. "I must have been in the rest room when you admitted to changing your loyalties, sir. I don't think I heard that part. You also seem to be very much in control of yourself. I don't see any evidence you are being controlled by our enemy, although you did shoot Jake."

"Yes, I did do that. I believe you will find I am suffering from exhaustion, stress, and a bit of dehydration and undernourishment. I fully intend on checking myself into the infirmary when we get back for a full evaluation. I'm sure Jake knows we are out here by now and we are taking a long time to get back onto the shuttle. I assume it's because you're giving me an ultimatum to let Jake fly us back and that I'm going to voluntarily report to the infirmary or face charges."

Lexi gave the Captain a quizzical stare. "I suppose that would be an appropriate discussion to be having especially if I don't know your true motivations. I also suppose you and I ought to be upset with each other." "I suppose we should, but before that happens I need to say one more thing." David stepped forward and grabbed Lexi's hand. "Thank you for giving me this chance. I'd really like to know why, but if you'd rather not go there, we can move on."

"Captain, I – I owe you my life for one. I – I guess I don't distrust Arni as much as I should. He's never done anything to bring harm to this crew or anyone else. I'm not ready to say I'll follow him, but I guess I'm not objecting to you following him."

David nodded. "I understand, and I will do whatever is needed to protect you and the others."

Lexi looked concerned. "You know you're taking a lot of responsibility on yourself."

"Do you want me to make regular appointments with you? You would have to keep them off the record. It's the only way to be sure you're protected."

"Let's just see how it goes. I'll make that call later."

David released her hand and holstered his weapon. "Are you ready to go?" Lexi nodded, then she turned and walked off the bus. As soon as David stepped off the bus he headed over to talk to Colonel Bernt. Colonel Bernt was standing near the shuttle entrance. He waved the Colonel away from the door way to keep their conversation private. When Lexi saw the two pull back she stopped at the bottom of the steps up to the shuttle and turned towards the two men.

David saw her stop and decided it was time to put their cover story into action. "That will be all, Lieutenant. Return to your station and leave the Chief to me. I'll be with you in a minute!"

Lexi was startled by his gruffness for a moment, then realized what he was doing. She responded with an appropriate, but equally gruff, "Yes, Sir!" She stomped up the steps and headed into the shuttle. She glanced at Jake, who was looking like he was ready to strangle anybody he could get his hands on. As soon as their eyes met, Jake had a million questions and started spouting all of them. Lexi moved towards the co-pilot's seat and started getting ready for launch. She tried to look angry, punching buttons with as much venom as she could muster.

Lexi finally turned around to answer Jake once he had lost some steam. "Chief, when the Captain comes aboard he intends to let you pilot the shuttle, but I strongly suggest you mind your manners. In the mood he's in, he's just as likely to shoot you again to shut you up. As soon as we get back aboard the ship, I've ordered him to report to the infirmary for a full medical evaluation."

"What good is that going to do? He's lost his mind. He SHOT me! He's obviously under the influence of Arni Liontari." Jake flexed against the binders on his wrists and glared at the two guards who were still watching him.

The guards looked at each other and one of them addressed Jake's assumption. "The Intercessor influences all of humanity, but he doesn't force the actions of any. If your Captain is acting oddly, it's because he chooses to."

The second man joined in. "From the time we've spent with you, perhaps your Captain was justified in shooting you." The two men laughed while Jake turned red and bristled.

Lexi gave the men a look that told them how little she appreciated their help. "Jake, just do what the Captain says. I'll take care of the Captain. He's been under an incredible amount of stress, please don't add to it."

Jake let his muscles relax. "Fine, I'll behave."

A moment later the Captain and Colonel Bernt stepped inside the shuttle. The Captain glared at Jake. "Chief, I'd like for you to pilot the shuttle back to the ship. Can I count on you to follow orders this time?"

Jake glanced at Lexi, who only returned an icy stare. "Yes, Captain. I apologize for disobeying orders earlier. I was only concerned for your welfare and for Lt. Flint's welfare. It won't happen again, sir."

Jake suddenly realized his apology came out backwards. He hadn't meant to say he would no longer care what happened to the two of them. "I'm sorry sir, that came out wrong. I meant I wouldn't disobey orders again."

David had a hard time keeping a straight face while watching Jake squirm. He glanced over at Colonel Bernt whose mouth twitched as well. The Colonel turned and nodded at his men to release Jake from the binders. The two men complied, then left the shuttle quietly. They really wanted to make fun of Jake a little more. They knew better. Jake rubbed his wrists then did some quick stretches before moving to the helm.

David watched him carefully, then shook the Colonel's hand again. "I appreciate the assistance, Colonel. If you happen to run across Rachel Johan or Captain Parker, please give them our regards. I really hope we can get past the rocky beginnings with the Commonwealth and start laying a new foundation of friendship. I meant what I said about the release and return of the last of the prisoners being a goodwill gesture from the Commonwealth."

Colonel Bernt returned a blank stare. The Captain had not said any such thing. The Colonel decided the Captain was saying this now for the benefit of his crewman. "Captain, I'm a soldier, not a diplomat or a politician. I'll convey your message to Ms. Johan and Capt. Parker, but I have no interest in your mission."

David escorted Colonel Bernt to the door. Colonel Bernt reached the ground and turned back to look at David. He whispered a quick and quiet, "Best wishes, my friend."

David nodded his thanks then closed the hatch. He took his seat and began to buckle in. He ordered Lexi to contact the ship. He reported to Brynna they were preparing to return to the ship. "Are the scanners clear, Commander?"

"Yes, Captain, no activity noted on long or short-range scanners." "Acknowledged. Stay clear of those satellites and wait for us to come to you. Let us know the instant you see anything unexpected. Most importantly, do NOT try and rescue us if this goes wrong. Don't let Ensign Dominick shut down those satellites, even if it gets us killed. Are we clear on that matter?"

Jake gave a startled look to Lexi, then the Captain. Lexi quickly shook her head at him, so he wouldn't start asking questions.

Brynna didn't hesitate despite the fact she didn't agree with the orders. "Understood, Captain."

David didn't bother to ask if she planned on complying because he knew it would be an exercise in futility. She would either obey his orders or she wouldn't. His questions were irrelevant. David closed the channel then ordered a channel to Moderator Tarmon be opened. "Moderator Tarmon, we are ready to depart Drean Air Space. My commander reports clear skies, may we be granted safe passage?"

"Stand by, Captain." They heard her click some keys on her computer. Momentarily she came back and said, "You are clear for departure. Captain, thank you again for bringing my father home." "Acknowledged, Moderator. You're welcome, ma'am. I enjoyed getting to know him and the others. I hope we will be able to improve on our relations in the future."

"With you, or the Commonwealth, Captain? I have a small amount of trust in you and your crew, Captain. I do not trust the Commonwealth." "I'm going to see if I can't fix things in the Commonwealth, so that you can trust us both equally." David's response was to indicate his intention of tearing down the evil in the Commonwealth, but it sounded to Jake like he intended to help them trust the Commonwealth.

Moderator Tarmon gave a brief, but heartfelt response before closing the channel. "I look forward to that day, Captain. May the Intercessor guide your journey."

"Thank you, Moderator. Chief, your flight path is programmed. Take us up."

The shuttle took off and headed out to sea then climbed through the atmosphere until it reached the cold vacuum of space. They all looked nervously at the satellites as they flew past them. Jake instinctively increased the shuttle's speed until they cleared its range. He didn't slow down until they reached the ship.

Jake contacted the ship for docking clearance. Brynna opened the shuttle bay doors for them and granted the clearance as requested. "Chief, why are you piloting the shuttle? Where's the Captain?"

Before Jake could answer the Captain spoke up. "I'm here, Commander. I ordered the Chief to pilot the shuttle because my abilities have been called into question. I will be reporting to the

Infirmary as soon as the shuttle is docked for a full evaluation. If you would care to stop by there and see me, I can give you a full report."

There was a definite pause before the Commander acknowledged the information. David knew she had burning questions. She knew better than to ask them now. "Acknowledged. I will see you shortly."

The shuttle landed, and the bay doors closed. As soon as the bay pressurized again, David got up and moved to stand between Jake and Lexi. "Chief, I think I may need to apologize to you. You did disobey my orders, and you deserved disciplinary action, but I probably shouldn't have shot you. You put all our lives at risk by stowing away on the shuttle. There was a chance this shuttle could have been destroyed and I didn't want to risk any more lives than absolutely necessary."

Jake had turned to face the Captain while he spoke. He turned just a little further to answer him. "Captain, I'm afraid I don't understand. Why did you bring Lexi? Why bring anyone else? Why did you come? You could have just sent me."

David had been holding on to a lot of anger over the last few weeks. Today he felt a great release from his anger. He knew if Jake had questioned him like this yesterday, he would have taken his head off for the insubordination. Instead he spoke rather matter-of-factually. "Chief, the Lieutenant and I are aware of certain pieces of information that, if known, could put all Drean lives at risk as well as… well, it could put the two of us at risk and possibly the rest of the crew. Chief, I don't need to explain my actions to you. This is need to know only and you didn't need to know. If I tell you, it puts you and probably Marissa at risk too."

"At risk from whom?"

David shook his head. "Jake, your curiosity is gonna get you killed one day if you don't get it under control. I'm not certain who's behind this. I intend to find out and put an end to it. That's all I can tell you for now. I really hope you can forgive me for stunning you, but I didn't want the Dreans to find you awake and alert. They would have been well within their rights to have us all arrested. I'm sorry for any discomfort you suffered. It had to be done. If you feel the need to file a complaint against me, then do so."

David didn't wait for his reply. He turned quickly, punched the shuttle hatch release and two seconds later he was gone. Jake gave Lexi a perplexed look. "So, what do I do now?"

"Do you feel the need to report him?"

"I don't know. I do think he was out of line, but I suppose I set myself up too."

"Jake, if you report him, your disobedience of orders will come out. This could feasibly come back and bite you worse than him. Yes, he assaulted you, but you disobeyed a direct order. If I were you, I would let it go. If the Doc gets him fixed up, then everything can get back to normal. If the Doc can't straighten him out, we can look at other options later."

Lexi got busy doing her post-flight check list. She didn't want to spend any more time discussing this with Jake. She was afraid she might say more than she needed to. Jake noticed she was done giving advice and finished his part of the post flight check list. He was no longer angry, just confused.

EPILOGUE

Supreme Executor Luciano Hale stood alone in his office staring out his office window. He suddenly felt another presence. Without looking behind him, he knew who was there. "It's been awhile. Why are you here?"

A voice answered. "You know why I'm here. Your time is almost over. You took them from me and now I'm taking them back."

Luciano looked down for a moment as though he had heard a disappointing truth. A fire began to build in every fiber of his being. He pulled himself up to his full height and turned to face his longtime adversary. "You'll never win them over. I've given them three hundred years of peace. I've eliminated war and hatred. I spread the wealth to supply all those in need. I've created something good here. No one is power hungry. I've filled their needs. I did this. I did it! I did!"

"And what have you robbed them of? What has it cost them? I'm not concerned about what you have given them, only what you've taken from them. I've taken the first step in giving it back to them."

Luciano slammed his fist down on his desk. "NO! You didn't! I took steps to prevent it! How? When? Who let it happen?" His face was now blood red, and he continued to lean over the desk propped on his hands. He picked up a data pad and slung it angrily across the room. He wasn't attempting to hit his visitor. The pad struck a decorative vase on the other side of the room causing it to shatter. In a moment, the color in his face normalized. He looked up and addressed his visitor more calmly. "I knew it. I didn't want to admit it, but I knew the day the stars went dark. I knew you had succeeded. This still isn't over. I'll fight you until the very end."

His visitor seemed unfazed by the Executor's tirade. "They were mine before you interfered, and they will be mine again."

Luciano stood back up into his full stance. "Not all of them, I will take as many of them with me as I can and there's nothing you can do about it."

"I gave them that choice and you tried to take it from them. If they choose to side with you, well, that is unfortunate, but it is their choice to make. I will take back as many as I can."

Luciano's eyes were cold, hard and dark. "I will destroy them myself before I see them side with you."

His visitor turned to leave. "You may try, but you will not succeed." As suddenly as he appeared, the man was gone.

Luciano shouted after him. "I'LL STOP YOU, ARNI! I WILL STOP YOU!"

Continued in
TREASONOUS ACTS

REGGI'S WRITINGS

TREASONOUS ACTS
THE DEFENDER SERIES

Thank you for reading this story, we hope you enjoyed it. We invite you to explore the rest of the books in The Defender series. Reggi's other books are available through your favorite book retailer! If you don't see it on the shelf, ask them to order it for you.

Tell us what you think!

Leave a comment online with your favorite book store!

Visit us at ReggiBroach.com for the latest information!

Search for "Reggi Broach Defender" in your favorite search engine.

THE DEFENDER SERIES

BIRTH OF THE DEFENDER
PREQUEL

How did it all start? How could anyone put something like this together? Did anyone design this or did it just "happen"? What brought David's parents together? How many lives did the birth of Arni touch? These seemingly unconnected events on opposite sides of the galaxy sets Pateras' plan in motion.

THE MISSION
BOOK 1

Captain David Alexander commands an Explorer Class Starship known as the SS *Evangeline*. Their Commonwealth assigned mission is to locate and identify a new enemy encroaching on Commonwealth territory before it's too late. Their new enemy has unidentifiable technology that turns people against their own government. No methods of persuasion have proven effective in restoring the enemy conscripts. The Supreme Executor of the Commonwealth, Luciano Hale, has authorized extreme sanctions. He wants the Liontari forces stopped, at all costs.

THE DEFENDED
BOOK 2

The Crew of the *Evangeline* continue their Commonwealth mission to make allies of the non-space-faring planets in the galaxy. Drea III is a technologically advanced world shrouded by a dark history with the Commonwealth. Drean officials agree to hear the crew's proposal of an alliance with the Commonwealth. A series of startling discoveries land the crew in jail, charged with several capital crimes. Captain Alexander finds himself caught between his Commonwealth mandates and protecting an entire planet from disaster. David does the only thing he can. He throws himself on the mercy of the courts, defending his crew to his last breath. The secrets keep growing older and deeper. What else can be learned? Who is responsible for so many secrets? Who is Captain Alexander – really?

TREASONOUS ACTS
BOOK 3

Who enjoys the story of a good boy gone bad?

Captain David Alexander is just such a man. He followed the rules, dotted every "i" and crossed every "t." Service to the Commonwealth Interstellar Force was his life… until now.

Treason; the only crime punishable by death. The entire crew wavers in their loyalty. Only one man remains true, Security Chief Jake Holden. Can he save them from themselves? Can he stop Captain Alexander from taking the entire crew down? Can he protect the primitive world of Tudoren? If he can't, Admiral Robert Deacons, David's uncle will have to. Can he arrest or execute his own nephew?

IN EVIL'S GRASP
BOOK 4

Betrayed… Imprisoned unjustly… His body racked with pain…

Evil voices whispering… Taunting him…

Pateras gave him a mission. Can Captain Alexander go on? Can he survive this darkest night of the soul? The desire to die grows stronger with each passing moment. His crew now believes he is either dead or their own betrayer.

Pateras prevents the Captain's captor from executing him outright. The one who betrayed him returned as an angel of light offering him a way out… a way to die.

MISSION ABANDONED
BOOK 5

The crew of the Evangeline are now united in following Pateras. The entire Galaxy is out for blood – theirs. The military base on Romajin was destroyed as the Evangeline escaped the solar system. Ten thousand men and women are dead and Chief Security Officer Jake Holden stands accused of the crime. Supreme Executor Hale tries to coerce Jake into returning to his service by any means necessary.

A new army of super soldiers is dispatched to destroy the Evangeline and other potentially wayward crews. Captain Alexander seeks out the other eleven ships to warn them. Will his best friend from the Academy believe him? Can he convince them of the danger before the Nefil arrive? What about the local population? Will they become casualties of war?

BIRTH OF A REVOLUTION
BOOK 6

Captain Alexander finishes searching for the other eleven Explorer Class Ships. Their Drean allies set up a secret meeting for all the ships willing to come. Captain Alexander proposes an alliance of the renegade ships to confront the Commonwealth. The odds of success are phenomenally against them. Will they agree to his proposal or will someone report them to the Commonwealth?

The fear that someone will discover them keeps everyone looking over their shoulders. Captain Alexander has more than the Commonwealth looking for him. An ugly secret is revealed as enemies from his past get lucky. Trapped in a maintenance duct under a mine shaft with Lt. Marissa Holden in labor, David's life is in the hands of men bent on settling an old score. The crew searches frantically for their missing people but the only one who can save him is another figure from his past. Can this man be trusted?

QUESTIONS OF TRUST
BOOK 7

The newly formed Pateran Resurrection Movement is severely outnumbered and outclassed. The potential for traitors in their ranks remains. Captain Alexander is immediately plagued with a manpower shortage aboard ship, along with a confessed Commonwealth spy. Arni, not one prone to violence, has asked one thing of the newly formed alliance; destroy the Nefil base on Ahnak III.

What else could possibly go wrong? Captain Alexander is elected to be the lead Admiral in the new alliance. Being nearly the youngest of the Explorer Fleet captains, David feels inferior to his peers. Personal tragedy strikes the new young Admiral adding to his load. Executor Hale allows a secret out designed to hurt one person, the new Admiral. How much more can Admiral Alexander take before he crumbles under the pressure?